# RAMPAGE

Justin Scott is the author of twenty-six novels, including *The Shipkiller* and *Normandie Triangle*, the Ben Abbot detective series, and five modern sea thrillers under his pen name Paul Garrison. He currently co-writes the Isaac Bell series with Clive Cussler. He lives in Connecticut.

www.justinscott-paulgarrison.com

## ALSO BY JUSTIN SCOTT

### THRILLERS

*The Shipkiller*
*The Turning*
*The Man Who Loved the Normandie*
*A Pride of Kings*
*Rampage*
*The Nine Dragons*
*The Empty Eye of the Sea*
*The Auction*
*Treasure Island: A Modern Novel*

### ISAAC BELL NOVELS WITH CLIVE CUSSLER

*The Cutthroat*
*The Gangster*
*The Assassin*
*The Bootlegger*
*The Striker*
*The Thief*
*The Race*
*The Spy*
*The Wrecker*

### THRILLERS AS PAUL GARRISON

*Fire and Ice*
*Red Sky at Morning*
*Buried at Sea*
*Sea Hunter*
*The Ripple Effect*
*The Janson Command*
*The Janson Option*

### BEN ABBOTT MYSTERIES

*Hardscape*
*StoneDust*
*FrostLine*
*McMansion*
*Mausoleum*

### MYSTERIES

*Many Happy Returns*
*Treasure for Treasure*
*The Widow of Desire*

### MYSTERIES AS J. S. BLAZER

*Deal Me Out*
*Lend a Hand*

# RAMPAGE

## JUSTIN SCOTT

HARPER

*Harper*
An imprint of HarperCollins*Publishers*
1 London Bridge Street,
London, SE1 9GF

www.harpercollins.co.uk

This paperback edition 2017
1

First published by Grafton Books 1986

A catalogue record for this book
is available from the British Library

ISBN: 9780008221997

Set in Sabon by Palimpsest Book Production Limited
Falkirk, Stirlingshire

Printed and bound in Great Britain

MIX
Paper from
responsible sources
FSC™ C007454
www.fsc.org

*a* Gloria Hoye
*mio amore, mia bellezza, mia amica*

# PROLOGUE

*The Privateer*

The witness before the President's Commission on Organized Crime wore a hood over his new face. Metal detectors had greeted spectators entering the columned rotunda of Federal Hall in Lower Manhattan and US marshals had erected screens to shield him from the TV cameras. He testified through an electronic voice distorter, which made him sound like a cheerful child in another room.

The commissioners – business people, criminal justice professors, congressmen and women, and law enforcement experts – faced him from tiered tables covered by periwinkle-blue cloth. Counsel directed questions from the centre of the front table. A grizzled old judge chaired from the back.

Christopher Taggart, the youngest commissioner by far, sat in front. The seal of the commission, prominently displayed, had a Latin motto that meant, the lawyers told him, Pluck Out Evil By Its Roots. He was armed for the task with a pad for the notes he kept in a clear hand, a gold pen that he began tapping impatiently, and a microphone, which he seized with sudden exasperation.

'Mr Counsel? This witness isn't telling anything about the Mafia that Jimmy Breslin hasn't already published in the *Daily News*.'

Members of the press laughed and counsel, an urbane, former federal prosecutor vaulting the rungs of government service two at a time, doled out a smile with the correct proportions of respect and superiority. Christopher Taggart seemed to have forgotten again that he asked the questions, witnesses answered under threat of contempt citations, and commissioners listened politely.

'Be assured, Commissioner Taggart, that this witness is eminently qualified to assess the effect of the Federal Organized Crime Strikeforce on the Mafia.'

The witness, a bold man with the garrotte before he entered the Federal Witness Protection Program, hastened to agree with the chief counsel. Taggart assumed he enjoyed these occasional outings and wanted to be invited back. The mouth hole in his hood flapped and the cheery child sounded earnest. 'Two years ago I was a *capo* in the Cirillo family here in New York.'

'But you were already in the slammer last year when the Strikeforce indicted every boss of the Mafia's ruling council,' Taggart shot back. 'The important question is, who's taking their place? I don't see New York's Mafiosa lining up for unemployment.'

'You're gonna see more and more surprising guys testifying for immunity,' the mobster promised. 'The Strikeforce is flipping some heavy hitters. They're scared shitless – excuse my French – about who's going to inform undercover. Even the Cirillos, every place they move, the FBI or the Drug Enforcement Agency's waiting with an army because they've infiltrated the street crews. It's *war* out there and the mob is losing.'

Taggart interrupted again. 'The agents are doing a great job. But the mob still controls heroin, cocaine, unions, extortion, hijacking and gambling. When the Strikeforce puts one leader away, five more step up to replace him. Who's taking over? Mr Witness.'

'Hey, you don't knock 'em off in a year or two – or even ten. But don't think it's a bed of roses for the bosses. It's not like changing mayors. They gotta fight each other for the job.'

'As a businessman, I'd like to see my law enforcement tax dollars going to more than making "Cosa Nostra" mobsters uncomfortable.'

'I just wanna say I never heard the words "Cosa Nostra" except on tele-vision. What I was in, we called it the rackets.'

'And I'm calling a recess,' Judge Katzoff interrupted. 'Would the marshals clear the room?'

A dozen marshals escorted the man in the black hood from the witness table, cordoning him with their bodies. An easel displaying a chart of orga-nized crime leadership in New York City crashed to the marble floor with a loud bang. Federal agents plunged anxious hands into their jackets and handbags.

Taggart smiled. He was dressed like a rich, busy man, blessed with a stylish woman or two who looked after him; his navy-blue suit, expensive and conservative, off the rack from Paul Stuart, was greatly enlivened by an interesting shirt that enhanced his blue eyes, and an Italian silk tie and handkerchief. His blond hair was short and fashionably groomed in the style he called stockbroker punk. The harsh television lights revealed a faint scar that creased both his lips, and another that furrowed his brow.

'Mr Taggart,' the chairman said, when reporters, technicians, and elderly spectators had trooped from the rotunda, 'I'm on a tight schedule.'

'I've got four Manhattan skyscrapers on tight schedules, Your Honour. For all I know, they've fallen down. I haven't seen 'em since our dog-and-pony act hit town Monday. I didn't volunteer to showboat. I joined this commission to expose organized crime and find ways to hit back. But all we're doing is rehashing old news for the benefit of TV. We're asking this turkey to tell us what we already know about old men who've already been arrested.

The old judge, who had made a name for himself jailing Vietnam war protestors while Taggart was in junior high school, flushed.

'What about the new ones?' Taggart demanded. 'Do you know how smart they're getting? Last night, the New York State Organized Crime guys busted a Cirillo bodyguard who was carrying more anti-bugging equipment than a KGB agent. They buy the same sophisticated surveillance receivers, bug alerts, and telephone analysers that the government does. There's a new breed, as vicious as the old, but hipper, and getting harder to catch. These guys are not going to fall for a mike in their girlfriend's panties.'

'I'll instruct counsel to schedule a technical witness,' the judge replied drily. 'I'd rather hear about the government leak on that Sicilian deal.'

'*What leak?*'

Katzoff looked at the staff members who had collected around his chair at the centre of the rear table. They looked at each other in panic.

'Who told the press that the Strikeforce had asked the Coast Guard to survey a Greek freighter? The ship happened to be carrying Sicilian heroin, which moved to another ship when the story broke.'

'I can explain, Your Honour,' said the commission's chief investigator, a slick New York Irishman in his thirties, who had been temporarily detached from the Drug Enforcement Agency. He circled the witness screen, shaking his head at Taggart. 'Your Honour, somebody in the Treasury Department wanted to be sure he got credit for his agency. It was a stupid bureaucratic screwup, but those things happen. What I want to know is how the hell did Commissioner Taggart find out about it? It wasn't in the paper about the dope.'

'I do my homework,' Taggart shot back. He turned around and faced his fellow commissioners. 'Look, when I asked my friend Governor Costanzo – or should I say my father's friend?' He hesitated, and those who knew him best, glanced away. 'When I asked Governor Costanzo, "Get me on this Crime Commission, get the President to appoint me," I did it because I believe that the Mafia, or the rackets, or call it what the hell you want to, threatens everyone in the country. I build buildings and I see Mafia extortion every day. They'll kill construction, like they killed the New York Harbor. The investigation I was talking about that got leaked would have been the biggest Cirillo bust since the Strikeforce got their last underboss. What can our commission recommend to prevent such fuckups? You'll notice, unlike our tame witness, I'm not asking you to excuse my French.'

'All right,' said the judge. 'Let's break for noon recess.'

Taggart stuffed the morning's press releases in his briefcase and hailed the chief investigator. 'Hey, Barney. Lunch?'

'You paying?'

'Sure. You got it last time. How 'bout Windows on the World?'

'Last time was Blarney Stone.'

'So live a little.'

'Seriously, Chris. How the hell did you know about the leak? Did your brother tell you?'

The smile went out of Taggart's eyes and he said coolly, 'You know damned well Tony never leaks. Especially to me.'

'I didn't mean it that way,' Barney apologized hastily.

Taggart threw his arm around Barney's shoulder, gave him a slow grin and a friendly finger. 'Hey, I'm just a businessman.'

'I know, I know. And you hear things.'

'From guys like you who talk too much. Hoods and cops, you're all the same, you can't keep your mouths shut.'

At the restaurant atop the World Trade Center, Taggart took a table facing uptown. It was a muggy May day and the skyline appeared hazy and distant. Taggart's gaze fixed on it nonetheless, and in the powerful north light Barney noticed that his big hands were impeccably manicured, the nails buffed to a satiny sheen.

'What's it like looking out there and seeing your own buildings?'

Taggart's glittering eyes, powerful Italian nose, and sensual mouth gathered in one of his infectious grins, reminding Barney that he was barely thirty years old. 'Almost as much fun as being a cop.'

While drinking their second martinis Taggart asked casually, 'Did they really find the leak?'

'Better. They found the dope.'

'Nice going. How?'

'Criminal intelligence.'

Taggart laughed. 'In other words, you turkeys got a tip.'

*    *    *

'Hey, hey. Who's this?'

Jack Warner, a burly police detective attached to the Strikeforce, opened one eye at the whisper in the dark. When the camera clicked, he opened the other and heaved himself out of the musty chair where he had dozed intermittently through the long night. Another car was approaching the abandoned parking garage that he and three federal agents were watching from a defunct metal-working shop on the other side of Forty-fifth Street. Thirty pounds of Sicilian heroin that the Strikeforce had lost track of earlier had surfaced in the garage, or so said a tipster.

The FBI agent in charge fired off a second round of film and stepped back to give his partner from the Drug Enforcement Agency a look. The telescope was aimed through a hole they had peeled in the tin that covered the door. A street lamp glinting between the boards that covered the window lit the room dimly.

'I don't know him,' the DEA agent said.

Warner waited his turn while an IRS criminal investigator stooped over the telescope and adjusted the focus. He too shook his head. 'Never seen him before.'

'Jack will know,' the FBI man said. 'Warner, get your ass here. Who's this guy?'

Jack knows. Damned right Jack knows! Thirty–eight years old, eighteen on the New York Police Force, with fourteen in Organized Crime Control, Jack Warner knows more than anybody about the Mafia. He knows who's up, who's down. He knows wiseguys their own mothers don't know. But he especially knows that tonight's hot tip is very hot indeed, because he phoned it in himself.

Warner rotated the eyepiece a quarter turn to compensate for the nearsighted IRS man. A car's image hardened in the lens – a black 1986 Chevy Caprice straddling the sidewalk, with New York plates 801-BD, the driver in profile, big nose and pompadour hair, was checking the block. The door of the supposedly empty building slid up and the car moved into darkness. At four o'clock in the morning, during false dawn before the Memorial Day weekend, the street was so quiet they could hear the metal door rattling in its tracks.

'You know him?' The FBI agent asked.

Warner yawned. 'That's a Cirillo hitter who runs security for their stash pads. He's been moving up lately. Started out bouncing in their clubs.'

His Strikeforce 'colleagues', as Warner enjoyed dubbing the Feds, exchanged testy looks. All night the cop had been batting a thousand.

'Is there any hood in New York you *don't* know?'

'That's what your local policeman's for.'

And no help from the tip, thank you, for he was proud that he had recognized the hood legitimately. It was a point of honour with him that he knew more about the Mafia than the Feds. He practically lived with the wiseguys, one jump ahead of the Mafia – two jumps ahead of the cops. Like his brother the priest who complained that he served two masters, God and the bishop, Detective Warner also had two bosses, the New York City Police Department and another who paid better.

'You know you look like one of them?' the IRS man grouched. 'How do you pay for that shit you're wearing?'

Good question, Warner thought; and if you don't like my clothes, you'd hate my Swiss bank account! It was a hot, muggy night and Warner had removed his suit jacket, exposing, in addition to his belly gun, a pure cotton shirt tailored to his girth, gold nugget cufflinks, and a brand new black and gold Baum & Mercier wristwatch. His shoes, hand made in Italy, had set him back three hundred bucks each.

'I been a cop eighteen years, so I make a decent buck. All I got to spend my salary on is one rent-controlled room. But don't worry, Internal Affairs gets on my case every time I take a girl to dinner, so if I ever go on the take, they'll be the first to tell you.' Good answer, he thought.

'It always looks funny on a cop around dope.'

'But at least I don't look like a cop,' Warner replied mildly, 'Half the wiseguys in town figure I'm on their side. Guys like to talk and I listen.'

'I don't look like a cop, either.'

Warner's quick eyes catalogued the hair too long over the ears, the tie that had turned up at Christmas, and the shoes cracking under the shine. 'You look like a guy paying bills for a wife and three kids in the suburbs. Good cover. Suits you.'

He peeked through the crack in the tin, but the street was empty. It was dumb to piss off anyone who might know something useful some day. 'Hey,' he apologized, 'when you love this city you want to own it – *hold* it! Like in your hand. Guys try different ways. A politician runs to be mayor. The actress wants her name on Broadway. Big builders like Trump and Taggart they change how the sky looks. But the only way a cop can own the city is *know* it. Knowing who's who makes me feel like New York is mine.'

The telephone rang. They jumped. Ma Bell had come across. The FBI agent answered, listened, covered the phone and asked Warner, 'Would you mind, Jack?'

An assistant United States attorney, one of the Strikeforce prosecutors, was writing warrants for the bust. Warner gave the kid the background, street names, and home addresses of the heroin traffickers they had spotted going in the garage.

'You wearing a computer?' the lawyer asked.

'Yeah. The FBI gave it to me. Fits in my heel.'

It was an axiom of the drug trade that deals and dealers were always late. But the arrival of a stash pad guard suggested to Warner that things were going to break, so he offered to relieve the man on the telescope. He knew, of course, the general drift of what was going down, but it was impossible to know everything, because lately strange things were going on in the rackets and a lot of people on both sides seemed to be running around with a bag on their head.

The phone rang again. It was the FBI agent's supervisor pressing his man for a prediction. Warner motioned for the agent to cover the mouthpiece. 'He's worried about holding a ton of agents over the holiday, isn't he?'

'Sure.'

'Yeah, well, I figure the Maf probably wants to take the weekend off, too. Tell him it's coming down any minute.'

'Are you *sure?*'

'We've busted so many suppliers they're hurting for product. They're not going to sit on that stuff.'

The agent promised his supervisor an imminent bust and hung up gingerly. 'Jesus, I hope you're right.'

'Hey, hey! Here we go.' A van was turning onto the sidewalk; the horn blew and the door opened. Warner stepped back to let the Feds look through the telescope. 'That's the lab I told you about.'

The Strikeforce backed a theatrical hauler's truck into the garage's Forty-fourth Street driveway, where it looked in place, if thoughtlessly parked, just down the street from the banners of the New Dramatists Guild and the Actor's Studio.

On Forty-fifth, the agents blocked one garage door with a Con Ed truck and the second with barricades behind which they started to drill holes in the street. Forty agents in bulletproof vests crouched inside the vans, with cutting tools and battering rams. When the police had quietly saturated the Ninth and Tenth Avenue ends of both blocks, the FBI man in the metal shop started to call the shots, with Jack Warner watching over his shoulder.

Both vans reported they were set, as were the cops. 'Okay, let's–' the FBI agent started to say.

But Jack Warner seized the telephone. A blue Buick was rolling towards the garage. 'Hold it! We want this guv.'

'Who's that?'

'That's Nino Vetere's car, but it can't be him. One of his geeps, in case somebody needs to be killed.' The Buick blew its horn at the barricades. The driver shouted not to block the fucking entrance, and the agents attired in workboots and yellow Con Ed hardhats obligingly lifted their saw horses.

'Give him a minute to check the stuff out,' Warner cautioned. 'Maybe the bastards'll get some on their fingers.'

Then, in an act of bravery that gave Warner the shivers to think about, an athletic DEA agent had herself lowered silently from the roof, five storeys down a shaft into the car elevator. She wrapped her ample thighs around the head of the hitter guarding the entrance, stuck a gun in his ear, and asked him to throw the switch that raised the door. Twenty agents piled into the building while the drug distributors were occupied running chemical tests in the back of their van.

For a minute it looked like a clean bust.

Then the blue Buick came screeching out of the darkness, scattering the agents in the doorway and flinging the young woman over its bonnet. The car skidded on howling tyres onto Forty-fifth Street and raced for Tenth Avenue. Warner, who ordinarily stayed out of the action to maintain his cover, charged after it. Somebody in that car was either very stupid or very desperate, and he had to know which.

The Buick ran onto the sidewalk when it reached the Corrections Department bus blocking the intersection. A quick-thinking patrolman filled the space with his prowl car and the Buick crashed into it, bounced off a wall, and stopped.

Cops with riot guns surrounded the wreck. They pulled a bloodied figure out in handcuffs, and Warner was astonished to see that it was Nino Vetere himself. A heavy-duty Cirillo crew leader, maybe number one, Vetere reported directly to underboss Nicholas, the elder son and heir apparent of Don Richard, the chief of the clan.

Agents were staring with their mouths open in disbelief. One did not find major Mafia guys on the street. No wonder he had run. Vetere was already in deep, deep trouble, awaiting trial on federal racketeering charges. Now, with a major heroin arrest, he was looking at the rest of his life in jail, and the Strikeforce prosecutors were going to pound his balls to flip.

His testimony would be golden, Warner knew, since he knew how the Cirillos ran their family. If they convicted Nicholas on Vetere's testimony, old Don Richard, who was trying to retire, had no one left to control the family but Crazy Mikey, his younger son who was aptly nicknamed.

Warner approached an FBI agent he knew well. 'Better get his family into protection, or he won't deal.'

'We're miles ahead of you, Jack. The marshals are on their way.'

'Great! What about his girlfriend?'

'What?'

'His girlfriend. It's not enough protecting his wife and kids. He won't testify if the Cirillos can get to his mistress.'

'I didn't know he had one.'

Warner wrote down her name and address.

But he was baffled by what in hell Vetere was doing at a heroin buy in the first place. Mobsters as high as him were supposed to stay miles above the product. They dealt in money twice removed – and even that they didn't actually *touch*.

Someone had set him up, Warner had a feeling he knew who.

* * *

Blue shades of evening darkened the city. At the base of the Taggart Spire a bare bulb was already burning in the gate shack, as were Park Avenue's street lamps and lights in the surrounding buildings, but so tall was the partially-built skyscraper that the upper works still blazed red and gold in the sun.

The construction site was quiet with the workmen gone. A tall plywood fence muffled the sound of traffic and the sweet clicking of high heels on the sidewalk, and the job seemed deserted except for the night watchman and his German shepherd, which closed its eyes when it recognized a perspiring Jack Warner swagger through the gate.

'You believe this weather?'

'Radio said cooler tonight.'

'Yeah? What kind of Memorial Day they gonna sell us? Gimme a hardhat.'

Warner knew that the watchman was a retired cement truck driver. The old guy probably figured him for a Taggart Construction front-office superintendent, or a union boss, or even one of the mob hoods who stopped by for their payoffs.

'We'll keep the elevator.'

It rose noisily through the cavernous lobby shell, ten storeys of empty space – Taggart's 'fuck you', Warner thought, to the price of square footage in midtown Manhattan and to Taggart's nearest competitors, the smaller Trump and Olympia towers on Fifth Avenue, the IBM and AT&T buildings on Madison, and the Citicorp complex to the east. The Spire's interior walls were taking shape on the lower office floors. Higher up, the floors were open to the glass skin. The fiftieth to seventieth floors were not yet sheathed and their decks were bare concrete. While the very top floors – destined to be apartments, and still sprouting three V-shaped derricks – stood wide open, raw lattices of steel through which the wind gusted freely.

A figure waited on the highest girder, a thousand feet above Manhattan. His narrow steel perch, cantilevered beyond the columns that supported it, thrust thirty feet into empty air. He swayed at the end, on the very edge, leaning into the wind.

Christopher Taggart turned from the sunset, half his face shining, half in darkness. 'Join me.'

Warner shivered. He looked down and regretted it instantly. This side of the building dropped sheer to the sidewalk, and they were too high to distinguish people in the dusk. The taxis were specks chasing hairs of light.

'How about you meeting me half way, Mr Taggart?'

'Chicken?'

'If I were, at least I'd have wings.'

17

Taggart laughed appreciatively and headed in from the precipice. His light, rolling gait, broad shoulders and a lean waist reminded Warner of a boxer. Warner edged out to the pillar and by the time he had reached the nearby upright, Taggart was leaning casually on the other side.

'Don't move!'

Taggart swung around the pillar and expertly patted Warner's chest, back, and legs; next he felt his waist for a Nagra recorder inside his belt. Warner, who took the same precautions with his contacts, submitted without complaint.

'How in hell do you stand it up here?'

'One time when my brother and I were feeling our oats, my father hired us out as iron workers. We were scared shitless, but more scared he'd belt us with a two-by-four if we didn't have the balls for it.'

'My old man beat the shit out of me, too,' Warner said. 'Musta been seventeen before I was big enough to deck the bastard . . . I still don't mind saying I'd like to meet elsewhere.'

'Elsewhere? How about one of the tables the Strikeforce bugs at the Brasserie?'

'You know what I mean.'

Taggart swung back to his side, peered around the column, and looked Warner in the face. 'I know this is the most private place in New York, Detective Warner. Start talking.'

'I was all day with the prosecutors breaking down Nino Vetere. Nino said he wanted to score big to take care of his children before he got convicted on the RICO charge.' The reference was to the Racketeer Influenced Corrupt Organization act; RICO, for short, cost twenty years and the Strikeforce lawyers brushed their teeth with it every morning. 'Nino was looking at life or damned close, so he sings and turns in his crews. "No way, Barf Brain, that's not enough. Give us more. Give us the guy running the Cirillos. Give us Nicholas Cirillo." And he finally says, "Okay, get me out of this and I'll show you how old Don Cirillo's still running the family through Nicholas." '

Warner looked at Taggart to gauge his reaction; Taggart stared through him. 'I know most of this from the radio. I can guess the rest.'

*Guess this,* Warner thought, again watching closely for reaction. 'Nobody knows where the dope came from. The original Sicilian stuff went south when the Feds leaked. The street says it was sold in Florida. Which sounds like somebody brought in new stuff and *gave* it to the Cirillos, pretending it was the stuff they had paid for. Who the hell gives away five million bucks of heroin?'

'Who cares?' Taggart snapped impatiently. 'Vetere and Nicky Cirillo are old news. What did you find on the Rizzolos?'

'The Rizzolos are being their usual weird selves.'

18

Taggart had some particular interest in the Rizzolos, which Warner hadn't figured out yet. They were a small Brooklyn family who were sort of odd man out, the smallest of the New York crime groups – maybe a hundred 'made' members and four hundred soldiers – and also the tightest, and very independent. They had broken from the Cirillos, and when the Cirillos had hit back, the clan had made what came to be called the Rizzolo War so bloody that the Cirillos had finally backed off and left them alone. Their response to the Strikeforce had been just as unpredictable.

'Strikeforce hits their bookie joints, but nobody's there. They just went out of business – empty store fronts, not even a piece of paper. They even took the phone jacks. It's the same with the numbers bank. So the Strikeforce hits that big coke operation I told you about that Eddie Rizzolo stole from the Columbians. *Nada.* Like their street guys are bus drivers and waiters, period.' Course they can't shut down forever.'

Gazing at the setting sun, Taggart asked, 'Have you figured out who's running the Rizzolos?'

Warner shrugged, uncomfortable with the idea, yet moved by the evidence. 'Maybe you figured right. The sister might be the real boss. Eddie "the Cop" and Frank are just plain dumb guys. Like you said, since the Strikeforce put old Don Eddie away, somebody's been running the Rizzolos just fine.'

'She sounds like an interesting woman.'

'Listen, Mr Taggart.' Jack was getting used to the height, as he did each time. So long as he could hold on to something solid.

Taggart turned his head, alert to a new note in Warner's voice. 'What?'

Warner took a determined breath. 'Things are moving real smooth on my end.'

'Then what's your problem?'

'The thing is, Mr Taggart. I think I been with you from the start on this, right?'

'Early on.'

'And I think you'll agree I'm pulling my weight and then some. What you know of the mob, you know through me. I been your expert. I been your man in the field, your contact. I–'

'You want a gold star, Jack?'

Warner took another deep breath. 'I know what you're doing.'

Taggart waited.

'The bust this morning was a set up,' Warner said.

'So?'

'What do you say we cut the shit? I know what's going on. You been using my information to turn in the bosses.'

'*Your* information? You're a cop. If your information is so good, why don't you arrest them yourself?'

'You're getting information from other people, too. The Crime Commission, other cops you hang out with, federal agents, and connected guys you're tight with – yeah, I know about them – and construction guys you do business with. Maybe even your brother.'

'Not my brother!' Taggart said sharply. 'Tony is one hundred per cent straight. He always has been and he always will be.'

'But yes to the others?'

'What do you want?'

Warner was startled; Taggart's question was as good as a confession. He said, 'I want in.'

'In?'

'Share. I want a piece of it.'

Taggart's reply was deceptively soft, but Warner wasn't fooled. The builder's whole body seemed rigid with tension; he could almost feel him stiffening through the pillar. 'What if I told you I'm not doing it for the money?'

'You're not doing it for the money?' Warner shrugged. 'You're so rich you don't want money? Then you won't mind sharing the profits.'

'What if there are no profits?'

'No profits? Who you kidding? Crime pays, man. It pays big – I figure half's fair. Huh?'

Taggart stared across the Hudson for a full minute. The sun slipped into an envelope of cloud and the sky flamed behind the New Jersey hills. Warner looked around anxiously. The air was clearing as the humid heat lifted. To the east stars were rising over Long Island. In the southeast, the lights of a single freighter ploughed into the black spread of the Atlantic Ocean. The wind was accelerating, dry and cool. His perspiration-damped shirt felt suddenly cold.

'Jack, you still carry that money clip I gave you?'

'What? Money clip? Yeah.'

'Let me see it.'

Warner pulled a gold Tiffany clip from his trousers. His initials, in diamonds, spelled how well he had done over the years selling information to Christopher Taggart. Taggart pulled his own clip from his pocket and transferred five folded C-notes to Warner's. 'Cab fare,' he said with a fathomless smile. 'Let me see your wallet.'

As Warner passed Taggart his pigskin wallet, he flipped it open to flash his tin – a blunt warning not to try to buy him off cheap. Eighteen years and he still felt the surge. An NYPD shield asked a potent question: Do you want to fuck with a man who has twenty-thousand partners?

20

Taggart put wallet and shield in his pocket.

'Why –'

'So you don't drop 'em.'

A long arm streaked out of the sky as Taggart whirled around the pillar and his big hand fell like a hammer. The blow enveloped Warner's face and with two hundred pounds behind it flung him into the air.

Warner felt the column wrenched from his hand. Then he was falling. The black sky whirled into city lights, building tops, blazing windows. The street looked like a dark ribbon and nothing was between it and his falling body. He screamed.

He was brought up short, hanging upside down by one foot. Warner looked up through his flailing legs and saw Taggart's immense hand clamped around his ankle. His blue eyes had turned dark with fury.

'*Don't you ever hit me for a payoff!*'

'Please.'

'You got that?'

'Please, Mr Taggart.'

'Say *yes*.'

'Yes. Yes. Yes.'

'You *are* doing a good job, Jack. But not good enough to shake me down.' He pulled him towards the girder. Warner reached and stretched and at last touched the sun-warmed steel with his fingertips. But Taggart jerked him away.

'Jack, maybe I ought to let you go.' Taggart jerked him up in the air.

'No!'

'Like this!'

To Warner's disbelief, Taggart opened his hand. He fell, screaming. It seemed he was falling forever. But Taggart grabbed him again, swung him back and forth. Warner's head was bursting with blood, his chest pounding with fear. Somehow, Taggart must have learned about his files. If he didn't admit to them, Taggart would drop him.

'I got notes,' he screamed.

'Blackmail?'

'No. No. I wouldn't use them. It's just my information.'

'Where?'

'In my room.'

'Where in your room?'

'In the wall behind the fridge. I wasn't going to use them. Honest.'

Viewed upside-down, shaded scarlet by the sunset, the broad angles of Taggart's face seemed to soften sympathetically. The swinging slowed, the awful arc diminished.

'I know, Jack. You only want more money. Don't worry about it, I'll be buying plenty of information. You'll give me the notes?'

'God, yes.'

He felt himself swung in from space and laid prone on the steel. He wrapped both arms around the girder and moaned his relief. Taggart knelt beside him, shaking his head. 'You damned fool,' he said, not unkindly, 'you've wet your pants.'

When he could walk again, Taggart helped him off the girder and led him solicitously towards the elevator. Warner couldn't stop shaking. His brain was roaring with blood and fear. 'I thought I was dead,' he mumbled.

Taggart laughed. 'Jack, how could I throw an NYPD detective off my own building?' He clapped Warner on the shoulder and handed him his shield and money clip. 'Go home and get those notes. And Jack? . . . I don't give second chances.'

Warner took that as fair warning not to voice the question that was still driving him crazy.

If Christopher Taggart wasn't in it for the money, what the fuck was he doing with the Mafia?

# BOOK I

*Slaughtered Saints*
*1976–1984*

# 1

Christopher Taglione remembered the day for its crisp heat and its promise. Nothing, it seemed, could be better, and nothing could ever go wrong. He bounded out of the hole, the enormous pit they were excavating between two buildings in midtown Manhattan, and hit the sidewalk running, signalling the next truck. Sweat glistened on his bare chest, poured between the cement spatters that spotted him like a grey leopard. His hair was long then, gold flying from the rim of his hardhat. A great-looking woman smiled at his exuberance and he grinned back – a star, twenty-one years old and future partner in Taglione Concrete and Construction.

His father's trucks filled Fifty-sixth Street, enormous concrete ready-mixers that towered over the taxis inching past, and thundered at the pedestrians scuttling between their lofty wheels and the plywood construction fence that rimmed the hole. It was the summer of the American Bicentennial and Mike Taglione had painted his fleet patriotically in grateful celebration. Red and white stripes swirled around the chassis, and white stars spangled the blue mixers, rising in a jaunty heaven as the huge barrel-shaped tanks rotated half-turns to make the concrete flow.

Tony Taglione, Chris's dark and slender brother who was two years older and sixty pounds lighter, came charging up the ramp hot on Chris's heels. Tony's jet black hair, long like Chris's and the younger men on the job, was held out of his eyes by a sweatband fashioned from a Tall Ships tee shirt, which had started the morning white but was now as grey as his jeans, his heavy, laced construction boots, his battered gloves, and skinny chest. They were working side by side and, as usual, in a race.

'That's my truck.'

'You're next.'

The woman who had enjoyed the sight of Chris's youthful exuberance stopped and stared at the dark-eyed Tony with frank and open interest. Tony slowed to return a practised smile and Chris stepped into the street, pumping his fist, and re-established his claim to the lead mixer. The driver was leaning half out the window to express admiration for another lady in a loose summer dress.

'*Frankie! Move that truck.*'

The behemoth swung ponderously across the sidewalk, splintering the planks wedged against the curb, and groaned down the steep earthen ramp, with its air lines sighing and brake drums protesting the weight. Chris harried it into the pit, exhorting the driver and impatiently tugging the massive bumper.

Posters on the ramp gate depicted the emerald green office building taking life – Taglione Tower; Thirty Storeys; Michael Taglione, Owner-Builder. Down the ramp, men and machines were deepening the hole and erecting wooden forms for the concrete footings. A chain-saw blared, the forest-sound incongruous until the city walls banged it back like shrapnel.

'Let's go, let's go, let's go. You're good. Come on!'

His father was experimenting with a new building concept called fast-tracking, in which the stages of construction were overlapped to save time. Thus Chris and Tony were pouring foundation piers in the middle of the hole even as excavation continued around the edges. Beside the ramp a tread-mounted pneumatic drill drove a long steely tongue into a granite ledge, tearing the stone apart with a quick-time *bang-bang-bang*. Back hoes seized shattered granite, chunks of old cellar walls, and rusty pipes from the former building, and hoisted them into dump trucks, which drove out of the hole on flattened springs. Half a block away, the blasters' whistle blew, the ground shook, and steel mats jumped like startled dogs.

Chris guided the mixer into position and jumped for the chute as the driver climbed down from the cab and started the barrel spinning. The big truck roared; the concrete hissed, tumbling inside, and the stars on the barrel spun in a blur. Chris manhandled the chute over the dark maw of the pier hole, which was bored deep into the bedrock. A wooden frame that rimmed the hole would contain the wet concrete until it set, forming the top pads on which the iron workers would raise the building's steel columns.

Thirty feet away, Tony was furiously urging his truck to the next pier. 'Come back, Rocco. Back her up. Come back, come back. Whoa!'

Chris grinned at his brother's expression as Tony watched Rocco, bull-necked and bullet-headed, descend ponderously, the live ashes of a hangover smouldering dangerously in his eyes. Rocco squinted at the sun, rubbed his temples, belched, and strolled to the back of the truck where the mixer controls and the pour lever were located. Tony waited, exasperated, and when Rocco paused again to relight his stogie, brushed past him and goosed the throttle himself.

'Don't strain yourself, speedy.'

'Watch the mouth, kid.'

'Get off your fat ass if you don't want to hear it. We got schedules.'

'Frankie, take over,' Chris snapped, breaking into a lithe run.

Rocco reddened to his bristly scalp and lunged for Tony, who had turned his back to nurse the machine. Just as he reached him, he felt an arm drop on his own shoulder, a firm tug, and then Christopher Taglione was walking him away from his truck, asking amiably, 'So Rocco, you getting married or not?'

Rocco looked at the big, rangy kid with the arm wrapped around his shoulder like a length of hoist cable. If he really wanted to dig in, he might have stopped their forward march, but then what? Chris, who had been full grown since he was fourteen, seemed to have added a few more inches this past year at college.

'You know, one of these days Tony's gonna get his mouth handed to him.'

'No,' Chris countered, still gripping Rocco's shoulder, still steering him away, still smiling. 'He's got *me* to look out for him. That's what brothers are for. Right?'

'Yeah, well, he's gonna pull that shit on the wrong guy when you ain't around and he's gonna get his ass busted.'

Hardly a thing about Chris changed, Rocco noticed. His grip was firm and his smile friendly. Maybe his eyes turned a little grey, though it could have been the way the hot sun crossed them as he faced Rocco with utter conviction.

'If you ever run into that guy, Rocco, tell him for me he's going to have the kind of trouble that never forgets.'

Rocco was surprised at how much he believed Chris. He wished he hadn't got into this. Somehow, he'd done more than threaten the guy's brother; he had blundered into some private territory where Chris was dangerous.

'Forget it. My head's killing me.'

Chris's eyes flashed in the sunlight, bright blue again. 'Hey, there's a reason to get married – no more hangovers. I'll have your truck out in a second. Take a break.'

Rocca sat down on a form, muttering that if his old man owned the company he'd be at the beach. Chris ran to help Tony with the chute.

'I can fight my own battles, Bro.'

'I know you can fight them. Winning them worries me.'

'I can take him.'

'Oh yeah, Godzilla? Then who drives the truck? Go!'

Tony scampered to the pour lever and Chris shot him a triumphant grin as twelve cubic yards of cement, broken stone, sand and water erupted from the mixer. Tony threw him a shovel to speed it along. The concrete rattled down the trough and cascaded fifty feet to Manhattan's core.

'Not bad for college kids.'

'Hey, Pop! Hey, look at you. Tony, check out the threads.'

Tony peered over the chute. 'Goes great with the hardhat.'

Mike Taglione dodged a puddle of the spilled concrete that splattered his sons, planted his fists on his hips, and beamed at the pour. He was decked out in his blue 'meeting suit', a fine old gabardine whose broad lapels had come back into style around 1970 and was ordinarily unearthed for nothing less than contract signings and permit hearings. Chris spotted a silky new tie, fashionably wide and probably bought by his secretary who had the hots for him, a ceremonial white handkerchief in his breast pocket from the same source, and a whiff of the aftershave lotion dispensed at the Waldorf Barber Shop. He was even wearing his gold watch; the last time Chris and Tony had seen that had been at their mother's funeral.

'Where the hell are you going?'

Mike Taglione drew an old red handkerchief from its hiding place in his back pocket and pretended to flick the dust off his shoes. 'While you college geniuses hump concrete, your dumb hod-carrier old man's been invited to testify before a United States Congressional Housing Committee.'

'You been indicted?' Chris said, ducking futilely as his father belted his hard hat with a lightning hand.

'I'll indict you, wise guy. Congressman Costanzo called up. Could I *please* catch the first plane to Washington to tell 'em about the new concrete?'

'I guess those contributions paid off,' Tony said quietly.

Proud and thrilled for his father, Chris said, 'Congratulations,' and reached to hug him.

'Hands off the clean suit, you dirty guinea. Jeez, if only Irish could see me now.' Irish had been his pet name for their mother, Kathleen Taggart. 'I'll be back tomorrow. Arnie's watching the job, so you guys watch Arnie.'

'We got it, Pop.'

'Secretary know where you're staying?'

'Yeah, well uh, Sylvia's gonna' fly down with me to ...'

Chris laughed. 'Take notes? It's about time, Pop. Three years.'

'Yeah, well, no big deal.'

Tony's face clouded and Chris shot him a warning glance. When his brother turned judgmental, as he had now, his dark intelligent eyes burned beneath his pale high brow as surely and sternly as a Jesuit priest's. 'Have a good time.' Chris fired a second warning look at Tony, who went along, muttering, 'Sure, Pop. Have fun.'

Mike grinned and cast a satisfied eye on the bustling foundation site. Suddenly his expression changed. 'Here comes that greaseball Rendini.'

Chris saw Joey Rendini, a heavy-set man in a business suit, standing just inside the gate. He looked around, spotted them, and swaggered down the ramp. Chris knew that Joey Rendini was in the rackets. He controlled a Teamsters local and was connected to the Cirillo's, the biggest of the New York Mafia families. He was, as Chris had often heard his father yell, a pig when it came to payoffs, abusing to the hilt the power that the Cirillo connection gave him.

'The greaseball walks like he owns my job.' In Mike Taglione's Brooklyn-tuned lexicon, 'wops' and 'guineas' were fellow countrymen, respectable Italians or Sicilians, but 'greaseballs' were the greedy, hard types of any nationality who tried to horn in on legitimate businessmen.

'Until you say no,' Tony said, 'you'll pay him forever.'

Keyed up by his father's anger, and frustrated because he couldn't do anything about it, Chris turned on his brother. 'Grow up! A little grease is a sensible investment. It gives people incentive to do a good job.'

Tony, who seemed to have inherited their mother's strict Irish-Catholic morals, said flatly, 'It's illegal.'

'There's a middle ground,' Mike Taglione said. 'The trouble with Rendini is he's so greedy he turns grease into blackmail.'

'No, Pop. It's like Watergate. You're straight or you're crooked. There's no middle.'

When his father turned away, Chris leaped to his defence. 'That's cool for you, if you're going to be a lawyer. But me and Pop, we gotta face the fact that Rendini can pull the drivers off any job we contract.' Alarmed by the angry flush darkening his father's face, he stopped arguing with Tony and said, 'Take it easy, Pop.'

Rendini picked his way across the beaten earth, grimacing at the dust and splashed cement. He was a darkly handsome man in his thirties, overweight and perspiring freely. Mopping his plump face with his sleeve, he called, 'Hey Mike, we had a meeting.'

'Something better came up. What do you want?'

'We gotta talk.' The mobster glanced at Chris and Tony. Chris gave him a cool nod, but Tony glared.

Mike Taglione addressed Rocco, who was hosing his chute. 'Get that truck out of here.' He waited, silent, while Rocco hastily coiled his hose and drove away. 'Okay. Talk. My boys and me got no secrets. Chris is going to work with me when he's done with college, and Tony's going to be my lawyer.'

'Yeah, well, this wildcat strike looks like it's heating up.'

'Spell that another payoff?'

'Spell it how you like, Mike. You know the rules.'

Mike Taglione shook his head. 'Rules change. This time it's *my* building. Thirty years I been pouring foundations, and general contracting. But this time

I'm the developer, and this job is all Taglione from the door knobs in the crapper to the pea stone on the roof.'

'Mike, what are you busting my balls for? So you're moving up in the world. Congratulations.'

'You know where I'm going right now? I'm going to the United States House of Representatives in Washington DC.'

'So?'

'So I think I earned the right to say, "Go fuck yourself." '

'Don't be dumb, Mike. I don't know if I can control my drivers.'

'Rendini, if you tell the poor bastards to squat, all they can ask is what colour.'

'My drivers –'

'Hold it! They're your *union members*, 'cause they got no choice, but they're *my* drivers.'

'We're talking money, Mike.'

Mike Taglione laughed. 'Money? I been paying you for years, you fat greaseball. You dog me on every job.'

Rendini shrugged. 'I don't care if you're going to Washington. I don't care if you're eating supper with President Gerald T. Fucking Ford. You know the rules. You wanna play, you pay.'

Chris shot a glance at Tony, who was regarding Rendini with open hatred, apparently unaware their father was rising onto the balls of his feet, telegraphing his sometimes violent temper. Yet his voice stayed calm, so detached that Chris wondered if he had somehow convinced himself that he had finally risen above the dirty side of the business. 'You pull one driver off my job and I'm going straight to the US Attorney.'

'You nuts?' Rendini blurted.

Chris was dumbfounded. The New York cement business was a collusive industry, with bidding often controlled by the few outfits that ran it. Quality material got delivered on time, but the US Attorney had more than once expressed the government's interest in how they had arrived at the price; whoever visited his office for a frank talk stood a chance of leaving in handcuffs.

'You nuts?' Rendini repeated, his mouth agape, and Chris wondered what in hell his father had in mind.

Mike Taglione laughed, suddenly enjoying himself, and grinned at Tony. 'Maybe I'll take the advice of number one son here and ask for immunity. Maybe I'll answer every question the US Attorney can think up.'

Tony clapped him on the back, leaving a grey handprint. 'Nice going, Pop.' Frightened, Chris cautioned, 'Pop –'

Rendini cut him off with quiet menace. 'While you're there, Mike, ask for protection. You and your kids might need it.'

His father threw a lightning right cross, faster than the eye. Chris barely sensed a blur before he heard the impact. Rendini flew backward and landed flat in the mud, blood spouting from his nose. Mike Taglione advanced, his balled fists floating like wire springs. *'Get off my job.'*

Men came running. Chris and Tony moved shoulder to shoulder, Chris in the boxer's crouch his father had taught him and Tony seizing a length of reinforcing rod. But by then it was over. A driver, one of Rendini's clique, helped the union man up, and he staggered away, holding his sleeve to his face. Taglione watched, rubbing his hand, until they disappeared behind the street fence at the top of the ramp.

Chris said, 'That wasn't too bright,' and Tony said, 'Pop, I didn't mean to push you into –'

'Nobody pushed me. Rendini got what he deserved. Should have done it years ago.' He looked at the men who had gathered. 'All right, fellas. Show's over. '

'Pop?' Tony looked awed. 'Where'd you learn to punch like that?'

Mike Taglione gave Chris a wink that warmed his heart in the hard years to come, and explained gently, 'Nobody *gave* me the concrete business, Tony.' Then he laughed, and the laugh stayed with Chris a long time, like an echo in an empty room. 'I must be getting old, I hurt my hand. ' He fanned it in the air and sucked a knuckle. 'Shit, hurts like a son of bitch. Hey, what's wrong with you?'

Chris said, 'Why don't we ride out to the airport with you?'

'Bodyguard? That's all I need.' This time he winked at Tony. 'You hit some hood with *that* fist and Tony'll spend his law career defending you from a murder rap. No. I'm paying you guys to pour concrete. Back to work.'

'Pop. Please.'

'I'll be fine. Take care, both of you. Go home together. Take a couple of your buddies with you. This'll blow over. I'll get Congressman Costanzo to talk to some people. Don't worry about it. Okay?'

He pulled out his watch and started across the excavation with his head held high and shoulders thrust forward like an adventurous bull.

'Look at him,' said Chris. 'Looks like he just got laid.'

Mike Taglione turned and waved at the bottom of the ramp. Then he cupped his hands and yelled over the clatter of the pneumatic rock drill. 'Keep an eye on Arnie. Takes him one day to throw a job off a week.'

A mixer rounded the turn and started down quickly.

'Where the hell's he going?' Chris said. 'Pop! *Move!*'

31

Free-wheeling, with brakes and engine silent, the concrete mixer hurtled down the ramp, pushed by its tremendous load to twenty miles an hour in the short space between the street and the rock drill at the bottom.

'Pop!'

Chris raced towards him, shouting and waving his arms. Mike Taglione whirled, saw the danger. His reflexes were superb. He gathered his legs, pivoted and jumped in an astonishing liquid motion. Chris thought his father had made it, and had he been wearing his regular work boots instead of what he called, 'cab-catching shoes', he would have escaped. But the smooth soles skidded on the earthen ramp and he stumbled. The truck's bumper slammed into his chest. His head snapped back and his hardhat disappeared under the wheels with a loud crack.

He fell to the dirt, rolled a short distance, and reached towards Chris who was running full tilt. Chris seized his outstretched hand. They locked fingers, as he reversed his headlong plunge, dug his heels in and pulled. He felt the shocks reverberate through their straining arms as the truck ground his father's body beneath its wheels.

# 2

Through the long burial Mass, Christopher Taglione fixed his eye on a stained-glass window his mother had contributed to her church. It was fashioned after Giotto's 'Lamentation Over Christ'; weeping disciples and angels hovering in a stone-blue sky mourned a naked, bleeding Jesus. Before his father's murder, Chris thought the window looked a little silly with its gaudy stigmata. Now, it seemed false. None of the haloed mourners looked angry. Where was their rage? His own fury was gorging his throat.

The sun came out as the priest droned on, streamed through the window, and laid a cold blue shroud over their father's casket. The two halves of the family sat separately, like at a wedding; Italian construction workers and Irish cops. All the Tagliones were on the left. On the right were the Taggarts, led by Uncle Eamon in the dress uniform of a police captain.

Chris could hardly breathe. His anger burned like a hungry fire, shooting jagged heat-bolts that attacked the air itself in a ruthless search for fuel. He hated this church. His anger struck during the homily. When the Irish priest mispronounced their name, Taglion*ee*, Chris felt Tony stir beside him. Then he compounded the insult by remarking that Mike Taglion*ee* had died cruelly in his prime.

'Mike Taglione didn't die,' Chris retorted in the front pew. 'He didn't *die*. He was murdered.'

A woman screamed, their Aunt Marie, who heaved her grief like something palpable caught in her body. Her cry unleashed a storm of bereavement and Mike's sisters shrieking the family's loss, for death to these women was a thief. Their men sat silent, as they had been expected to for centuries, their faces like dark stone, and hearts bound against the whims of a capricious nature.

An old man glanced curiously at Chris and Tony, for in his vanished world the sons sought vengeance. He hardly expected a vendetta in America in 1976, and certainly not from college students, but old ideas lived in his memory as the ancient perfume of Sicily's dry soil and hot sun lingered in his nostrils.

Chris looked across the aisle at Eamon Taggart, his mother's brother. He was a broad-shouldered handsome Irishman with salt-and-pepper hair, pale

33

blue eyes, and the noncommittal gaze of a man who knew how to get along. Uncle Eamon nodded back, which Chris interpreted as Eamon's promise that Mike Taglione had friends among the cops who would not take his murder lightly.

They carried Mike's casket – Chris, Tony, Uncle Eamon, Uncle Vinnie, Arnie Markowitz, and Mike's brothers, Uncle Pete, Uncle Johnny, Uncle Tom – to a grave beside his wife's in the churchyard. Only a block from Queens Boulevard, the cemetery was sheltered by the church, a brick rectory, and a high wall of reddish stone; a quiet place that seemed to be miles away from the city. Chris took Tony's hand and felt him trembling. Except for a clear report to the police, his brother had been virtually silent since the killing. Yet he joined the Hail Mary's and Our Fathers with a strong voice as they lowered Mike's casket into the ground.

Uncle Vinnie, Mike's favourite brother-in-law, rode home with Chris and Tony in the lead car. At times Mike's rival, often his partner, he was a prosperously fat man and the most 'Italian-Italian' of the family. He had stayed the longest in his old neighbourhood, in a Little Italy railroad flat, years after the others had left Brooklyn and lower Manhattan for the comforts of detached houses in Queens and nearby Long Island. Chris had always looked to him for a tenuous link with an ethnic past which was more vivid in the movies than in his parents' house. His jowly face was doughy with grief.

Outside the house the street was filling up with the businessmen's late model Lincolns and Cadillacs, and the civil servants' old Chevies, and Plymouths. The feast would be a huge gathering and Chris didn't think he could handle it yet. 'Tony, cover for me, okay?'

'Where you going?'

'The job.'

Uncle Vinnie said, 'You shouldn't, Chris. Everybody's coming.'

'It's okay, Uncle Vinnie,' Tony said. 'We'll cover.'

He thought that the rock drills, the bull-dozers, and backhoes in action, and the endless line of churning mixers might make his father seem less dead, and his departure, as Father Frye had euphemized it, less final. But when he arrived at the job he realized why Uncle Vinnie had tried to stop him. The hole was deserted.

Chris ran from the limousine. Inside the ramp gate he found a guard and Arnie Markowitz, his father's long-time project manager, who had come directly from the funeral and stood now on the ramp, gazing sadly at the raw mud where his father had choked out his life. There was a deathly stillness about the excavation which even the drone of mid-Manhattan could not penetrate.

'What happened?'

'The bank pulled out.'

'What the hell for?'

'Your pop ran a one-man show. What's Taglione Concrete and Construction without Mike Taglione?'

'Me. I'm here. Me and Tony.'

'Tony's going back to school. And you should too. Hey! Where you going?' Chris spun on his heel, his barely controlled rage suddenly directed at a specific target. 'To the goddamned bank. I'm going to finish my father's building.'

'Forget it. The bank doesn't know you. They'll make you fill out forms.' Arnie seized his arm. 'Why don't you talk to your Pop's friends? He's owed a lot of favours. Come on, we'll go to your house and eat.'

Chris stood stiffly atop the ramp.

'Come on, Chris.'

'Get in the car. I'll be with you in a minute. I want to be alone a second.' Arnie left and Chris looked at the silent machines. A man in a business suit approached from the sidewalk. 'I just want to say I'm sorry about your father, Chris. We talked when he was trying to get his building started. If you have any problems give me a ring. Maybe I can help.' He handed him his card.

'Like what?'

'I heard about the bank. I can set you up with a short term bridge loan till you wrap up your regular financing.'

'How much?'

'Short term runs about twenty-four per cent. But I'd need a fella to sit in and keep an eye on things.'

'How about Joey Rendini?'

'Huh.'

*Fuck you.*

He turned his back – it was that or hit the guy – and slammed the door of the limousine with an eerie sensation of reliving his father's early days when Mike Taglione had forged his iron rales of survival. No loan sharks. No silent partners. 'You believe that guy?' he asked Arnie. 'Fucking shylock hits on me the day of the funeral?'

'He's a criminal. You want nice manners?'

\*    \*    \*

Lambs' heads made the funeral feast. Uncle Vinnie had brought the cloven skulls in the morning from the Manhattan markets, wrapped in newspaper; now, hot and savoury, they steamed on the sideboard with bowls of tripe and macaroni. So many leaves had been inserted in the dining table to accommodate the mourners that the lower end thrust into the living room, where a second crowd were balancing plates on their laps. The house was hot and alive with the babble of talk his father had loved.

Chris's Uncle Pete, a teacher, greeted him tearfully. 'There are some guys make you feel you're part of something big. When they go, you wonder what it's all about.'

Chris wondered which of the men hunched over their plates could help get credit for the job. Their bond with Mike was strong. Other uncles spied him, kissed his cheeks and led him to the head of the table. Tony, ignoring a full plate and deaf to the blandishments of his aunts, was deep in conversation with Uncle Eamon. The police captain jumped up as if relieved by the interruption and said, 'There you are, boy. Take my chair.'

The women brought Chris a plate. Uncle Eamon flinched from the *contadino* food and retreated to the bar, a table of bottles in the living room, leaving Chris and Tony in the care of Uncle Vinnie, who squeezed between the brothers with a refill.

'Eat.'

Chris took a bite, couldn't swallow, and pushed his plate away. 'The fucking bank shut us down.'

'It figures.'

'What should I do?'

'That's a tough one, Chris.'

'Can you help me get money?'

'Black money.'

'Pop always said no shylocks. I already told this one to get lost.' He showed Vinnie the loan shark's business card. 'Know him?'

'Shit, yes. He's a Cirillo shylock.'

'He said he knew Pop.'

'He knew *Pop*?' asked Tony.

Uncle Vinnie said, 'You know how it is. Mob guys cosy up to legit businessmen.' He glanced around and lowered his voice. 'They know they're shit; they want someone important to tell 'em they're not. But don't forget, they also want a piece of your action. A couple of years ago, when your father was putting the Manhattan building together, everywhere he went this guy showed up with a big smile.'

'What did Pop do?' Tony asked.

'What could he do? As nice as he could, he ignored him. You don't want a guy like that thinking you insulted him. He probably bought your father a drink and now he goes around saying they're buddies. You were right to stay away from him.'

'I guess so, but I still have to raise the money.'

'You sure you want to get involved at all? You're going to have your hands full with the cement, unless you want to consolidate the cement. Why don't you come in with me?'

Chris caught the flash in Tony's eyes. His brother knew shit about the business, but he was sharp enough to warn him that Uncle Vinnie's offer, part *famiglia* – looking out for family interests – was also the sharp, cold ethics that won men like him and Mike Taglione pieces of the New York cement business.

'If I don't finish Pop's building,' Chris said, 'the greaseballs win.'

'There will always be wiseguys.'

'Not always,' said Tony.

'The rackets have been around a long time,' Uncle Vinnie retorted sternly. He chewed a forkful of tripe and said to Chris, 'Aren't you going to finish college?'

'Fuck college. You think I'm going to study business so I can get a job working for someone else? We already got a business. I'm a lucky guy. My pop built a business.' His eyes filled and Uncle Vinnie looked away.

'Let me talk to some guys.'

Later, he led Chris into the living room where a grey-haired patrician banker was waiting with Arnie. Both the banker and the Taglione project manager looked uncomfortable. 'This is Pete Stock, Chris. He's a real estate officer at the bank.'

'We've met. Thanks for coming today, Mr Stock.'

'Of course, I came. I've dealt for years with your father on his Queens' projects. I'm sorry that the bank had to withdraw credit on the big building.'

'I want to finish my father's building.'

Stock shook his head. 'Chris, you're plunging head first into a deeply troubled market. Manhattan's getting overbuilt.'

'We're preleased. And Aetna's pledged to buy it in two years.'

'That's fine for Aetna. They don't risk a dime until you're finished the building and actually filled it with tenants.'

'But we're preleased. We've got tenants.'

'You've got tenants *signed,* which is how your father got Aetna. But you still have to get them in. So, in other words, the bank is taking the risk on your performance – *your* ability, now that your father is gone, to meet schedules and contain costs and control labour. It's a big job for a college student.'

'I can do it. I've worked with my father since I was fourteen. We had big plans to move Taglione Construction into Manhattan development.'

Stock swished the ice in his drink. 'Chris, Manhattan real estate is even tighter than the cement business. It's been controlled by a handful of developers for decades. Men who can walk down Fifth Avenue, or Second Avenue or Eighth Avenue, and tell you the history of every building on the street, from the day the land was assembled, to who built it, financed it, bought and sold it, leased it, renovated it, and tore it down and built a new one. . . I hope you understand that I'm trying every way I know to discourage you.'

'We were going to be guys like that. . . Can you give me credit?'

'We'll bring in a man to run the job.'

'*No*. Then it's not our job. No way. I can do it. My father must have told you he was going to make me a partner.'

'At least fifty times.' Stock looked pained. 'Listen, your father's friends are leaning hard on me, very hard. But if you insist on going alone –'

'I do.'

'Then the best I can do is persuade the bank to extend interim financing for two months. If you haven't performed by then, it's all over.'

'I can do it.'

'But you have to agree to put the trucks up as collateral –'

'The trucks?' Chris echoed, dismayed. 'We've already put up all our property.'

Stock sighed, clearly uncomfortable with his own terms. 'That's what my superiors will demand. I'm sorry. If you still feel this way Monday, come by the office and we'll do the paper work. But at this point I want you to listen to your father's project manager.'

'Don't do it,' said Arnie. 'Without the trucks you got nothing.'

'Yeah, I know, but –'

'Your father's trucks. That's all you got.'

In his mind Chris saw them parked in rows at their East River plant, astonishing in their number. By the time he had been old enough to count there had been enough to be called a fleet. 'I have to think, Mr Stock.'

'That's precisely what I want you to do. Goodbye. Good luck. And again, I'm so sorry we've lost your father.'

'I'll walk you out,' said Arnie.

Chris stood where he was, his mind reeling.

A tiny old man tugged his sleeve. He looked down at Alphonse Castellone, who gave him a toothless grin. 'Leesa trucks.'

Alphonse Castellone was unbelievably old, totally uneducated, and as primitive as a Sicilian cowherd. But he had pioneered heavy equipment rental in New York and was very rich because of it, which Chris and everyone else in the room respected mightily. Already, his aunts and uncles were watching with relief and pleasure the private conversation of the grieving son and the wise elder.

'They're my father's tracks, Alphonse.'

Alphonse replied with the bluntness of age. 'Your Pop was the last dummy in the city to own equipment. So what you lose your trucks? I buy 'em from the bank and leesa back. I leesa ya anything. I leesa shovel, I leesa grader. I leesa whole goddammed tower crane. But I canna leesa *contacts*. I canna leesa smarts.'

'Sellin' cement is knowin' who's who and what's what. You already got that from your Pop.' He looked around the living room, nodded at the people watching respectfully, and said, 'Fuck the trucks.'

Chris felt his lips part in his first smile in three days. The old man was right. Arnie had utterly no understanding that his father's contacts were the real value of Taglione Concrete. Alphonse patted his arm. 'You did a good funeral. Your father woulda liked it. It's over, now. Go do some business.'

He tore after Stock and cornered him in the foyer. They talked over the details for a few minutes and the banker reluctantly honoured his offer. Then Stock left amid a general exodus of business associates and friends. Shortly, the family too began to trickle away, the few Irish first, Italian cousins next, and finally teary aunts and sad-faced uncles. The women instructed Chris how to heat up the food they had left in the refrigerator, and the men clasped the young brothers in their arms.

Uncle Vinnie was the last to leave. He sent Aunt Marie ahead to the car, which was parked down the short front walk at the kerb. 'You need anything, anything at all, you telephone. I'll stop by the job Monday, Chris.'

'I'll be at the bank.'

'So I'll walk you over. See you early. Hey, Tony. You call if you need me, right?'

'Thanks, Uncle Vinnie.'

Chris stood with Tony in the front door, holding each moment like heart-beats. Uncle Vinnie gripped the iron railing as he climbed down the front step. His shoes clicked on the walk. The street was quiet but for nightbugs humming in the trees; the sidewalk was softly lit by street lamps which cast dull pools of light filtered by the leaves. Far off a highway murmured like a river.

Uncle Vinnie's Cadillac settled deeply on its springs. His door thunked shut, blacking the courtesy lights which had shone briefly on Aunt Marie's unhappy face. He started the engine and turned on the headlights. The power steering whined and as he slowly pulled away and around the corner, the taillights blinking through the neighbour's privet hedge. Tony turned into the house and Chris followed, holding the door open a moment longer before he closed it.

They were alone.

★　　★　　★

'Look how they cleaned up. Like nobody was here.'

'Aunt Marie had the vacuum going.'

They stood looking around the empty living room, then at each other. 'Want a drink?'

'Yeah.'

Tony poured Johnnie Walker Black Label at the table set up for a bar. The ice-bucket, a gold plastic container made to look like a barrel, was empty. They headed for the kitchen. The big refrigerator icemaker was empty, and the crushed ice dispenser in the door was out as well. Chris found an old tray in the freezer. He smacked the shrunken cubes out in the sink, filled their glasses with a handful, and headed for the living room.

'Want to go downstairs?'

Downstairs was a wood-panelled family room where, since their mother died, they usually ate supper on trays, watching the TV news with their father. Tony started to turn off the living-room lights.

'Leave it, man.'

Chris settled on a puffed couch, beige like the carpet and covered in a shiny cloth. This had been their mother's room, her special place for special events. It had a big glass coffee table, couches, and chairs flanked by enormous lamps. Shortly before she died, she had hung a picture of the Pope over the fireplace.

Before the cancer, she had enjoyed giving parties, and their father had knocked out a wall so the living-room el-ed into the dining-room, like a suburban house. Her grand piano filled the other end; it had been unplayed for years, although Tony had taken lessons. The polished brown top was down and on it stood a realistic model of the Fifty-sixth Street building as it would look nearing the end of construction; the lower floors were sheathed in soft green glass and most of the steel frame was erected. On top was a little derrick hoisting a steel beam from a miniature truck with TAGLIONE written on the side.

'Remember when he got the model?'

'That was one smart architect. He knew that toy gave him Pop's business for life . . .'

They sat silently, looking around the room.

'Life,' Tony repeated bitterly. 'We said dumb stuff like that when Mom died too.'

Chris said, 'You know what I never got until now? He protected us when she died. When did *he* cry?'

'Ask Sylvia.'

'*Get off it, man*. That just started.'

'Chris, you are so fucking naive. Pop was balling her for years.'

'No way,' Chris retorted firmly. 'She had a guy until after mom died. She told me once. They were both lonely.'

Tony softened abruptly. 'Hell, she's a good-looking woman. Pop was lucky to find her.'

'Speaking of good-looking, did you check out Cousin Mary Jane?'

Tony grinned. 'I wanted to jump on her right in the church. Remember when we met her at Uncle Eamon's the first time? What was she, six? I was eight. You were six? We had the most incredible fight in the car on the way home.'

'Pop called us horny bastards. I thought Mom would croak . . . Shit, now I'm saying it.'

'Remember when he caught us at Uncle Vinnie's?'

'Everybody at the kitchen table eating spaghetti.'

'Except us in the front room with what's her name.'

'I don't think he ever told Mom.'

Chris went to the piano and reached behind the model for a picture in a tarnished silver frame. 'Mom when she met Pop. Is that Mary Jane today?'

Tony took the frame and studied her picture. 'The Mick side is dynamite.' 'Tagliones aren't bad. You notice Lucille?'

'The *elephant?*'

'No. Not Uncle Vinnie's Lucille. *Little* Lucille Taglione.' Every branch of the Tagliones had a Lucille, named for their great grandmother, a mythic figure from the old country who had died a year ago at age one hundred. Little Lucille belonged to Uncle Pete.

'What are you robbing cradles? She's fifteen.'

'I'm not saying *jump* on her, but in a couple years she's going to melt some eyeballs.'

'A little bottom heavy.'

'Baby fat. It goes away when they have sex.'

'It does?' Tony looked at him. 'Oh, bullshit. Christ, you had me believing you.'

'Remember the time you asked Pop if it was true when I told you that dragonflies fuck flying?'

'He belted me for saying fuck –'

'For an older brother you were pretty dumb.'

'I didn't know how else to say it. Then he came out to the pond with us. Remember?'

That was upstate in the Catskills, where they spent summers with their mother. Mike drove up on weekends; Chris and Tony would lead him barefoot and sinking in the wet grass around the pond Saturday mornings to show him the frog eggs, snakes, and baby fish they had discovered during the week. Chris remembered the water squelching around his father's toes, the way he rolled up his pants and how white were his feet and legs, while theirs were brown from playing in the sun.

Tony threw his head back and gazed at the ceiling as if he were seeing the mountain sky. 'Dragonflies swooping together twosies and threesies, really

41

getting it on, laying eggs in the water and having a fine time. Pop watched about ten minutes, not saying a word. Finally he looked at you – real serious, his eyebrows got thick – looked at you, looked at me, and he said, "They're dancing." '

'When he walked back to the house we heard Mom laughing. . . God, I wish. . .'

'What did Uncle Vinnie say about the building?'

'He set me up with a guy at the bank. They want the trucks for collateral.'

Tony shrugged. 'You going to?'

'Would you come in with me?'

'I'm going to law school.'

Chris wandered back to the piano and stared at the model of his father's building. He twined his fingers through the threads that represented derrick guys, the cables which supported the derrick mast. The model builder was a nut for detail, right down to the spider, the round fitting atop the mast where the guylines converged.

The funeral day began rushing though his memory – the window, the priest he didn't like, the shylock, and the stilled machines. His hand clutched and snapped a cable. He put down his glass and tried to tie it. But his fingers were clumsy from the scotch and trembling from exhaustion, and he snapped another. The mast started to lean; before he could stop it, it snapped a third thread of its own weight.

'What are you doing to Pop's model?'

'Nothing.' Chris gave up and released a fourth and fifth cable and laid the derrick gently on its side, resolving to repair it when he was sober. 'What did Uncle Eamon say?'

'They're investigating.'

'That's what the cops tell strangers.'

'He'll stay on it.'

'I wish I had stopped Pop! I saw he was mad. I should have pulled him back. I could have stepped between them.'

'It was too late. It was over in a second.'

'I didn't think.'

Tony crossed the room and removed Chris's hand from the model. 'Pop was way too fast. I didn't even see that punch. Did you?'

'I saw him go up on his feet. I should of known when I saw him go up on his feet. He was so fucking fast.'

'I wish he had taught me to box,' Tony said sadly. 'He'd always say, I was too light, wait 'til I got bigger. Said he was afraid he'd hurt me. He never hurt you. You were younger and he taught you.'

'I had the weight,' Chris said lamely. 'He knew if he slipped I could take a punch.'

'He waited too long.'

'What are we going to do about Rendini?'

'What do you mean?'

'He killed Pop.'

'I told you, Uncle Eamon −'

'Aren't sons supposed to avenge their fathers?'

'Avenge?' Tony looked at him like he was nuts. 'Sons sleeping in sheepshit in Sicily, maybe. Not Americans.'

His brother's hand fell away from his and Chris suddenly felt so alone that he started to cry. 'I should have stopped him.'

'You couldn't.'

'If I'd moved a second sooner I'd have pulled him away from the truck.'

'You got there ahead of me.'

Chris shuddered. He could still feel his father's grip go dead in his hand. Tony said, 'I'm going to bed.'

'Oh, stay up, man.'

'I can't. I'm crashing.'

Chris watched his brother ascend the stairs; Tony was self-contained, a small, tight package, like a sealed, permanently lubricated electric motor humming along forever. Chris laughed. Tony turned. 'What?'

'The last thing Pop said was to take care of you.'

'I can take care of myself.'

'No kidding.'

'Hey, Bro? He said the same thing to me about you. Good night.'

'How soon before you have to leave for school?'

'I'm leaving the job tomorrow.'

' *What*? I thought you had two months.'

'Congressman Costanzo stopped by before you got back.'

'He did? Hey, that's really nice of him.'

'He said he was sorry he couldn't make the Mass, asked about you, said all the right things. Anyway, I hit him up for a job.'

'Doing what? Hey, I need you this summer at least.'

'He's recommending me for a student internship in the criminal division of the US Attorney's office. I'm going over tomorrow for an interview.'

'Tomorrow's Saturday.'

'They don't punch a time clock. I'm sorry about the timing, Chris. It's a great shot for me. If I get in there now, I'll have a leg up when I graduate.'

'But you were going to be Pop's lawyer. Not some Fed's.'

'That was Pop's idea, not mine. Good night.'

'Jesus Christ, Tony. We always thought –'

'*You* always thought and *he* always thought. Nobody asked me.'

'It's our company. Pop made it into something big.'

'I don't care about making money. I want to serve.'

'Serve? Serving fucking who? Serve us.'

'I'm going to serve the law. I want to be part of it. Not just dodge around it'.

'I don't believe you. You sound like a goddamned priest.'

'Chris, I'm sorry. This is a fight I was supposed to have with Pop two years from now. Good night.'

Stunned, Chris got up and took a slug of scotch from the bottle. It burned going down. He tipped the bottle again, but he knew he wasn't going to get any higher tonight. Just a headache in the morning. He turned out the lights and climbed the stairs. Tony's door was closed. He had left his bed unmade but an aunt had made it. He flopped on top of it and stared at the ceiling. He got up and went down the hall and looked at his parents' bed. Then he took a shower and climbed into bed.

He lay awake in the dark and for some reason thought of Greenpoint – their taste of the street the end of his junior year of high school, a few months after their mother had died. They had started hanging out with a group who had an apartment in Greenpoint – a 'crashpad' in the dated parlance of the middle-class American hippie drug scene that had finally seeped down to the Italians and Irish of Queens, even as the originals were getting haircuts and going back to school. Grass and acid and ludes fuelled the scene, coke or the Procaine mixes that passed for it, and whispers of heroin nearby; couples joined, split, realigned, like the dragonflies. Chris and Tony, fleeing their mother's death, had plunged into the free and easy difference of it all, the obliteration of time, and the dull kick of working angles dealing dope.

It hadn't taken their widowed father long to realize something was wrong. His reaction had been typical. He had driven to Greenpoint early one morning and collared his sons, who had crashed on a mattress with a girl from the Bronx. Clamping a big hand around each neck, he had marched them down the stairs, tossed them into the Lincoln, and drove to Wall Street, where one of his friends was superintendent on a sixty-storey tower. He pulled tools and gear from his trunk, shiny new stuff, straight from the supplier.

'You wanna get high? I'll make you high. Here's your hardhat, spud wrench, bolt bag, gloves, and shoes. Put 'em on.' He handed his friend papers from the Ironworker's Union. 'Here's their tickets. This guy's your boss. I'll pick you up at quitting time.'

'Hey, Pop,' Tony protested.

'You want to go college, you're going to pay for it. You can see your friends on the weekend. Meanwhile, a lot of people did a favour for this. Don't make me look like an asshole.'

Chris, too, started to resist, until he was stunned to see fear on his father's face – it flickered in his eyes and made his jaw work. The special bond they had always shared helped him understand that tough Mike Taglione was alone and helpless, and was desperately trying the only thing he knew how. He told Tony to shut up.

The super pointed at a spot five hundred feet in the sky. 'Dougherty's your pusher. Boss of the raising gang. Grab a keg of bolts on your way up.'

The keg weighed two hundred pounds. They manhandled it to the top, where Dougherty, a grizzled veteran of thirty-five and some six inches taller than Chris, put them to work carrying small beams for the detail crew. It had been a turning point, forging a new family out of the lost sheep 'Irish' Kathleen Taggart Taglione had left alone. They got hooked on the macho work, and by the end of the summer were bulging with muscle and had been promoted to bolter-ups, installing the final bolts where headers and columns joined over the city. Next summer they had advanced to connecting the girders. Only this year they had come back to the concrete to pour foundations because it was their father's special building.

And in Greenpoint, Chris thought, as he drifted off, most of the kids they'd hung out with were still hanging out. A few had ODed, and one had been shot while making a buy in Harlem.

He was asleep when the phone rang. He came up groggy, felt around on the floor, found it under his extra pillow. The luminous clock said three.

'Chris?'

'Yeah?'

'Uncle Eamon. You awake?'

'What's the matter?'

'I had to call you before you read it in the paper.'

Chris sat up. 'What happened?'

'We found the driver in a garbage can.'

'Dead?'

What do you think?'

'What about Rendini? He's the one who told the driver to do it.'

'He didn't tell him in front of witnesses. So with the driver dead, the scumbag is scot free.'

★    ★    ★

Eamon Taggart and Mike Taglione had met in Korea; after the war, Eamon had introduced Mike to his sister. In the sheer ignorance of his bigotry, he had never dreamed that the tall blonde Kathleen could be attracted to his dark barrel-chested Italian war buddy, and he had been stunned, even betrayed, when Mike and 'Irish' married. But they had stayed friends of a sort, and when she died, it was Eamon who brought a bottle and sat with Mike through the night.

Now he perched on the edge of their father's chair with his captain's cap on his knees, and tried to explain why the police couldn't arrest Mike Taglione's killer. Tony listened silently. Chris hammered him with questions he could not answer.

'How can you believe that driver lost his air brakes?'

'The driver said he did. By the time we got to the truck, they weren't working.'

'There were fifty men hanging around that truck! Rendini's people had time to mess up the lines.'

'*You* know that. *I* know that. But we can't *prove* it.'

'But the driver was one of Rendini's hoods. Didn't you say he had a record?'

'He's *dead*. We can't offer immunity to a dead man. I wish I could say we'll bring Rendini to trial. But we won't. We can't, as much as we want to. But it'll be a long while before they hit you for another payoff, I guarantee it.'

'But Rendini had the motive to kill my father.'

Uncle Eamon sighed. 'Chris, just between you, me and Tony, Rendini didn't likely act on his own. A Cirillo crew leader might have been waiting in the car. He might have okayed killing your father. But I'll bet even he called upstairs to an underboss on the mobile phone.'

'The Cirillos gave orders to kill my father on the *CB radio?*'

'They don't come right out and say it.'

'I can't believe they'd say it on the radio,' Chris protested, fighting the idea that the murder went above Rendini. It was too complicated. How many names and faces could he hate?

'Chris. They talk carefully.' Chris glared stubbornly and Eamon sighed again. 'Look, when your Pop and your Uncle Vinnie get together to sell cement, do they – *did* they – come right out and say, "I'll bid so and so and you bid such and such less?" No. They talk around it.'

Chris started to protest the slur. Eamon ignored him. 'Same thing here,' he continued blandly. 'You know what I'm saying . . . Take my word for it. Rendini's just one little link in a long, long chain. You wouldn't believe the command charts the organized crime squad has drawn. They look exactly like a corporation's.'

'Show us,' Tony said.

'Beg pardon?'

'Let's see them.'

Eamon drove them to One Police Plaza.

The Mafia's command charts drawn by the Organized Crime Control Bureau were draped on easels like architectural renderings. Chris recalled how his father had practically danced with anticipation at the first plans presentation for his Manhattan tower. A young, heavyset detective was waiting for Eamon.

'This guy knows more than anybody, right, Jack? Jack Warner, my nephews Tony and Chris Taglione. Show 'em what you do here.'

'Yes, Captain.' Warner did not mention their father, but it was clear by the chart he chose to illustrate that he knew what had happened. 'Here's the Cirillos, the biggest of the New York families. The family Joey Rendini answers to. Rendini is here, pretty high up 'cause that union local is a real money earner. I'm pretty sure he's a soldier, a "made" guy, but maybe just an associate. These guys here are what they used to call *capos;* the young ones call 'em crew leaders. Above 'em are underbosses. This Salvatore Ponte, called Sally Smarts, is *consigliere,* counsellor to the boss himself, old man Cirillo. "Don Richard", he calls himself, but he used to be just, "Little Richie", 'cause he's a runt.'

'Who are these two?' Tony pointed at blocks beside Don Cirillo.

'Michael, "Crazy Mikey", is Don Richard's younger son and chief enforcer. He acts as his father's personal, private hitter. Crazy Mikey loves his work. Wears a little coke spoon around his neck shaped like a sawn-off shotgun – sort of his badge of office. Nicholas is his older brother; the one with the brains. They're Don Richard's heirs. When he retires, they inherit, *if* they can hold off the underbosses. But you gotta remember the chart's only about half right.'

'Why?'

Uncle Eamon said, 'You're part Italian. You know how tight your families are. How do we infiltrate? Even using Italian cops is tough. Everybody knows who everybody is. It goes back to the old neighbourhoods.'

'It sounds like you're saying we're criminals because we're Italian, Eamon,' Chris interrupted. This was nothing new from the Irish side of the family; nor, he wanted Eamon to know, had he missed the sideswipe about bid rigging.

'Your people are tight,' Eamon continued blandly. 'They know who went to jail, who went into the service, who went to college, who stayed home, who joined the Force. Isn't that right, Jack?'

Chris noted that Jack Warner tactfully dodged Eamon's question. 'Also, the balance of power is constantly changing. When we do infiltrate, or persuade an informant, we often find we've connected with people who've already been edged out of power. The Cirillos are getting stronger and stronger with alliances and takeovers.'

When a telephone rang, Warner answered, excused himself, and left the room quickly.

Uncle Eamon said, 'It's a long chain. And tough for the law to break.'

'The law sucks.'

'Often,' Eamon agreed.

'I'd like to kill them with my own hands.'

'That's a normal reaction.'

'I mean it. I feel like sawing the barrels off a shotgun –'

'I'll not hear that talk, Chris.'

Chris's mind leaped to an old, untraceable weapon he had bought at a country tag sale. His father's work bench at their Catskill cabin had a heavy vice; hacksaw the barrels, throw away the blades, vacuum the metal filings, dump the vacuum bag . . . He looked his uncle in the eye and made what he knew was the most careful decision of his life. 'Sorry, Eamon. I just feel so angry.'

'Revenge is a normal desire. Of course, you want to get even.'

Tony had been studying the chart intently, tracing names with his finger. 'That's precisely the same stupid thing Rendini did,' he said. 'Instead of suing Pop for a punch in the nose.'

'What?' At this new resistance from another quarter, his own brother, Chris felt himself starting to lose control again, felt rage searing his throat.

'Revenge is crazy,' Tony replied coolly. 'That's what courts are for. The law is the only civilized way to get even.'

Chris spewed the rage at his brother. 'Didn't you hear Uncle Eamon say the law can't touch them?'

'It's practical, too. Not just civilized. If you take revenge on a killer, the killer's friends will take revenge on you, and back and forth and back and forth. But when the *law* catches a killer, the whole bloody chain is broken.'

'You sound like a fucking text book. Jesus Christ, Tony, I'm talking about *Pop.*'

'So am I.'

Uncle Eamon said, 'Tony's right. You go ahead. You live, you forget.'

'*I'll never forget.*' The brothers locked eyes, the grey-blue and the dark in sombre harmony.

They had spoken as one.

\*     \*     \*

He put up the trucks as collateral for a sixty-day bank note. But even as he signed the paper on Peter Stock's desk, he saw the future in a terrible instant – even if he could finish his father's building, he would never lose his rage.

The bank advanced him two million dollars to bring men and suppliers back to the job. The final construction cost required over twenty million. A brief respite, but the sharks smelled blood in the water. A second Cirillo shylock called for the same offer of short-term money at twenty-four per cent.

The accountant who was steering Taglione Concrete and Construction over the mud flats of probate joined with Arnie to advise that he abandon the project. 'You want I should tell you something, Chris? Your *father* shouldn't have gone into that fucking building. There's another recession coming, and we're still not out of the last one. Real estate's dead.'

'Real estate goes up and down in cycles.'

'Three blocks away that turkey on Fifty-seventh Street's been standing half-built for six months. Jobs are shutting down all over Manhattan.'

'Not this one.'

'How you going pay for it?'

'I don't know yet.' He was too angry to be worried. And he had much grimmer thoughts in his mind.

Business and the dreams he had dreamed with his father were one thing – but murder was another.

★　　★　　★

He called a staff meeting. Arnie, Ed the accountant, the bookkeeper, the foreman of the mixing plant, and Sylvia Marx filed gloomily into his father's office. Their faces and silence reflected their doubts that Taglione Concrete and Construction really existed without Mike at the steering wheel. Chris had to admit he felt a little silly sitting at the scratched metal desk.

'We got some pretty screwy files,' the accountant reported. 'Your dad kept a lot in his head.'

Chris knew his father had run a one-man show. He was haunted by his father's arcane business habits, yet instincts he had never tapped were welling up from memory. First and foremost, his father always had an answer. Chris stood up, put his hands in his pockets, sat on the desk, and told the sad-faced accountant, 'Start new files.'

Ed exchanged an incredulous look with the bookkeeper.

'Buy one of those little computers. We had one in business class at school. They ran about thirty grand and they're great for keeping track.'

'*Buy* a computer? With what? A lot of your Dad's customers figure with him gone there's no rush to pay their bills. We're crunched for cash. I don't even know if we can make the payroll.'

'Sell a truck.'

'You mortgaged them.'

'Thirty-four, thirty-seven, eighty-six, and one-fourteen were in the shop. I forgot to tell the bank we owned them.'

The accountant smiled.

'Sell it to old Alphonse. *Lease* a computer. Feed it our delivery invoices for the last six months. Give me a list of who owes us what by the end of the week.'

As they filed out, Sylvia Marx hung back. His father's secretary was a fiftyish blonde, a former Copa dancer with stunning legs. At the funeral she had stood off to the side, not sure of her place. Grief had cut hard lines in her pretty face.

'What's up, Sylvia?'

'I know the accounts that owe us the most.'

Chris visited the worst of the worst at a job site in the financial district. The steel was halfway to the sky, which meant they had owed on the foundation pour for a long time. He pushed into the main office trailer, introduced himself to the project manager.

'Sorry about your father, kid. What can I do for you?'

'I'm collecting our outstanding accounts.'

'And I'll bet we're standing way out. Right?'

'Right.'

'And you're pressed for cash?'

Chris admitted he was.

'Well, I know exactly what you're going through, because so am I. . . Tell you what. You want to clear things up? I can try and raise maybe about forty cents on the dollar.'

'Forty cents? But –'

'Help me out and help you too, right?'

'No. That's not even cost.'

'That's the best I can do for you.'

'Forty cents is ridiculous. You owe me a legitimate debt.'

The project manager stopped smiling. 'You want to settle for thirty-five?' Defeated, Chris returned to the office and told Sylvia what had happened.

'Get a haircut.'

'Nobody cares about long hair anymore, Sylvia.'

'Sure. All the builders' kids look like you.'

'So?'

'You can't afford to look like a kid. It's showbiz. You gotta look the part.'

'It wasn't looks with my father.'

'Your Pop was born with a part. Anybody looking at Mike Taglione knew this was one tough, smart, straight guy. Looking at you they see a nice college kid with long hair. You're big, but you look a little too sweet to hit anybody.'

'They could be wrong about that.

Sylvia gave him a shrewd look. 'Maybe.'

'I don't even *know* a barber. Girls at school cut my hair.'

'That I can believe. Why don't I make an appointment with your Pop's barber? And meet me at Paul Stuart's afterwards.'

Chris watched his image change in the Waldorf-Astoria barber shop mirror as his hair slid down the satiny sheet like yellow straw. He looked a little like a stranger and a lot like his father. His nose seemed bigger, and his brow grew broad and high. Freed of the shadow of long locks, his glittering blue eyes became the most prominent feature in his face.

Chris went to the coloured bottles in front of the mirror, opened one after another, sniffing the contents. 'This one.'

'That's what your father liked.'

'Right.'

'Very nice,' Sylvia said when he walked into Paul Stuart's. She took his arm and led him to the second floor.

'People are staring at me.'

'They think you're my gigolo.'

'Christ, Sylvia.'

'I used to take all my fellas shopping, but your father, God bless him, absolutely refused to buy clothes.'

He bought a suit and Sylvia chose a half dozen shirt and tie combinations.

'French cuffs are not really appropriate for daytime wear, madam,' the sales clerk remarked.

'The guys on his dance card aren't up on their Emily Post.'

Later, she revealed why she had insisted on the French cuffs. 'I already bought these for your Pop's birthday. I want you to have them.'

Chris opened the unmarked box. Two big cuff links burned white on a black velvet bed. 'Are these diamonds?'

'Don't worry about it. I know a guy.' She worked them into his cuffs. 'Kinda loud, but your Pop woulda liked them.' She stood back and admired the effect. 'You'll probably outgrow 'em, get conservative when you're a big success. Now go get 'em!'

Chris visited the next job on the debtors' list, found the project manager's office in a tenement across the street, and presented his bill.

'Hurting for cash, are you?'

'I'm just straightening up some loose ends before I start a new building.'

'What new building?'

Chris shot a French cuff, exposing a flash of diamond. 'I can't go into it yet. My father's partners are very nervous – afraid somebody'll bust in on the deal. Now if you can just give me a cheque.'

'Is that the same building your father started?'

'Another,' he embroidered the lie, looking hard at the guy. 'I want to clear things up with you.'

The guy scratched his head. 'It's kind of a heavy number.'

Chris shrugged. 'I won't bust your balls. I'll let you give me half now and half next month.'

Heart in his throat, he sat back as if he had the day to spend, and watched the man actually write a cheque. He forced himself to straighten his other cuff instead of lunging for it.

★　　★　　★

'Dinner,' he told Sylvia. 'To celebrate and thank you.'

He chose the Palm because he remembered his father mentioning it, but the restaurant was one Mike had taken her to and the evening turned sombre. They talked about how much they missed him. Sylvia got drunk, but covered well until the cab, where she cried. Chris said he wished he could kill the bastards. At her door she kissed his cheek and said, 'Finish your Pop's building. That's the best revenge.'

★　　★　　★

'You have only one month left and no way to raise more money and Arnie's already behind schedule.' The accountant nudged the bookkeeper, who nodded grave agreement. 'But you did great on collections and we're billing like a real business. So you don't need banks. You're fine if you just get out of that fucking building.'

Two problems. And both were Arnie. His father's old project manager couldn't hack it. And to make things worse, the bank knew. He went back to the best run of the jobs he had dunned to talk to the project managers, who ran the business end, and the superintendents, who bossed the field. Ben Riley was the first he clicked with, a blunt-spoken, middle-aged superintendent who reminded him a little of his father. Riley was sufficiently charmed by his brash approach to repair to a bar, where he ordered milk for his ulcer – a common superintendent affliction – lit a cigarette, and passed one to Chris. Nervous, Chris dropped it. Riley ground it under his boot and gave Chris another. 'The building business is bids and schedules. You know didley about bids, zip about managing supplies, and zilch about labour. How do you expect the banks to lend money to somebody who can't guarantee a schedule?'

'I know a lot about building. I know that labour's going to try to fuck me over and suppliers are going to try to steal me blind because they think they can. I think I know from my father how to control them, but the bank doesn't believe it, so I need help.'

'You sure do.'

'I'll top what these clowns are paying you by ten per cent, including your incentives. Plus I'll pay you a two-month bonus up front in cash.'

'You're *not* kidding.'

'I'm too young to kid. I'll be at the job tomorrow morning.'

Again and again, he raided his competitors until he had hired four top managers to do the job his father and Arnie had done alone – two top field men and two in the office.

'Fancy window dressing,' Arnie grumped. 'They're tripping over each other. You got enough bosses on the payroll to build the fucking pyramids.'

'Window dressing for the bank's sake,' Chris mollified him. 'With all these heavy hitters running the job, they can't bitch about Taglione Construction being one kid. Now you gotta make me look good by whipping the cement into shape.'

'Hey, wait a minute –'

'I can't do it myself, Arnie. And anything I'm doing hangs on the cement business making money. These guys'll run the building, you run the cement.'

'You're easing me out.'

'Arnie, you were a week behind schedule.'

He moved the Brooklyn headquarters into trailers at the foundation site so he could personally oversee the project. When the staff complained that his father never made them work under such rough conditions, Chris dipped again into Mike's reserves of goodwill. 'The sooner we finish the building, the sooner we get indoors. Besides, how can I learn to build Manhattan skyscrapers in Brooklyn?'

When his notes came due, his new managers had the foundation poured ahead of schedule and steel rising out of the hole. He put on his new suit and went to the bank, confident that Taglione Construction's performance had proved itself creditworthy, and proud that the interest cheque in his pocket proved he had put Taglione Concrete in the black. He failed to register that Peter Stock's receptionist was emptying her desk drawers into a shoulderbag.

'Chris Taglione to see Peter Stock.'

'Mr Stock is no longer with the Bank.'

'*What*? Where'd he go?'

She looked up, her face bitter. 'Where do you think? The unemployment line.'

'Fired? Christ . . . Well, can I see his boss? Who's his boss? Sphunt?'

'Sphunt's fired, too. *Everybody's* fired.'

Chris looked around, noting belatedly that the corridors were in disarray, with pictures off the walls and boxes on the carpet. 'Who's in charge?'

'Mr Bunker.'

Through the open door Chris saw a man about his age unpacking a cardboard box. He wore shirt sleeves, a narrow tie loose at the neck, and wire-rimmed glasses. Chris knocked on the door frame and stepped in. Bunker said, 'You're late.'

'No, I'm not.'

'You're from Wharton.'

'Taglione Construction.'

'I'm looking for my assistant.'

'I'm looking to roll a note. Taglione Construction. You're backing my Fifty-sixth Street tower.'

'Was this one of Stock's deals?'

'Sure. My father dealt with Mr Stock for fifteen years.'

'Bye bye.'

Bunker pulled a framed diploma from a cardboard box and hung it on one of the many picture hooks Stock had left on his wall. It said that Bunker had graduated from the Harvard Business School three months ago.

'You mind telling me what's going on?'

'The bank has eaten too many loans,' Bunker replied, straightening his diploma. 'About two hundred million dollars worth, to be precise. So they're cleaning house. They fired everybody in the real estate department and hired me to pick up the pieces.'

Chris sank in a chair and stared in disbelief.

'My bank has to do this now?'

'Well, it's obvious you possess one quality a builder needs – total egocentricity. Not just *your* bank. *Every* bank.'

'What?'

'Every bank in New York has, as of this morning – or will, as of tomorrow – fired its entire real estate department. It seems some very cosy relationships have sprung up between real estate officers and developers.'

'How the fuck do you think we got buildings built?'

'You got too many of them built. Nobody said, Stop. So you've got twenty million square feet unused, empty, and unrentable.'

'My building's preleased.'

'There's another recession coming. Are you sure your tenants can afford the space?'

'We can't just stop. We've promised to supply the space.'

Bunker reached into his box and pulled out a coffee mug. 'It suddenly hits me, this is what I went to school for. Guys like you and Stock get so cosy nobody asks the hard questions.'

Chris stared at him. 'So you're going to run an uncosy department?'

'Right. Nobody's pulling friendship to jolly me into dumb loans.'

Bunker removed the last item from his box, a Hewlett-Packard calculator, and set it beside the mug.

'Let me ask you something?'

'And then I must excuse myself.'

'How are you going to know who's honest?'

'Credentials.'

'And who keeps their word?'

'Track record.'

'That's the past. Track records and credentials tell you what's *already* happened. Cosy is knowing about it now.' A childhood and adolescence of conversations half-heard at family dinners and job-site trailer offices started galloping onto his tongue. 'How do you know who's maybe getting into trouble with some building inspector? And who's about to get slapped with a mechanics lien 'cause he stiffed his employees? And whose contractor is overbooked? Who's undercapitalized? Who's got union problems? Who can't hack it anymore? Whose subs are about to go broke?. . . Cosy pays, man. You gotta be in touch. Otherwise you miss the good deals and only the people everyone else knows to avoid will come to you. Now I'm bringing you a good deal. I am preleased, thank God, and I'm running ahead of schedule. The slowdown means I'm getting breaks on everything. And my building is small enough so even if some of my tenants back out, I won't be killed.'

'So what's your problem?'

'I need money. My old man was – died, and everyone thinks I'm a kid. All I'm asking for is the money they would have loaned him.'

Bunker looked at him for a full and silent thirty seconds. Chris glared back. Couldn't anybody see what he knew was true?

'Let me find your file.'

Bunker returned with a thick folder which he spread on his desk and read for five minutes. Finally he looked up. 'This is a bitch.'

'I don't owe that much,' Chris protested.

'That's the bitch. You don't owe us enough money to have any leverage.'

'What?'

'This morning I told a developer he owed us forty-six million dollars. He said he was aware of that. I asked when he proposed to pay it. He said as soon as the market gets better. I said that's not good enough. He said, then take my building. Then he said, fuck you, and hung up. Because he knows as well as I know that the bank doesn't have any use for a half-built unleased building.'

'But he *will* pay you,' Chris said. 'If you were ballsy, you'd lend him the money to finish his building.'

'You say ballsy and I think twenty million unused square feet.'

'He's not a dead beat, he's just temporarily in trouble. Like me.'

'Unfortunately for you, Mr Taglione, you don't owe anywhere near forty-six million dollars. So your troubles aren't the bank's.'

'But I do have leases if I can just get the thing built.'

Bunker tapped the papers with his pencil and poked his calculator again. 'The fact is, your father does seem to have minimized the risk . . . It's a fairly creative financial structure.'

'Pretty good for a hod-carrier.'

'Beg your pardon?'

'Something he used to say.'

'It's obvious he was more interested in completing a building than reaping a large profit.'

'He wanted to get his foot in the door.'

'Yes, I can see that. It's a good location, too. It's this goddamned market that worries me . . . Do you mind my asking how your father died?'

Every instinct screamed that this slick Presbyterian would not lend money to a wop in a Mafia feud. Bunker looked at him. 'You said he died.'

'A construction accident,' Chris murmured, the lie burning in his stomach. 'A truck. Never knew what hit him.' Another lie, to lay him to rest. If only that were true he might not hate so much; but Mike Taglione had known exactly what had hit him and why.

Bunker removed his glasses, covered his face with his hands and peered between his fingers. 'I don't believe I'm doing this, but provided everything you say checks out, we'll roll your notes another sixty days, and extend the next stage of credit.'

'Just like that?'

'Why not? I'm the entire real estate department, except for my assistant from Wharton, who apparently can't find the building.'

Chris felt like a door had opened on a sunny room. He reached across the desk. 'Thank you. I'll never forget.'

Bunker shook hands mechanically, as if they had told him at school he was expected to indulge native customs.

# 3

The brothers went out for a farewell supper the chilly September night before the day Tony returned to Cambridge for his first year at Harvard Law School. Chris suggested driving into the city, but Tony insisted on his favourite, Abatelli's, an Italian restaurant on Woodhaven Boulevard. While Tony drove their father's Lincoln, Chris stared moodily at the sidewalks; children were running home from the neighbourhood shops with loaves of bread, milk, and the evening paper. He dreaded living in the empty house without his brother. He knew already that he would sleep most nights on a couch in the office trailer.

'Why do you think Pop did it?' Chris asked. 'Why'd he tell Rendini to go fuck himself? After all those years of paying off.'

'I don't want to talk about Pop.'

'Yeah, but why? I gotta know why.'

Tony sighed. 'Why'd he suddenly go from building Queens apartment houses to a Manhattan office tower?'

'I think Pop made a mistake by not paying.'

'No, he didn't. Will you get off it?'

'You mean that? He didn't make a mistake?'

'He did the right thing. His only mistake was doing it too late.'

Chris clung silently to his brother's judgement.

Tony laughed softly. 'You know, we're switching roles at last. Here I am twenty-four years old, starting law school, and I'm finally becoming big brother, and you're becoming the dumb kid.'

'It took you long enough, runt.'

The restaurant was deep and narrow, with three long rows of tables set with white tablecloths under replica Tiffany lamps. Joe Abatelli greeted them as regulars, for Tony had insisted on eating here two or three times a week, but tonight the expression on Joe's square fleshy face seemed guarded, Chris thought, and his greeting an ambivalent-sounding, 'Back so soon?'

'Tony can't stay away and my Pop always said this was the best guinea meal in the city.'

Joe put them at a table far in the back, Tony facing the door, and Chris the service bar. He beckoned a waiter and hurried away.

'What's his problem?'

'Knife fight in the kitchen, maybe.'

They drank two fast Scotches, as the restaurant filled up, and Chris started to relax. The booze seeped warmly through his shoulders and into his back, a warm, easy release. Hunting their waiter for another refill, he happened to be glancing towards the entrance when a sensual dark-haired girl glided in on the crest of a large family.

His throat tightened and his mouth went dry; for one clear, icy moment he forgot his father, the job, everything. She was very young, in her middle teens, slight, with pretty legs and small, round breasts. Her lips were full, her eyes large and very still. Her dark skin seemed to glow and her hair was like a long, silky drift of black night.

Tony looked up from his menu. 'Check it out!'

'I saw her first – she's mine!'

Tony gave his sharp tone a look. Then he smiled and said, 'We'll see.'

'I'm not kidding, Bro. This is one time you keep your hands off or I'll break your head.'

'Oh yeah?' Tony said with another teasing smile. 'You might have to get on line. Catch her big brother. He looks like an ape somebody shaved. Christ, she has two of them. And look at her old man!'

Her father was shorter than his sons, but easily as broad, and despite his fear that Tony would move in on him, Chris laughed. 'Alphonse could lease those guys to chew rocks. Hey, her mom's cute.'

'Kind of like Sylvia.' She had Sylvia's carefully made up and dressed look, as if she too had been in show business, but she was petite like her daughter.

'Mom must have some genes to hold off daddy's. That has go to be the most beautiful girl in Queens. Let's trade seats.'

'I wouldn't give you this seat for three hundred dollars. Turn around and stop staring.'

Joe Abatelli sat the family near the front. The parents placed the girl between them, while the brothers sat with their backs to Chris and Tony.

Tony flashed his best smile.

'What was that for?'

'She looked at me.'

Chris glanced over his shoulder. Her enormous eyes were violet. 'I am definitely in love.'

'She's only about fifteen.'

'I will sleep in her garage for three years.' He stopped Joe as the owner went by calling orders to his bartender. 'Hey, Joe, you got a line on those people?'

'What people?'

'The far-out girl with the huge ugly guys.'

Joe pulled away. 'I hear he owns the Blue Bus Line,' he said coolly.

'She's his daughter?'

'I don't know 'em. They're from Brooklyn.'

What are they doing here?'

What are you, a detective? They came to my restaurant. I'm very complimented. I hear they own restaurants, too. In Canarisie.'

Chris grinned. He felt spacy, high on the Scotch, and abruptly happy, as if a weight had lifted and he could be twenty-one for a night instead of businessman of the year. 'I'll pay you eight hundred bucks for her phone number.'

'I'm busy.' Joe hurried off.

'What's with him?'

Tony shrugged.

'How about another drink?'

'Think she's old enough to drive us home?'

'Drive *me* home, man. Is she looking?'

'At me.'

'Let's change seats.'

What are you gonna eat?'

'Cheesecake on her breasts.'

Tony waved for the waiter. 'How you doin'? Veal chop for Chris. Steak for me. Split a caesar salad?'

'Big one. And clams. Want to have clams first?'

Tony said, 'We'll start with clams. And we'll have another drink.'

'Doubles.'

The waiter wrote it down and left.

'What's she doing?'

'They just got company.'

'Who?' Chris didn't want to waste a turn around when she was distracted. Who came in?'

'I'm not sure.' Tony looked tense, alert, like a hunter sniffing the wind.

'What's going on?'

'I said I'm not sure.'

'I'm checking this out. I'll get some cigarettes.'

'No! Stay there. Have one of mine. I'll tell you what's happening.'

'Who came in?'

'Another family. I'll tell you when to look. Papa, mama, and a guy about our age. Joe's pulled the tables together. Everybody's up, shaking hands. Now!'

Chris pretended to wave for a waiter. The new arrivals were Italian, too, but looked like out-of-towners. The father was wearing a pastel leisure suit with a lot of gold, and the woman, suntanned to a mahogany brown, bulged in pink slacks and a flowered blouse. The son, a quiet-looking kid with troubled eyes, said hello shyly to the beautiful girl, who replied without a smile.

Their waiter came back with the Scotch. Tony asked, 'Who just came in?'

'I don't know 'em.'

'Joe knew they were coming. What'd the reservation say?'

'I don't know, man,' he replied, hurrying away.

'What's Miss Universe doing?' Chris asked.

'Reading her menu.'

'You think they'd sell us their daughter?'

'Lease her.'

'We could say we're orphans starting a new family. We need a sister.'

'Funny.'

Their waiter returned with raw cherrystone clams and hot bread. Chris started to turn around again. Tony said, 'I'll watch, you tell me how the job's going.'

Chris filled Tony in briefly on his loans from Bunker and the latest scheduling victories achieved by the managers he had hired for credibility. Tony's dark eyes kept flickering towards the front of the restaurant. 'It sounds like you know what you're doing.'

'No. But no one else seems to, either. So I keep moving and they keep running after me. Funny thing is, I know now that's how Pop operated. He always seemed to know what he was doing, but he couldn't. Nobody could. It's all a moving target. Sure you won't join me?'

'I told you, I'm going to be a prosecutor.'

Chris glanced over his shoulder. She was looking down at her precisely folded small hands, her face shielded by her long, shiny hair. The second time he looked she was nibbling like a cat from a plate of antipasto. There were several big platters of the hot antipasto on the table and the group seemed to be prolonging it as an ice breaker. When he looked a third time, her father said something, and her brothers turned around and gave him a hard look. Their waiter rescued him with a thick veal chop that covered most of the plate.

Later, halfway through his steak, Tony said, 'I can't figure it out.'

'What?'

'That's a meet of some sort.'

Chris turned around again. She looked up, straight at him, her violet eyes blazing defiance. Then she surprised him with a small, private smile, and he smiled back. Her brother noticed and Chris turned away before he caused her problems. Tony was smiling too, and he suddenly realized he didn't know which of them she had smiled at.

'It's about her,' he said. 'They're marrying her off.'

'What?'

'And she's fighting it.'

'Nobody does that shit anymore. Order some wine. I gotta make a call.'

Tony was gone a long time. Chris buttered breadsticks, picked at his salad, and stole glances at the girl. She got up as if to go to the ladies' room. The same direction, he thought enviously, that Tony had gone. She was gone awhile and when she came back, she gave Chris a stoned smile, and he realized she had escaped to smoke a joint. Tony returned and Chris asked, 'She come by the phone?'

'Yeah, she's going to spend the weekend with me at the cabin. After I teach her what to do with it, she'll marry you.'

'You didn't even say hello.'

'Actually, I was too busy talking to the guys at the office.'

He clinked his glass to Chris's and said through his smile, 'There *is* a meet going on at that table. They're connected.'

'Bullshit. Racket guys don't meet with their wives.'

'I thought the Blue Line Bus sounded familiar. Miss Universe's father is Eddie Rizzolo. He runs south Brooklyn and chunks of Queens. Gambling mostly, books and numbers, and he's got his paws in freight forwarding at Kennedy and LaGuardia. A little hijacking on the side. He's got a kind of loose partnership with the Cirillos. I keep hearing that this is a mob joint. Now we get to see the bastards.'

'Fuck,' Chris blurted, his emotions flip-flopping as they had all summer. 'What are you taking us to a mob place for?'

'I want to see these fuckers with my own eyes – hey, who's this?'

A little man in his sixties scuttled in the door and made for the joined tables, apologizing profusely. His thin ginger hair looked dyed. His suit was too large and his face sagged as if he had lost weight recently; his movements, however, were quick with nervous energy. Chris thought of a tiny shrew he had seen in the country, flinging itself on giant beetles, which it ripped apart with teeth and claws.

His voice carried. 'I'm so sorry. Business. I couldn't get away.'

The fathers and the brothers shot to their feet, protesting they themselves had just arrived. The mothers bobbed their heads with confirming smiles. The girl watched gravely, still as granite. Joe came running and solicitiously guided the newcomer to the head of the table.

'Sit, sit,' the little man smiled, and they dropped like stones.

'Somebody big,' Tony said needlessly, and then, more to the point, *'Turn around, Chris.'*

He did, his heart pounding. 'Hey, Joe!' Joe was hurrying towards the bar again, calling for another Pinot Grigio. 'Who's that came in?'

'I don't know.' He passed by again, the wine bottle in his hand. While he was fumbling with the foil and cork, the waiter dropped a bill on Chris and Tony's table. 'What's this? We haven't even finished. We're going to have dessert.'

'Joe wants you to pay.'

'What are you talking about?'

'You're bugging him with all your questions. He's got a big night going and he doesn't have time for it. The drinks were on the house.'

'What is this? All I'm asking is about a girl –.'

The waiter leaned closer. 'You ought to shut up, Chris. Do you know who just came in? You ever hear of Don Richard Cirillo?'

'Bullshit,' said Tony. 'He never comes out.'

'He's out now, man. Sitting right there. So why don't you both shut up.'

Chris turned completely around and stared at the man who controlled the biggest single piece of the rackets in New York: narcotics, gambling, extortion, and a number of union locals that his father – and now he – had to deal with. And one teamsters' local in particular, run by Joey Rendini.

Tony pinned his arm to the table. 'No.'

'I'll kill that fucker.'

The waiter backed away – 'Jesus, what did I say?' – and Joe Abatelli raced to their table. 'Please, Chris. I don't need this kind of trouble.'

Chris started to stand up. Tony wrestled his arm with both hands and muttered through his teeth to Joe, 'You know what happened to my father. Why the hell didn't you say something when we came in?'

The restaurateur looked wild with panic. 'I didn't know. I just knew these people were meeting. Neutral territory or some fucking thing. I didn't know *he'd* set it up. Gimme a break, Chris. Let me get through the night. Don't start trouble.'

'We're leaving,' Tony said. 'I don't want to be in the same room with those creeps.'

'Thank you, Tony. Thank you. Thank you very much. I'm sorry about this, Chris.'

'What's the meeting about?' Chris asked.

'Hey, come on.'

Tony turned on him, harshly, 'Joe, a second ago you're thanking me. You owe me. Answer Chris. What's it about?'

Their father's credo: Take nothing for nothing. *Give* nothing for nothing.

Joe whispered, 'I think it's two families been fighting. Don Richard brought 'em together. I appreciate your leaving now.'

'I want dessert,' Chris said.

'Chris, Tony. Please. Here, I got this.' He snapped the bill off the table, crumpled it in his hand. 'You just take care of the tip.'

Chris repeated his request in the firm, but polite voice he employed on the job and he was quite suddenly not a twenty-one-year-old kid to be shooed out of a restaurant. 'I want dessert. My father ate here. Tony and I come two and three times a week. This is our place. You can't kick us out for some rackets guy.'

Joe went white. 'Get him what he wants.'

The waiter ran for the pastry trolley and rolled it swiftly to their table, silver serving pieces ringing against the platters. Chris stared at the dark cakes, the cannoli flecked with red and green citrons, the striped Napolean. A single crumb would choke him. 'Forget it. Let's get out of here.'

'Too late,' Tony muttered. Cirillo's party were staring as Don Richard got up and walked towards them. He picked up a chair in his wiry, brown-spotted hands, set it between Chris and Tony, and sat down. He looked straight at Chris with eyes like coal. 'They told me you been bothering the girl.'

Tony said, 'We did not bother the girl.'

Don Richard ignored him. 'Now you're bothering me,' he said to Chris.

'Do you know who I am?' Chris asked, controlling the impulse to hit him only because he was so small and old enough to be his grandfather.

'No. I want you to behave in this restaurant or leave.'

'*Behave*? *You* tell *us* to behave? Your people –'

'I didn't come here to talk. I came here to ask you nicely to stop bothering a family party.'

'Your people –'

Don Richard cut him off with savage gesture. 'Outside!'

Chris surged to his feet. 'Let's go.'

'I'll catch up,' said Tony. He headed quickly for the men's room.

The Cirillo leader paused at his own table. 'Excuse me, a few moments.'

Chris kept going, the girl's level stare a hard diamond light in the centre of the red haze boiling across everything he saw. He pushed through the foyer and onto the dark street, and turned to face Cirillo as he came out the door. 'Your people –'

'Kid, I don't know what your problem is, but I'm telling you nice to leave us alone.'

'You tell me to *behave*? Your hoods *killed* my father.'

'What?' The little old man propped his spotted hands on his skinny hips and looked up innocently at Chris. 'What are you talking about? Who's your father?'

'Mike Taglione.'

'Never heard of him.'

'Joey Rendini killed him.'

'Who?'

'He works for you and did it on your orders.'

'Sonny, the last guy I killed was before you were born. I ain't in that business no more.'

'Now you pay people –'

'Hey! I been nice. You're attackin' me. Fuck you.' Cirillo pointed a finger towards the street. Two strong-arm men came swiftly from a car. 'He's not allowed back in the restaurant.'

Cirillo turned on his heel and went inside.

'Get out of here, kid,' one of the men said.

Chris had ceased to think. It never occurred to him that the Scotch had gone to his head, that Tony had disappeared, or that even one-on-one either of these men were formidable. They were as tall as he, heavy in the belly, and eight or ten years older; the restaurant neon flickering red and green highlighted thin lines of scar tissue which creased their brows and spelled heavyweight hopeful.

'Fuck you.' He started back to the restaurant.

The two men glanced up and down deserted Woodhaven Boulevard, calculated the distance to the nearest pedestrians, and moved swiftly in concert. One stepped lightly behind him. The other tossed a sharp jab at his face. Enraged, Chris blocked it, feinted with his left, and threw a hard right cross, the first combination Mike had ever taught him.

The strong-arm hit the sidewalk with a surprised grunt, shook his head, and bounced back to his feet like a rubber ball. 'Good hands, kid.'

His partner rabbit-punched Chris in the back of the neck and sunk a fist into his kidney. The pain staggered him. They pinned his arms behind him and shoved him around the comer where thick trees darkened the street lights. A tall, rangey man stepped out of the car, flexing his hands, and sauntered after them.

'We can handle it,' said one of the men holding Chris. And his partner cautioned, deferentially, 'It's okay, Mikey. Maybe you better go back to the car.'

'Shut up!' The man they called Mikey stepped closer, fingering a gold coke spoon, which was fashioned in the form of a miniature sawn-off shotgun. Chris couldn't see his face in the shadows, but a soft profile of blow-dried hair and a slick looking jacket might have belonged to a rich young Italian-American bachelor cruising the discos, one of the new, young entrepreneurs who had perhaps expanded the family grocery store or restaurant into a high-profit fast food joint. Chris's eyes locked, however, on the finely tooled spoon dangling from a gold chain. Mikey. *Crazy* Mikey? Don Richard Cirillo's enforcer son.

A bony fist – studded with rings – flickered out of the night and smashed his mouth. Chris levered himself against the men holding him and kicked back. Mikey dodged most of it and attacked like a whirlwind, punching and kicking. Chris tried to protect his balls with his legs and braced his work-hardened stomach muscles to absorb the body punches; Mikey changed tactics and all the heavy work in the world wasn't worth a damn against the flurry of hard jabs that tore Chris's cheek, blackened his eyes, and cut his lips.

Dizzy with pain, he sensed Mikey pause, planting his feet, and knew he was winding up to hurl a deliberate roundhouse to break his nose. It flew from the shadows like a stone. Chris managed to slip it partially, but it still tore a furrow along his cheek and banged his ear. Mikey kicked him in the stomach. The air whooshed out of his lungs and he hung helplessly between the two men holding him. Mikey fished a set of chrome knuckles from his pocket, swiftly removed his rings, and worked the knuckles onto his fist.

'Chris!' Tony yelled from the street.

'*Get away!*'

Tony skidded around the comer, launched himself, and hit Mikey airborne, dragging him down in a cursing tangle. They both got up and Tony swung wildly. Mikey doubled him over with a punch in the stomach and whirled on Chris, who was kicking in another futile effort to break the hold the other men had on his arms. A police siren screamed suddenly, drawing close. Light flashed on the knuckles. Cold metal tore into his face. The three men smashed him to the sidewalk, and ran.

Chris crawled towards Tony. When he saw the streetlight through the trees he was vaguely aware that Tony was turning him onto his back. Then there were red lights and cops and Tony was announcing calmly, 'I'm Tony Taglione. I called Captain Taggart.'

\*    \*    \*

'The trouble with you,' Eamon said later in the car, 'is you're arrogant.'

'He killed my father,' Chris slurred through battered lips. It had taken ten stitches to close a cut on his mouth and three on the rim of his eye. He ached everywhere and the teeth on the left side of his mouth felt loose. Tony was still hunched up, clutching his stomach, his face dead white.

'Let the Law do its job – no buts!' Eamon retorted angrily. 'I don't care who he is, or who you think he is, he's got the same rights as anybody else. The only person allowed to interrupt his dinner is a police officer with a warrant.'

'But no cops are doing that. Cirillo's free.'

'You want to pull a "Deathwish"?' Tony asked scornfully. 'Bronson blows away the Mafia boss? Bullshit. The Mafia's a system. It's not one guy. The Law's a system for that job.'

'The one punching me was called Mikey. Isn't that Cirillo's son? The one they call Crazy Mikey? Eamon, I couldn't see much of his face, but he had a little coke spoon like a gun. Remember? Show me pictures.'

'Go to bed,' said Eamon. 'Sleep it off.'

'I'm not drunk!'

'Then you've got no excuse.'

★   ★   ★

He vowed never again to blunder into a fight he couldn't win.

Ten weeks later they tested him.

The Teamsters' shop steward who spoke for Joey Rendini asked for a private meeting. Chris knew, despite Uncle Eamon's assurances to the contrary, that the Cirillos were about to end their self-imposed period of respect for the dead. He sat at his desk trying to control the expression on his face while the shop steward spelled it out.

'We got a problem with the ready-mix drivers, Chris.'

'How bad?'

'There's wildcat talk.'

Chris picked up a pencil and slowly drew a circle around the date on his calendar. It was four and a half months since his father was murdered. He had been waiting for this, wondering how long they would wait – and how he would react.

# 4

Their timing was no mystery. His building was precisely at the level, sixteen storeys, when he had to start pouring the concrete decks to stiffen the steel frame. Without that 'diaphragm' to hold it together, the structure would wobble and rack as he built higher.

Concrete was his own product, and yet he was powerless to supply it if the Mafia made his drivers walk. He shoved his hands under the desk to hide them. He was learning to control his face, almost without effort, but his fingers were rattling against each other. He wanted to break the shop steward's arms. But then he heard his own voice coolly expanding his options, declining to fight when he couldn't win.

Since the fight at Abatelli's, he was constantly surprised by the coldbloodedness of his rage. It still surged wildly out of his heart, like the jagged bolts of an electrical storm, but he was developing somewhere in his mind a sort of transformer, which channelled his anger into usable energy and protected him from its deadly backflash.

'Why don't you work up a list of your men's demands?' he asked calmly, maintaining the charade of labour relations. 'Then see what your needs are.' The bribe. 'And I'll talk to my people.' A warning not to make it too expensive. 'I'll get back to you.' A second warning, that he might not pay. And then, buzzing Sylvia on the intercom, a blunt threat. 'Sylvia, call Riley. Tell him to bring in that truck of cable we got in Long Island City.'

This was to let the shop steward know that if worse came to worse, Chris could keep working by guying the steel frame with cable and turnbuckles until he got concrete. His iron workers could continue to erect steel, and he could even prepare the decks to pour when the strike was over. Not that he wanted to; cabling cost a ton in time and labour and was only a temporary expedient. But it served to remind the shop steward that they were all in this together. He dismissed him with a curt, 'Get back to me,' and sagged behind his desk, physically ill.

*You pay to play.* He knew now, he thought bleakly, why his father had lost his cool with Rendini; he had been simply unable to stand paying bribes any

67

more. Grease, sensible investment, and incentive were all bullshit words to pretend it didn't tear a man to pieces to be forced to give away his work for nothing. He was still shaking that afternoon as he drove Tony to Kennedy Airport to go back to school after an uncomfortable Thanksgiving break. 'I swear, if Rendini had come himself, I would have killed him.'

'Tell 'em to go fuck themselves.'

'That might work in Harvard, kiddo. But I have to deal with these people.'

'That's the same mistake Pop made.'

'I gotta follow my gut. And my gut is stuff I learned from Pop.'

'You're perpetuating the system that killed him,' Tony replied coldly.

'And you're getting high and mighty about a scene you don't understand and have never worked in. This isn't hopping around atop the building with a spud wrench. I'm talking about keeping the job alive.'

'Maybe distance gives me a clearer eye. Maybe the reasons for the excuses don't show up at long range. Maybe you're too close to it to understand what you're doing to the rest of us.'

'Doing to the rest of who?'

'The whole city. The country. Democracy is fragile. You undermine it with your payoffs and bribes.'

'I'm talking about business.'

'Business? Look at the water.' They were driving on the Belt Parkway, skirting the lower bay of New York. A tug ploughed seaward and a few rusty freighters stood at anchor. Otherwise, the broad blue bay looked as empty as the sea.

'What about it?'

'Where'd the ships go?'

'What ships?'

'Remember when we were kids Pop would drive us around the docks, show us the ships? The harbour was full of ships. Remember the Eire Basin, the Atlantic Basin, the whole West Side? They're all gone. The mob's longshoreman unions wrecked the shipping business. The best harbour in the world is empty. How would you like to see that happen to construction?'

'I don't know what you're talking about.'

'I'm saying, if you don't like moral reasons for honesty and responsibility, look at the practical. Responsibility works better.'

'I'm *taking* responsibility. I'm trying to save Pop's company.'

'Parading around in a fancy suit? You're just picking up where Pop left off. Compromise.'

'Are you blaming Pop for what happened?'

'Pop fed the Mafia just like you are. Bribe money is power. People like you and Pop give the Mafia its power. They grow on guys like you and Pop.'

'I'm going to knock your fucking head off if you don't stop talking about Pop that way.'

'Why don't you stop the car and try it?' Tony shot back. 'But it won't change the issue. If you pay those bastards, you're going to cross a line you can never come back. They'll own you forever. And you and I are going to end up on opposite sides.'

'We're family.'

'Don't pull that shit on me. Family's the same excuse Pop used! Got himself killed, didn't he? Left us –'

Tony slammed his hand against the door, and for a second Chris saw beyond his own anger to the grief Tony was finally allowing to well up. 'Can't you see,' he continued with a trembling mouth, 'that the one thing that makes this country safe to live in is that citizens are more important than families?'

'Including brothers?'

'Especially brothers. People with every opportunity like you and me, we have a responsibility to make things better, not worse.'

'What is it with you? You only see things *your* way. Who the hell appointed *you* judge of better and worse?'

'It's not an appointment,' Tony said coldly. 'The job's there for the asking.'

'Maybe the job ought to have tougher requirements. Compassion, maybe. A little understanding of ordinary people?'

'Ordinary people have the same responsibility as the rest of us. Truth, honesty, no compromise.'

'How'd you get so hard-assed?'

'Watching you suck up to the people who killed my father.'

Chris swung hard, a backhand blow heavy with rage. Tony snapped his head away, fast, but Chris's high school ring tore across his cheekbone. When Chris saw the blood on his face he froze, squeezing the wheel, despising himself.

'I'm sorry,' he said, begging forgiveness, burning to kill Rendini. And Rendini's bosses and their bosses. Right up to Don Richard. Make them lose what he had lost.

'You're bleeding . . . It hurt?'

'Just get me to my plane.'

Tony found a tissue in the glove compartment and pressed it to the cut.

'I'm sorry I hit you.'

'Yeah.'

'You shouldn't have said that.'

'You got a problem with the truth?'

Chris drove slowly the last mile and a half, past the colour-coded parking lots. He remarked upon a Boeing 747 crossing an overpass they drove under, but Tony was silent. Chris passed the last lot and drove straight to the departure door.

'Aren't you going to park?'

'You got any more to say, write me a letter.'

Tony looked hurt, but it quickly turned to anger. 'Let's get something straight. I'm going into public service. You're going to be a problem for me if you're illegal.'

'I won't be any more problem than Pop was.'

Tony shoved his way out of the car and through the terminal doors. Chris watched his form fade into the mass of shadows rushing beyond the glass. He ran into the terminal and found Tony on the check-in line. 'Hey, we're all we got left . . . I want to hug you goodbye.'

Tony forced a smile. 'Hands off, you dirty guinea. You want the women on the plane to think I'm gay?'

Chris embraced him, surprised how small Tony felt. 'Get good marks.'

'And you straighten out your act.'

'Maybe I'll change my name.'

'That'll fool everybody but you and me.'

Chris backed away. 'See you at Christmas?'

He waited for some sign that the two of them were more important than an argument about payoffs, but all Tony gave him was a high-beam stare and a remote 'Sure. Christmas.'

Hurt and mad, lonely and sick with remorse, Chris stopped at the churchyard. He sat beside the thin grass covering the new plot and stroked the turf on his mother's grave. He wondered if the aching he felt for his father would subside the way it had when she had died. But no one had killed her; there had been no one to blame but God and disease, no target for rage.

'Pop, what the fuck should I do?'

Stupid question. Pop had always said, 'Pay the bastards when you got no choice.'

When the shop steward reached for the banded, used twenties, Chris clamped his hand on his wrist. 'Pass the word – no pigs. I'll follow the rules, if you guys do. But if you fuck up my building or ask too much, or threaten me or my brother, you'll kill the goose that lays the golden eggs.'

'Hey, Chris, I think –'

'Tell your people what I said. They already killed my father. I got nothing to lose.'

\*   \*   \*

The air lay still behind the cemetery walls, cold and sweet with wood smoke from the rectory. Dew glistened on the fallen leaves. He had stopped as he often did early in the morning on his way to work. He knelt and brushed the leaves from the grave, and he tried to commune with his father.

'How are you getting on, Chris?'

He jumped. Father Frye, his mother's priest, had crept out of the rectory and stood over him. Chris kept his head down and continued brushing the leaves with his hands.

'Tony's gone back to school, Father. I've dropped out to run the company.'

'I'm sure your dad would be pleased. I'm told your building is progressing nicely.' His breath hung in the cold air, like cartoon balloons.

'On schedule.'

'You must be the youngest general contractor in New York.'

It had been a dry autumn and the new grass was taking slowly. He rejected the notion of hiring a gardener. Let it follow its own course. 'What can I do for you, Father? I'd like to be alone here.'

'I was going to visit you soon. We should have a talk.'

'About what?'

'Your mother, you may not know, was a faithful supporter of Sinn Fein in the years before she died.'

'I know she contributed money to Irish causes near the end of her life.'

'Enormous sums.'

'Penance,' said Chris. 'Because she couldn't get my father to take your church seriously.'

His mother had embraced the Catholic hierarchy in the Irish-American manner, cherishing the belief that a direct line existed from priest to pope to God; she had fallen deeply in its thrall as she lay dying. Chris's father had been the opposite, heir to the Southern Italian peasant or *cantadino* tradition of family first and damn all outside authority, be it government or the Catholic church; he had had little patience and less respect for priests and bishops.

The priest ignored the jibe. 'I've been asked to convey the sympathies of certain parties. They want you to know that they understand it was your father's money your mother contributed and are grateful.'

'She was dying. How was my father going to stop her?'

'Perhaps he found it easier than accepting the Church,' the priest smiled. 'It all works out in the end.'

'By "certain parties", you mean Provos, don't you? Terrorists. She had some strange types visiting the hospital. My mother's money went for guns, did it?'

'Your mother believed in getting the job done.'

'My mother was half nuts with pain and fear. She could just as easily have left her money to a cat.'

'Your mother knew exactly what she was doing.'

'No, she didn't. But the point is, now they're wondering if the money's going to continue flowing to the Old Sod?'

'I imagine the thought crossed their minds,' Father Frye admitted with another sly smile. 'You *are* executor of your parents' wills.'

He had never surrendered the idea of revenge. It sustained him that one day, somehow, he would destroy Rendini. But his experience in business – distancing himself from the day to day details – shouted louder than before that the *method* he imagined was foolish. Were he to actually pull the trigger, he would set the entire police apparatus against himself; detectives, patient men with decades of learning like Uncle Eamon. Sure he could be clever, put his quick mind to bring invention, stack the details – yet the odds were with the cops.

He looked at the priest and found himself on familiar ground. Why not hire a professional just as he hired superintendents, project managers, lawyers? Even interior decorators, he thought with a thin smile, that made the priest squirm. A professional outside American organized crime? Chris loaded his voice with heavy insult and asked the priest, 'How do I know my money will ever get to the IRA?'

'Are you suggesting –'

'You've got a great setup for a con game here. Wrap the church in the Irish flag to shake down the orphans of dead contributors.'

Father Frye bristled, but he kept icy control – a man above insult when serving his cause. 'If you came to my church, my parishioners would set you straight about my dedication to Ireland.'

'I want *proof.*'

'Proof?'

Chris took a breath, acutely aware that he was on the edge of changing his life. 'Bring me proof.'

'What sort of proof did you have in mind?'

'Bring me someone convincing.'

The priest puffed up. Chris thought of a mean little boy playing soldier. 'Convincing is it you want? All right, Chris. I'll convince you.'

\*     \*     \*

John Ryan, quiet-spoken, middle-aged, ordinary looking but for his icy blue eyes, was in the country illegally. He met Chris, as the priest had promised, in an Irish bar on Second Avenue, where British liquor bottles were marked off-limits with a diagonal red stripe. Chris took him to a Jet's game and spent the afternoon and a long supper feeling him out. Late that night, he dropped him back at the rectory, still unsure how to rate a killer.

'You're looking for something,' said Ryan.

'Maybe.'

'Father Frye told me what happened. I think I can guess.'

'Meet me at Charley O's for lunch tomorrow.'

He drove to the job, climbed into the control cab of a crawler crane, and sat the rest of the night trying to assess how capable John Ryan was. At dawn, when the gleaming black and chrome commercial garbage trucks were racing down the street and he still hadn't made up his mind, he realized that he now put less time and thought into the gambles that were thrusting his father's building out of the ground. At lunch he showed John Ryan a photograph of Joey Rendini. 'He lives in Brooklyn. When the papers say he's dead, the IRA collects five thousand dollars.'

The gunman ran his blunt fingers over the face. Three days later Rendini was sprawled across the front page of the New York *Post,* shot twice in the knees and once in the back of his head.

★     ★     ★

Nursing an Irish coffee in the smoky warm winter afternoon gloom of Charley O's, Christopher Taglione waited with one heel hooked firmly on the bar rail, his eyes set just as firmly in the middle distance. He looked reflective and older than his years, but he was in fact gravely confused.

A glance at the handful of regular customers who reigned between the end of lunch and the start of the cocktail hour roused his fleeting concern; he should have been more careful where he chose to pay the gunman. But fear and cunning were far from his mind. Why, he wondered, was he not supremely satisfied that he had righted a terrible wrong?

He shivered and swallowed more of the hot, sweet, boozy coffee. He had to admit he felt less triumphant than sick. Yes, he had wanted to erase Joey Rendini, but the shooting in the knees amounted to torture, and his images of vengeance – the sawn shotgun barrels clinking to the workshop floor, Rendini's face disappearing in a torrent of pellets – had not encompassed pain. He realized, too late, that he didn't even want Rendini killed so much as made to suffer terrible loss, as he had suffered loss.

Ryan came in at last, his lined cheeks ruddy from the cold. Blowing on his thick workman's hands to warm them, he nodded hello to several drinkers. The bartender poured Murphy's, no ice, without having to ask. Again, Chris was reminded that this association could be dangerous. Yet Ryan was no fool. He pretended not to notice Chris at first, and when he did he said casually, 'Well, young fella, how are you?' and drew him just as casually towards an unoccupied corner.

Chris took fifty one-hundred dollar bills in an envelope from his breast pocket, passed the envelope under the table. What should he say, he wondered. Congratulations?

Ryan went to the men's room, presumably to count the money. Chris waited in turmoil. His father's murderer was dead. What was wrong? Ryan looked surprised to see him still there when he came back.

'Tell me what happened,' Chris demanded.

'The man begged for his life. He swore he wanted only to beat up your father. He claimed that the order to kill your father came right from the top.'

'Who on top?' Chris asked angrily, his earlier misgivings forgotten. 'Who gave the order?' Ryan could be drumming up business. But Uncle Eamon had raised exactly the same possibility. Wasn't a Mafia murder an endless chain of wrongs?

'He would not say,' John Ryan replied, adding simply, 'I believe he was in fear.'

★   ★   ★

Taglione Construction topped out his father's tower with an American flag Mike Taglione had bought a year before he was killed. When Tony came down from school for the bitter-sweet topping-out party, Chris showed him the newspaper clipping and waited anxiously while Tony read the story. Boldly, he longed to share his revenge.

'Yeah, I heard. Too bad.'

'What do you mean?'

Tony sighed. 'This might sound strange to you, but I've been running on a sort of fantasy that after I graduated Law School I'd get Rendini in court.' He smiled thinly. 'I guess I'll have to settle for his bosses.'

'Aren't you glad he's dead?'

'I wish he were in prison.'

'That never would have happened.'

'Now we'll never know.'

Chris clung to the right of his less-than-satisfying efforts. 'At least Pop can rest easy.'

Tony's face was a cold mask. Up came the highbeam stare. 'Don't you think Pop deserves more than one scumbag shooting another scumbag?

# 5

'Rand,' the English policeman introduced himself.

Chris settled warily behind his father's old desk.

Inspector Reginald Rand, according to the card which Chris started rolling between his fingers, appeared to be in his forties. His black hair was greying at the temples and he wore a trim moustache, also greying, and a tailored suit. He had a powerful grip for a slim man. His eyes were remote flat pools shielded by reflections.

'What can I do for you?'

'Scotland Yard's Special Branch has killed an IRA terrorist.'

'So?'

Rand took out a Charley O's matchbook. Chris shoved an ashtray in his direction. The policeman gave it a thin smile, opened the matchbook and showed him the inside. It had two matches left. Two more lights and John Ryan would have thrown it away, along with Chris's telephone number scrawled on it in pencil.

Chris touched the desk for strength. Through his fingers he could feel the building pulsing as the tower crane hoisted concrete to the upper decks.

'Maybe he was looking for a job.'

Rand cast a dubious eye at the six-button phone anchoring the twenty-fifth storey floor plan.

'Do your workmen ordinarily contact you directly, Mr Taglione?'

'Taggart.'

'Beg pardon?'

'I'm changing my name to Taggart. My brother may go into politics and building can be a dirty business.'

'Very well, Mr . . . Taggart. I repeat, do your workmen *ordinarily contact you directly?*'

'I don't know if you've ever worked with your hands, Inspector, but workmen pass the word on jobs. Maybe my name fell into the grapevine.'

'Oh, I'm sure it did.' He smiled. 'But *which* grapevine?'

'What was his trade?'

Rand's smile went out like a light. It was a definitive announcement that he was taking the gloves off, and Chris felt his second rush of panic.

'Understand, Mr *Taggart,* my interest is not casual. I *must* know what he was doing in this country. And I will before I leave.'

Chris started to protest. Rand cut him off. 'Sir, your father was killed in a questionable, shall we say, "traffic accident". A union officer with whom your father had feuded was subsequently kneecapped and shot dead. Now I find your telephone number in the possession of an Irish terrorist.'

Chris thought crazy things, even killing the cop and running away, or denying everything. He felt young and scared, and very stupid, but most of all, he felt hot panic coursing through his limbs and leaving devastation in its wake.

Rand raised his hand as if to ward off a wild blow. 'You realize I'm here unofficially. I only just got off the plane and took a taxi into Manhattan. If I make it official I'll have to confer with all sorts of United States immigration agents, the FBI, police, what have you ...'

*Had he heard right?* Christopher Taggart stared enquiringly into the flat pools of the Englishman's eyes, trying to pierce them for meaning. Had he heard what he thought he had heard? He rose unsteadily and went to the iron safe where he kept grease. He came back and stacked five grand on his father's desk.

Rand looked at it a long time. He held up two fingers. Chris doubled it, with a deeply relieved smile. Rand stepped to the desk, stroked the surface, traced squares around the money with his finger. But he didn't touch it.

'I'm not yet convinced this would be in my best interest. You see, I know your mother contributed generously to the IRA, but *you* haven't. I'm hopeful that means you can help me perform my duty, which is to protect the British public from Irish terrorism. If so, we can shake hands on this transaction and part as gentlemen.'

Chris nodded; they were nicely in synch. Rand was saying, Convince me you are not an IRA supporter; then, for ten thousand dollars, I will forget that you paid a terrorist to kill the man who murdered your father.

'The guy did a job for me,' he admitted. 'Private. Nothing political. Nothing to do with England or Ireland.'

'An entirely private matter? I *will* enquire further, you know.'

'It was exactly what you guessed.'

Rand inspected him with a hard, penetrating stare. Abruptly he nodded.

'Excellent. I was concerned, of course, that the IRA was preparing political attacks in the States. One has desires' – he smiled at the money – 'but one also has commitments. Well, I think this has worked out very nicely all around, don't you?'

'Has anyone else made the connection?'

'Your police certainly haven't. And my sources indicate the mob hasn't either.'

'What kind of sources does a British cop have in America?'

'The same sort of cutthroats I cultivate in Europe, Africa and Asia,' Rand answered with a modest smile.

'Then I'm in the clear?'

Rand stuffed the money into his raincoat. 'Completely.'

Impulsively, Chris thrust out his hand. 'My name is Chris.'

Rand hesitated, finally took it. 'Reggie. But may I say something, Chris?'

'Sure. This is the classiest shakedown I ever had.'

'Thank you. You've been a damned fool, though. Be more circumspect next time you need such assistance. Make your arrangements through a third party. It was sheer luck I killed your gunman, you know. If I'd arrested him instead, he'd have sold you in a flash to save his own skin.'

'I hadn't thought of that.'

The remoteness in Reggie's eyes dissolved a little and he looked genuinely concerned. 'And now you're trusting *me*. What if I were wired? For God's sake, man, what if I were a homicide detective with a phony British accent?'

'What makes you think my office isn't wired? What makes you think this shakedown isn't on tape?'

Reggie reached under his belt and pulled out what looked like a telephone beeper. 'This. It pulses if that sort of thing is going on.'

Chris stared, secretly delighted by the older man. His spectacular success in the building trade had stifled his father's friends, and even the bankers were treading softly. No one dared push advice on a man with the magic touch. He hadn't realized how lonely he had become, or how young he sometimes felt.

'I guess I've been kind of stupid,' he admitted.

Reggie returned a long, hard, calculating look. Chris shivered with anticipation, sensing that in Reggie's world his magic touch meant nothing. 'You're not stupid, so much as very young and, please forgive me, appallingly arrogant. If you persist in acting as if you can walk on water, you'll end up either in prison, or dead.'

'Want a job?' Chris asked.

'Thank you, no. I have a job.'

'How about dinner?'

Rand shook his head. 'I think I'll just fly on home before anyone notices I'm missing.'

'I'll drive you to the airport. There's a good restaurant on top of the International Building.'

Reggie looked dubious, but agreed to a ride. He was booked on an eight o'clock British Airways flight, but fate intervened in the form of a two-hour delay caused by a Heathrow baggage handlers' slowdown. So he let Chris take him to dinner. In the car Chris had pumped him about his work but had found out little. At dinner Reggie asked about the construction business and seemed intrigued. Finally, over coffee, Chris blurted, 'I want to kill them all.'

'Impossible.'

Chris blinked. Unlike Uncle Eamon's policeman lectures, Reggie Rand was merely making a practical comment.

'I want to get them all,' Chris repeated.

'Shooting them isn't the answer. "They", as you call them, are a system. A society. A shadow government.'

'How do you get a society?'

Reggie hailed a waiter.

'No, no, this is on me,' Chris protested.

'Thank you. I thought I'd have a glass of port. Would you like a brandy?'

'No. I'll try the port. Never had it.'

Reggie asked what brands the waiter had.

'Sandemann, Harvey's —'

'Croft?'

'Maybe.'

'Excellent, tawny for myself, ruby for the gentleman. You'll like it better first time.' When it came, Chris tasted it and said, 'Like Marsala.'

'Yes, very much so. . . Have you ever wondered why ports and sherrys come from Spain and Portugal yet have English names?'

'Never thought about it,' said Chris, anxious to return to the subject of revenge.

'Two systems collided. In the eighteenth century, English wine merchants started buying the Spanish and Portuguese product in quantity. A small portion of a vineyard's output, at first; more the next year, as the taste for it grew in England: and more after that, paying whatever price the grower asked. Eventually, they bought the entire crop. That went on for a few years. Suddenly the merchants refused to pay the price. The vineyards had nowhere else to sell, because the wine merchants had seized control of the entire market.'

'Why'd they change the names?'

'They married their sons to the Spaniards' beautiful daughters. Just bloody absorbed them.' Reggie raised his glass, gazed through it at the mile-long blue lines of runway lights beyond the window, and smiled at Chris. 'Of course, it was all legitimate business. Neither society was evil and indeed both benefited. . . Now, the society you propose to attack is evil. And it has the strength of evil, which is the strength that comes from answering to no one.'

'There's gotta be a way to beat them.'

'There *are* ways,' Reggie said mildly. 'Mussolini did it in Sicily. But are you willing to be evil to beat evil?'

'I'm willing to do anything.'

'Then you ought to very seriously consider doing nothing.'

★　　★　　★

His rage grew cold, intense, as laser fire. He kept waiting for his achievements to be enough, but they never were. Every time he paid off, he paid the Mafia system that had killed his father. For it was his father crushed by his own truck that remained the centre of his existence; the minutes holding his father's hand as life seeped away were the source of his rage; and Mike Taglione's tears were the fuel of Chris's determination to wreak terrible vengeance.

Atop the tower one evening, he compared the Mafia to a construction derrick that at night kept working, secretly snatching materials off the street, and building them into the tower, making itself part of the tower. Cables guyed the derrick mast, each guy like a New York Mafia family. Cut enough guys and the derrick would topple into the street.

Six months after Reggie Rand shook him down – almost a year to the day since his father had been murdered – Chris's accountant came in while he was watching the evening television news. The accountant had a list of reasons why Taggart Construction shouldn't bid to general contract a new corporate headquarters on Madison Avenue, a job which would begin about the time they finished Mike's building.

'I know your father, God rest his soul, would be very proud of you, Chris, but this time, you could blow the whole shooting match. The architect's gone bananas and the client knows it, so the late penalties are like Stalin's.'

'It's a class project,' Chris retorted wearily. 'If I pull it off, I'll draw class clients.' The fact was, with his father's building nearing completion, he didn't know what he wanted to do next. Despite a full year since the murder, his mind still replayed it as vividly as if his father had been killed this morning.

'If you don't pull it off we'll be selling pencils on the IRT –'

Suddenly Chris gestured for silence.

A Belfast riot was big on the television news. A Special Branch inspector was accused of murdering an Irish prisoner, and Chris had recognized Reggie Rand marching in grand silence through a gauntlet of reporters outside Scotland Yard.

He bought British newspapers and followed the story. Reggie had surprised two IRA Provos in a remote cottage outside Londonderry and in the ensuing gun battle he had shot both. Later, a third man hiding in the eaves claimed upon his arrest that he had seen Reggie gun down a man who had already surrendered. The London *Times* took no sides, the mass-circulation *Sun* demanded a medal for the Special Branch officer, but the moderate *Guardian* spoke what was likely to be the government line, praising the 'officer's resourcefulness and bravery, which are however, not licence to take the law into his own hands.'

Chris announced a vacation. His accountant blinked. 'What?'

'I'm dead tired. I got to get away.'

'It's about time. This has been a hell of a year.'

Chris nodded vaguely. 'Yeah. Just don't fuck it up while I'm gone.'

He telephoned Tony to ask if he would watch things for him, but Tony had been invited back for another summer internship at the US Attorney's office. 'Where you going?'

'London.'

★　　★　　★

He found Reggie Rand in a Victoria Street pub near Scotland Yard. As at their first meeting, they operated in complimentary modes. Chris left when Reggie spotted him, walked to the Thames embankment, and stuffed a train ticket to Cambridge behind a pay phone.

The following afternoon he waited in a student beer garden on the Cam, slouched before a pint at a scarred wooden table in an open window. The place was packed with Americans over for the summer semester. The low ceiling echoed the roar of conversation, the air was thick with cigarette smoke, and the floor smelled of beer. The students looked like ghosts; it seemed much more than just a year since he had lived like this, talking, drinking, smoking too many Marlboros and making notes on thoughts he no longer had time nor inclination to think.

Reggie wandered through the crowd with a Newcastle Brown Ale. He had dressed his part in rumpled corduroys and a heavy knit tie, looking like a don on the prowl for a student bedmate.

'Thanks for coming.'

'You seem at home here.'

Chris patted his faded Fordham sweatshirt. 'School is school. I saw your problem on television. Sit down.'

Reggie sat and trickled his ale from the bottle into his glass. 'Decent of you to remember.'

'It's going against you,' Chris said. 'What are you going to do?'

'Not to worry. The Yard is delighted to give me my full pension if I'll only retire. Friends have offered some interesting armanent work.'

'Selling guns?'

'Something like that.'

'Do you still have your "cutthroat" sources?'

'They weren't issued by Her Majesty's government, if that's what you mean.'

'I'll top those offers.'

'Oh?'

'I'm looking for that "third party".'

'You still demand revenge?'

'I have to. The law can't.'

Reggie lowered his ale, untouched. Somebody started banging a guitar and he leaned closer so Chris could hear. 'Yesterday I made inquiries. Your business is thriving. You're on your way to becoming a man of wealth and power. Why court these "darker enterprises"? Your enemies are mired in the gutter. The sky is yours. Isn't completing your father's building revenge enough?'

'Not when my father can't stand on the sidewalk and look up at it.'

Reggie shook his head, and said gently, 'I'm afraid I'm somewhat over-qualified to contract gunmen. No, Chris. You set this meeting up very well. In fact, I rather admire your flair for the clandestine; you've read your Le Carré. Though I'd have chosen a less conspicuous jumper. But I've no interest in finding you another gunman.'

'You think it's beneath you?'

'It's as if I hired Taggart Construction to erect a garden shed.'

'No, no, no. I'm looking for more than gunmen.'

'How's that?' Reggie glanced idly out the open window where the shallow river lapped the beer garden terrace and picked up his ale.

'I'm building an organization.'

'What sort of organization?'

'An organization to destroy the Mafia.'

'You don't say?'

'I didn't fly three thousand miles to fuck around,' Chris snapped angrily. 'Or crack jokes. I'm making a legit proposal.'

Reggie deflected his glare with a mild apology. 'Terribly sorry. But the Mafia employs, shall we say, perhaps thirteen thousand men in America – the majority in the so-called five families of New York – and its power has grown for four generations.'

'Nine thousand associates in New York,' Chris said, 'and less than nine hundred made members. They're not as strong as they seem, nor as organized. They have as much trouble getting along with each other as they do with the cops. But their real weakness is that they're city kids – street fighters – not soldiers. Their leaders are wide-open, vulnerable to the kind of terrorist violence common in the rest of the world – car bombs, rockets, automatic weapons.'

'They control their streets.'

'Listen. I got in a fight with Cirillo's strongarms last year. I was too mad to be scared of two on one, and I took one guy out right off. So they brought in another, made it three on one, and beat my head in. That's how the mob intimidates its victims and protects itself from competitors, but ganging up on somebody is about as far as they can go. They depend upon the protections of a free society. The Police Commissioner is not allowed to send tanks to level their homes or hang them from lampposts the way Mussolini did. He beat them because they weren't soldiers. Look what I did with a single IRA man.'

'Let's say you manage to identify and slaughter their leaders. New leaders take over. That's hardly destroying the Mafia.'

'I know that! That's why I came to you.'

'You may hold an exaggerated opinion of my talents.'

'I have a plan, Reggie.'

'And I suspect you're going to tell it to me.'

'If you're trying to piss me off, you're doing a good job of it. Will you shut up and listen?'

The flat pools which were Reggie's eyes glazed over like ice.

'In one sentence, young man, what is your plan?'

'Support one Mafia family in a take-over war against the other four.'

Reggie looked at him and the pools began to glisten. 'Destroying all five in the process?'

'Right.'

'What are your weapons?'

'Three weapons. Imported violence. Drugs. The law.'

'What do you want from me?'

'Number one, violence. I want you to hire soldiers we can slip in and out of New York on a one-time basis – IRA gunmen, Palestinian bombers, French mercenaries, professional fighters, terrorists.'

'A shadow Mafia?'

'Exactly.' He liked Reggie's phrase. 'A shadow Mafia to destroy the real one. Number two, drugs. Drugs are Mafia currency. I need a big, steady supply of heroin as a weapon to burrow into their networks. They want it, man. They need it. They're as addicted as the guy who shoots up with a needle. I'm going to hook them to me, then cut 'em off.'

'A la our wine merchants? What's your third weapon?'

'The law. You'll do international, Interpol and whatever else you know. I'll do New York. I'm going to set them up and turn them in. And I'll use the law for information. I'll put Organized Crime Control cops on *my* pay-roll for intelligence information.'

'Never trust a crooked policeman,' Reggie smiled.

'I'm trusting you. Every man has his price.'

'Don't ever forget his limits. He also has a magic number, that amount after which he will cease to work for you – another thing not to forget when establishing risky contacts.'

Taggart smiled back. 'That's the kind of expertise I want from you. Along with violence, drugs, and risky contacts.'

'Recruit a Mafia family. Take over the Mafia. Destroy the Mafia. Then what?'

'Hand the leftovers to the cops.'

'The leftovers being the family you provoke against the others?'

'What's left of them.'

'Then close down shop and walk away?'

'Of course.'

Reggie smiled and his eyes flattened with private knowledge. He started to say something, but juggled it first in his mind; obsessed with revenge, Taggart seemed a little nave on the subject of walking away. Instead of pursuing it, Reggie stated the obvious. 'It would take years.'

'I've got years,' Taggart shot back. 'Everybody's always telling me how young I am. So I've got plenty of time.'

'And money.'

'I'm starting to make money.'

'And of course,' Reggie mused, 'at some point your operation will start to generate money itself.'

'Maybe it would. I suppose so.'

Again Reggie was struck by Taggart's blind side. Did he really not consider the mind-boggling profits, the millions for thousands, that successfully smuggling large of amounts of heroin would yield? Apparently not, for he was forging determinedly ahead again, like a tank skirting the observation points on the high ground in favour of a direct route to its target.

'But I need your international "cutthroats", Reggie. I need your fighters, smugglers, informers, thieves, hijackers –'

'Killers.'

Chris met Reggie's eye. The flat pools had formed again and he felt his own gaze reflected. 'I'm hunting killers. Nobody knows that better than you.'

'The odds are against you. By a great margin.'

'I'm going to beat them.'

'A very great margin.'

'I'm still going to beat them. They took my father. I'll take away what they care about – power.'

'But they didn't kill *my* father, more's the pity. You'll forgive me if I ask what is in it for me?'

'Exactly what you want.'

The Englishman's brow rose sharply. 'And what is that?'

'The way you're heading – gun salesman, security expert – you'll end up so bored you'll shove a thirty-eight in your mouth. I read about you. You've done it all. You've been in action your whole life. You're the best. I'm offering you a shot at –'

'What is it you think I want?' Reggie's soft voice turned softer and quieter, pulsing with menace. Having turned the tables with a shrewd guess that broached the Englishman's reserve, Chris had also loosed demons. Demons that convinced him that Reggie was the man to direct his war.

'Roam the world. Write your own rules.'

'A privateer?' Reggie sounded amused.

'Backed to the hilt! No one to answer to but me.'

'That would make you the privateer, and me merely your vessel.'

'Come on, Reggie. Let's stop dicking around.'

'Why, may I ask, not just hire a competent killer to eliminate the top Dons?' 'Because I realized you were right. It's the system more than single men.' Ironically, his brother's diatribes against revenge had finally convinced him, though not in the way Tony intended.

'New criminal groups will pop up. And remnants of the old.'

'But not institutions. The new groups will be weak and the law will beat them.'

Reggie nodded agreement. 'I'm told your FBI is gearing up for a major campaign against organized crime.'

'Glad to hear it.' Taggart grinned. 'I'll take all the help I can get. Nobody ever said this is going to be easy.'

'They'll crack down on you, too, if you're not careful.'

'But I am careful. I hire only the best. Welcome aboard, Reggie.'

Reggie sighed. 'One million dollars per year.'

'*What*'

'My price. Cash!'

'A million –'

'I don't intend to haggle with a businessman. That is my price. Out of it I'll foot the initial expenses. Cutthroats do expect to be paid, you know.'

'Wait a minute. I'm not saying you're not worth it. But I don't have it now. I'll pay it, but in the future. Give me, say, five years. That's a lot of money to make disappear from a legitimate business.'

'Generate it out of your drug smuggling,' Reggie replied, suddenly sarcastic. He pushed back his chair.

'I'll pay you a hundred grand a year,' Chris countered, wondering where in God he would get it. 'And pay you the rest once we're rolling.'

'You're missing the point, mate. I seriously doubt you'll still have this crazy idea in your head by the time you're earning that sort of money.'

He stood up, his ale still untouched. Shaking his head in disbelief, he said, 'I suppose I should be complimented you thought of me.'

'It's not crazy. It'll work – look. Imagine a construction derrick atop a building. The building's society. Right? Now imagine it at night. Everybody's gone home, but the derrick keeps working when nobody sees it – like the Mafia – snatching things off the street and building them into the building, making itself part of the building, part of society. Cables guy the derrick mast. Each guy holding the mast is a New York family. Let's say five guys, five families. We're going to cut one guy after another, and when we cut the last one the derrick's going to fall into the street.'

'I don't intend to be standing under it when it lands.'

'We'll be on top of the building looking down.'

'If you still believe that when you can afford me,' Reggie replied drily, 'we 'll chat.'

Stunned, Chris watched him walk out of the pub. Disappointment turned swiftly to anger and he hurried to the train station, heading for London and the airport, seething that the Englishman had treated him like a nut. Reggie was already on the platform, waiting for the same train. Taggart took it as an omen. He went up to him and promised, 'I'll be back, you son of a bitch. And we *will* chat – if you're still the best.'

Reggie sighed. 'For a hundred thousand dollars I'm sure I can find someone to shoot Don Richard and a few others.'

'*No.* I want to take more than their lives. I want to take their *belief* they can do it. I want to make it too tough to start over, too hard to be in the rackets. Too dangerous, too risky and too scary. I want them to cease to exist.'

# 6

He costed out his attack on the office computer, as if he were estimating a bid on a building, and discovered logic behind Reggie's demand; perhaps his fee wasn't out of line. In fact, it appeared that Reggie Rand's million dollars a year would be only a small portion of what revenge upon the Mafia might cost. And between raising the money and creating the shadow Mafia, it would take years; perhaps a decade. In a sudden leap of the imagination – grim in its concept, but exciting in that he could indeed conceive it – he embraced the reality that he might be well in his thirties before his father was fully laid to rest.

The only way he knew to raise the fortune he needed – every penny of which he would have to hide from the IRS – was to succeed as a major developer on a scale that his father had never dared dream. He had to build many buildings, not just one at a time, and also had to extract a much bigger profit than bank financing would allow. The answer was joint ventures. But to attract joint-venture investors, he initially had to make his name with some hot buildings on bank mortgages. He set up a meeting with his best and probably only hope, Henry Bunker, who behind his prickly faade was a cautious man.

After greeting Chris in his office, Henry Bunker removed his wire-rimmed glasses and gave him a tart glower. 'You took a vacation.'

'You make "vacation" sound like Legionnaires' Disease.'

'Is your building on schedule?'

'No.'

'What?'

'Two weeks *ahead,* as if your little spies hadn't told you. Pittsburg fucked up or we'd be up three weeks. Where do I sign?'

Bunker called his secretary for the notes due, and wiped his glasses while Chris signed them. After she left to make copies, Chris sat back and smiled. 'Let's get down to the real reason I came by today.'

'The *real* reason?' Bunker put his glasses back on. 'What do you mean, the real reason. I thought you're trying to finish your father's building.'

'I'm top heavy in management. My guys have expensive time on their hands.'

'Fire them.'

'I hate to break up a hot team. Why don't we work out something with the people who hold the mortgage on that Fifty-seventh Street building?'

The banker gasped. 'Chris, you came in here to try and save your father's building in the midst of the worst real estate depression in memory, and now you're trying to start another?'

'You know the one I mean?'

'Yes. It's standing there like a half-built tombstone.'

'Let's finish it.'

'Have you any idea how much money they're owed?' *He* apparently did, because he started scribbling numbers and pecking at his Hewlett-Packard.

'If you were stuck with that mortgage,' Chris replied, 'you'd sell your sister to get out of it.'

'I would not sell my sister during a recession,' the banker replied drily. 'And we are most definitely looking at a recession.'

'*They're* looking at a recession,' Chris shot back. 'They screwed up the building. But I've got the top people to ran the job right. We'll close it in before winter and start renting in the spring. You've got the cash. We can buy it for a song.'

'There's no one to rent it to when it's done,' Bunker objected. 'Who's going to live in it?'

'If we can't rent it, we'll sell it as co-operatives.'

'To whom? I'm frankly not sure that this is the right time to invest heavily in Manhattan real estate.'

'Real estate is cycles. We're in a down cycle. Now's the time to get in before the next up cycle.'

'Cycle theories are dreamed up to generate sufficient hope to prevail over intelligence.'

Chris surged towards the door and Bunker flinched at his size in sudden motion. 'Come on,' he barked, his father echoing in his voice. 'Let's take a walk.'

'Now?'

'I'm going to show you the next cycle.'

'How old are you, Chris?'

'You want to come with me? Please.'

'The reason I ask is I'm too young to be here and something tells me I'm older than you.'

'Just a half-hour walk. I'll buy you lunch.'

'You can't afford it.'

But he agreed to let Chris tour him up Sixth Avenue. It was a crisp, clear summer day, the avenue thronged with people walking during lunch hour, and New York – thank God for his pitch – sparkled.

'What am I supposed to be looking at?'

'Faces and buildings. All these young executives. Guys and girls like us. All these office towers just finished.'

'And half empty.'

'I'll talk about that in a minute. But all these people are commuting for hours to get here.'

'From the suburbs.'

'You want to live in the suburbs?'

Bunker shuddered.

'Neither do they. They want to five here. They want to walk to work.'

'You can't write off the suburbs.'

'I don't have to. The Arabs have done it for me. The suburbs have passed their high point and can't grow any more. The roads are clogged. Nearby land is running out. And single family housing costs are going crazy. But at the same time there are more people. My class at Fordham had twice as many students as ten years ago. The baby-boom kids are coming up. They're going to flood this city and need places to live, starting with that tower on Fifty-seventh Street.'

'Are you sure it's big enough?' Bunker asked sarcastically.

'As soon as we finish it, let's go to Columbus Avenue. It's just waiting to be developed.'

'If Lincoln Center didn't get that wasteland developed, nothing will.'

'Sixth Avenue will,' Chris promised. 'These people have to live somewhere.'

'Chris, your theory depends upon renting these office buildings, and right now it's more likely we're going to see deer in Times Square.'

'No. Money's coming this way.'

'That's news to my bank.'

'The world is going to hell. Half of it's shaky dictatorships, the other half's already in revolution – right?'

'Basically.'

'But even the most miserable places have people with money. Where they going to put it?'

'Hong Kong.'

'So the Chinese Communists can take it?'

'Beirut.'

'Which will blow up if things get worse with Israel?'

'London.'

'With England nationalizing anything not in running shoes?'

'Geneva.'

'Swiss vaults, while inflation whipsaws it? Definitely not. They gotta make their money work someplace they can count on. That leaves the only stable democracy where the government has a healthy respect for money – the US. And where will these money people buy apartments, start businesses, and rent offices? The money capital of the safest country in the world – *New York*. So let me ask you –'

'What were you studying in college?' Bunker interrupted.

'My father told me I could study anything as long as I read the newspaper. Let me ask you something?'

'What?'

'Why don't you and me get in on the ground floor before the safe and easy boys come back into the market?'

'Damnit, how old are you?'

'I'm twenty-two, for crissake. How old are you?'

'Twenty-three.'

'Wanna shake on it?'

\*    \*    \*

On Thursday nights the cops picking up college credit at Fordham's Manhattan campus gathered after class in Jimmy Armstrong's Saloon on Ninth Avenue. They ran the New York Police Department gamut from sergeants hoping to become lieutenants, to lieutenants gunning for captain, to detectives in homocide, burglary, and organized crime control. Christopher Taggart took to waiting for them around ten o'clock, his big hand wrapped around a glass of Murphy's from which he drank sparingly.

Having been reared around his Uncle Eamon, he was comfortable with cops and knew how to put them at ease. One trick was to honour partners and treat the sour, unfriendly, gloomy cop as politely as his cheerful, outgoing buddy. Another was not to ask questions. But the best device was to seem so rich and powerful as to not need anything from them.

When they asked, 'What course are you taking?' the answer, 'I'm putting up a building over on Fifty-sixth,' did wonders.

'Office building?'

Taggart shrugged. 'Thirty storeys.'

'My brother's in construction. He's an electrician.'

'Is he good?'

'Busts his ass.'

'If he ever needs work, send him over. I'm Chris Taggart.' He shook hands.

'Nick Pomodoro. My partner, Charley Dobson.'

Dobson glowered.

'Chris is building a building over on Fifty-sixth.'

'Oh yeah? When are they going to do something about that one on Fifty-seventh? There's planks blowing off in the wind.'

'I just took it over.'

'Oh, yeah?'

'I'll have her closed in by Fall. What do you guys do?'

'Homicide.' This was worthless in terms of Mafia intelligence, but it was an opening to more cops.

'Nice work if you can get it.'

'Steady,' Nick agreed, and even Dobson ascended from his gloom to remark, 'It's a fucking growth industry.'

Taggart returned Thursday night after Thursday night, gaining their confidence until he was less cop buff than one of the boys. A street crimes sergeant needed a bridge loan to close on a new house before he sold his old one; Taggart obliged. A mounted patrol sergeant everybody liked was forced to retire at sixty-five; Taglione Concrete put him and his horse in charge of security at its sprawling East River plant.

On Wednesdays he regularly hit a cop bar behind the new Police Headquarters downtown. Tuesdays, a spaghetti joint next to the Fifth Precinct. On Fridays, religiously, he joined Uncle Eamon for end of the week drinks with his brass hat cronies. And Monday nights it was back to Armstrong's Saloon to catch the captains trickling in from the John Jay College of Criminal Justice.

That summer, just before night classes ended, Taggart Construction contributed to the PBA's widows fund. Taggart loaned the Taglione family's Catskill acreage to several PAL-supported Boy Scout troops for wilderness camping. And in the Fall, he formed the Mike Taglione Memorial Foundation which bought a thousand bullet proof vests for the NYPD.

\*　　\*　　\*

He borrowed a page from Sylvia's showbiz book and invested serious money in his business image. He toyed with the idea of a flashy car like a Rolls-Royce, but settled instead upon what he described to his decorators as a 'blow 'em away' office in the partially completed Fifty-seventh Street tower. Unfortunately, he didn't make clear who his image was aimed at, so he scrapped it and tried to explain again.

'My old man always drove a big white Lincoln–Continental.'

'So fucking what?'

Chryl Chamberlain zipped her drawing case shut with a vicious buzz. Her partner, Victoria Matthews, glared angrily and gripped a clump of her red hair as if to yank it out. A year out of Pratt Institute of Design, they were outraged that a Taggart demolition crew was stuffing their first effort into dumpsters.

'I still think you're tops. I'm trying to explain what I need.'

'Not very clearly,' Chryl replied icily.

Taggart wondered whether he would toss them out with their design if they weren't two of the most beautiful girls he had seen in his life – women, actually, in their late twenties, who had retired from modelling to study architecture. But for hair colour – Chryl was blonde – they might have been sisters, with their lovely, lean faces, straight noses, and long bodies that seemed to drape over furniture as if each piece had been built with them in mind and gently inserted underneath. They had a habit which enchanted Taggart; one would lightly rap the other with the back of her half-closed hand, their heads would bob, and a word, a look, or a laugh would flicker between them. Today, however, they weren't laughing.

'My Pop used to say, "Most guys humping a guinea cadillac –" that's a wheelbarrow – "think they're smarter than the boss. My car makes 'em wonder." '

'But you just threw half our job into a goddamned dumpster.'

'And handed you a cheque for your full commission.'

'It's not just the money.'

'That's right. I won't smile at something that doesn't work. Do you get what I'm saying about my father's car? Forget taste. What you did looked great, beautiful.' He cracked a small smile and tweaked the dragon's tail. 'Soho chic –'

'You son of a bitch!'

'But it doesn't work for me. At this point I gotta go for impact. I've got a problem making money people believe me. I've got great ideas, but they think I'm a kid. I have to get their attention before they'll listen. Can you try again? Can you design me an office that makes a joint venturer scratch his hard head and wonder, Maybe we should be nice to this kid?'

'What's a joint venturer?'

'A guy in control of a hundred million dollars, such as the assets of an insurance company. An investor I gotta convince to go with me on a new project.'

'How old are you?'

'Old enough to take you both home and screw your brains out.'

'That's offensive.'

'Asking my age is offensive. I just *paid* you for a job I didn't like. Now I'm giving you a blank cheque for your biggest commission since you graduated. And you're still bugging me about how old I am? Just like the joint venturers.'

'That doesn't give you the right to act like a clod.'

'And speaking of brains, it shouldn't take too many to figure out that if your design gets me more buildings to build, you'll get commissions for lobbies and plazas and offices. That doesn't give me clod rights either, but it would be a hell of a lot of fun. We can do some good buildings.'

Victoria rapped Chryl's shoulder, and they exchanged a speculative glance. They were very tight, so finely tuned to each other that Taggart couldn't read them.

'Okay, I'm twenty-one.'

'Sounds old enough to me,' Chryl said. 'We'll put our heads together for a boyish fantasy.'

'One more thing.'

'What?'

'It has to be moveable. I'm a builder, and I want my office where I'm at.'

'We'll make you a new one.'

'No. I want that image to come with me. You know how kings used to move from castle to castle to keep an eye on things?'

'Carrying their tapestries with them,' said Victoria. 'Right. Okay, we'll come up with a *royal,* boyish fantasy.'

Chryl touched her with her knuckles. 'Do we call him "Your Majesty"?'

' "Clod" will do,' said Taggart, and they were friends.

★   ★   ★

He got lucky and connected with a federal agent who would serve him for years. An assistant business agent of the Cement and Concrete Workers' Union hit Arnie Markewitz for a payoff at the East River plant, and Arnie, who could be very street smart, sensed something was wrong and passed the guy up to Chris. The business agent started talking in circles, trying to get Chris to finish his sentences for him.

'I don't understand,' Chris finally interrupted. 'Do I have a labour problem or don't I?'

'I think it's fixable.'

At that point, custom deemed it appropriate to lay money on the table. But Arnie's warning, and the heightened senses Chris had begun to cultivate scheming his revenge, told him something wasn't kosher.

'So fix it.'

The business agent backed out with a frustrated look. Chris went down the stairs after him and followed him around the corner. A sedan was double parked on Eighth Avenue. It had long, whip radio antenna. Inside was a man, barely visible behind tinted glass. The business agent shook his head as he passed. Taggart leaned on the roof of the car and knocked on the window until the glass was lowered an inch.

'Was that prick wired?'

'What?'

'I'm Chris Taggart. You're trying to sting me for bribery. What are you, FBI?'

The agent tried to look serious.

'If this is what my taxes go for, I'd rather buy an aircraft carrier.'

'Take it up with the IRS. What did I do wrong?'

'You sent the wrong guy. The turkey can't act. Every time he opened his mouth he was reading from your script and then he expected me to read it back. If I changed one word, he almost dropped his teeth. What you get on him?'

'None of your fucking business.'

'Hey. I just helped you do your job better next time and you're yelling at me. I'll tell you something else. You're wasting your time. I don't pay bribes.'

'Can I quote you on that?'

'I'll sign an affidavit.'

'Better discuss that with your lawyer.'

'I'll ask my brother. He's interning with the US Attorney's office. Well, this blows the afternoon. How about a beer?'

*   *   *

'Close your eyes.'

Long, perfumed fingers closed his eyes. Chryl took one hand, Victoria the other, and they led him into his new office. He heard the door close firmly and the lock click.

'Ready? Open.'

'Outta sight!'

'We can't decide whether to call it "Clod Chic", or "Guinea Cadillac". What do you think?'

'I love it.'

'You would.'

They had mingled Japanese electronics and expensive-looking European antiques. An entire wall sported the latest executive toys: stereo, multi-screen television, and video games. In the centre a leather ottoman faced burled walnut bookshelves. Anchoring the business end was an art-nouveau desk with lines that flowed like a lake.

'The carpet's for class,' said Chryl, as Victoria demonstrated the electric curtains and multi-level lighting. 'John D. Rockefeller bought it second-hand.'

Victoria touched another button. The bookshelves opened and a king-sized bed was lowered with a sigh.

'I love it.' He walked around, toying with the electronic control panels. 'What happened to my books?'

'Since you persist in putting your own books in the shelves, we've had them leather-bound. As you get new ones, your secretary will send them to the bindery. Including those tacky paperbacks.'

The first electrical contractor to set eyes on the desk said, 'No wonder you're jewing me down. What did that fucker cost?'

'Somebody's gotta pay for it.'

A Morgan Guaranty vice-president Bunker had introduced him to said, 'I saw that piece in Christie's last month. I wondered what lucky devil would get it. Very nice, Chris. Very, very nice.'

Even the cold-eyed Bunker was impressed. 'Yet another reason to get richer, sooner.'

Chris reported to Chryl and Victoria that it worked. 'For a ten thousand buck desk the guy's talking about syndicating a sixty-million dollar condo. People want to believe.'

'Did he ask how old you are?'

Chris touched her mouth. 'I said you two could vouch for me.'

Victoria sprawled on the leather ottoman and laid three lines of coke in the etched grooves of a gold 'thirties Dunhill cigarette case. She held it towards him.

He shook his head. 'Do you guys ever try sex without dope?'

Chryl peeled off her designer jeans, stepped out of her panties, and pressed a button that simultaneously closed the drapes and lowered the bed. 'Chris, you're a credit to your gender, but often nobody's home. Something's in your head. So we put something in ours.'

'What do you mean?'

Their *ménage* dated from the night they celebrated finishing the office. They had taken a sort of possession of him, like a mutual Christmas gift, and the several years they had on him often made him feel like a kid. He watched Victoria squirm out of her slacks and tried to concentrate on saying, 'Hey, I resent that. I really like you. I'm half in love with both of you.'

Chryl touched another switch and the light turned golden, flickering on her shapely legs as she crossed the carpet and stretched over the ottoman with a silver straw.

'There are times I don't know where one of you begins and the other ends.'

Victoria smiled over her shoulder. 'Don't think we're complaining. We're quite capable of filling in the spaces. We also like you dearly.'

'I get lost with you.'

Victoria looked unusually serious and said quietly, 'I wish that were true, Chris. We'd make you a bigamist. But you're lost in something else.'

For fiery moments, time disappeared with them, and memory dissolved. Their first night he had lain spent, unable to remember why he had gone to

England. But the next day, when they showed the office to their parents, he had ached that these well-dressed strangers should see what his father would have loved.

# 7

He began to revel in his work, moving surely and swiftly again, as when he first took over his father's building, fuelled by the larger goal. Now, everything he did served the single purpose of creating wealth and power to destroy the Mafia.

Uncle Vinnie offered to bid partners for a Newark Airport runway contract if Chris would front the project. Chris suspected Vinnie was holding hands with somebody in the Port Authority who had foreknowledge of the bids, but he didn't ask because he needed the money. He bid what Vinnie told him; Taglione Concrete undercut the local competition and landed the contract.

He rescued another half-built derelict on upper Broadway for a song, and continued scouting Columbus Avenue properties between Lincoln Center and Seventy-second Street. When his accountant iterated the banker's contention that it was 'a wasteland', he extended the search to Eighty-sixth Street.

'I have heard,' Henry Bunker complained when Chris hit him up for mortgage money, 'that the one decent restaurant above Seventy-second Street maintains an armoured car for its customers' convenience.'

'How about another walk?'

After a twenty-minute walk from Bunker's Sixth Avenue office, and an excellent meal, Chris showed him the bill. 'Expensive restaurants mean expensive apartments. The waitress says the armoured car's in the shop for reloading, but I want to show you something.'

He led Bunker up grim-looking blocks of Columbus to a basement bar he had discovered on Eighty-sixth Street. The bar was called Strykers, and Chico Hamilton was playing that night. Bunker, who regretted admitting to Chris that he had a severe weakness for jazz, agreed to stay for a few beers. After three sets he was making noises about getting up in the morning, when Chet Baker walked in with his trumpet.

Baker played 'The Thrill is Gone'. Then he put down his instrument and sang it. And Henry Bunker, wiping his eyes and complaining about the cigarette smoke, promised to review Taggart Construction's proposal for a Columbus Avenue apartment tower.

On the way out they ran into a black narcotics detective-sergeant Chris knew who invited them to a narc party in a Village loft. The detective shared a bottle of Southern Comfort she had in her purse in the cab downtown, and they landed thoroughly ripped on Washington Street at two o'clock in the morning. Upstairs was wall to wall cops – NYPD, DEA, Treasury. Taggart introduced Bunker to some friends. Suddenly he stared at a group laughing loudly.

'What's the matter?' asked Bunker.

'Want to meet my brother?'

Tony had a beer bottle in his hand and a sharp grin on his face. He said something and four cops cracked up. When Chris approached him, his grin faded and he looked as astonished as Chris had felt. 'What the fuck are you doing here?'

'What about you?'

'I'm a guest of that lady over there. This here's Bunker, my banker. Bunker meet Tony Taglione, first-class prosecutor on the make and number-one brother.'

Later, when they were alone in an all-night coffee shop on West Fourth, he asked Tony, 'Are you on a case with these guys?'

'Cops bring their investigations to prosecutors they want to work with,' Tony said. 'I'm making friends.'

'Drugs?'

'Drugs make the best cases. The wiseguys get crazy around the money. And freaked by the prison terms.'

*  *  *

From the night they bumped into each other wooing the cops, Christopher Taggart followed his brother's law career with wary fascination. Tony, it seemed, was advancing in a sort of legal parallel with Chris's own march for revenge. Congressman Costanzo had helped get him the summer internship in the Southern District US Attorney's Office and Tony had been asked back the next summer. By that time he had transferred from Harvard to Columbia Law School, claiming he wanted to be near the New York action. The next summer he had interned with the public defender. He worked for the Manhattan DA, ground out good enough grades to clerk for a Federal judge, a former crusading organized-crime prosecutor, passed the New York Bar Examination, and then landed a job with the Justice Department in Washington.

For two years the brothers met at Christmas and weddings and funerals. Then one day Tony telephoned from Washington, as excited as Chris had ever heard him, and announced he was coming back to New York.

'Gonna work for me, Bro?'

'No way! Criminal Division of the Southern District. I want you to come to my swearing-in.'

Taggart managed to stammer congratulations, but when he hung up the telephone his heart was pounding. He went to the window. As usual, Chryl and Victoria had moved his office to the building he was currently erecting. Madison Avenue was streaked cement grey a hundred feet in both directions from the gate. His heart was still going like a jackhammer. He saw a dangerous opportunity, risky as hell, but too good to resist.

\*     \*     \*

He was clear in his conscience that he had never pushed Tony in this direction, that his brother had arrived at the US Attorney's office of his own free will. But he had promised his father he would take care of him, so he said, the morning of Tony's swearing-in, 'Before you go and pledge your life away, I'm asking you again – please join up with me as general counsel and a full partner in Taggart Construction.'

Tony looked at him with fiery eyes.

'Four hundred grand a year,' Taggart persisted. 'Hot and cold running secretaries. We'll make a great team, man.'

'No! You've asked me before and I've told you before, I don't want corporate practice. I'm a prosecutor.'

'Still gunning for the Mafia?'

'Don't ask me again.'

'I promise,' said Taggart. He threw his arm around Tony's shoulders and they went upstairs to the executive floor for photographs with the US Attorney.

Taggart had met Arthur Finch at the last Al Smith dinner and had been impressed. Scion of an old New York railroad family, Finch had ignored the careers of foundation directorships, Foreign Service, or Ivy League academia traditionally favoured by inheritors of huge private incomes. And though he looked like a clubman in his staid Brooks Brother's suits and dull neckties, and spoke with a voice redolent of boarding school and regattas, he had waded into government lawyering with a steely determination the equal of any striving Italian or Irishman. The youthful prosecutor regarded himself as conservator of his office's eighty-year-old tradition of disinterested law enforcement. He was famous for icily correct rages when confronted by incompetence, laziness, or any hint of political subversion of the legal process. He was also, persistent rumour had it, running like a cheetah for governor of New York State.

Finch administered Tony's oath of office before a hundred assistants in the office library. Taggart's eyes filled as Tony pledged to uphold the United States Constitution and the laws of the land. The casual gathering of the prosecutors to welcome another to their band was strangely moving, but the source of his emotion was a sudden fantastic vision of his father alive beside him, wearing his blue meeting-suit and a broad grin and stage-whispering proudly that from now on they had better be damned careful talking business around the breakfast table.

Finch announced that Tony would be specializing in Organized Crime business extortion, then joked, with a wink at Taggart, that any plans to convert the US Attorney's St Andrews Square offices to a highrise condominium had to be cleared by Washington.

Chris saw Tony's face mask up and the mark his ring had gouged on his cheek turn angry red. Tony had long ago put his inherited share of the company in the blind trust required of public servants, but Christopher Taggart had become too flamboyant a New York character for his name change to distance Taggart Construction from Tony Taglione. The delicious irony was that from the day he took his first job with the Justice Department, few wiseguys dared demand a payoff from Tony Taglione's brother.

They went down to Tony's new office. It was cluttered with cartons of books, his backpack, and the former occupant's desk, chairs and telephone. Tony told his paralegal assistant he would greatly appreciate a typewriter before lunch, and turned to Chris. 'Lunch is out. I have to get to work.'

Taggart handed him a gold-wrapped package he had stashed with the receptionist. 'Happy new job.'

'Since I'm on the public payroll, I gotta be careful what I accept from rich businessmen.' It sounded like a joke, so Chris kidded back dutifully, 'If you report it on your income tax, it's going to knock you into another bracket. Go on, open it.'

Tentatively, Tony removed the wrapping and opened the box, revealing a dark leather briefcase with solid gold comers. He turned it slowly in his hands.

'I figured it's time you stopped carrying a backpack,' Chris said. He pointed out the combination locks and Tony's initials, A.M.T., embossed in gold. 'The hinges suck, like on all of them, but Saks'll fix 'em. Do you like it?'

Tony set it on his desk, crossed his arms, and stared. 'I'll look like defence counsel.'

'Look inside.'

'Cheri and Vicky pick it out?'

'I did.'

'Seems more their style.'

Stung, Taggart said, 'Hey, what do you have against Chryl and Victoria?'

'Nothing.'

'You hit on every other girl I had since I was twelve,' he said heatedly. 'Why won't you even talk to them?'

'I don't do that stuff anymore,' Tony replied seriously. He startled Chris by putting a hand on his arm. 'Chris, I'm not as crazy I used to be.'

'If anyone in this family is crazy it's me, not you.'

'Chris, they all see me straight-arrow, but you know. Come on, Bro, we've been places.'

It was as intimate an exchange as they had shared since the night of their father's funeral, six years ago, and Chris shook his head in disbelief. Tony was such an innocent – Kathleen Taggart's altarboy son – thinking that their Greenpoint escapade and the occasional Queens Boulevard drag race was heavy-duty sin.

'But I'm over that,' Tony continued earnestly. 'Now when I have to prove something to myself I do it right here at this desk and in that courthouse across the plaza. Kicking criminal ass beats stealing my little brother's girlfriends.'

Tony took his stunned silence for argument. 'Bro, it doesn't matter anymore that you're bigger than me now, or Pop liked you better, or I didn't want the business. Okay? We have our own lives. Our own women.'

'Pop didn't –'

'Drop it! Please. Pop's not here to defend himself and you can't speak for him.'

'Okay . . . But would you do me one favour.'

'What's that?'

'Try to be nice to Chryl and Victoria? Whatever you think, they are magical women and they're very, very important to me. Like, I would have really liked to bring them here today.'

Tony flashed a teasing grin that flung him back to childhood. 'Do they switch mother and playmate roles? I mean who makes breakfast and who stays in bed?'

'Is rapping a brand new assistant United States Attorney in the mouth against federal or city law?'

'God's law.' Tony glanced at his watch. 'Listen, this is a real nice briefcase, but I gotta get to work.'

'Not yet.' Chris shut Tony's door and locked it. 'Open the briefcase, Bro. Look inside.'

Tony gave him a puzzled look, and shrugged. The catches released with a soft click.

'Calfskin, so wrap your lunch in plastic. The salesguy said they taught you at law school what to put in the pockets . . . See the secret compartment?'

Tony traced a line of stitching that rimmed the inside of the lid. His finger went unerringly to the release, the maker's seal, and it popped open.

'How the hell did you figure that?'

'I'm a sneaky guy . . . What's this?'

Tony pulled a manila envelope from the compartment.

'Your real gift. Check it out.'

Tony opened the envelope and spread a half dozen sheets of typed paper on his desk. 'What is this?'

'Your first case.'

'What are you talking about?'

'Names.'

'I can see that.'

'With addresses and phone numbers.'

'Who are these people?'

'Guys in the Concrete Workers and the Teamsters who've been hitting contractors for payoffs and kickbacks; and contractors who're buying sweetheart contracts.'

'Where'd you get it?'

'And they're hitting on the union pension funds.'

'I said, where'd you get it?'

'I'm around. I hear stuff.'

'Rumours.'

'It's better than rumours. I hear one thing, I hear another. I put a few pieces together. Sometimes they add up. Sometimes they don't.' He picked up the last sheet of paper. 'See this?'

'What is it?'

'Codes.'

'For what?'

'I don't know. But this guy, I'm told, imports heroin.'

'This says anchovies.'

'Look who he sells the anchovies to.'

Tony turned the page. 'Vitelli Pasta 'N Things. Atlantic Avenue.'

'Owned, I hear, by a guy named Eddie Rizzolo.'

Tony reached for his phone. 'Let's sit down with my boss.'

'No.'

'What do you mean, no?'

'Keep me out of it.'

'I can't just take this.'

'Why not?'

'I have to tell the C.D. Chief where I'm getting it.'

'No, you don't.'

'You're telling me the rules?'

'Wait a minute,' said Chris. 'Just hold it a second.' Even if the Chief of the Criminal Division didn't throw him out on his ear, his plan to betray certain mobsters to the US Attorney required a degree of secrecy that only Tony could supply him. 'What if I were a street hood who you turned stoolie? You think I'd risk talking to more than just you? What would you do if I said, "I ain't talking to no boss"? You must have some method of protecting a confidential informant.'

' "Deep Throat",' Tony admitted. 'No attribution, no testimony.'

'Call me your Deep Throat. If I hear anything else, I'll inform you, and only you. In the meantime, maybe you can get probable cause on this. Maybe get a wire up.'

'Kind of cosy with the vernacular, aren't you?' Tony asked shrewdly and Taggart realized he had got to him just in time. Two years tougher and his brother wouldn't buy it.

'Treat this like when an agent brings you a case. All you have to ask is, "How can I make a case?" '

Tony looked at the door. 'Chris.'

'What's the matter? I'm a legitimate source. You can vouch for me if they ask. Tell 'em you've known me your whole life. I'm sure there are plenty other non-criminals who pass information to your office.'

'But usually with a reason. Like they want to get even or knock off a competitor. Or they want what someone has.'

'Clowns like these killed Pop.'

'I remember.'

'So I'm getting even. What's the matter with that?'

Tony divided the papers into two piles, crossed his arms and stared at them as he had at the briefcase. 'I'll tell you what's the matter. The construction stuff is one thing. I imagine you get hit for payoffs. I pray to God you're not paying them. But I understand that you know who's crooked and who's straight.'

'I know who's crooked,' Taggart agreed with a smile.

'But this dope stuff.' Tony picked up a typewritten sheet. 'This is like an agent affidavit. How do you know this?'

'I'm around.'

'Around criminals?'

'Guys talk. I listen.'

'Who are you hanging out with?'

'What is this, the third degree?'

Tony looked at him. He was dead serious. 'You better believe it.'

'Hey, I'm just a businessman.'

'Businessman don't come in here with dope deals.'

'Bullshit. Guys with money are offered deals all the time.'

'Not straight guys.'

'Wait a minute. I'm just a businessman. But I got two reps around the city. One for being honest. And one for live and let live.' He clasped his hands together, doubled his index fingers, and pointed them at Tony. 'But *you* know, and *I* know, that they owe us.'

'They owe the law.'

'In this case it's the same thing.'

'Where'd you hear this?'

'I'm in a bar one night. Somebody starts bragging he knows a guy who knows another guy who opened the wrong crate of anchovies, and he nearly got shot for it by the Rizzolos . . . Doesn't the name ring a bell?'

'Sure, Eddie Rizzolo runs South Brooklyn. He used to be linked to the Cirillos.'

'What else? Don't you remember? Blue Bus Line?'

'Yeah, they own a legitimate bus company. It gives them enough profit to file real tax returns.'

'Restaurants? Canarsie? Remember the little doll in Abatelli's?'

'Miss Universe. The night you got your head beat in.'

'Her father. When I heard the name I remembered the connection between Eddie Rizzolo and Don Cirillo, so I started paying attention. I paid a guy for the codes he overheard in the Rizzolo's restaurant. And now, whenever I hear something I listen. Real close. When I get home I write it down. I write down his name, what they called him – "Bugsy" or "The Beast" or Eddie "the Cop", whatever the fuck. I write down where he's from and what family somebody whispered he was connected to. I got a research guy in my office who checks things out for me. My secretary looks up addresses and businesses. Then I talk to my friends in the cops. Sometimes what they say fits what I heard someplace else. When I get the same rumour from two sides I end up knowing more than either side.'

'How'd you find the guy who sold you the codes?'

'What are you busting my hump for?'

'How'd you find him.'

'They killed Pop, goddamnit. I got a right.'

'How'd you find the guy who sold you the codes?'

Chris contrived to look embarrassed. He turned to the window, gazed a while at the ramps looping onto the Brooklyn Bridge, and finally admitted in a low voice, 'I hired detectives.'

'Detectives?' Tony asked scornfully. 'Are you nuts? What are you, a one-man gangbuster?'

'Hey! I'll spend my money the way I want to. I'm not breaking any laws.'

'Okay, okay.' It was Tony's turn to study the bridge. Finally he said, 'What do you expect? You waltz in here with a name and I'll authorize the FBI to arrest the guy?'

'Tony, you know and I know the FBI has tons of organized crime investigations going. So does the DEA. So does NYPD, the State Police, Labor Department, IRS, Customs. The agents and cops do the planting and the prosecutors harvest. All I'm doing is pointing you towards some wiseguy you might not know about. If it looks like the beginning of a case, use it.'

'Do you mind me asking why you didn't give it to the cops?'

'Cops? Why should I give it to strangers when my brother's in the Criminal Division of the Southern District US Attorney's office?'

'Uncle Eamon –'

'He's ready to retire. Besides, cops don't have the clout that your office does. What's your problem, Bro? Are you telling me you don't want me messing around in your career?'

'I'll take any source I can get,' Tony replied hastily. 'But I just got here. It took you time to put this together.'

Taggart laughed. 'I waited for you. I had faith you'd get where you were going. Tony, what you got to lose? Put Rizzolo away and they might even invite you to join the Strikeforce.'

\*　　\*　　\*

Three office buildings, a midtown hotel and a Westchester shopping centre later, Christopher Taggart returned to England. He stayed at the Savoy because Chryl and Victoria told him he would like it. He visited the British Foreign Office to discuss building a new Manhattan British Consulate. He met the managers of the royal estates to negotiate erecting a hotel tower on one of their valuable and vastly under-utilized midtown Manhattan properties. He wrote Tony a postcard, 'London's picking up. Might buy it. Congratulations on making Strikeforce. (signed) Deep Throat.'

Although he was twenty-nine years old, when he stepped out of his hotel on the last day of the trip with a knapsack slung over one shoulder, he still looked more like a professional graduate student than the Manhattan developer that *New York Magazine* had dubbed – quoting a rival builder – 'the slickest new dude in the Big Apple'.

He drove southeast from London to a country pub outside Maidstone that Reggie Rand frequented for lunch the rare times he was in England. The bar was thick with young car salesmen and insurance agents, but the former Scotland Yarder was seated alone at a table in the bay window, reading his newspaper by the drizzly light and smoking an expensive cigar. A plate of cheese and pickled onions sat untouched beside a freshly poured Newcastle Brown Ale.

He looked prosperous; the Burberry trenchcoat folded on the bench beside him was new, and his blue suit looked like a twelve-hundred dollar job Chryl and Victoria had talked Chris into having made at Kilgour, French and Stanbury. The British Racing Green Jag parked in front was registered to the arms trader that employed him.

Seven years had passed since Chris had shared his plan with Reggie in the student pub on the River Cam, but physically, Chris was relieved to see, the Englishman appeared not to have aged. He had a little more grey in his hair, perhaps, but he was still lean as a knife and either remote or dangerous, depending upon how the light caught his eyes.

Chris tossed his knapsack on the Burberry. 'Remember me?'

'I certainly do. What's this?'

'Open it.'

Reggie unzipped the flap, turned the opening to the window, and closed it again. 'It appears to be money.'

·'Your first year's salary. A million bucks. Cash.'

Reggie looked at him, the flat pools of his eyes seeming to ripple. His moustache twitched as he shook his head with a rueful smile. 'I'm rather taken aback. You passed my little test.'

'Let's get something straight, Reg. When you work for me, I don't pass your tests. You pass mine.'

Reggie Rand might have bridled, but he could not help but smile at Christopher Taggart's earnest audacity. 'How long has it been since your father died? Eight years?'

'Eight years since the Mafia murdered Mike Taglione.'

What a strange young man, Reggie thought; equally strange were his own emotions. Widowed for decades by the last German V-2 to fall on London, he had learned to enjoy his life alone and the dalliances that went with it. But of late, as he rocketed through his fifties, he had begun to take notice of children and wished, sometimes, that he had fathered a son.

Then along came this driven, vengeful, frightfully clever American – and an orphan to boot. It was too bizarre. 'I made no promise to work for you.'

'You need a job.'

'You're misinformed.' He thrust a proprietary hand towards the window, indicating boundless opportunity to the south and east – Africa, the Levant, a festering Orient. 'There's a world full of angry natives out there, many of them violent. I'm doing very well arming them, thank you.'

'Your business card says Hovercraft, but in fact you're the senior rep with Breech Arms Ltd of Slough.'

Reggie's eyes narrowed fractionally. 'That's not common knowledge.'

'I just bought an interest in Breech.'

'I beg pardon?'

'I'm a director through a Luxembourg holding company. I thought it might be handy for writing end-user documents. I'm going to get you fired. So like I say, Reggie, you'll need a job.'

'What have I done to deserve your largesse?'

'There are four men in the world I could have hired, but each of them told me you're the best. We want only the best.'

'We.'

'I've got a great start on cop contacts and a pretty good intelligence profile on the current state of the mob. The feds are starting to romp all over them. We're going to finish the job. I'm nearly ready for your cutthroats. But first, we've got to get some dope flowing. The American market imports about four tons of uncut heroin a year. We need a ton for bait.'

'Two thousand pounds of heroin? Why, if I had the ability to get rich importing heroin into America, would I do it for you?'

'You *can* do it. I checked. Selling guns, your contacts are even better than when you were a cop. You're tight with people from Amsterdam to the Golden Triangle. You know the Chinese Triads and their Swiss bankers and the shippers and airlines that mule the dope in and the money out. But you never run dope. Remember, when you shook me down in my office you said, "One has desires, but one has obligations." You seem to be a guy with a code, Reggie.'

'And you're still prepared to spend millions and years more for revenge?'

'I'm projecting three years. Two more to get ready and a year to fight.' Reggie drained his ale in measured swallows. He pulled a cotton handkerchief from his pocket and dabbed his moustache, which was perfectly dry. Then he smiled like a man who had seen the future and liked the look of it.

'You appear to have matured, Mr Taggart.'

\*     \*     \*

Two years separated the day in Kent that Taggart hired Reggie from the night on Forty-fifth Street when they betrayed Nino Vetere to the Strikeforce. In that time Taggart had laid the groundwork for his Shadow Mafia. He strengthened his political connections and boosted the prestige of Taggart Construction by starting the Spire; he continued playing 'Deep Throat' for his brother, Tony and he penetrated the heart of law enforcement via the President's Organized Crime Commission. Reggie shuttled tirelessly between Europe and Asia, forging links to terrorists and mercenaries, and connecting with international heroin merchants. Under Taggart's direction he established financial conduits in Switzerland, Luxembourg, Singapore and the Cayman Islands and corporate fronts to shield Taggart's legitimate business. The

Englishman subverted Mafia spies in Sicily and New York and formalized Taggart's cop and agent friendships by placing the officers on his own payroll; when the two years were over, the cops were still friends with Taggart, but worked, secretly they thought, for the Englishman with the bulging wallet and empty eyes.

Taggart's opening gambit – the set up of Nino Vetere – appeared to be a success. Nino Vetere cooperated with the Strikeforce prosecutors that hot Memorial Day Weekend and turned in Nicky Cirillo: New York's most powerful crime family was thrown into sudden disarray. But it was only the beginning and that night when Taggart suspended the treacherous Jack Warner from the top of his Spire, he already knew that his biggest challenge loomed. He still had to seduce a Mafia family into waging his war of vengeance.

# BOOK II

*Sweet Kiss of Revenge*

# 8

A white dress of soft jersey cloth, which never quite touched her hips though it moved as if it might, high-heeled shoes, and silken jet hair turned heads when Helen Rizzolo jumped down from her chartered Cessna. The pilot, who had made no headway with his silent passenger, tried again, but his eager smile got lost in the off-putting solemnity of her gaze. She refused help with her bag and hurried towards the hangar, where a lone taxi waited.

The driver didn't ask her destination. There was only one place to go – the federal prison, whose colourless stone walls dominated these remote western New York flatlands just as a medieval castle cowed a town. They hassled her at the main gate, as usual, but once inside a guard captain on her payroll showed Helen into an attorney-consulting cell and made a show of closing the barred spy hole. Her father stuffed his cap between the bars anyway, and scooped her into his huge arms.

'Sweetheart.' Eddie Rizzolo buried his face in her hair, and she stroked his head until at last he stepped back, holding her shoulders in his hands, shaking his head and grinning delightedly. As always, he stared at her face as if desperate to memorize her features for the long days to come. She noticed that he hadn't shaved in days, which wasn't like him.

'You look tired, Pop.'

'But you look gorgeous. Jesus, it's good to see your face. How's your mother?'

'Okay.'

'Hey.' He took her chin in his thick fingers. 'What's the matter?'

She couldn't say that his hair seemed thinner than at the time of her last visit, or that it had turned nearly white since his conviction, so she forced a big smile. 'Everything's okay. I just wish you were coming home.'

'You live to gain,' he replied, seriously. 'And to gain you sacrifice. Right? It's the only choice we can live with.'

'I know. I'm not complaining.'

'How are your brothers?'

'We'll talk.'

'Trouble?'

She shrugged. 'I can handle it. It's you I worry about. Are they treating you all right?'

He looked away.

'What's wrong?'

'A guy pulled a knife on me.' He raised his sleeve. His forearm was bandaged from his wrist to his elbow.

'*What?* We paid –'

'Maybe we paid the wrong ones,' he said quietly. All of a sudden he looked frightened, and she had never seen that before. Her throat gorged with helpless anger. 'We'll get on it, Pop,' she promised fiercely. 'We'll take care of it.' He looked away again, his brows working. She took his hand. 'Does it hurt?' 'No. Yes! I don't know.' Then his expression relaxed and he gave her a strange smile. 'I'm doing fine. I'll be home any day, now.'

'Home? What do you mean, home? What happened?'

He glanced at the steel door, and shook his head. No bribe could guarantee they weren't being bugged. Wives and daughters were, after all, time-honoured couriers and sometimes she suspected that the Feds ordered the guards to accept the bribes to trick her father into speaking freely. She made him sit so she could lean close to his ear and whisper, 'What do you mean, *home?*'

Even in his prison uniform, even using prison soap, he still had the sweet smell which was her earliest memory of him. But it was odd that he hadn't shaved. He was usually as neat and precise as she.

He smiled vaguely. 'I'll be home as soon as I'm better.'

'Better? They didn't tell us you were sick.'

'My, my. As soon as my . . . my . . . my . . . gets better.'

'You mean your arm?'

'No. No. My . . .'

'Pop? *What* gets better. What are you talking about?'

'My, my, you *know!* When the doctor says my, my, my . . . So I can go home from the hospital.'

She felt fear seep into her body. She shivered. 'What hospital? What do you mean?'

'Well, you know, this hospital. This. . . I. . .' His eyes roved over the room and settled on the bars in the door. His voice trailed off. Suddenly he looked afraid again, as if he had finally heard the empty ring of his own words in the crazy way she was hearing them. He blinked, walked around the table, and stared at her. Then he asked in a small, puzzled voice, 'Why are you crying, sweetheart?'

* * *

After leaving the room, she screamed at the guard captain: ' *What is wrong with him?*'

'I don't know, Miss. I really don't.'

'Has he been to a doctor?'

'Couple of times. Said he felt funny. We took him there right away. Don Eddie has no trouble here.'

'What about that knife?'

'We took care of the guy. It was just a scratch.'

'It frightened him. He's different. I want to talk to that doctor.'

'I don't know if he's around today.'

'Find him, goddamnit!'

She paced in the captain's office, running her nails through her hair, sinking into helpless terror. When the captain returned with the news that the doctor would see her, she said, 'I don't know what, but something's wrong. He's confused, he doesn't know where he is.'

'Like a little senile?'

'*I didn't say that!* He's only sixty years old.'

She tore frantically through her bag and hurled a roll of hundred dollar bills on the captain's desk. 'Listen, you take care of him until he gets better. If he gets confused like that, he can't defend himself.'

'I'll watch him as close as I can. It might help if I had a little money to pay a few more guards.'

'You'll get it tomorrow. As much as you need. But if anything happens to him . . . You'll die.'

'Hey listen, lady –'

'You want to try me?' She stepped towards the captain, the blood rising in her face, her lungs filling, and he backed up. Helen took a deep breath. '. . . Pass the word. Whoever hurts my father, dies! I don't want him *touched*! Now please, take me to the doctor.'

The doctor, who had not been bribed, treated Helen as he would have the relative of any inmate. 'What's wrong with him?' he asked casually. 'I would guess arteriosclerosis. Hardening of the arteries.'

'He's not even sixty.'

'Then call it Alzheimer's disease. That strikes men young. I don't know a darned thing about it except I can promise that it's never going to get better.' 'But that's crazy. You don't understand. He's always been healthy. He doesn't smoke. He hardly ever drinks and then only wine and –'

The doctor glanced at his watch. He was very young and managed to look

113

sour and bored simultaneously. 'If you look back a few years you might see flashes of strange behaviour started then.'

Memories slammed into her. Little lapses, apparently unimportant in the daily rush of events – lost in Manhattan, one time; failing to recognize a bodyguard, another.

'Can I get him out on this?'

'I'm not the warden. But it's an easy thing to fake.'

'He's not faking.'

'I'm not a judge either, Miss. Or a parole board.'

He was enjoying her agony. She collected her strength, putting her thoughts in simple order. She spoke to this monster as if he were a child. 'You're a doctor. And under these circumstances, my father's only doctor. My family has influence. What can my family do for you in return for taking excellent care of my father?'

The young man laughed. 'How about getting me on the staff of a real hospital?'

'The day my father comes home on a medical.'

'Are you kidding? You should see my record.'

'I don't care if you carry AIDs. Take care of him and I'll put you in the best hospital in the country.'

She left the prison, stunned and grieving for her father. Only after her plane had been airborne for hours and they were heading down the Hudson River at eight hundred feet altitude, was she able to admit that whatever happened next, from now on she could count only on herself. It was frightening.

When she saw the city spires beginning to thrust through the murk, she tapped the pilot's shoulder. 'Westport.'

'Connecticut?'

'Yeah. And I want to call Brooklyn.'

\*　　\*　　\*

She found her Uncle Frank haranguing his 'boys'. He greeted her with a big surprised smile, and resumed his pep talk, gesticulating with a baseball bat and strutting like a rooster with a round belly and a balding head.

'I know they're big,' he bellowed, 'so you gotta hit hard. Back each other up. And please, please, please think before you throw!'

He thrust the bat into their circle. Nine young men with 'Frank's Excavating' emblazoned on their uniforms piled hands on it and gave a throaty cheer. Frank sat beside her as they found their mitts and trotted onto the field in the fading light of a Westport evening.

'They're going to kill us,' he confided. 'You picked a hell of a day to come. Stubby's is romping the league.'

Stubby's Bar and Grill's leadoff batters, full-bellied moustachioed men, each bigger than the next, were warming up. Fifty or sixty people watched from the low bleachers, while on the sidelines Greenman's Olds and The Car Store teams rehashed their game just ended. Lights came on, turning the brown infield mocha and the grass emerald; the air was warm and heavy.

Gloomily, Uncle Frank watched his pitcher lob slowball warmup pitches. 'Move back!' he yelled at his short stop and motioned his outfielders to move further out. He huddled with his line coaches, then returned to the first row of the bleachers, which served as his dugout.

'Beer?'

He pulled two from the cooler at his feet and popped the tops.

'What brings you to the country?'

'Softball?'

He eyed her shrewdly. 'Oh yeah? What's wrong? Have you seen your father?'

'*Play ball!*' The umpire stepped behind the catcher. Stubby himself addressed the plate, cast a condescending eye on Frank's pitcher's first effort, and fouled it over the left field line, through the dense weeping willows that bordered the field, and across four lanes of Route One. Frank's pitcher threw four balls in a row, and Stubby walked.

'Is it your father? Hey, hey, sweetie, what's wrong?' She was crying and he put his arm around her. 'What's the matter, sweetie?'

'He's sick. He got stabbed. Not badly, but it seemed to set him off. It might be Alzheimer's disease.'

'They letting him out for it?' Frank asked coolly.

Frank was her mother's eldest brother. He hated the rackets and had violently opposed the marriage of Helen's parents; he hadn't spoken to her father in thirty-five years.

'They said he's faking. I'll get lawyers on it. He acts like he's eighty-five or something.'

'If he does have it, he's probably better there than at home.'

'It's dangerous there. He can't protect himself.'

They sat awhile in silence, watching Stubby's runners circle the bases. Finally, Uncle Frank sighed. 'Is there anything I can do?'

Helen shook her head. 'I just had to tell you.'

'How's your mother taking it?'

'She doesn't know. I've got enough on my hands without her going crazy. I'm not going to tell her. Don't you.'

'You two still fighting?'

'You know how it is.'

115

'Yeah.' Uncle Frank dried her eyes with his handkerchief. Then teased her knee, making her squirm. 'Like mother, like daughter.'

'She's *your* sister.'

'Sweetie. When are you going to get out?'

'What out?' Helen asked coldly, on guard now and her tears forgotten. 'I'm not in.'

'This is Uncle Frank, so don't tell me you're not in. Those lunk-head brothers of yours couldn't empty a can of tomatoes with instructions on the bottom. If your father's really sick, it's all going to fall on you.'

'Restaurants don't run themselves, Uncle Frank.'

'I'm not talking about the joints,' he snapped fiercely. 'And I'm not talking about the bus company. I'm talking about –' He glanced at the crowded bleachers and lowered his voice. 'You know what I'm talking about. Get out! Get out while you can.' His eyes glistened and he took her hands. She pulled away, but he seized them again, hard, and tugged her around to face him. 'You're not even my kid, but you're my favourite kid. You know? Since you was this high. You was *my* little girl.'

For as long as she could remember, she had come up here with her mother. In Uncle Frank's house – much more than in her own home, where her father often disappeared unpredictably – she felt treasured. Her uncle adored her as only a man with no daughters could love a niece. Here she felt safe. Even though he was leaning on her, she was glad she had come tonight.

'I've seen this coming,' he said. 'You're getting sucked into it worse every day. And your goddamned father has allowed it.'

'My brothers need me.'

'Screw your brothers!'

'I have a duty. What is the saying?' She whispered in Sicilian, ' "A wife is one thing. A sister something more." '

'Don't give me that peasant crap. Get out of it! Make a life for yourself. Be some kind of real person. Like you almost did when you went to college.'

'I didn't fit in there.'

'I know it was hard. What do you think I gave you the car for?'

She smiled; her parents had refused to let her live in a dorm the first semester, so she had commuted every day from Canarsie to Bronxville. When Uncle Frank found out, he gave her a red Fiat Spider.

'I needed wheels.'

'You had wheels, driven by a gorilla. I gave you your own car to make you feel like one of the regular kids. You almost did it before they dragged you back.'

'They sent him to jail. I had to come home. Mama was –'

'Your mother – who I love – was as bad as him. She should of told you never to come home. Go to school. Be a person.'

'That's the past.'

'It's not too late. Do it!'

Helen tried to meet his eye. He was no fool and knew her well enough to suspect that it wasn't only for her brothers and mother that she served her father. That perhaps she was tempted by the power that masqueraded as responsibility – and even relished it.

She pretended to watch the game and Uncle Frank pretended to change the subject. 'Hey, what do you think of my pitcher? Nice looking guy?'

'He's gorgeous.' She had noticed him before the game began; he was tall and dark with thick black hair, sleepy eyes, and a body to swim on. Which raised the problem she had faced since her father went to jail – if she dated a guy who wasn't connected she had to hide her true life, and if he was connected he would try to steal her business.

'Thirty years old, divorced. She was a bimbo. A guy that good looking gets bimbos when he's too young to know better. He got the kid, a beautiful child you could die for.'

Helen indulged herself with a long look. He was absolutely beautiful, an Adonis compared to the beer bellies fielding. He pursed his lips slightly each time he wound up, a nice movement, like a probing kiss. Uncle Frank nudged her, grinned slyly and apparently changed the subject again. 'Did I tell you? Your cousin is finally going to be a dentist?'

'How long has he been in college?'

'Longer than Enrico Fermi.'

'Congratulations.'

'Congratulations? Now I got no kid to take the business . . . But this guy pitching? I send him out to dig a septic, I know he's going to bring the machine back in one piece. I'm thinking maybe I should make him a partner.'

'Who takes care of his little kid?'

'His mother. Real Italian. Good family. But it would be nicer if he was *my* family.'

'Sure. Who gives their business to *stranieri?*'

'Lemme introduce you.'

'*What?* Frank –'

'He's a husband for an Italian girl. Strong when he should be, but a pussy cat inside. What do you say?'

'He's in Westport. My business is in Brooklyn.'

'You make a clean break. You sell the joints. You sell the buses. You leave your brothers the other stuff. You move up here, buy new businesses, and live in my house 'til you see if you like this guy.'

The funny thing was how easy he made it sound. 'What about my mother?' 'Connecticut's not Hong Kong, you know. It's an hour's drive, you can visit. Besides, you make bambinos with that fella and your mother'll be here like a rocket.'

'Frank, what are we talking about? I don't even know this guy.'

'I'll introduce you. You don't like him, I know others. Nice people – straight.'

'Like you.'

'Fucking A straight. I want to see the stars at night I look out the window; there's the sky, not a bunch of security lights. I hear a noise in the backyard and the cops come. It's a raccoon. Everybody has a nice laugh. I give 'em coffee. I got a stranger at the door, he's waving a brush, not a gun. It's the real world. You pay your taxes. You do a little better than your parents did. You have some fun.'

'What's fun? I have fun.'

'Yeah? Tell me about it. If you take a guy like my pitcher to bed, and it feels like something special, you don't worry about him being busted selling dope.' She gave him a smile, teasing. 'All this bed, you make it sound tempting.' 'What do you think I moved my family for?'

'You're in another world.'

'It's a *better* world. See my boys playing? They graduated high school. They married their girlfriends.'

'Just like Canarsie. So?'

'But *you* can't do that in Canarsie. Everybody knows you're on the wrong side. Here you can start new.' He nodded the length of the low bleachers at the people watching Stubby's massacre his team. 'See their parents. Look at those girls, younger than you, with pretty babies.'

He jumped up. *'Hey! Nice out.* Watch the first baseman when he comes in.' Stubby's team took the field and Frank's Excavating trotted to bat. The first baseman kissed a pretty girl and scooped their two-year-old into his arms.

'See? This is what real people do, Helen. They have fun, they work hard. They don't kill, they don't hurt, they don't push dope.'

A blond all-American sort of guy with the name 'Brace' stitched on his uniform greeted the couple, took the giggling child, and held him overhead. 'How's the bambino?'

'Hear that? They even talk Italian. Let me introduce you.'

'Uncle Frank, what are you doing to me?'

It was make believe. At home she was bogged down in a seemingly endless war with the other families, while the Strikeforce prowled the edges, picking off the weak and growing stronger every day. But here, tonight, with the air so soft and warm and the colours perfect, anything seemed possible. She looked again and wet her lips.

'Okay. Introduce me.'

Uncle Frank motioned his pitcher over and gave him some unnecessary advice. Dark eyes flickered towards her, filled with humour, maybe knowing passion. Helen smiled back.

Uncle Frank, transparent as a windshield, abruptly took notice. 'Hey, Rudy? Ever meet my niece, Helen?'

Rudy cocked his head, obviously comfortable with women who enjoyed his looks, and just as obviously enjoying hers. 'Hi.'

'How you doing?'

Rudy shook his head at the score board where the umpire was arranging double digits. 'We're not always this bad. You up from the city?'

As if she needed confirmation that this was not a sudden impulse on Uncle Frank's part. 'Canarsie. Are you always the pitcher?'

'The other guy ran the backhoe over his foot.'

'How'd he do that?'

Rudy glanced at Uncle Frank, winked at Helen. 'I don't know if your uncle wants to hear this again.'

'Tell her,' Frank grouched, then wandered off to confer with his leadoff batter. Rudy sat beside her and leaned close. 'Your Uncle sends him to dig a pool at a big rich house down by the water. The homeowner's daughter comes out sunbathing. He lifts the pods and starts moving the machine a little closer to the deck. She "forgets" she loosened her top and starts to sit up. He forgets he's still in gear. She goes, "Oooh", grabs her top, misses by three inches, and he creams his foot.'

Helen laughed. 'Is that true?'

'Oh yeah. See, everybody sits in their own house here and hubby or daddy goes to work and in comes this guy with no shirt on a machine. Happens all the time.'

'Where's your cast?'

Rudy grinned. 'I'm too old for kidstuff.'

'Rudy! Rudy!'

'You're up.'

'Excuse me. Gotta get a hit. Hey, we're going out for pizza, after. Wanta come?'

She looked at him, liked his arms, liked his eyes, and thought, what the hell. She could stay the night at Uncle Frank's if it got late and run the country streets in the morning. 'Sure.'

'Later.'

119

He hefted his bat and swaggered to the plate. The umpire called the first ball a strike and she booed with the crowd. Uncle Frank returned to the bleachers, his face troubled.

'He's really nice.'

'I told you.'

'What's wrong?'

'Don't look now, but your hood brother is here.'

'What? Where?'

'He's in a van, over there.'

Her stomach clutched. Eddie here without warning meant there'd been more trouble.

'I'm sorry, I gotta go.'

'Get rid of him. We're going for pizza after the game.'

'I can't.'

'Get out. Get out.' Frank grabbed her hand. Helen pulled away and hurried towards the driveway.

Eddie's van was black with smoked glass windows, a little beat up and consequently as ordinary as the thousands of vans that plied the outer boroughs and suburbs. Even the beefed-up tyres to support its bombproofing looked like last winter's snow tyres. She spotted a second van Uncle Frank hadn't noticed and, parked at a distance, a car with three guys who looked like federal agents.

Behind her she heard Rudy connect with the sharp crack of a solid base hit. The little crowd cheered and she wanted to turn around and see how he did. But Pauly, her brother's bodyguard, seemed very nervous; he gunned the engine and popped open a door for her.

She got in and they started to roll.

*　　*　　*

Her brother, Eddie 'the Cop' Rizzolo, was a strapping man in his thirties with fine jet hair and an open, sensual face swelled by food and wine. Physically, he looked like a bigger, younger version of their father, but he had neither the shrewd intelligence nor the ambition that made Eddie Sr a leader – *had* made him a leader, she reminded herself. Those days were gone.

Eddie's ordinary-looking van was luxuriously appointed, with leather seats, a bar, a TV, and a partition between the passenger compartment and the driver. He put down his Johnnie Walker Black Label, pulled her close with a kiss on her cheek, and turned up the sound on the Cable News.

'Just in time for the bullshit. President's Commission on Organized Crime.'

'What's wrong?'

'Catch this first.'

'What happened?'

'It's okay. I'll tell you in a minute. Look at this.'

She and her brothers had already concluded that the Commissions' witnesses were way out of it: they described the past while the Federal Organized Crime Strikeforce was breaking down doors in the present. The camera panned the men and women at the periwinkle blue tables while the chairman closed the hearing and thanked them for their work. They looked like they thought they should look, serious – all but a smiling blond guy in front who seemed familiar.

She tapped the screen with a red nail. 'Who's that?'

'Taggart. The builder.'

'Taglione's brother?'

'That's him. You musta seen him at the trial.'

She said nothing, but she had seen him long before her father's trial. In fact, he'd never been at the trial. The camera cut back to the chairman, who scheduled the next hearing in Atlantic City. Eddie laughed, flipping it off. 'So next month they'll get laid and play craps.'

'Hey, you're white as a ghost. Are you okay?'

Eddie raised the hand he'd been hiding. It was pillowed to his elbow in an enormous gauze bandage.

'Oh, my God! Eddie.'

'Fucking Cirillos sent some blacks to hit one of our numbers on Knickerbocker. Too bad for me I was there. Blew my fingers off. Two of 'em.'

She stared at his bandage, her stomach churning.

'No big deal. I'm checking out who did it.'

'That's why there's Feds in the car behind us.'

'There are? I guess they figure I'm going to shoot somebody back. They figure right.'

'No. We don't want another war.'

'What do you think this is?'

'Later. After the Strikeforce.'

'Later? The rate the Cirillos are sucking up Brooklyn, they're going to be charging us rent on the house.'

Helen glanced at Pauly. He was driving nervously and watching them in the mirror. 'I thought the Strikeforce getting Nicky Cirillo would slow them down.'

Eddie shrugged. 'Not if Crazy Mikey comes up on top. Then we'll see a real fight.'

Her brothers still couldn't understand that it took more than guts, muscle, and snap decisions to fill Don Eddie's shoes. They were like proud, brave bears, ferocious in battle, yet doomed to be puzzled by the events which led to the fight, and mind-blown by the diplomacy which would end it.

She closed her suede bomber jacket because the van was ice cold. Eddie noticed right away. 'Cold?' He turned down the air-conditioning, threw his arm around her, and snuggled her close, like her father. Her heart flew to him.

'How's Pop?' he asked.

'Not so good. Some guy pulled a knife on him.'

'**What?**'

'It was taken care of.'

'It goddamned better be.'

'It's tough. The blacks own the prison.'

She realized with an almost giddy sense of triumph that she had already decided not to tell Eddie and Frank about his condition. They listened to her because their father approved the arrangement. They never visited, so they'd never know. She kept a private place within her where she told the truth about things of the heart. But though she loved her brothers, this was business; her family simply could not survive their leadership. Thus she had lied about her father, so they could all survive.

'We got black friends,' said Eddie. 'Spanish, too.'

'Maybe you better talk to them again. There's a limit to what we can buy from the guards. I think maybe we should –'

She had a funny feeling that Pauly was listening. She pressed the partition button. The glass hummed shut.

'Wha'd you do that for? Pauly's like my right hand.' Eddie flourished the bandage with an ironic laugh.

'There's some things to talk about.'

'Sit on it 'til we're home with Frank. You sure they took care of the knife?'

She started to reply, but Pauly was still bothering her. Like most no-class Italian guys she knew, Pauly took his image from the movies. *Saturday Night Fever* a decade gone, he was still failing hard at a Tony Monteiro image in a black leather jacket, white shirt, black pants. A real *gavonne*. Who else would drive her brother around for ten years? But why so nervous tonight – the tense set of his shoulders? This wasn't his first war. He kept cocking his ear towards the intercom. She touched the switch. It appeared to be off.

She looked at him. Pauly's eyes were flickering like snake tongues in the rearview mirror, and suddenly Helen felt herself reeling from her third, sickening jolt of the day. What if the Strikeforce had turned Pauly? That was their style. Get right to the top. What if her brother's bodyguard were wired? What if he had fixed the intercom so that he was transmitting every word that she and Eddie spoke to the Federal agents trailing the van?

Helen opened the vanity, lit up the mirror, and calmly examined her makeup. She was naturally dark, and tanned from running in the sun, so she

122

used no blusher, only violet liner for her large solemn eyes, and red lip gloss that tracked the curves of her mouth.

'Pop was wondering if you want to promote Pauly.'

'What? Since when does Pop get into running my crews?'

'He says Pauly's earned it.'

Pauly, the dumb *gavonne,* proudly squared his shoulders.

★   ★   ★

Early the next morning, Eddie Rizzolo entered the Florida room in the back of the house that Helen used as an office. She was dolled up in a tight silk blouse, tighter jeans, and the open-toe, high heels with thin straps that Eddie's girlfriend, who was jealous, called 'fuck me shoes'.

Helen looked up from a computer screen she was filling with financial spread sheets, swivelled her chair, stretched her perfect legs, and gave him her full attention. He knew she weighed a hundred pounds and stood all of five-one without her spikes, and he towered over her, but when she fixed her violet eyes on him, he felt as if she filled the room.

'Was Pauly wired?'

Eddie nodded.

'Feds?'

'Southern District Strikeforce.'

'What are they doing over here in Brooklyn?'

'They cut a deal with the Eastern District – joint investigations.'

'Great. Was he alone?' Meaning, had the Strikeforce wired other Rizzolo lieutenants to transmit conversations with their bosses?

'Guaranteed. We had a little talk, first . . . It's a bitch with somebody you like.'

'How long was it going on?'

'It just started, thank God.'

'Thank God . . . How'd they get him?'

Eddie rubbed his mouth. He saw where she was going and didn't like it. 'Pauly had a little heroin action on the side.'

Her eyes flashed. 'So they waved twenty years at him and he flipped?'

'His little cousin was in on it. That nice kid, Joey? The Feds told him they'd get the kid, too. Pauly got scared what the fags in jail would do to little Joey, so he flipped. They had him by the balls.'

'Did you know about Pauly's heroin action?'

'I didn't really know

She levelled her gaze on him, cold, silent, waiting.

'I guessed, but I stayed out of it.'

'Eddie. We've agreed – no heroin! It's how they got Pop. It's not worth the heat. You've got to stop acting like one of the boys. You make 'em think you're just another guy, so there's no respect, there's no fear. You think Pauly would have dared pull that on Pop?'

'Yeah, well, maybe they know I'm not that smart.'

She made a face, motioned him over, pulled his head down to her and kissed his cheek. 'Do me a favour? Remember something?'

'What?'

'Remember you're not alone, okay? It's you and Frank and Pop. And me.'

*       *       *

Yesterday's unseasonably muggy heat had given way to a clear, chilly morning. After dead-heading some pansies in the backyard, she glanced up and surprised her smoky reflection in the bulletproof plastic that her brothers had attached to the jalousie windows. A trick of the light made her face appear clear against a murky background, like an old-fashioned studio portrait of a passionate girl with serious eyes. She moved to touch it, but the shift caused the glass behind the plastic to appear and the narrow slats seemed to slice her face into many parts. She shivered, shook her head violently, dropped the petals on the grass, and went back inside.

She cleared the computer in which resided the legitimate books for the Rizzolo's bus company, wedding palaces, and dance clubs. The blank screen stared back, another mirror. She got up to tend her plants, but water was standing in their drain saucers, and the jade leaves were turning yellow. She punched some Corelli out of her stereo, but it did not sooth her and she turned it off. She stared at the oil portrait of Joannes Baptistsa Guadagnini that she had bought when she went to Italy to help after a big earthquake there. Her 'patron saint', but even the great trickster of the Cremonese violin makers could not make her smile today.

The light was making her crazy; it looked dirty because of the bullet-proofing. Her brothers were proud of the off-set mountings which allowed her to crank the slatted windows to let in air, but as with many things Frank and Eddie did, execution never quite matched intention. The special plastic had grown cloudy since her father had led them through the last mob war, when they broke away from the Cirillos. It was so murky that her Canarsie neighbourhood appeared to be underwater, while at night the glare of the security floodlights on the postage stamp front lawn, the driveway, backyard, and alley was diffused like a snowstorm.

Ordinarily, when she felt trapped, she had many escapes – the old farm their grandfather had bought upstate in Westchester, a whaler's mansion on the north fork of Long Island which the connected side of her mother's family had owned since Prohibition, and a summer cabin in the Adirondacks. Cousins, people she liked, lived on handsome estates in the New Jersey hunt country, where she was welcome, even courted; for even the best Sicilian families had divorced sons in need of remarriage. And there was always, of course, Uncle Frank in Westport; and now, his handsome pitcher.

Once, when she got the itch to really break loose, she had boarded a plane alone to an isolated Club Med on Martinique, and for a week that still shimmered in memory she lived like somebody else. But since the Strike-force, nothing was ordinary, and she wasn't going anywhere until things got a lot better, which didn't look soon.

She fled upstairs, removed her spike heels and peeled out of her jeans and blouse. She hung up her clothes, put her heels in a shoe bag, and tossed her panties in the hamper. She confronted the mirror in her high school dressing table and regarded her body with pleasure. She was slight yet strong, fine rather than delicate. She chose a grey sweatsuit piped with lavender and tied a matching lavender sweatband around her head.

Eddie and Frank fell silent when she strode into the family room. Frank was even bigger than Eddie, a quiet, yet robust man of great and often indiscriminate appetites – quick to anger, quick to forget. They looked guilty about something, and Frank, who, unlike Eddie, could never lie to her, glanced anxiously at the unlisted telephone.

'I'm going running.'

'It's dangerous to make it a habit, Helen. You set up a pattern and they're waiting.'

'I have to get out.'

Frank, whose street crews were responsible for the Canarsie area, sent reluctantly for her bodyguards. He cast another guilty glance at the telephone.

'What are you two up to?'

'Nothing.'

'Come on.'

Eddie looked obstinate, but Frank said, 'This guy got in touch.'

'No dope deals.'

'*Fifty* keys,' Eddie shouted, waving his bandage.

Frank said, 'The price is going through the ceiling with the shortage. We could use the cash, Helen. Let me go upstate and dig up some bread.'

'You guys! You got a Strikeforce just waiting to nail you. Did it ever occur to you that phone's probably bugged?'

'I swept it this morning,' Eddie retorted, and Frank added, 'We didn't say nothing.'

'Besides,' Eddie said, 'the Feds can't just call us up to buy it. That's entrapment.'

'Now you're lawyers. Listen, lawyers, you buy, you possess. Then you say hello to some guy the Feds wired and you're conspiring to sell it. I told you no deals, no business.'

'But this is different.'

'We have an agreement, Eddie. You and Frank and me. When they put Pop inside we agreed. You and Frank run the business, but I make the decisions.'

'I'm talking about running the business. You're moving into our territory now.'

Eddie looked very determined and started pacing. Frank pushed his closed fists together, causing muscle to swell in his upper arms; his way of shrugging. Eddie, as usual, was the problem.

'Frank, did we have a deal?'

'Yes.'

'Would you tell Eddie, please.'

'Come on.' He pushed harder and his knuckles turned white.

'Did we?'

'Yeah. We made a deal.'

'Did Pop go along?'

'Sure he did.'

'Eddie. Did you agree, too?'

Eddie broke off pacing. 'Yeah.'

'Did Pop go along?'

'Sure. He knew we was a couple a dummies.'

'Hey.' She went to Eddie, her heart filling. She tugged him towards Frank, and put her arms around both of them. 'You are not. And I'm lucky to have you.'

'Bull.'

'I couldn't do any of this without you.'

'All you need is a couple of dummies to bust heads. You could do the whole thing yourself.'

'I couldn't. And I wouldn't want to. This is us. Right?' Teasing, she dug her nails into the rolls around their waists. 'You want to come running? Get rid of those guts?'

Eddie pulled away. 'What if we rip it off? This guy's a schmuck.'

'Yeah,' Frank said. 'How about it, Helen? Can't we just steal it?'

The listed telephone rang in the kitchen. They waited, glaring at each other. Their mother appeared in the doorway, holding a towel, and Helen thought, as she often did, I'll never be that beautiful when I'm her age. Despite ribbons of grey in her hair, she had a show girl's body and a face every boy in the family fell in love with as he came of age. Helen was never sure whether her mother really missed her father, or preferred being sole boss of the house. She must miss sex, not that they ever talked about it. Like they didn't talk about business, either. Even the time the Cirillos blasted the picture window with shotguns, and the *Post* had Don Eddie's picture on the front page, she had clung to the fiction that her husband was a bus company executive.

'Some girl named Marcy on the telephone.'

'Marcy Goldsmith?'

'Some Jewish name.' Her mother shrugged. 'She says she was your room-mate in college.'

'Tell her I'm out.'

'Don't you want to say hello?'

'Mom. Please.'

'Okay. I'll lie.'

'Thanks.'

Eddie started to speak as soon as she left, but Helen stopped him with a gesture. 'Wait. She'll be back.'

'How do you –'

'I know.'

She returned, perplexed. 'Marcy says you're alumni.'

'Didn't you tell her I'm out?'

'We got talking. She sounds like a nice girl.'

'Tell her I'll send a cheque.'

'Don't yell at me.' She turned to Eddie and Frank. 'You guys hungry?'

'Yeah, Mom. Sure.'

'I'll bring you something.'

Eddie waited until their mother had gone again. 'What do you say, Helen?'

'No.'

Outside, two of her best men waited in a car. A third, a young zip from Sicily, warmed up in running shoes. She flopped beside him on the grass and did stretches, aware that grandmothers and widowed aunts were flutter-ing curtains up and down the block – Helen, the wild one, was at it again. The houses to the left and right were occupied by Rizzolo lieutenants, as were those that backed on them from the next street. The grouping offered a sense of security, but the street was no fortress if the Cirillos provoked a really bloody war.

'Let's go!'

Helen jogged out of the neighbourhood, trailed by the car and the young zip, and took a road that cut across a marsh, through the park, and onto a path beside the Belt Parkway. The clear sun sparkled on Jamaica Bay. A land breeze, dry and chill, swept the shore. When the car had to cut ahead to intercept her at the next entrance, she motioned the zip to catch up. He was cute, with a little angel smile, but appropriately tough. What a way to blow a family apart,

Helen thought; sleeping with a bodyguard. Brought up by decent people, he knew his place and never once threw anything remotely like a pass. Respecting that, she treated him with the same cool remoteness as she did all her family's retainers, and when she ran with him she wore baggy sweats to play fair.

She wished, as she often did, that there was some way of getting regularly and happily laid without jeopardizing her empire. A sudden dazzling white smile made her look like a gypsy girl, in a few more good years she could afford to buy Club Med. But then, the handsome French kids would be employees and it wouldn't be the same. Besides, thanks to the Strikeforce, the Rizzolo enterprises had stopped growing for the first time since she had taken over.

'Pennsylvania Avenue.'

Two miles and she was feeling good, up for the long way back, another three miles. The bodyguard tinkered with his Walkman, which had been altered to serve as a radio connection with the car, and he repeated the direction into a dummy earphone.

Two runners came the other way.

Helen and her bodyguard automatically closed ranks to make them split and go around. They were jocks, big and muscular. The one on her side – a handsome Irish guy who looked like a fireman – gave her an appreciative grin, which she fell for hook, line and sinker, smiling back even as his partner practically tore her bodyguard in half with a fist to the stomach.

The zip went down with an explosion of breath, blood, and vomit, clawing for the gun in his sweats. They were ready for that, too. One of them got to it first, pulled the gun, and ripped the wire out of the radio. The other caught Helen as she lunged towards the highway. She screamed for help. A car screeched to a stop. Two men inside. It seemed like a miracle until they held the back door open while the runners forced her onto the seat.

She fought, kicking, biting, screaming. One threw himself on top of her. She levered her knee into his groin. He yelled and rolled off. His partner grabbed her by the shoulders. She laced into his wrist with her teeth, kicked a third man in the face, and threw herself at the door. She got the handle open. But they pulled her back and slammed her face down on the seat, where they pinned her bucking hips and jabbed her with a needle.

# 9

Twelve miles to the north-west – as Helen Rizzolo's captors sped towards Kennedy Airport – Christopher Taggart's white Rolls-Royce Silver Spur rounded a Harlem street corner, crunching broken glass beneath its tyres. Reggie, his face hidden by doper shades and the polished visor of his hat, drove slowly down the block of derelict houses and dusty trees. Taggart sat stockstill in the back, staring at the one way bronze windows that made Harlem appear to bask in a golden sun.

Heroin addicts gazed at the corner, waiting for their man. Some were crying; some waited stoically in holes battered through the cinder blocks that sealed the gutted brownstones; the strongest clambered up rickety stairs for a better view. All stared in the same direction, like spring flowers tracking the sun on a cold day, and no one gave the gleaming car a second glance. Their man came on foot and he was late, if he was coming at all, for junk was getting short.

Reggie repeatedly checked Taggart in the mirror, but his regular smile had died, and he hadn't barbed him with a joke all morning.

'You know, sir, heroin trafficking is like child molesting in that one takes the most advantage of those least able to resist. On the other hand, you're not likely to entice Mr Cirillo with butterscotch and toffee.'

The first rule of the dope trade was never do business with anyone recommended by the person with whom you were already doing business; your associate has turned informer and his new friend is a cop. Taggart had to get Crazy Mikey Cirillo to break that rule.

'This sounded a lot better in theory.' He had crossed lines by the very nature of his vengeance and expected to cross many more before he had destroyed the Mafia, but dealing junk was less like crossing a line than changing sides. The thing that kept rattling in his head was whether, if by some miracle they were to meet, his father would accept his goal as justification.

Reggie gave him a look, a reminder that heroin was Mafia currency, and Mafia power was wired to supply. Which made the Mafia just as dependent as the addicts on the street, and as ripe for exploitation.

A shiver rippled up the block, the junkies stirring as one, like grass in the wind. Taggart turned to the back window, expecting to see their dealer, but Reggie, alert to his mirrors, said, 'We have a police car overtaking us. Two officers driving a brass hat.'

The NYPD blue and white sedan shot alongside. The siren blipped and the cop in front gestured to pull over.

Taggart lowered his window. 'Hi there, Captain. Hunting pussy?'

'Chris! What the *hell* are you doing here? I thought you were some damned pimp.' The precinct commander stuck his arm out and they shook hands from car to car. 'You trying to get killed riding around in that?'

'This baby's a lot safer than yours. I look like a local hero. You look like the enemy.'

'What are you shopping for, a place to build a parking lot?'

Taggart winked. 'Captain, if you were a very rich man I'd take you for a tour of the Columbus Avenue properties I bought in 1977. Harlem's getting hot. Now's the time to buy.'

'Get your chequebook. I'll sell you my station house.'

The cars moved off.

At last the dealer came, carrying a gun, because the shortage had driven the price of a 'dime' bag up to fifteen dollars. His own connection had been an hour late with half the bundles he had promised, and his price had risen to one hundred and twenty dollars for ten bags, up from the normal seventy.

\* \* \*

Downtown, Harlem's biggest black heroin distributor gazed mournfully through the iron bars of Gramercy Park as he discussed the dope situation with a Cirillo family crew leader. 'If your people don't connect with my people soon, I'm going elsewhere for product.' He was lying, in that he was already looking. The Cirillo *capo* repeated that he would have heroin soon. He nodded at the statue of Edwin Booth for something to say. 'What's the line on this guy?'

'His brother shot Abraham Lincoln for freeing the slaves.'

Beyond the park, through the far fence, the distributor noticed a beautiful white Rolls with bronzed windows cruising past the Gramercy Park hotel. He had to get one of those; he had two cars already, a black limo and a red Corniche convertible, but neither looked like that white sucker.

\* \* \*

The *capo* tracked Crazy Mikey Cirillo to one of the family's whorehouses, a Flushing brothel that catered to a big afternoon crowd. Mikey, who should have been attending to business, in the crew leader's opinion, was putting on a show – a boxing match in a small ring in the basement. His hard-edged,

130

handsome face was flushed with excitement, and the *capo* presumed he had just had a hit from the little gold sawn-off shotgun dangling around his neck. Shouldering through the mob around the ring, he reported the black distributor's threat. Mikey's expression turned menacing.

'Later.'

'Mikey, the guy's not kidding.'

Mikey cut him off. 'I'm taking bets. Sherry or Rita?'

Two naked women were warming up on the ropes, a big, buxom blonde and a smaller brunette. Reluctantly, the *capo* appraised them. 'The blonde.'

'You'll lose,' Mikey grinned. 'Little Rita's a killer.'

'This trouble can't wait, Mikey.'

Mikey hit the bell with a ball peen hammer. Thirty johns in suits and sportjackets cheered, and the girls tripped into the ring.

Because the light gloves hurt, Sherry and Rita had a long-standing agreement to pull punches. The johns didn't give a damn. They were happy with spread-legged falls and undulating struggles to rise from the canvas. Besides, as Sherry had explained to Rita, if anybody got bored, they could go upstairs and get laid, which was what they had come for in the first place; the nude boxers were only a floorshow. But today, Crazy Mikey made one of his unpredictable visits and tumbled to their arrangement.

His face clouded as he watched Rita pretend she had taken a roundhouse to the jaw. She flung her arms high, flopped to the canvas, crawled to the ropes, writhing like a snake, and dragged herself back to her feet with the enthusiastic support of the johns. Mikey rang the bell signalling them into their corners.

The johns crowded around, towelling them down, plunging champagne bottles between their lips, spilling the stuff on their breasts. Mikey leaned close to Sherry and whispered, 'A big one for first blood.'

'You're kidding.'

He crossed the ring to Rita, a tough little Spanish brunette with pointy breasts, and repeated the offer. Her eyes widened. 'A thousand dollars?'

'All you got to do is make her bleed.'

He hit the bell again and the girls bounded out of their corners, the webbing of the rattan stools imprinted on their flesh. Sherry, the blonde, still seemed reluctant to really punch, but Rita went for the face. Sherry peekabooed. The smaller Rita flailed at her gloves.

'Go for the body!' Mikey yelled.

Rita stepped back, planted her feet, and sunk her glove into Sherry's belly. Sherry dropped her hands with an astonished gasp.

'Hit her!'

Rita swung again, slugged Sherry in the face. Sherry sat down hard on the mat, crying. Blood trickled from her lip.

Rita pranced, clasping her hands overhead and shouting. 'I get the grand. I get the grand. Pay me, Mikey. Pay me.'

'Hey, Sherry's not out,' her champions protested.

'Don't worry,' Mikey assured them. 'Fight's just getting started.'

The johns piled into the ring, heaved Sherry onto her stool and poured champagne over her head. Mikey inspected her lip.

'You all right, sweetheart?'

'I can't believe she hit me,' Sherry sobbed, wincing as the champagne stung the cut.

'What are you, nuts?' Mikey laughed. 'For a thousand bucks she would have blown a monkey.'

'It's one thing to fuck for money. It's another thing to hurt your friends.'

'Everybody's got their price.'

'I don't.'

'Sure you do. The winner gets five grand.'

'Forget it.'

'The loser spends a month on the third floor.'

Sherry gaped at him. 'A month?'

'Every night. All night. Go for it, doll.'

He whispered the same to Rita and the happy grin slid off her face. The third floor serviced rich kinks. A gorilla stood guard to make sure none of the girls went to the hospital, but short of that the customers got to do what they paid for; ordinarily the girls rotated. Neither Rita nor Sherry *had* to obey Mikey and his manager, but if either left the Cirillo brothel she would find the rest of New York – the bottomless bars, the sex clubs, and the porn flicks – locked tight, which left the option of marrying a doctor or working the trucks in Long Island City.

They came out slowly, measuring each other.

'Mikey!' the *capo* protested. 'We need product!'

Mikey tarned, cold and deadly, and the *capo* recoiled, realized too late that he had made a mistake. Crazy Mikey was no fool just because he happened to act like a spoiled rich kid. Goading a couple of girls into maiming each other might be merely a distraction while his brain shifted to overdrive to fathom what had gone wrong in the dope trade.

He reached for the gold coke spoon. Though barely an inch and a half long, it broke at the breech like a real shotgun, revealing a tiny cache of white crystals. Mikey snorted, closed the breech and let it fall against his chest. 'I'm doing it,' he said softly. 'Now get the fuck out of here.'

As he watched the girls pummel each other's faces, Crazy Mikey realized he had begun to get over the shock of his brother Nicky's arrest by the Strikeforce. Three days ago he had been pulping a bookie who had screwed the family, when the word came and a bunch of long-faced guys had whisked him away like he was suddenly president of the United States. His father, Don Richard, had commanded him to take over Nicky's duties. He said he had faith in him. Later, the crew leaders told him bluntly how bad the dope shortage really was.

There was something going on that Mikey didn't understand. Everybody said the shortage stemmed from two years of Strikeforce busts. They had included the Pizza Connection, the Anchovy Connection, the Sicilian Connection, the Pizza Connections Two and Three – even the fucking Nepal Connection. And now the Forty-fifth Street Garage Connection which had led to the crew leader Vetere turning in Nicky. The arrests of wholesalers and importers had begun to squeeze New York's heroin supply just as the junkie population had increased. That's what everybody said.

Except that the Cirillos had been major importers and distributors for thirty years and Mikey knew a lot of smugglers. Many who hadn't been busted complained of hijackings, unexplained accidents, and mysterious betrayals. Add those stories up and something weird was going on. What, nobody knew. All that was sure was that product was short and getting shorter. He opened the gold sawn-off again, raised it to his nose, thought twice, and emptied the coke on the floor. Fucking up his head wasn't going to make his problems go away.

News of Mikey's plight flowed relentlessly to his father, despite the fact that the old man was, in theory at least, retired. Within hours, his *consigliere* reported the threatened defection of the black Harlem distributor. They discussed it over iced tea on the patio of Don Richard's home on a Staten Island hilltop. His thin red hair had lost some colour in the decade since his dispute at Abatelli's with Christopher Taggart and he stooped a little, making his shrunken frame seem smaller.

Manhatten lay across an empty harbour. Sea green Wall Street towers hid the Metropolitan Correctional Center, but in his mind's eye Don Richard could see his older son's prison as if the towers weren't there. Forget the lawyers' promises. They were bluffing. His elder son was going away for years; in terms of controlling the vast family – the only terms that counted – Nicky was as good as dead.

Don Richard's *consigliere* warned that dozens of Cirillo *capos* were itching to fill his shoes.

'Mikey can handle it.'

'You know I love Mikey like he was my own,' the *consigliere* argued, 'but he's not ready.'

Don Richard shook his head. 'He's a fast learner and he wants it. That's the most important thing. Even if he don't know it yet, he wants it. Like I wanted it.'

'He's the baby, your youngest,' the *consigliere* countered. 'We expected less of him and he grew more slowly for it.'

'Bullshit,' said Don Richard. 'That's nut doctor talk.' He denied he had a soft spot for his youngest son – he was simply too hard and ambitious a man himself to admit such a weakness. In fact, his faith was rooted in memories of himself when he was Mikey's age. Surely he had been as silly and arrogant, and look how far he had come *without* the advantage of the tall and handsome looks of a natural leader.

Mikey would perform when he had to, despite a soft childhood as the son of a rich and powerful boss. Don Richard was so sure that he decided to stay aloof of the heroin supply problem. His *consigliere* repeated that rebuilding their shattered import network was too stern a test for Mikey, that Don Richard must come out of retirement to help. Don Richard ignored that advice, as Christopher Taggart was betting he would.

The old man noticed, through the chain link fence on the road, a huge white Rolls-Royce. He glared, offended that some cheap Columbian cocaine dealer was house-hunting in *his* neighbourhood.

In the car, Taggart said, 'Head for the airport. Let's see what Ms Rizzolo has to say for herself.'

---

'The shot's worn off again,' Reggie said. 'I ought to give her another before she hurts herself.'

'Wait.'

Fascinated and a little awed, Christopher Taggart studied Helen Rizzolo through a one-way glass. Reggie's women had strapped her ankles and wrists to an oak chair, which was bolted to the stone floor. They had been careful not to hurt her, but no one had imagined the ferocity with which she would fight the unyielding leather, wrenching and twisting, her slight figure corded with straining tendons, and her face a mask of finely controlled rage. Her eyes met their own reflection in the mirror that camouflaged the view port, but she just kept struggling, as unselfconscious and determined as a leopard in a trap.

'I'm ready,' Taggart said.

Reggie touched his arm. 'I beg you to reconsider.'

'We've been through this. She controls the Rizzolos. I can control the Rizzolos through her. They are tough, ambitious, and hate the Cirillos. As we hit the Cirillos, her family will pick up the pieces and recruit their soldiers.'

'Ask yourself why you've chosen this woman.'

'She has no criminal record. Her family's attracted the least Strikeforce heat, since Tony jailed her father. She's innovative; she's against drugs and is perfect to take over gambling. Plus, she needs help.'

All true. Starting with the thin lead Taggart had given his brother, Tony Taglione had made his name at the Southern District by convicting Don Eddie Rizzolo. When the Cirillos tried to move in on their territory, Helen's brothers fought back in a bloody struggle which still smouldered and was exacerbated by mutual accusations of Strikeforce informing. The latest round had been the Cirillo's shotgunning of Eddie Jr, who had, as was his wont, survived.

'She's also very beautiful. You've had your eye on her since her father's trial.'

*Before,* thought Taggart, studying her through the glass. *Long before.* Like a sketch that captured the essence of the painting to come, the woman Helen Rizzolo had become had lived in the face of the girl Taggart had seen ten years ago in Abatelli's restaurant. She had grown an inch or so taller, perhaps, and womanhood had made her arresting beauty even more exotic, but her qualities had been there – the power in her deep, still eyes, her fierce pride, and her heart-stopping sensuality. He was unwilling to admit to Reggie that he was smitten at the sight of her today as he had been when he was only twenty-one. Yet he was confident that in the past ten astonishing years he had grown capable of savouring her at a safe distance.

'I'm not going to blow my whole scam 'cause I like the way she looks.'

'Chris, while I was making our Sicilian arrangements, I had the great privilege of a love affair with a woman there. They never forget, they never forgive. If she ever realizes how you plan to use her family, she will destroy you.'

'I'm Sicilian, too.'

'One quarter.'

'That quarter's working overtime.'

He pulled a black ski mask over his face and entered the room. She stopped struggling the instant she saw him and Taggart thought again of an animal, a predator whose every move embodied the dual purposes of attack and defence. She acted as an animal conserving strength while assessing a new threat; patience replaced the rage in her dark violet eyes.

'Helen, no one's going to hurt you.'

'Take these things off me.'

'Will you listen?'

Her eyes flickered over the stone walls, the small shuttered window, the solid plank door he had shut behind him, and his mask. If she was frightened, it didn't show. 'Do I have a choice?'

'No.'

'I'll listen.'

Taggart unbuckled her ankles and then her wrists, prepared to defend himself if she kicked. She stood up, quietly massaging her wrists. 'My clothes are clean and I've been bathed. Who touched me?'

'A nurse and a doctor, both female, were with you all the time.'

'What about the guys who grabbed me?'

'They went home.'

'I'm thirsty.'

Taggart poured water from a pitcher on a rough table by the door. She drank half and continued to draw small sips from the glass as they talked. 'Who are you?'

'A friend.'

'Listen, *friend,* do you know who I am?'

'Helen Rizzolo. You're here because I admire how you run your business.'

'Ransom?' Helen laughed. 'You grabbed the wrong person. I don't run anything. My family owns restaurants and a bus line – neither of which are doing well enough to pay ransom. My brothers run them. I handle the books, which is why I know they're not doing too well.'

'It's a good story, Miss Rizzolo. The Feds believe it – at least the part about you not running things. More to the point, so do your rivals – the other New York families. They can't believe a woman could head a tough Mafia family. But the truth is that *you,* and you alone, control the Rizzolo betting shops, the numbers, the extortion, and the hijacking. Your brothers just carry out *your* orders.'

'Are you crazy?'

'*You* shut down the bookie joints when the Strikeforce hit. *You* stopped the war with the Cirillos. Yesterday, *you* ordered that one of your soldiers be, shall we say, "terminated", when he was discovered wired with a Strikeforce transmitter.'

'I don't know what –'

'Your brother Eddie's crew leaders beat his head in with a baseball bat after Eddie was done questioning him. It was considered too vital to be left to ordinary soldiers.'

'I don't –' She reeled suddenly and dropped the water glass. It shattered on the stones. Taggart caught her as she sank to one knee amid the shards. Her body, which appeared delicate, was in fact as firm and resilient as a finely braided wire rope. She wrenched loose and bowed her head. 'I'm okay. I'm okay.'

'I'll get the doctor.'

'No. Just let me rest.' She knelt, shaking her head. Taggart kicked the shards of broken glass into a corner.

Helen tried to stand, pulling herself hand over hand up the chair. Taggart reached again to help, encircling her in one arm. She stiffened and shrugged him off coldly.

'Why do I get the feeling that you're FBI?'

'Come here.' Taggart stepped to the window and opened the shutters. The whitewashed stone wall was two feet thick. Outside, sheep dotted brilliant green hills under a lowering sky. 'Look.'

'Where are we?'

'The west of Ireland.'

'Ireland?'

'It's not FBI territory.'

She touched the thick, wavy glass. 'How long was I out?'

'Sixteen hours.'

'Do you realize my brothers are tearing New York apart looking for me?'

'They started to, but we convinced them to wait quietly.'

'We? What is this?'

Taggart left the shutters open. 'Let's talk business.'

'What kind of business.'

'Organized crime.'

Helen walked unsteadily to the chair and sat down. 'I don't know who you are. I don't know what you want. I don't even know what you're talking about.'

'I'll talk and you listen. There's no risk.'

'I want to go home.'

'Business first. The government has busted the council and the situation in New York is that the old Mafia – the rackets, call it what you will – is washed up. The Federal Strikeforce is winning. I give you five years tops.'

'Not me. I'm not the Mafia. If I ever meet someone in the Mafia, I'll tell 'em what you said.'

'It's going to take you awhile to get this,' Taggart replied patiently. 'Just listen . . . Demographics were killing you even before the Strikeforce. You haven't enough soldiers any more to run your operations and protect them from your enemies. Italians are the new Jews in New York. Their kids are going to college, so they're no longer cannon fodder for Sicilian warlords.'

'I don't know who you are or what you want, but just for the sake of conversation, don't you think that college-educated Sicilians might be more capable Mafiosa?'

'You're becoming too organized. All your lawyers and MBAs and accountants make you an easy target for the Strikeforce. Just like tax evasion got Al Capone, RICO and dope convictions are getting a better organized generation. The old Dons never adapted to the changes. Their heirs, your father's generation, aren't much better – sitting around swapping stories as if electronic bugging didn't exist. And your generation is hopeless. Maybe they're smarter about bugs, but when they get arrested for something, they talk to the cops. So who's going to replace them?'

'I don't know what this has to do with me.'

'Your father, for example.'

Her eyes flashed and Taggart was surprised to see pain in their depths. The next instant, however, they were blank again, revealing nothing.

'Don Eddie,' he continued, 'is a long-term resident in federal prison because the modern veneer he adopted played right into the government's hands. He let a smart accountant talk him into laundering heroin profits – which was theoretically a better idea than burying them in a hole in the ground. Your father was right to try it, but the Feds found the records. So even though they couldn't pin the heroin on him, they got him on the heroin profits. I don't mean to make light of your father's situation, but his misfortune might help you and I understand each other.'

'What's your point?'

'Do you agree that the *system* is a mess.'

'Whatever you say.'

'But the *market* is still growing. Ordinary people's appetite for criminal services is insatiable. They still want to borrow money, get high, gamble, and pay strangers to lay them. These services are currently earning one hundred billion dollars a year.'

She fixed him with an intent and sombre gaze. Her extraordinary beauty pulled him like a whirlpool. Taggart felt himself sucked down, getting lost in her eyes – he turned away. She said, 'That's an exaggerated figure.'

'Settle for eighty? Eighty billion dollars a year is the gross national product of Austria. Or the total p.a. gross of General Motors.'

'What do you mean, *settle?*'

'I'm taking over.'

'Taking over what?'

'Organized crime. All of it – everything. I'm filling the vacuum left by the Strikeforce.'

'With what?'

'That's where you come in.'

'Me?'

'The Rizzolos will run the street in New York, Long Island, Westchester, Fairfield County, Jersey. Everything the five families control is yours. I'll protect and supply you from the top.'

'*What* are you talking about?'

'On the street level, you will sub-contract, as it were, supplying the labour for extortion, shylocking, numbers-running, whorehouses, porn, and muscle

138

for the unions. On the upper level, I will eliminate your rivals and provide banking services and protection.'

'You're dreaming.'

'Am I?'

Helen stood up and started pacing from one stone wall to the other. 'You think you can do all this?'

'Not without your help,' Taggart said.

He sat down in the chair to put her at ease. She stepped behind him and massaged her wrists, a pretence to draw the long sliver of glass she had secreted in her sweatshirt sleeve when she had dropped the drinking glass. She held one end in the cloth, slipped her other arm around his throat, and slid the point of the shard through the right eye of his mask.

Taggart froze. The glass glittered a centimetre from his eyeball.

'*Who are you?*'

'You can't get out of here.'

'The hell I can't. You're walking me through the front door. Who *are* you?' 'Don't you see what I'm offering?'

'Offering? What if I don't want it? You'll just let me go?'

'Why not? You can't tell the cops.'

'You're crazy. This whole thing's crazy. You can't just move in. There's a war in New York. Strikeforce on one side, the rackets on the other. And you think there's room in the middle? *Don't move!*'

He had started to reach for her hand.

'I've already done it. Trial runs. Smuggling, wholesaling, money laundering. And today, kidnapping.'

'You can't –'

'Ms Rizzolo, you're leader of the most secure, best run crime family in New York. A few hours ago you were jogging in your own neighbourhood surrounded by your best bodyguards. You woke up tied to a chair in Ireland.'

'How?'

'I hired an experienced IRA kidnap team to sub-contract the job. A second contractor brought you here. When you've agreed, you'll be sent home, having crossed international borders *four times* without anyone the wiser. I've done all this without maintaining armies the way you do. Don't tell me there's no room in the middle.'

'You're stalling me. I don't believe you. Tell the truth!'

She sliced the skin that rimmed his eye. Blood trickled down the mask. 'My sub-contractor thought you were a piece of cake compared to the British politicians they've snatched. He said your security was a big joke.'

'The truth!' She cut deeper. He jerked from the pain. She moved the sliver to the surface of his eyeball.

'*Reggie!*'

Reggie, who was watching through the one-way glass, stepped into the room, his Remington P51 cocked like an eleventh finger between his clasped hands.

Taggart said, 'Reggie will be the richest retired Special Branch officer in the history of the British Empire – provided I remain alive – which makes him, among other things, the best bodyguard in the world. He's been a killer for thirty years. He's going to kill you in one second if you try to hurt me.'

Helen Rizzolo let the glass sliver fall to the floor, where it broke again. Reggie backed out of the room and closed the door. Taggart stood up.

She eyed him fearlessly.

He seized the sleeve of her sweatsuit, pulled it to his face and dabbed the blood. 'I won't hit you, for the same reason your kidnappers were ordered not to rape you. The job I'm offering demands respect.'

'May I ask what a non-rapeable Sicilian-American girl is worth to the Irish Republican Army?'

'Fifty M-ls and enough ammunition to slaughter a British regiment.'

'You got a bargain.'

'Damned right I did! That's what I'm trying to tell you. Sicily isn't the only source of drugs and murderers. Helen, there are cities in Asia and Africa, whose names we'll never know, where millions of people play the lottery every day and the prize is a ticket to America. The whole Third World is an endless supply of hungry sons and daughters. They'll fight, they'll kill, they'll fuck, they'll mule drugs. They'll do anything for a meal or a lucky break. Don't you see it? I can *import* violence – when and where I need it.'

Taggart released her sleeve, but neither he nor she moved.

'The world is much more violent than we Americans are. If a Conforti or a Cirillo, or even a *Strikeforce,* messes with my people, I can hire a sub-contractor to blow them up, machine-gun them, or kill them quietly with a knife. Radicals, mercenaries, whatever the job calls for. When my murderers are done they go home, clutching whatever little treasure they wanted – guns, explosives, money.'

'Then what do you need me for?'

'The *street.* I'm not going to hire Palestinian bombers or South African guerrilla fighters to slap around a welsher. That's where your people come in. Your people take the street. I'll attack the other families' leaders. You'll never worry again about a rival family. Your soldiers can concentrate on business instead of defence.' He smiled suddenly, hot on his own juices, because he was getting through to her. 'Well?'

'I have to think about it.'

'You're wasting your time and mine. You know your answer.'

'Don't push me!'

She went to the window, rested her chin on her folded hands on the stone sill, and gazed out at the fields of sheep. A mackerel sky was drifting in from the sea and the sunset was tinging it pink. The scenery looked like a holy card the nuns gave for being good. She hungered suddenly to be out of doors. Taggart asked. 'Why don't we go for a walk?'

'All right. I'd like that.'

She gave him an ironic smile when he handed her a lavender windbreaker in her size. 'Thought of everything?'

A stone path gave onto the fields, where deepening grass rippled in the steady sea breeze. She held her face to the wind and the sun and picked up speed. Taggart strode easily beside her, learning her moods. The fields spread along a crumbling rim of cliffs. Whitecaps dotted the dark blue sea lough below. Miles to the west, the Atlantic stirred. Helen drank it in, pausing now and again to stare with frank pleasure. Her silky black hair fluttered about her cheeks. The wind swept it back.

Taggart feasted on the remarkable beauty of her profile, the richness of her mouth. Sexually, the heat shimmered off her, yet he felt an enchantment more complex, brushed by forces unknown in his experience.

Reggie trailed at a distance, flourishing a walking stick, which concealed a four-ten squirrelgun loaded with buckshot.

'Does he think I'm going to throw you off the cliff?'

'Reggie assumes the worst, always.'

'I already took my best shot.'

Taggart grinned. 'He's a little put out because he missed you palming the glass. Did they teach you that in your father-in-law's casino?'

'You know too much about me.'

'You heard my offer. You think I'd make it blind?'

'Who told you?'

'I prefer my informants to remain living a while longer.'

Helen shrugged. 'Did Reggie plan my kidnapping?'

'No. It was exactly like I told you, sub-contracted. A package deal, deliver one Helen Rizzolo, unmolested, to the general aviation terminal at Kennedy.' 'If Reggie is English, why would he give the IRA guns and ammunition?' 'Reggie makes his own arrangements – just like you will – but if I know Reggie, that particular branch of the IRA is going to have a problem. Make up your mind, Helen.'

'What about the Strikeforce?'

'I'll take care of the Strikeforce. You won't have to worry about them anymore.'

'That's a little hard to believe. The Strikeforce belongs to the US attorney.'

'I can handle them.'

'Let me explain something, Mister. If the Brooklyn or Manhattan District Attorney comes after my brothers, our lawyers handle it. One way or another, they can deal with it. But if the United States Attorney for the Southern District of New York gets on their case, it's "Oh shit". Who do you think got my father?'

'Tell your brothers to stop using the phone in the bus barn. The Strike-force is tapping it from a street vault on the corner.'

'You're *inside*?'

'I can also assure you that the Rizzolos are low down on their hit list at the moment. Taglione is concentrating on the Cirillos.'

They found a sheep path worn to the stone and followed it towards a promontory. 'You must give me a sign,' she said thoughtfully. 'Something by which I can trust you.'

There was a rhythm to this dance and Taggart knew suddenly and surely that the time had come. He led her to a lichen-covered rock wall and sank to one knee before her. Then he pulled off his mask and placed it in her hand.

'Look at my face, Helen.'

Helen Rizzolo stared. At last he had astonished her.

'I know you!'

'My name is Christopher Taggart. I build skyscrapers. I own Taggart Construction and Taggart Realty. I am a director of the Association for a Better New York. I'm a charter member of the Mayor's Commission for Growth in the Eighties. My new Park Avenue spire will make Trump Tower look like a box of Saran wrap. When you get back to New York you can look at my picture in the newspaper and my address in the telephone book.'

'I know,' she whispered.

'Maybe you saw me on TV,' Taggart said, wondering whether she remembered their brief encounter ten years ago at Abatelli's. 'I happen to be a member of the President's Commission on Organized Crime.'

Helen's face turned blank with distrust and she asked, harshly, 'How'd you get appointed? Your brother? Your name isn't Taggart. It's Taglione. You changed it when Tony Taglione became a prosecutor. Who do you think you're kidding? Your brother put my father in prison.'

'And now I've just put my entire life in your hands,' Taggart countered. 'Until you say yes, I am at your mercy.'

'No,' she said, with devastating accuracy. 'Your *plan* may be at my mercy; maybe. But not you. I can't touch you. Who would ever believe this conversation?'

'Only you have to believe it. I'm all your prayers answered. I'll free you to operate by your best instinct and observation, instead of fighting a hundred years of Sicilian history.'

'What are you doing this for?' she asked suspiciously. 'You're a rich man. You run things.'

'I intend to be richer.' Taggart had concluded that only wealth and power were motives that would make sense to this empress of the Rizzolo clan. Certainly, if he were her, he would not throw his lot in with an avenger. 'A lot richer. Which is what you're going to be if you join me. A lot richer. And a lot more powerful.'

She searched his face, hunting God knew what? But while Taggart waited, quelling his impatience, Helen was, in fact, less concerned with his motives than the opportunities he offered her family, and the risks. *His* family was the problem. Tony Taglione.

'Is your brother in on this?'

'Christ no.' Taggart shook his head emphatically. 'If my brother had a tape of this conversation, he would send me to the electric chair.'

She believed him, but didn't understand. 'Why does he hate you?'

'He doesn't hate me. He loves me, deep down somewhere, but he's a law and order guy. He's what used to be called a moralist.'

'Yeah, fine, but you're his brother.'

'Tony sees life like two tunnels. Right and wrong. Once you're in one, you can't transfer to the other.'

'I don't get it. He's your brother.'

'It's his way,' Taggart said simply. 'Our family is half construction workers, and half cops. Tony got the cop half.'

She still didn't understand and knew she never would. 'Then who do you have inside his Strikeforce?'

'I have many contacts in many agencies, and in many families. That's all you have to know. *Capish*? Do we have a deal?'

'I expect trust from a partner.'

'Sub-contractor. I don't take partners.'

'I'm not interested in being a sub-contractor,' Helen replied coldly.

'I'm not doing business that way. I've chosen you over the Cirillos, the Bonos, the Imperiales, or the Confortis. The Rizzolo family will survive the Strikeforce and prosper. But on my terms.'

'What if I refuse.'

'It's a deal breaker.'

'You're asking a lot.'

'I'm offering the whole goddamned city of New York.'

'You're asking me to put my family under your control.'

'No. I will tell you what needs to be done. *You* will control your family.'

'And you will control me. I don't like it.'

Angrily, Helen faced the now darkening sea lough. Yet her anger was merely from pride, which she could not afford to indulge. Her father, she knew, would never make a deal with an outsider. But he was weak now, helpless, while she, beset by the other families and the Strikeforce, was on her own; for if the power of the Rizzolos was not yet all hers, the responsibility surely was. She had little to lose and much to gain; besides, a deal was a deal only as long as it served both sides. She faced Taggart with a smile. As her father used to say, it was a choice she could live with.

Taggart saw that patience had again curtained the diamond hard light in her eyes, which he suddenly realized was not at all at odds with her extraordinary beauty, but its foundation. For an eerie second he saw something else that almost made him shiver, but the feeling evaporated when she stretched her sleeve over her thumb, wet it with her tongue, and dabbed his face where the cut had opened up again. 'We're going to have to find a better way to meet.'

Taggart laughed. 'Is that a yes?'

'Your terms *sound* generous, but you're asking a lot back . . . My family is very fortunate to put such a powerful friend in our debt.'

Taggart smiled at the old-fashioned Sicilian belief and thrust out his hand. Gravely, she slipped her fine and pliant fingers between his. He held them for a moment, savouring the victory. He had won an army.

# 10

On a warm June night, two weeks after returning from Ireland, Taggart met Reggie high atop the bare steel of the Taggart Spire to assess their response to the heroin shortage. Work lights illuminated the columns and headers that framed the space Taggart had chosen for his triplex penthouse and the great derricks stood silent against the stars. Below and beyond, New York sprawled, its lights a dense carpet in the centre, thinning gradually north and west and south into the suburbs. Easterly, they stopped abruptly at the dark wall of the sea. Jets descended on the edges and long trains flowed in measured procession.

Taggart walked into the wind; Reggie trailed like a cat, reporting on feelers extended into the Cirillo's heroin pipeline. Taggart listened with a heady feeling that for each light scattered in their millions there was a switch that he and he alone could turn on or off as he pleased. For in the dark between the lights, the men and women of his shadow Mafia were making temptingly generous overtures to the hard-pressed Cirillo drug traffickers.

Among them, Taggart and Reggie decided that night, a Californian named Ronnie Wald, looked best.

★   ★   ★

'We're talking pure,' Ronnie Wald told the Cirillo soldiers sent to check him out. 'Pure and plentiful.'

Reggie Rand's agents had discovered the slick West Coast dude in a California prison. Essentially a con-man, and a good actor as any con-man had to be, Wald was tough enough to survive fourteen of his twenty-eight years inside. He wore three broad rings on his right hand, which served as knuckles in a pinch, and was good with the knife he carried in his alligator boot.

The Cirillo soldiers didn't like him, his suntan, his fancy boots, or his bleached jeans, and didn't trust him. But the street said he had stuff to sell in heavy-hitter quantity.

'Ninety-four point eight per cent. Run it through your box.'

Wald opened his hand and flashed a generous sample in a baggie.

'If you like it, we can talk numbers.'

The Cirillos recoiled. The Strikeforce, the DEA, the Federal Organized Crime Drug Enforcement Taskforce, NYPD and the State Police, half the fucking world, were busting wholesalers left and right, and this Wald clown was flaunting heroin in broad daylight like it was coke in a pitch-dark disco and they were a couple of girls who'd fuck for it.

They looked up and down the West Side block for the fourth time in a minute. It was a hot, sticky evening; the Puerto Ricans were drinking beer on the stoops and young executives were walking home with paper bags of takeout food and their jackets slung over their shoulders. Half the buildings on the block were being renovated and the gaping windows and lattice scaffolding made a thousand hiding places for Feds with binoculars and gun mikes.

'Let's go for a ride.'

Wald shrugged. 'If you got the time, I got the time.'

They got in the Cirillos' car, a rented T-bird, and headed up Amsterdam, outta there before the Puerto Ricans and junior executives whipped out machine-guns and FBI badges. Wald took his bag out again and dangled it like he was pushing Carvel flavours. 'This'll stand forty. You know?'

'I know how to cut junk.'

'So what's your problem?'

The soldiers exchanged looks. The one not driving said, 'I'm gonna pat you for a wire.'

Wald showed his teeth. 'You can't be too careful.' He leaned forward while one of them hung over the seat and frisked his back and waist and legs. When he was done, Wald dropped the baggie on the front seat. 'Check it out. Meet me at a Hundred-fourth and Broadway tomorrow.'

'If it's good.'

'If it's good,' Wald mimicked amiably. 'Listen, my men, you better get used to dealing with class.'

He got out of the car and walked away.

'Gotta be a Fed.'

Wald's sample checked through the hot box at ninety-four point eight on the nose. The Cirillo soldiers discussed Wald and his dope with their *capo,* who relayed the information in veiled terms to Mikey Cirillo. Crazy Mikey drove around Manhattan half the night, cruising the clubs, worrying. Even the heroin's purity seemed damning. If Wald were a Fed wouldn't he supply a top sample? On the other hand, Wald's name had popped up in other deals and no one yet had a bad word for the prick. What it came down to, Mikey knew, was he needed product. The whole fabric of supply was falling apart like a rotten towel and his distributors were looking elsewhere. He telephoned the *capo:* 'Keep going.'

'Keep going' meant find out how much Wald could deliver. And if it all hit the fan and the *capo* got caught and the Feds waved twenty years in the face, what could he testify? Crazy Mikey Cirillo said, 'Keep going.'

Maybe his smart brother, Nicky should have been this careful.

*   *   *

Taggart and Reggie concluded Wald had tapped a direct line into the Cirillo insulation, a line which could lead to Mikey Cirillo himself. While others continued courting Cirillos, they decided to let Wald sell five kilos of heroin at one-hundred and fifty thousand dollars a kilo, and repeat the sale in a few days.

Then the Cirillo soldiers asked Wald if he could supply larger amounts.

'Five keys a pop is plenty private enterprise for me, thank you. My boss hears I'm diddling around with these little side deals and I'm in trouble.'

The Cirillo soldiers looked at each other. 'Side deals?'

'Hey, don't get me wrong. I don't mean he doesn't know I did it. But enough's enough.'

'We'd like to meet this guy.'

Wald laughed. 'Forget it.'

'Well, maybe my boss would like to meet him.'

'If your boss can buy fifty keys a pop, you send him around.'

'Tomorrow.'

Wald looked surprised.

'Tomorrow,' the soldier repeated. Who the hell did Wald think the Cirillos were?

'I'll see what I can do. Riverside and a Hundred-sixth.'

Their *capo* was wary and insisted on cruising the meeting spot for an hour ahead of time. He didn't like the spot. It was a busy intersection, the junction of the wide One Hundred and Sixth, Riverside Drive, and a service road. Tough to keep track of the traffic and sidewalks and the park.

'Drop me at Broadway. Pick these clowns up, lose a tail, and then get me.'

'What if they won't come?'

'Fuck 'em. This looks like a setup. Don't say anything stupid. If he has stuff with him, leave.'

Wald was waiting at Riverside. 'Where's your guy?'

'Where's yours?'

'Waiting for us.' Wald waved up a cab. 'We figured you for this paranoid shit.'

Reggie Rand stepped out of the cab wearing light slacks, a shirt unbuttoned down his hairless chest, a gold chain, sunglasses and a grey-flecked beard. He slipped into the Cirillo car, too quickly for a photograph. Wald climbed in

147

front. The soldier floored it, and raced up Riverside on the yellows, scattering pedestrians.

Wald said, 'You're gonna get a ticket.'

'Funny.' He doubled back and picked up his *capo* on Broadway. The *capo* got in the back next to Reggie. 'Pull onto a side street,' he told the driver. 'Check 'em out for wires.'

'Wait,' said Reggie.

'What?'

'I said wait.'

Shortly after he had joined up with Christopher Taggart, he had studied with one of the New York theatre's top voice coaches to call up a flat American accent on occasions like this. 'Let's shake hands hello first.'

He extended his hand. The *capo* took it warily, trying to probe his glasses with his glittering black eyes. Reggie smiled. The whole purpose of this meeting, and of the transactions to follow, was to impress the Cirillo hierachy with his ability to import heroin on the top level. If this *capo* didn't eventually lead Taggart to Crazy Mikey, the whole scheme was a waste.

'Okay. Frisk us and get it over with.'

The *capo* patted him down thoroughly. When he found the gun on his ankle, Reggie said, 'Look, but don't touch.'

'Mine's clean too,' said the soldier at the wheel.

'Drive.'

'How much do you want?' Reggie asked bluntly.

'Huh?'

'How much do you want to buy? What quantity?'

'Fifty . . . uh . . . units.'

'Sir. This is your car and you've taken the liberty of frisking me. Do me the courtesy of saying kilos.'

'Are you crazy?'

'Stop the car. Stop it, I said!' It eased to the kerb at One Hundred and Fifty-second Street. 'Would you be more comfortable if we walk around the block? Just the two of us?'

The *capo* nodded.

'Have your man follow. This neighbourhood's a bitch.'

They started down the steep slope to Riverside, trailed by the car. They walked uptown a block, and finally, as they trudged back to Broadway, the Cirillo *capo* admitted that he wanted to buy fifty kilos of heroin.

At the comer, Reggie said, 'Excellent. Come up with six-million-two-hundred-and-twenty-five-thousand dollars and it's yours.'

'We gotta work out a consignment deal. A third down?'

'I don't mean to sound rude, but consignment is for friends and I don't even know you.'

'Who the fuck are you to say you don't know me. You know who I represent. Who are *you*?'

'I'm a man with fifty kilos whenever you can pay for it, sir. Good evening.' He signalled Wald, aware that England had crept tartly into his voice. The Cirillo *capo* did not appear to notice.

'Hold it. For cash? Four million.'

'At one-twenty-five a kilo you've already got your break.'

'Four and a half million.'

Reggie pretended to ponder the offer. 'Can you save me laundry bills?'

'Bearer bonds.'

'Five million in bearer bonds. Have your chap work it out with mine.'

The *capo* blinked and Reggie concealed a smile. Considering the terrible shortage on the street, both the price and, equally important, the quantity, were golden. The Cirillos had reason to rejoice.

The next afternoon, Wald and the Cirillo soldier checked in separately to the Palace Hotel carrying identical Lark suitcases. In Wald's room the Cirillo soldier set up a portable lab in the bathroom, spooned random samples of the fifty kilos from Taggart's stockpile and heated them in test tubes. The heroin melted at two hundred and thirty degrees and remained white, indicating it was at least ninety per cent pure. When he signalled that he was satisfied, Wald scrutinized the stolen bearer bonds under infra-red and ultra-violet light, and when *he* was satisfied, counted the negotiable paper with the fastest hands the soldier had seen outside Atlantic City.

That same night, a Nigerian United Nations envoy in Reggie's pay delivered the bearer bonds in his diplomatic pouch to Switzerland, where Taggart's full system of international contacts went into play.

The diplomat turned the bearer bonds over to a broker who sold them as previously instructed and delivered the proceeds to an officer of Geneva's Union Bank with instructions to deposit them to various accounts. Upon confirming receipt of those deposits, a Chinese heroin distributor with Dutch citizenship, and a member of the Triad, Green Pangs, arranged for three-hundred kilos of processed Burmese heroin to be released at a remote landing field near the Thai border in the Golden Triangle.

A Thai air taxi brought it to Bangkok airport, where it docked alongside an AirVac twin-jet air ambulance, diverted from a legitimate medical run. Resuming its legitimate journey, the AirVac plane picked up a Mobil executive who had broken his back on an Indonesian oil rig and flew the injured man to American facilities in the Philippines.

AirVac was owned by a consortium of American corporations based in Luxembourg and controlled by EuroLand, a real estate company held, through a string of holding companies, by Christopher Taggart. Taggart had bought the ambulance business, secretly, when the recession of '83 had sharply reduced the market for extremely expensive corporate executive emergency medical care. Routinely engaged in legitimate medical evacuations, the silver jets with the green cross on the tail were a common sight in the private aviation sections of major airports. No one bothered them, other than to ascertain that hospital-bound patients weren't carrying plague, and they crossed borders with a minimum of Customs inspection. Thus had Helen Rizzolo been smuggled out of Newark Airport disguised as a rich Belgian in a coma and brought into Ireland as an oil executive injured in a North Sea drilling accident.

In Manila, a fresh crew, ignorant of the jet's hidden cargo, continued east with a New York executive in the glover trade who had been shot in a brothel. In New York it was visited, briefly, at Newark Airport by Reggie Rand, a director of AirVac Holding, who left with a panel truck full of heroin sealed in body bags worth hundreds of millions to Crazy Mikey Cirillo.

# 11

Visions – The Club, on Queens Boulevard in Forest Hills, was an expensively redecorated movie theatre with chairs in the balcony, a main dance floor of glass, and a second showcase dance floor on the raised stage. Taggart paid twenty bucks at the door and bought a five dollar beer at a glass bar, which was filled with water and goldfish and changed colours with the lights. A hot-looking joint, yet for this space and the money spent, Chryl and Victoria, who kept threatening to design a club, could have done a knockout.

It was early and the place was overrun with women who got in for half price before eleven. He danced with several who asked him to, while he located the peephole where the owner kept an eye on the action. Taggart traced it to her office, guarded by a well-dressed bouncer in a silk shirt and heavy gold chain, the kind which, Reggie said, had a weak link to break away in case somebody made the mistake of fighting the guy.

'Can I help you?'

'Tell Ms Rizzolo, Chris is here to see her.'

Her office was stark white, clean, and soundproof but for the insistent bass thumping through the wall. As the bouncer ushered him in, Helen stood up behind a table desk, which was cocked towards the smoked glass window Taggart had spotted over the music station. She wore tight jeans and a shimmering white blouse and spike heels. Taggart wanted to tell her she had beautiful feet, but the alarm bells that had gone off in his head the moment he entered the club were clamouring that he was playing with fire.

'Come in, Chris. With you in a minute. That's okay, Sal. Thanks.'

Sal backed out and shut the door and she said, astonished, 'What are you doing here?' She gave no sign whether she had see him at the bar.

'You said we had to find a better way to meet.'

'I've been meeting with Reggie for a month. I thought that was the deal. What's happening?'

Acutely uncomfortable wherever a tap could be installed, he asked, 'Is the room clean?'

'It is and you know it.'

'What do you mean, I know it?'

'I found out who Reggie had among my people.'

'Reggie said I shouldn't come,' Taggart replied with a smile, doubting she had found all of Reggie's spies.

'Like another beer?'

'No thanks. We have to talk, but not here.'

'Where should I meet you?'

He felt light-headed and wanted to show off. 'Park and Fifty-sixth. I'll be at the main gate.'

'I'll be in a cab.'

Taggart turned to leave. 'Nice-looking club.'

'It's okay.'

He felt her eyes as he crossed the dance floor. His hands were shaking. This was crazy, but he couldn't help it – or didn't want to. He felt like he was back in school, romping around after a pretty girl the major thing on his mind.

When she got out of the cab at the Taggart Spire, he led her into the dark work site and aboard a freight hoist. 'Afraid of heights?'

'No.'

The lights blossomed like a flower the higher the hoist rose. At the top, Taggart took her arm and walked her to the edge of the plank floor. Overhead, the derricks soared, enormous dark V's against the sky. She looked around as if she liked it and he was glad he had brought her.

Taggart stroked a steel column. 'This is a dinosaur. They'll all be cement soon.'

'What did you want to talk about?'

'Are your brothers still buying it?'

Helen hesitated and Taggart tensed up. He needed them desperately. 'Are they?' he repeated. 'Reggie says he's not sure.'

She looked out at the lights. It was a month since Taggart's people had flown her back from Ireland, but she could still see the expression of astonished relief on Eddie's face when she walked in the front door, trailed by the FBI agents who had been waiting outside . . . Eddie threw them out, hugged her and listened dubiously as she promised to explain everything after a bath. While she was still in the tub, they sent her mother to ask the big question: Had she been raped?

'No, Mom.'

'Are you sure?'

'Mom!'

'Then what happened. What did they want?'

'They had a message for Frank and Eddie.'

'That's all?'

'Would you send them up, please? I have to talk to them.'

Her mother changed the subject, as only she could. 'Do you have to work so much with your brothers? Don't you miss having a guy?'

'You mean a guy to get laid?'

'Helen, do you have to talk that way?'

'Yeah, Mom. I miss having a guy. I miss it a lot. You want to send up Eddie and Frank?'

She could have added, but didn't because she didn't want to make her mother miserable, that she couldn't have a straight guy because her life would be secret from his, and she couldn't have a rackets guy, because he would try to take it away from her.

Her brothers trooped into her bedroom, closed the door, and stood around the bed looking very uncomfortable, as she intended them to. She had set the stage, propped up against the pillows in a fluffy bedjacket, sipping a glass of white wine.

'What happened?'

'Have you swept the house?'

'This morning, like always. No bugs. What happened? Who grabbed you?' 'The whole thing was a set-up. They just wanted to talk.'

'Talk?' Eddie exploded. 'They grab a girl off the street to talk?'

'Who are they?' Frank asked quietly.

Taggart had suggested an explanation. Helen modified it, hoping that a promise of independence linked to an opportunity to destroy the Cirillos would prove so tempting to Eddie and Frank that they would accept dealing with people they didn't know. She said, 'You know what the Italian police are doing to the Sicilians.'

'I know they got a big guy to squeal.'

'And what the Sicilians are doing to each other.'

'They're killing each other, just like the Cirillos are killing us. What does it have to do with who the fuck snatched you?'

'There's a new group of Sicilians who survived. They're getting out of Italy and going international. They're setting up the money in Switzerland and Luxembourg. They're recruiting the best from each country to join them. Italy, France, England, Jamaica, Canada, the United States.'

'Recruiting?' Eddie asked belligerently. 'Who the fuck do they think they are.'

'The future.' She held his gaze until he looked away. 'They don't trust the Cirillos. They want us to take New York.'

'Tomorrow soon enough?' Frank asked.

'They'll back us with everything we need. Hitters. Weapons. Information on the cops. Laundry–'

'Dope?'

'No dope. There are better ways to make money.'

'What do they want from us?'

'Partners they can count on; a door into legit corporations; and a skim on the laundry. But first we have to get rid of the competition. That means the Cirillos and everybody else.'

'The rest will fall in line after the Cirillos,' said Frank.

'What'd you tell 'em?'

'I told them I would tell you guys what they said. That's all.'

'What if me and Frank don't agree?'

She shrugged. 'I guess no deal.'

'But why'd they grab *you?*' Eddie demanded. 'Why not me or Frank?'

'They knew about me seeing Pop. I think they had contacts up in the jail. So they knew I knew the business.'

'I know the business, too. So does Frank.'

Helen hung her head and replied contritely, 'But you weren't dumb enough to go running every day. I was easy. Sorry.'

'It's a trick,' said Eddie. 'They're Feds.'

'They took me to fucking Ireland, Eddie. They kidnapped me. They're not Feds.'

'It still could be a trick.'

Helen had leaped at that opening, ensuring that they would never deal with Christopher Taggart. 'I'm the go-between. If it's a trick, what do they get? Me. As long as I'm the only one who talks to them, they can't touch you guys or the family.'

'I'm not letting my sister take a rap.'

'Nobody's taking a rap. It's no risk.'

Eddie made a face. 'Pop wouldn't buy that.'

'He already has,' she lied smoothly – her second lie about her father in less than a week. 'I went to the jail before I came home. I ran the whole thing by him and he said, go for it. Eddie, don't you see, these are smart people and they like the kind of tight family we are. We're natural partners.'

'I know we're good. What are they going to do *for* us?'

'We can tap into an international cash and information system,' she answered, embroidering the lie with details that might actually come to pass in the future when her family controlled New York. Christopher Taggart was right. Internationally-organized activities were the future. 'They've got scams going with government money that make heroin look like sand.'

'What kind of information?'

Helen had paused to sip from her glass. 'They warned me the Strikeforce has a tap on the bus phone. They're in the street vault on the corner.'

154

Eddie and Frank had liked that, had liked it a lot. . .

★   ★   ★

She turned now to Taggart. The wind drew a silken veil of black hair across her face. 'They're still going along, but they're getting impatient. They want results damned soon.'

'Tomorrow,' he promised, gazing with satisfaction at the shimmering city. 'Tomorrow?'

'Do you know the new Cirillo Brooklyn underboss?'

'He tried to kill my brother Eddie.'

'Do you know Tommy Lucia?'

'I know he's a Cirillo crew leader. A gambler. Number Two to the Brooklyn underboss.'

'Tell your brother Eddie to make a deal with Tommy.'

'What kind of deal?'

'Ask him to join the Rizzolos.'

'You're crazy. Tommy Lucia won't talk to Eddie.'

'It would double your book and numbers.'

Helen considered it. 'Yes, but only if Tommy Lucia brings the right people with him. What makes you think he'll break with the Cirillos?'

'Can Eddie handle it?'

'Of course he can handle it,' she said sharply. And then, in softer tones, 'I'll stay close. We'll be ready . . . How do I get down?'

'I'll take you.'

In the elevator, he asked, 'Would you like a drink?'

'No, I gotta go.'

Taggart found her a cab and she was gone.

Slightly dazed by his own audacity, he walked slowly towards Third Avenue to the Old Stand, where he could usually count on finding some off-duty cops from the Seventeenth Precinct. He stood at the bar, sipping an Irish coffee and thinking that he was glad he had done it.

★   ★   ★

Helen's cab driver was not pleased with a fare to Canarsie and less so when she told him to take the Belt Parkway. 'Lady, we're a lot better off going from Flatbush to Eastern Parkway to Rockaway Parkway.'

'I want to see the water,' she said, staring out the window and ignoring his next remark about the ferry.

Christopher Taggart was shaping up as a very lucky break. He had given her a chance to protect her family from the Cirillos, even as she consolidated her own power with her brothers. She would call the shots, and by the time she got her father home on a medical and Eddie and Frank finally realized he was no longer capable of being the boss, they would have already accepted that she was in charge.

When her cab crossed the Manhattan Bridge, the driver headed for Flatbush Avenue.

'I said I want to go on the Belt.'

'Screw you, lady. You're not going to tip anyhow, so I'm going my way.'

'Because it's Canarsie or because I'm a woman?'

He pulled the cab to the kerb, reached back and opened the door. 'Hop out.'

Helen glanced up and down the barren stretch of shops with closed gates and thought, this guy would really throw me out of the cab and leave me here if he could. She supposed she would be frightened if she were alone; but she was never alone and she said in a voice low with suppressed anger, 'Call your dispatcher, please. Tell him I'm a friend of Johnny Carroccio.'

The driver looked at her and the sheer certainty in her voice made him do it.

'Be nice,' the dispatcher radioed back. 'Be very nice.' The driver turned the car around and took the Belt Parkway. When the harbour came into the view, he asked, politely, 'Who's Johnny Carroccio?'

'He lends money for taxi medallions to people who can't go to the bank.'

'Good friend?'

'He works for my brother,' she replied and the driver fell into a profound and lasting silence.

Yes, Taggart had come along at a good time. Though tonight, she had to admit, he had worried her. He was lunatic to come and see her, and she wondered whether he was an amateur playing at the rackets. But the kidnapping had been masterful, precision work by a powerful international enterprise.

Belatedly, it occurred to her that she should have said yes to his drink invitation to find out what was going on in his head. Nice looking guy; nice manners. And he moved gently for a man his size. She had said no automatically. It was habit by now.

*　　*　　*

Tommy Lucia was a tough survivor of the Brooklyn gambling rackets. Longevity being one route to power in an unstable world, patience another, Tommy had got ahead by going along and by choosing his opponents carefully. His lone career with the Cirillos reminded Taggart of his own Uncle Eamon's successes in the Police Department. But while his uncle had retired after thirty years, Tommy Lucia still reported daily at the Caffe di Catania on Knickerbocker Street in the Bushwick section of Brooklyn.

The Catania had a front room with a long, clean counter, a modern espresso-cappucino machine, and four-colour posters of the Italian World Cup soccer team. In the back was a second, larger room where the regulars played cards at round tables. At six in the evening, it was like a village square as Sicilian men from all walks of life stopped in on their way home from work. Among them was the new Brooklyn underboss of the Cirillo family.

Tommy, his number one crew leader, stood by, pleased. With the RICO conviction of the underboss's older brother, the mantle of Brooklyn leadership had fallen on powerful shoulders. A handsome man in his sixties, Tommy's boss wore a fine blue suit, and a ring of snowy white hair circled his otherwise bald head. He greeted friends and neighbours amiably, embraced an old baker – laughing with him at the flour marks pressed on his suit – and sat down at a card game while younger men scrambled to bring him espresso.

Tommy knew a winner. Their gambling enterprises were flourishing as the new man extended books and numbers into parts of Brooklyn which were previously Rizzolo territory. When the hot-headed Eddie 'the Cop' had struck back, the new underboss's counterpunch had been masterful – suckering the greedy slob with a phony cocaine deal to lower his guard.

The fact that Eddie had lost only his fingers instead of his life could fairly be attributed to luck, and luck, Tommy Lucia knew was never more than a brief lowering of house odds. The new underboss would destroy Eddie in the end and reclaim the rest of Brooklyn from the breakaway Rizzolo clan. He might even edge out Crazy Mikey for boss of the underbosses and from there? Maybe when Old Don Richard died, overall boss; carrying Tommy on his coat tails.

The pay phone between the front and back room rang. A kid leaped to answer and handed it to Tommy. He listened, went back to the card table, and whispered, 'Somebody torched one of the Rizzolo's Blue Line buses.'

'Call your friend in the Rizzolos. Say I'm concerned they might misunderstand. Tell them we are sorry, and we had nothing to do with it. And put a couple of men out front, in case they don't believe you.'

Tommy dispatched some men to the sidewalk, then got on the phone. He had just made contact with his 'friend', who sounded sceptical, when the front door opened on three blond men in blue suits. 'The fucking FBI just walked in. Ill call you back.'

The men stepped up to the counter, set their brief cases on the floor, and ordered cappucino.

'To go?' the counterman asked hopefully.

'Here. You got a men's room?'

'Middle door in the back.'

One of them strolled between the card games, went into the bathroom, and strolled back a few minutes later. He and his companions spooned sugar into the cappucino and sipped it until a black sedan, with a government seal on the door, double-parked in front. Moving in swift concert, the men in blue suits opened their briefcases and unfolded stock-mounted machine pistols. Two stepped into the rear room and shot the underboss. A bodyguard tried to pull a weapon from his jacket and they blew him across the room. The third gunman turned his automatic on Lucia, who pressed against the wall and opened both hands, palms out; he thought he was dead for sure.

'On the floor.'

Tommy dropped to the linoleum, waiting for the bullets. But the guy just looked at him, like he was covering him, while his partners sprayed the walls. When everyone else alive was flat on the floor they backed out to the waiting car, from which protruded a gun covering Tommy's men on the sidewalk. The car pulled away, running red lights and speeding north.

The Italian neighbourhood gave way to Spanish. Then Knickerbocker Avenue entered a barren industrial district of canals and railroads. Less than a mile from the shooting, the driver turned into a deserted railyard, raced along side a string of flat cars, and stopped behind a warehouse. The men in blue suits got out, climbed into a shiny steel shipping container on a flat car. The automobile drove away. Shortly, a switch engine coupled onto the flat cars and hauled them through Brooklyn to the Atlantic Basin, where cranes swung the containers aboard a Swedish Mersk Line container ship, which sailed on the evening tide.

*　　*　　*

Tommy wasn't too surprised to get a message that evening from his 'friend' in the Rizzolos. He returned the call expecting threats. His friend sounded bewildered. 'I don't know what's going down. But I got messages for you.'
'What?'

'First, Eddie Rizzolo says he didn't do it.'

'Yeah? What's second?'

'There's a guy wants to eat dinner with you. Ten o'clock. Cafe des Sports.'
'Never heard of it,' Lucia said suspiciously.

'Neither has Crazy Mikey or the Strikeforce. It's on West Fifty-first between Eighth and Ninth.'

Lucia figured that the name meant sports, and a trophy cabinet in the brightly lit front bar confirmed it. A big guy, who acted like the owner and looked like an ex-soccer player, said, 'Oui, Monsieur, your friend is waiting.'

A self-assured blonde led him past customers who looked like showbiz people. Nobody connected in the joint, just people. She showed him into a cubicle couched between brick walls. Lucia was just thinking he liked the way she walked, when his eye fell on his host. There, at a table set for three in the private-most corner of the restaurant, his back to two brick walls, his enormous hand cupping a fragile-looking wine glass, was Eddie 'the Cop' Rizzolo.

Which made no sense at all to Tommy Lucia. Eddie waved him into the empty chair across the table. 'How you doing?'

'What is this?'

Eddie started to extend his right hand, smiled at his missing fingers and asked instead, 'You want a drink? I got a bottle of wine. If you don't mind French.' The self-assured blonde produced a glass, poured and asked if they would like to hear the specials. Eddie, apparently on his best behaviour, said to Lucia, 'Mind if I order? We talked about it earlier.'

Lucia glanced at the third place set beside Eddie, but apparently they weren't waiting. 'Go ahead.'

'We'll share the pâté and the celery *remoulard*.'

Lucia was impressed until he remembered that Eddie owned restaurants. 'Sound good?'

'Sure.' He wanted to throw the woman out of the cubicle, grab Eddie by his lapels, and scream, What the fuck is going on?

'What can you tell us about the scallops *provençale?*' Eddie asked.

Lucia listened to his head roar while she described the dish and Eddie interrupted repeatedly. He was getting the shakes, recalling the gunfire of several hours ago. One second his boss was alive, the next, dead on the floor.

'How about you?'

'You got steak?'

'*Au poivre?*'

'Go for it!' Eddie exulted. 'Double french fries for both of us. They got these good looking skinny ones – kind of like you doll.' He grinned at the hostess. 'And maybe some red wine for my friend when his steak comes.'

She left and, as it was a large table, a comfortable space separated them from the nearest diners. Eddie grinned, inviting his questions. Lucia caught his breath and stalled. No way Eddie Rizzolo was going to make him look like an idiot.

'Classy looking girl.'

'Her father's the owner.'

'It shows.'

'Always.'

Eddie sipped his wine and broke off a piece of bread. He was displaying a patience he had never been known for, acting like he could sit there all night. Lucia couldn't stand it any more. 'So what's going on?'

'We're all well. My sister's home safe, no harm done. My hand don't hurt no more. Are *you* all right?'

'Better than this afternoon.'

'Good. My father always says things can always get better; for worst there is no end.'

Lucia forced a smile and asked, as was proper, 'How are they treating Don Eddie?'

'My sister says he's fine. She sees him regular.'

'You said she's well. Who took her?'

Eddie looked embarrassed. 'A thing in the family. Can you imagine? It was good, of course, that they didn't hurt her. Not like getting snatched by Columbians.' He shook his head. 'Would our grandfathers have imagined the things we have to worry about?'

'It's a strange world,' Lucia agreed. He sipped the thin white wine, buying time, wondering how Eddie 'the Cop' got so smart so fast? Eddie had apparently gone to a lot of expense to advance him, Lucia, up the Cirillo hierarchy by blowing away his boss. Thank you very much. But Eddie Rizzolo wasn't smart enough, tricky enough, or even greedy enough to put such a scam together. He and his brother, Frank, had the slob tastes of your ordinary street hood – a full belly, a fast car, and friendly broads. Somebody was backing them.

The restaurant owner passed the cubicle and gave Eddie a nod. He waved back, and Lucia wondered, what next? 'I hope you don't mind,' Eddie said. 'My sister's in the city and I told her to meet me here. Okay if she joins us?'

She arrived like a windstorm, black mane flying, arms laden with packages, perfumed, flashing eyes. A rich little Italian princess, and one hell of a piece of ass.

Lucia smiled at her. 'How you doing?'

She gave him a cool nod. Sex might be written all over her, if you knew how to read it, but she wasn't giving any away. Dropping her packages on the empty chair, she sat beside Eddie and kissed him.

Tommy Lucia smiled again. She was his answer! Daddy's little go-between. Old Don Eddie was dealing from jail. His daughter would report. Must gall the hell out of Eddie to have a woman sit in on his meet. Relieved that at least he had an idea who was leaning on him, Lucia said, 'I think I'd like that red wine now, Eddie, if you don't mind.'

'No problem.' Eddie flagged down a waitress and asked for the wine list. 'How about you, hon? Something to eat?' Helen took her brother's arm like a little kid. 'Can I have a cappuccino?'

'If they don't got it,' said Eddie, 'I'll make 'em send out.'

Tommy figured Eddie would surely turn to business when he had finished ordering, but to his annoyance, Helen resumed the amenities that her brother had stalled with. 'We hear Don Richard is well.'

'Don Richard amazes us all.'

'Aren't the old guys great?' Eddie asked innocently.

'They're not old when they have their health,' Lucia parried, for he saw clearly where this was going. Fucking Rizzolos.

'Health is all,' Eddie agreed.

'And freedom,' said Lucia, jabbing Eddie with a reminder that his father was in prison.

A dark shadow floated across Eddie's broad face and he looked dangerous. But Helen nudged him lightly and he controlled himself. Lucia grinned; in the clubs the coke dealers' girlfriends used to hold the drugs to fool the cops, but now the girls sold the stuff themselves. Eddie better watch it or Helen might take over. Wondering whether she would join the discussion or merely report to her father, he said, 'There's a lot going down I don't understand.'

'Look at it this way,' said Eddie, tearing off another piece of bread and passing the basket to Lucia. 'If I wanted to kill you, I've had two chances today. Atlantic Avenue, where you had breakfast, and Woodhaven Boulevard, lunch.'

'Knickerbocker Avenue.'

'I already told you, that wasn't me.'

'Guys have found out I'm not so easy to kill.'

'Three, if you count I coulda gotten you on the sidewalk a minute ago. Four, if I cut your head off with this butter knife.'

'So you're doing me favours. Why?'

'I want to talk.'

Lucia made his face blank. No way he was going to put himself in the position of dealing with the Rizzolos behind the Cirillos' backs. Bad enough sitting in public with them. 'You're talking to the wrong guy. Don Richard –'

Eddie cut him off, switching to Sicilian, a language which conveyed multiple possibilities. 'Why don't we talk about Don Richard later? . . . Funny thing. Your boss getting shot kind of clears your way to running Brooklyn for the Cirillos. Doesn't it?'

'It'll go to Mikey,' Lucia replied in English, still wary.

Helen's Sicilian was as fluent as Eddie's, and more subtly insinuating. 'Crazy Mikey is busy selling dope in the city. What does he care about making book?'

Lucia couldn't help but nod agreement. Gambling was big and steady money; they had built empires on it, but it didn't turn guys on like dope. Mikey was hooked on the insane profits.

The restaurateur brought the wine Eddie had ordered, a '71 Bordeaux as rich as cream, and confided it was one of his last. Eddie waited until a waitress brought his sister's cappucino. Then he tilted his glass towards Lucia. 'The future.'

'What future?' Tommy asked coldly, determined to stop their advance before it got out of hand.

'Our future. We're in the same business, by and large. So we're dumb to compete when we could pull together. We got the same problems with the blacks and Spanish throwing their weight around. We got the same problems turning dollar bills into clean C-notes. We got the same problems laying off bets.'

'Russia and China got the same problems too. I don't see their future together.'

'Books and numbers,' Helen interjected quietly, 'don't do well in a war.'

'What war?'

Eddie held up his maimed hand. 'We got nothing but trouble if we keep shooting up each other's stores.'

'So what do you want, Eddie?'

'*You.*'

'Me? You want me to work for you?'

'We're looking for good people, Tommy.'

'I appreciate the compliment. But I am content where I am. What would I get that I don't already have?'

'Better than the Cirillos gave your boss,' Eddie answered. 'And better protection, too.'

'But only if you bring the best people with you,' Helen added. 'That's important. You must deliver your best. We'll take good care of them. Nobody will lose.'

'Except my friends the Cirillos.'

'The Cirillos are going to lose anyway,' Eddie sneered. 'Brooklyn, for openers.'

Lucia hid his contempt. The boast was Eddie Rizzolo at his loudmouthed worst. A man shouldn't talk about it, a man should simply do it. Nor should he give away his whole plan. He said, 'You're talking about a big step. I could lose everything. The Cirillos are big and you're not. I don't see them giving Brooklyn to you or anybody else.'

'Think about it,' said Eddie. 'Think about it 'til Tuesday.'

Lucia had a suddenly funny thought. If he were legit, this would be extortion. He stared at Helen, who was watching him intently. 'Give your tough brother's mouth a rest,' he said coldly. 'Why don't *you* tell me what happens Tuesday?'

She touched Eddie's beefy forearm, silencing him, and held Lucia's gaze so hard and so long that he felt a strange shiver in his spine. He knew three kinds of women in the world – whores, wives and mothers. But there was something

162

dark in Helen Rizzolo's eyes that said she was a thousand years old, the fourth kind – *Maghe,* a witch.

'Somebody might not tell you to lie on the floor, Tuesday.'

Don Eddie couldn't have put it better, Tommy Lucia conceded grudgingly; the old bastard had himself one hell of a go-between. 'You're strong-arming me,' he protested, 'Like I was a fruitstand buying protection.'

Helen returned a smile and the dark years receded slightly into the cool depths of her eyes. 'Look at it this way, Tommy. We're offering a choice you can live with.'

★   ★   ★

Taggart and Reggie watched the Cafe des Sports from a rented limousine, parked in a row of similar black, white and silver cars waiting for the theatres to let out. It was a block of tenements hung with fire escapes. Several had restaurants on the ground floor. An hour after Helen had gone in, Taggart noticed a man come out of a neighbouring building, glance up and down the street, and hurry towards Eighth Avenue, swinging his attaché case as if proud of a good day's work.

'Reggie, hand me the phone, please.'

Reggie gave it to him, shooting looks up and down the street for the source of the trouble. 'What's wrong?'

'Not a thing.' Taggart swiftly dialled the home number of a real estate broker who worked for him. 'Elliot, you're going to make us both rich. I just saw a broker for Wootten coming out of a tenement on West Fifty-first near Eighth. Unless he's screwing a hooker, they're doing an assemblage. Buy me a store with a long lease.'

Reggie retrieved the phone with a broad smile. In the past two years with Taggart he had learned enough of the Manhattan land business to know that when the developer-clients of Jones Lang Wootten had almost got their parcel assembled, they would find Christopher Taggart owning a leasehold in the middle of it, ready to negotiate a sale, a construction contract, or trade for a deal on some other property they were developing elsewhere in Manhattan.

Moments later Tommy Lucia emerged from the restaurant followed by Eddie Rizzolo with his sister holding his arm. Taggart watched Helen, whose gaze wandered about the street as she closed her cape against the evening chill of a mid-summer Canadian high. Eddie and Lucia shook hands to conclude their business.

'It's working,' Reggie marvelled.

'Of course, it's working. They're like sharks. All they know is to keep moving. . . Okay. It's time to make Crazy Mikey crazier. Have somebody drop a hint that the *capo* we're supplying is a big money earner.'

# 12

A Cirillo bodyguard was paid four thousand dollars to drop the hint and Reggie promised to double his fee if Crazy Mikey got demonstrably angry. At the risk of overkill, the spy chose a moment they were snorting cocaine in the stalls of an oceanfront Hampton Bays summer dance club. He' knew Mikey to get a little paranoid marching to a Bolivian drumbeat and indeed, when he mentioned casually that a certain *capo* was making some very impressive heroin buys, Mikey turned white through his suntan, the golden spoon fell from his fingers, and he bolted out the men's room door. Seconds later, his big, black Mercedes convertible was scattering parking lot attendants and burning rubber onto Dime Road. He sped back to New York, shouting on the car phone that the *capo* in question had better join him at the Flushing brothel if he knew what was good for him.

'I want to meet your man's boss.'

'I don't know if he's got a boss.'

'He's got a boss. Just like you have a boss. Set it up!'

Reggie seemed appalled when the *capo* approached him with Mikey's demand. 'Such a thing just isn't possible.'

The point of being a boss, he explained with infuriating deliberation, was that one did not take risks one could pay others to take. Why would his boss want to get involved?

The *capo* said, 'Mr Cirillo wants to buy a hundred keys a shot. But he don't want to pay up front. He agrees consignments are for friends, so he wants to make friends.'

'And he's a little touchy about you getting all the action, too, isn't he?' Reggie asked innocently.

The *capo* shrugged, but his dark eyes turned private.

Reggie decided he might be a man with a future in Mr Taggart's service. He held him off two weeks before announcing that his boss had agreed. 'But with tighter security than the Pope. Your boss is allowed one companion. I will be with my boss. If they have anything to discuss they will do it alone. Third Avenue and Sixty-eighth.'

Reggie's spy reported that Mikey was having second thoughts; he was worried that Reggie might be an undercover FBI agent and that the buys, as big as they had been, could be all part of a huge government sting operation. At the same time, Reggie learned from his British sources that Mikey's people were expecting an immense heroin shipment from London. Thus neither he nor Taggart were surprised when Crazy Mikey did not show for their meeting.

Taggart sent Reggie to Paris. He had befriended Kurt Spielman in the aftermath of the Munich massacre during the 1972 Olympics when 11 Israeli athletes were killed by Palestinian terrorists. The disillusioned Israeli had left Mossad to go freelance. Like Reggie, he had kept his body in shape and his contacts current. He had a deep affection for the dapper Englishman based on mutual tastes and Reggie's kindnesses over the lean years. Somehow, whenever things were hard, Reggie Rand could be counted upon for a job.

Summoned to Versailles, Spielman met his friend in a tourist restaurant which served an astonishingly good lunch. After they helped the waiter recalculate a bill equally astonishing for its creative currency exchange, they went for a walk in the palace gardens.

'What mayhem?' Spielman smiled.

'A hijacking . . . with a twist.'

Reggie gave him the details, airline tickets, expense money, and passports, and wished him luck.

Two days later, Spielman found himself with two hired hands in a bogus yellow taxicab trailing an Emory Air Freight truck around Kennedy Airport at two in the morning. Slipping out of the North Freight Terminal, the step van stopped at British Airways, then sped out of the airport onto the Belt Parkway and into the streets of Brooklyn. Spielman spotted a Mercedes leading the truck and an Oldsmobile taking up the rear, and he had his doubts about the dirty van following his own car. His men were veterans he had used often; nonetheless he repeated his orders to keep the violence to a minimum. 'Chase them, don't kill them, unless you have to.'

The car and the weapons – pump shotguns and automatic pistols – had been waiting in a long-term parking lot when they got off the plane. God willing, they'd be back in Europe in less than twelve hours. Ahead was a mile-long, straight road that cut between bulldozed blocks of abandoned factories. There were few lights and no traffic.

Spielman's driver blinked his high beams and pulled ahead of the Oldsmobile, the air freight truck, and the Mercedes. Spielman and his partner rolled down their windows. A quarter of a mile along, the driver jammed on the brakes, slewed through a screaming U-turn, and sped back towards the convoy. Spielman and his partner shotgunned the Mercedes, shot out the truck's windscreen and tyres. Then, while the Oldsmobile fled away, Spielman climbed out, shot the padlock off the back of the truck, and lifted the door.

'Choral'

The smugglers had buried their heroin in a legitimate truckload. There were easily a hundred packages, stacked floor to ceiling. At that moment, the van he had wondered about raced up, decanting men with guns.

Spielman jumped to the road, firing his automatic, while his men laid down accurate fire to hold the Mafiosa at bay. Spielman opened the gypsy cab door. A bullet tore through it, inches from his hand. He tossed a thermite grenade into the back of the freight truck and got in the cab. 'Go!'

He heard the familiar dull thud and when he looked back the truck and its contents were an orange pillar of flame.

When he heard about the explosion, Mikey Cirillo went crazy. 'They burned up the whole fucking truck!' he screamed. 'What kind of fucks do that?'

The *capós* who had to explain things to their Harlem and Bed-Stuy distributors gazed back silently. None of them had ever heard of a hijacker destroying what he couldn't take, but that mystery mattered not at all. Two hundred irreplaceable kilos – a quarter ton or two months' supply – had gone up in smoke. The Strikeforce bust at the West Forty-fifth Street garage, arrests in Sicily, more Pizza Connection indictments, several hijackings around the world, and now this. It might not be Crazy Mikey's fault, but what, they wondered, would Crazy Mikey promise next?

'Mikey, the blacks aren't standing still for this. Another few weeks I won't be able to park my car on the street up there.'

\*     \*     \*

The *capo* Reggie had been selling to apologized for the screwup. His boss, Crazy Mikey, really did want to meet Reggie's boss. Reggie said he would try to set another meeting. He made them wait a week. This time, Mikey showed. It was Reggie's first close look, and he wondered if Taggart had bitten off more than he could chew.

Despite his reputation for impulsive violence, Mikey had the self-assured air of a man who had grown up around power. His father, the elderly Don Richard, had been securely in command when Mikey was born and this showed in the arrogant set of his thin lips, the seemingly blasé expression in his dark eyes, the expectant look of a man used to getting his way. Rather, Reggie thought, like the English public school boy who breezed on to Sandhurst and an Army command.

It was easy to believe the underworld rumour that Mikey was growing into the job of chief underboss, and Reggie was reminded of how young Christopher Taggart really was. In fact, he thought with a thin smile as he climbed into Mikey's car, Mikey reminded him of Chris's hard-eyed brother, Tony, who might be better suited to deal with this sort.

'Tell him where to go,' Mikey greeted him coldly.

His driver's broad shoulders were bulked out by a fourteen-ply Kevlar bulletproof vest; his heavy hands and attentive intelligent eyes told Reggie he was the best bodyguard the Cirillo clan employed.

'Turn the corner . . . into that parking garage . . . down the ramp to the end. Park there.'

Mikey looked at the silver grey Citroën-Maserati. 'No way, I'm getting in your car.'

'I'm sorry. It's the only way.'

Crazy Mikey's eyes turned black and glittery. Reggie found himself hoping he would change his mind again. But he said, 'No bullshit,' then snapped some Sicilian at his driver, who lifted a powerful signal analyser from under the seat. Reggie unlocked the Citroën-Maserati, started the engine and warmed it up. The bodyguard sat in front with the analyser on his lap, and Mikey sat in back.

Reggie drove up the ramp onto the street, around the block and north on Third Avenue, searching his mirrors for the Cirillo chase car. It was a yellow cab, ideal camouflage in mid-town, but less so as they passed Ninety-sixth Street and entered Harlem. He turned on the radio, which emitted a shrill beep. 'Turn your transmitter off, please.'

The bodyguard looked at Mikey, who nodded.

'We agreed two on two,' Reggie said mildly. Mikey looked out the window. Reggie reduced speed until he was crossing intersections on the yellow light. The chase car followed suit, two blocks behind. Reggie nudged the accelerator; the Citroën burst to sixty. He crossed One-hundred-twenty-fifth, careered right down a long dark block past the city bus barn, took another right and a sudden sharp left, hooking across three lanes of traffic into the northbound lane of the Willis Avenue Bridge. A moment later he turned onto the Major Deegan Expressway, accelerated to ninety mph, exited onto the westbound Cross Bronx Expressway, and then drove south onto the Henry Hudson Parkway. Gliding sedately into a riverside parking area at One-hundred-twenty-fifth, he got out of the car and motioned for them to follow.

Mikey came warily, sticking close to the bodyguard, who handed him the signal analyser and walked with his hand in his pocket. Reggie was impressed; too few people realized a bodyguard wasn't a servant. He led them to the edge where the Hudson River lapped a crumbling bulkhead. A big open Cigarette-class ocean racer waited in the shadows beneath a broken light, guarded at a distance by several heavyset black men with fishing poles.

'What is this?'

'A boat.'

He had taken her from people in the Long Island cocaine run, and she was uniquely fitted for the night shuttle between the Patchogue River and points two hundred miles seaward of Fire Island. Her numbers were readily changed and each set was backed by forged documentation, but her real defences against hijackers and the law were speed, stealth, and, if they failed, a unique capacity for suicide. She was built of fibreglass and all metal fittings – rails, chocks, wheel, even the steering linkage – had been replaced with epoxy and graphite composites to offer the least radar target. The only metal aboard was in her engines, which were mostly below the waterline. If the boat were trapped, the hull was wired to blow a hole the length of the keel.

'Mind your footing.'

He showed the way with a penlight to the deep bucket seats set four abreast in the broad open cockpit, which was sheltered by a massive wraparound windscreen, and started the engines. The bodyguard checked his signal analyser, but again detected no transmitters. Reggie loosened the single line which held the bow to the current and flipped it off the dock cleat. When the river drew her off, he engaged the engines and she murmured quietly towards the dark.

He let her go for a half mile into mid-channel and turned upstream towards the George Washington Bridge. Blue garlands of catenary lights draped the orange line of the roadways; their reflections painted the water the breadth of the river. He opened the throttles. Now she thundered, her propellers cutting a luminous froth as she drove hard into a chilly wind.

'You're gonna drown us if you hit something.'

Reggie ignored him. The deep-V hull drove debris down and away from her shielded propellers. He turned off his running lights as the boat passed beneath the bridge. He continued upstream a mile, veering towards New Jersey. An eighth of a mile from the black wall of the Palisades, he stopped the engines and the boat glided and slowed, then drifted. When current and momentum held her in limbo, Reggie released the anchor winch, and let her fall back, setting the hook in the muddy bottom.

'Gentlemen?'

He unlocked the cabin door and lighted the step with his penlight. He closed the door when they were inside and turned on a single lamp which lit the small compartment with a dim red light. The cabin was surprisingly large, with a gleaming galley. Mikey glimpsed a bidet in the mirrored bathroom. He saw that it had been a real pussy barge until the bunks had been replaced with deep leather swivel chairs bolted to the deck. Now it looked like a conference room on a corporate jet.

Christopher Taggart had his back wedged in the U-shaped bow seat, his face deep in shadow, and Reggie noticed his hands were folded tightly.

'Sit down.'

A goddamned nigger, thought Mikey. But as he sank warily into the chair nearest the bow seat, he realized that Taggart was wearing a black ski mask and leather gloves; his skin could have been green for all he could see.

'What's with the mask?'

'If I were you, Mikey, I'd expect the man who sells me a hundred keys a pop to be very careful. In fact, I'd demand it.'

'You got a name?'

'No.'

'I don't like this.'

'We've made every effort to arrange a safe meeting. No one followed our car or our boat. Your own equipment guarantees no one is wired. No one can see us or hear us. What don't you like?'

Mikey looked around the cabin and repeated loudly for the benefit of a bug. 'I don't like this. I don't know what you're talking about. Let me outta here.' 'Mikey.'

'You're fucking Feds. Fuck you. I ain't done nothing but gone for a boat ride.'

Taggart turned his slit eyed mask to the bodyguard. 'What's your name, fella?'

Surprised, he answered, 'Buddy.'

'Well, I'm awful sorry, Buddy.' He nodded at Reggie who pulled the gun from his ankle.

Mikey couldn't believe his eyes. *'What is this?'*

Reggie repeated Taggart's 'Sorry,' and shot the bodyguard.

The Teflon bullet tore through Buddy's bulletproof vest and threw him out of the chair onto the deck. Mikey's ears were ringing and smoke burned his nostrils. He gaped at Buddy, whose face was dead white. He was moaning softly. Blood was spreading from his shoulder, soaking the front of his shirt. Reggie pounced on the wounded man and pulled Buddy's gun from his shoulder holster.

*'What!'* yelled Mikey unbelievingly. 'What the fuck did you do that for?'

'Would the Feds shoot Buddy?' Taggart asked him calmly.

'Why—'

'Now you know we're not federal officers.'

Mikey was coming out of shock but remained incredulous.

'You just shot a guy to show me you're not a cop?'

'You can trust us.'

'But —'

'We mean business, Mikey. We're looking for good men we can trust. We do not give second chances.'

Slowly, Taggart's purpose sank in on Mikey. He figured the guy for a Sicilian, though he was big for one and had no accent at all. One thing for damn sure, he wasn't a cop. And people called *him* crazy! 'But what about the stuff?' 'Let's step outside and talk. Take care of Buddy,' he said to Reggie. 'Tell him again we're real sorry.' Taggart knelt beside the wounded gangster, peeling bills off a roll. 'Hey, Buddy? You hear me? Sorry, man. Mikey will get you to the hospital soon as we're done talking. Here's five grand.' Taggart stuffed the money in Buddy's shirt. 'You'll be out in a couple of weeks. Take a vacation and recuperate – okay?' Taggart stood up and motioned for Mikey to follow him. 'Let's take a look at the stars.'

They stepped up to the cockpit and closed the door. Mikey could hear the river sliding past the tethered hull. Overhead were pale stars. Upriver it was black with sweet woodsmoke on the breeze; downriver were the lighted bridge, the glittering towers of Manhattan, and the scattered lights of the Jersey condos.

'You guys are nuts.'

'That's how we stay alive. What do you want to talk about?'

'Well, how much can you supply me?'

'A hundred keys a week.'

'What's it gonna cost me on consignment?'

'When I can deal on consignment, one hundred and fifty thousand a kilo.'

'I paid one ten last time.'

'That was last time. Figure one-fifteen for cash at the present rate.'

'What do you mean, present rate?'

'In my experience, prices fluctuate in every area, from source to freight.'

'I don't know about that. I have to talk to my people.'

'Look, man. I don't want to dick around with you. *You* are your people. Mikey Cirillo doesn't have to ask anybody's permission. Your guys are having problems getting stuff. I got plenty.'

'One-fifteen?'

'For cash. Those bearer bonds are fine, but I guess you don't get them that often. One-fifty on consignment.'

'Gold? Jewels?'

'I'm not a fence.'

'Steady supply?'

'Guaranteed. That's what you're paying for.'

'Don't leave me hanging.'

'You and me deal direct. Our people can handle the stuff and the cash, but you personally come to me when you want to buy. No chance of stings.'

'I can go with that.'

'And one more thing –'

'What?'

Taggart couched it as a threat, but it was really an invitation to Mikey to expand the Cirillo heroin operations. 'If you want to bring in another guy, *you* sell to him. I don't want to know from any third parties. No partners. I'm telling you right now, up front. If you come with a guy you know since you were in reform school and he's the son of a don who runs the Bronx, and he's made his bones and served ten years because he told the cops to fuck off, I'll kill him. Then I'll kill you. Clear? You deal with who you want to. I will only deal with you.'

'I don't like threats,' Mikey said quietly, thinking no Sicilian would ever be so blunt, and wondering exactly how much this guy could deliver.

'Then don't do anything to make me repeat them . . . Hey, what are we arguing about? Your worries are over. I'm your man. You get your hundred keys a week you can count on. You get a fair price. We oughta shake on it. . . Then we can take poor Buddy to the hospital before he bleeds to death.'

Mikey silently extended his hand and Taggert gripped it firmly. The guy talked like a Mick, he suddenly realized; a hearty Irishman.

'And who knows? Some day soon you might even want more than a hundred keys.' Taggart had his back to the bridge and saw the light glitter in Mikey's eyes.

Crazy Mikey was hooked – just as hooked as if he were shooting the junk himself.

★ ★ ★

Taggart and Reggie Rand cruised Mulberry Street in a ten-year-old Cadillac with rusted rocker panels and a tear in the vinyl roof. Reggie slouched behind the wheel in sneakers, greasy jeans, and a Moosehead T shirt; Taggart wore jeans and a leather waistcoat, flashing bare muscle through the open window. If they looked like anything, he thought, it was a couple of out-of-town dopers too dumb to know it was almost impossible to score in Little Italy. Twice they passed Paletti's, the steak house where Crazy Mikey's rival heroin distributor, Joe Reina, ate lunch, but they were early. Reggie turned onto Kenmare and parked with the engine running.

Taggart cocked his ear to the potently burbling dual exhaust. 'Rhapsody of a misspent childhood. We used to sneak my old man's Lincoln to the drag races. Two cars off the line.'

'Straight track?'

'Queens Boulevard. Tony and me would pull the mufflers and resonators to reduce back pressure. You should have heard it – six hundred cubes cooking. That car hauled freight.'

'I presume you tuned the carburettors to compensate.'

'Carbs, timing. Tony had a beautiful touch. Then we'd stash the mufflers in the trunk, and find some turkey with a hopped-up muscle car. Cameras were big that year. Also Cheval SSs, even Vets; Chevy was turning them into pigs those years. I'd bet twenty bucks and blow them away. We'd make two hundred bucks a night, then put the whole muffler system back together before we got home. I'll bet you had a souped-up Jag when you were a kid.'

'A Lancaster.'

'What the hell's that?'

'Four-engined heavy bomber.'

'In the Second World War? What, you lied about your age?'

'Among other things.'

'Okay, head up Mulberry again . . . My father used to take us down here on Sundays. It was jammed with families like ours coming in from Queens and Long Island and Jersey to look at grandma's old neighbourhood. See the clamhouse? Cars would cruise by all day, people saying, "Hey, where was Joey Gallo shot?" They still do, I guess.' He laughed. 'What a fucking heritage.'

As they crossed Grand Street, Taggart glanced east. 'There's our boys.'

\* \* \*

'Jews everywhere!' The Palestinian laughed. 'Why are we killing Italians?' His friend driving the truck returned an indulgent smile. Perhaps his own eye was less obsessed, or perhaps it was just that he had lived once in New York. Surely Grand Street on the Lower East Side teemed with Jews, but among the shoppers and shopkeepers were as many Chinese, Spanish, and blacks, not to mention bargain-hunting East Side matrons, West Side actresses, and suburban housewives of many hues and pursuasions. 'I suppose,' he said, 'to fry an egg, we milk a cow for butter.'

They drove carefully west, obeying traffic lights and waiting patiently when cars parking and garbage trucks blocked the street. Ahead was Little Italy, Mulberry Street, and Paletti's Steak House, where the Conforti narcotics importer, Joe Reina, was having his customary late lunch.

Neither Palestinian knew Reggie Rand, nor Rand's agent who had contracted their mission. Reggie had hammered out the bargain – four perfect blank British passports – with their unit leader in Algiers. All they knew was that after years of exile in a dusty training camp two hundred miles from Algiers, they were suddenly back in action.

They double-parked across the street from Joe Reina's limousine, took the radio transmitter, and unloaded some fish crates for appearance's sake.

\* \* \*

On their next pass Taggart directed Reggie to a parking space two blocks down Mulberry, from where he could see the sidewalk in front of Paletti's Steak House. It seemed to him that the limousine driver was eyeing the truck suspiciously, and he checked them with binoculars. The Palestinians were three blocks further up by a payphone.

Reggie dialled his cellular phone. The Palestinian answered in French and Reggie told him to sit tight.

Taggart watched the sidewalk; next to the restaurant was an Italian social club with a blank window, and up from it a plumber's shop, funeral home, another restaurant, and a hardware store. Below Paletti's, nearest their parking spot, was an empty storefront, from the cellar of which, he had learned from an agent he trusted, the Strikeforce conducted electronic surveillance of the steakhouse. Below the storefront were a laundry and a bakery. Across the street a row of tenements was being renovated. Sometimes the sidewalks were empty, but suddenly they would fill with people.

'You sure those clowns won't jump the gun?'

'Positive, Mr Taggart.'

'I don't want to kill a bunch of innocent people.'

'Not to worry, sir. The detonator requires two radio signals – theirs and mine. It won't go off by accident if some child comes down the block with a remote-control cabbage doll.' He opened his hand; in his palm lay a dull black box.

\*    \*    \*

Joe Reina's lunch guests were a Sicilian importer and the *capo* who headed Reina's network in the South Bronx. Everybody knew the Strikeforce had the restaurant bugged, but the steaks were tops and the fact that the Feds were listening make it off-limits for war.

This was a good thing because the current dope shortage, which was becoming the longest one Reina could remember, was making people crazy. Hijackings were becoming routine, and get-rich-quick freelancers were screwing people all over the place, so erroneous revenge couldn't be far behind. Conversation, of course, was casual, although personal contact was very helpful in understanding each other later on the telephone. Reina had observed that it helped to know a man's voice and face whe he was trying to talk a problem around a wiretap.

After they finished the meal with coffee and anisette, Reina said casually to his *capo,* 'You wanna order the check? I need a breath of air.'

He got up and thanked the restaurateur for a good lunch. The Sicilian followed him out the door. Reina paused on the sidewalk for a moment. Too many people were walking by. His driver hopped out of the limousine, but Reina waved him off and led the Sicilian down Mulberry and around the corner.

'So? Where's the stuff?' Reina asked.

'Already what I have is on the road,' the Sicilian said.

'By now it was supposed to be God, already,' Reina replied testily, referring to a twenty kilo shipment of heroin due weeks ago which should have been long sold and turned into money.

'This guy in Florida's giving me a big headache.'

'If this keeps up much longer I'm going to shrug my shoulders.'

'No, no. It's gonna work out. They just wanted that I should take this little walk.'

'Delivery is not your affair. It's their affair. You don't have to take a walk. They have to.' He stopped at a pay phone. 'Call them now. Tell 'em you want delivery, now!'

The Sicilian dialled the number of a pay phone outside Collins Avenue Pizzeria in Miami and pumped in quarters. When it was answered, he spoke in Sicilian and in code as well, because the FBI had Sicilian-speaking agents on their taps.

'How's the weather?'

'The weather got bad. It started to rain hard. Everyone went to take cover.' The Sicilian covered the mouthpiece. 'He says cops again . . . Is it still raining?'

'It is sleeting. Damned weather, it never ends.'

'Can we expect our tomatoes soon?'

'Soon. It would be better if you came down . . . to the . . . parking lot.'

'I can't do that this time. We have the documents.'

When he heard 'documents', Reina nodded gloomily. Money was not the problem; he had bags of the stuff, but never enough dope.

'We're waiting on you.'

'We will speak Sunday. Then I will know who is coming and when.'

'Excellent. It's my pleasure to have spoken with you. I wish you a world of good . . . I embrace you . . . Give my regards to everyone . . . Goodbye. Many things. Good things...'

The Sicilian hung up the phone, a thoughtful light in his eyes. 'He's lying. I don't think the stuff is ever coming unless I pick it up myself.'

Reina shrugged. 'You two guys have to decide this thing – and soon!' They walked back to the restaurant and stopped on the sidewalk. Reina waved to his *capo*, who threw money on the table and hurried out. Reina heard the telephone ring as the door opened. The owner answered it, waving goodbye through the window.

'Paletti's.'

'Listen,' said an electronically distorted voice. 'I'm going to say this once. Get your waiters and bus boys in the back. You got five seconds. Do you understand?'

Paletti looked out his front window. Through the sheer curtains he saw Joe Reina and the Sicilian talking while Reina's driver held the door. Beside the limo was a dark van. He said, 'Jesus Ch–'

'Five seconds.'

Paletti snapped his fingers. The bus boy and the waiter hurried to him.

'Into the kitchen! Hurry!'

Paletti followed them. Outside, Reina shook hands with his importer, who gave the *capo* a nod.

'We'll talk Sunday.'

Fire blew across the street. Windowglass disintegrated for a block on either side of the restaurant. A dust cloud filled Mulberry Street. When it cleared, the van and Reina's limousine were a smouldering wreck.

The Palestinians dropped their binoculars and transmitter into a sewer and walked to the subway station on West Broadway, where a girl who worked for one of Reggie Rand's agents led them onto the E train and helped them change to the JFK Express at West Fourth Street. At the airport, the Palestinians boarded the seven o'clock Northwest Airlines flight to Hamburg.

*     *     *

In New Jersey, a rival heroin importer named Vito Imperiale was crawling around his lawn uprooting crab grass when he heard the news on the radio. The bombing sounded to him like a Cirillo move since Reina had covered maybe a fifth of the New York market. Imperiale figured he would pick up some of the slack, but Crazy Mikey Cirillo was bound to take most. On the other hand, Mikey's eyes were bigger than his stomach, and soon he would be short of product. When that happened, Mikey would have several options: he could go out to Kennedy to meet the Lebanese and Pakistanis who stepped off the airplane with dope in their turbans, he could buy synthetic stuff and kill half his customers, or he could do business with old reliable Vito Imperiale.

As the radio reports got more specific throughout the afternoon, Imperiale was surprised to hear it had been a car bomb, which had caused damage up and down the block. That was pretty heavy-duty stuff, but then, it paid to remember that Crazy Mikey Cirillo wasn't called crazy for nothing. Imperiale had mixed feelings about his prospects. Being needed by Mikey Cirillo wasn't necessarily wonderful.

That evening, a crew leader arrived at the heavily-guarded suburban mansion. Imperiale was on the patio, slapping mosquitos and frowning at tufts

175

of grass he had pulled from the lawn; it had separated like straw because the Japanese beetle grubs were tearing up the roots.

'A Cirillo guy called me,' the crew leader reported. 'He said that Mikey says he didn't have nothing to do with the bomb.'

'Right.'

'He says Mikey might be interested in buying from us.'

'Sell the greedy bastard what you can, but keep him away from my sources.'

# *13*

The upper decks of the Taggart Spire were still bare steel, reddish and dull in the cold light of an autumn morning, but now, at the very top, a shiny ribbon of glass wrapped Taggart's penthouse and its cantilivred living room. Capped by glass, the tall, slim spire impaled Park Avenue like a diamond stickpin.

Taggart inspected the penthouse work, trailed by Ben Riley, the superintendent, who was taking notes and eyeing his watch as if it were a poisonous snake. Riley wore a quilted coat against the cold; Taggart had on a three-quarter coat of leather by Claude Montana. Steel girders shook as one of the V-shaped roof derricks fetched up another huge plate of reinforced, insulated glass from a truck on Park Avenue.

'The city ain't gonna give you a CO until the building's done,' Riley protested, trying to get him to change his mind about finishing the apartment early. He was having kittens, while trying to sheath, wire, and lay pipes in the penthouse before that work was completed on the lower floors. 'You can't live up here till the building's done anyway.'

'Fuck a certificate of occupancy,' Taggart shot back. 'It's my building and it's my apartment. The Mayor can shove his paperwork. All that's standing between me and living in my apartment is you.'

Across the city Taggart could see his current projects in varying states of completion – the half-erected frame of an apartment tower on upper Madison, another rising above Central Park on Columbus, and a dark hole on East Forty-seventh Street where a poured concrete substruction was nearing street level like a stack of bones. Those notches on the skyline were ordinarily a deeply satisfying sight, but this morning he was more interested in Reggie Rand, who had stationed himself behind the elevator and was dialling calls on a car phone he had brought up from the street.

The elevator clanged its arrival and Chryl and Victoria stepped off in hardhats, blue jeans, and black leather jackets, capturing the full attention of the glaziers and riggers who were manhandling a ten-by-twenty-foot sheet of glass that the derrick had hoisted alongside the deck. 'Christ on a crutch, the decorating broads,' groaned Riley. 'That's all I need.' He fled to the edge of the roof, bellowing at the riggers to steady the glass.

Taggart distractedly kissed each cheek offered. 'Ben's falling behind. Are you ready to decorate?'

'Decorate?' asked Chryl.

Victoria gazed thoughtfully into the glass room, framed it with her gloved hands. 'I see a single picture frame on that wall.'

'Off-centre,' Chryl agreed.

'Empty.'

'Not another stick of furniture.'

'Oh God, no! Total minimal.'

'A very thin frame.'

Knuckles rapped a shoulder; heads bobbed. 'An icy black line.'

'All right, all right,' Taggart said. 'I'm sorry, I meant design.'

Victoria slipped her hand inside his coat.

'*Mr Taggart!* ' Reggie called.

Taggart hurried to his side. Reggie unhooked a pager from his belt and showed him the number on its one-line screen. 'Bronx exchange. This might be my chap in Joe Cirillo's crew. I'm running down to find a coin box.'

'But if he's calling from a pay phone,' Taggart demanded impatiently, 'can't you use the car phone?'

'You pay me not to take chances.'

While Taggart had penetrated the heart of Crazy Mikey's heroin distribution, his parallel, and equally vital, campaign to overthrow Cirillo bookies and loansharks and to replace them with Helen Rizzolo's people was moving more slowly because gambling and shylocking were less centralized than heroin. The betrayals and apparent random attacks that Reggie had engineered had begun to unsettle the numerous Cirillo bookies and shylocks, but not yet sufficiently to convince many to shift allegiance to the Rizzolos. Taggart had called for another attack on the scale of the Caffè di Catania shooting that had induced Tommy Lucia to change sides. Reggie selected the biggest Cirillo shylock enforcer in the Bronx, and the most vicious, Crazy Mikey's cousin, Joe.

When Reggie returned Taggart joined him again at the elevator. 'What's up?'

'Joe Cirillo is planning a sort of public punishment for a Bronx industrialist. I think it's for us. With your permission, I'll bring in soldiers. I need a top team. No bolshies or starving natives.'

'That's your decision. But I'm coming along to watch.'

'I don't recommend that.'

'I'm coming anyway,' Taggart snapped, unaware that he had used the same tone of voice in over-riding his superintendent.

*　　*　　*

Joe Cirillo slid his fingers into a chrome knuckle duster. Working himself up, he ran the razor edge along the fleshy part of his other hand, drawing a thin line of blood which he tasted with his tongue.

'I'm making an example of this guy,' he told the six hitters crammed shoulder to shoulder behind him. 'When you borrow from us, you pay.'

A second van was parked behind them, awaiting his signal. Across the street was a long, low, mustard-yellow brick factory, a modem windowless building. It was just after the lunch hour and they had watched from a distance until the employees had finished their stick ball game and had gone back to work.

The hitters were big, well-dressed men nearing middle age, trusted soldiers, years senior to a routine beatup. In the past few weeks half a dozen Cirillo enforcers had been arrested while collecting outstanding debts, doubtless set up by informers. Until they somehow cleared the lower ranks of Strikeforce informers, a job like this was best done by guys who had a stake in the family. Joe knew from years of experience that the deadbeats wouldn't take long to figure out the shylocks were having trouble collecting. Thus the need for a demonstration the entire Bronx would remember.

'When money was tighter than virgin twat,' Joe reminded his soldiers, 'this joker borrows to build his factory. When he has union trouble, we get him a sweetheart contract. When he's got chemical shit, we make it disappear. But now he tries to fuck us.'

The factory owner was expected to carry a dozen Cirillo soldiers on his payroll, supply specially hollowed-out plastic toys to ship heroin, and make off-the-books cash interest payments weekly. He had performed until he got suckered into a high-stakes poker game in Atlantic City. The rest was history, to the tune of two hundred grand outstanding and, finally, a weekly interest he could not pay.

'The whole Bronx is gonna hear him scream.'

Joe's men looked as if they wished to discuss the fact that suddenly it was getting unhealthy to enforce collections. Not only were guys being arrested right and left, others were attacked in the streets. Two days ago a Cirillo crew leader overseeing a beating had been attacked himself by a black street gang; from his hospital bed he swore that it was a setup. They were waiting for him. Nor had the gang come to the defence of the welsher, who was a roundly hated white landlord.

One of the hitters summoned up the courage to say, 'Something's going on, Joe.'

Joe Cirillo looked at the guy. 'You got a problem?'

'Maybe it's more than bad luck that everyone's getting hit at once. Our guys are –'

'You want to go home early? You can leave now.'

'I'm just saying –'

'I don't want to hear it.'

'Joe, what if somebody's moving in on us. I keep hearing about the Rizzolos. I'm seeing Rizzolos where they shouldn't be.'

'What are you, some kind of *consigliere*? You're a fucking soldier. You beat up guys when I tell you to. You cross me and you go back to baking pizzas.' Joe stared him down. Then he motioned the others out of the van. 'Okay, get him ready. Remember, nobody leaves 'til I'm done pulping the bastard.'

Twelve men entered the factory simultaneously, converging on the front door and the side and rear loading bays. In the bright, carpeted lobby, the receptionist looked up with a smile that faded uncertainly. A burly black security guard dropped his magazine and went for his gun.

Joe Cirillo's men mobbed him, took his revolver away, and locked him to a railing with his own handcuffs. The factory owner heard the scuffle and stepped out of his office in shirtsleeves and loosened necktie. When he saw the hoods, he fled back through his door, which he locked, and pawed desperately at the telephone. They kicked the door open, rounded his desk, and slapped the telephone out of his hand. He backed against the wall, pleading and covering his face. Two Cirillos seized his fleshy arms and marched him out. Another dragged the receptionist along. Leaving a man at the door, they burst onto the low balcony that overlooked the main work room.

The plant, covering nearly a half acre, was washed white as a desert by overhead fluorescent lights and reeked of the sweet, cloying odour of hot plastic. Fifty men and women were working the extruder machines, presses, and bench drills. They looked up at their boss cringing between the large men holding his arms, and a dark wave of apprehension washed over the room until they and their machines stood motionless and silent. Workers in the back started to retreat to the rear doors, but the Cirillos were there too, herding the rest of the guards, whom they had surprised at lunch.

From the front entrance the arrogant click of heel taps on linoleum broke the quiet, and Joe Cirillo strolled in. He removed his wedding ring, as he surveyed the silent black and Spanish faces, and made a show of working his fingers into the chrome knuckles. Then he nodded and his men lifted the factory owner off the floor. He squealed in terror. But before Joe could go to work, one of the Spanish girls, a kid of eighteen or nineteen, charged up the stairs screaming and swinging a monkey wrench.

'Let her through,' Joe instructed.

180

'Rosa. No!' the owner cried, but she came anyway, swinging the wrench. Joe ducked under it. Her momentum dragged her to him, her hands locked on the wrench, the whole side of her body exposed from her ankles to her face. Joe measured his target and backhanded her with the knuckles and she went down, her cheek a bloody smear. The joker actually tried to hit him!

'Balling for help?' Joe sneered. His men heaved the guy into the air again. Joe stepped between his flailing legs, the knuckles cocked.

*  *  *

A block away, atop a three-storey bakery, the tallest building in the industrial park, Reggie Rand, who knew the police patrols down to the minute, watched his men go into action. They were French mercenaries, two brothers and their protégé, a young German boy. Reggie had flown them in, supplied the weapons they had asked for, and tonight would fly them back to France.

Taggart stood beside him, with hands in pockets and eyes like ice. From this vantage point they could see the plastics factory's front entrance and driveway, the Cirillos' vans, and a lower rooftop directly across the street from the factory. Reggie had pleaded that Taggart shouldn't be here, that his enterprise was so risky that he ought to take every opportunity to minimize his risks, but Taggart seemed more and more and more bent on taking chances.

Suddenly, on the low roof across from the factory, there was a hint of motion in the shadows. A moment later, shooting started inside the factory. Muffled by the cinderblock walls, the rapid firing automatic weapon had the muffled buzzing of a high-speed printer. A year ago, Taggart had ordered Reggie to put him through a basic weapons survival course and the noise, he recalled, was terrifying. Inside the factory, Taggart knew, the shattering reports of an unsilenced Uzi on full automatic sounded like a war.

'Surprise.'

He watched the doors with grim satisfaction. A few more attacks like this and the Cirillo loansharks were out of business. The Cirillo soldiers came boiling out the doors, white-faced, arms and legs pinwheeling as they fled. Some trailed, staggering, and one collapsed on the sidewalk. Those who could raced to their vans. Reggie pointed to the roof-top across the street. 'Watch the German. He's superb.'

A figure popped over the parapet and levelled a short, blunt weapon on his shoulder. His captain arose easily beside him, covering with a stock-mounted automatic pistol in the unlikely event the boy should need help.

*Whooom!* A rocket struck the rear van, blowing the Cirillo enforcers back just as they lunged for the doors. The explosion hurled them to the street where they writhed, burned, or were too stunned to seek cover. Joe Cirillo, the last man out of the building, gaped incredulously at the inferno. His bullet-

181

shattered arm hung like a stick, the chrome knuckles still attached to his fingers. He shambled into his own van screaming, 'Go. Go!'

The van leaped forward, scattering the men who tried to get in after Joe, and squealed for the comer. *Whooom!* The van turned to flame, slewed across the street, leaped the kerb, and crashed into the factory wall. Joe Cirillo rolled out of the passenger door and crawled into the gutter. The burning van exploded thunderously. The explosion threw him across the street, where he lay, twitching feebly, as the flames reflected red off the chrome knucks still attached to his hand.

★   ★   ★

That night, after the police and fire department had left and he had picked up Rosa in the emergency room and put her in a cab, the owner of the plastics factory propped his feet on his desk and figured things were looking up. He was clear. Whoever had attacked Joey Cirillo had done him a big favour. Everyone knew that he had had nothing to do with it. But with all the cops around, the Cirillos couldn't take a chance on trying to hurt him again. One of the security guards knocked on his door. He still looked embarrassed for screwing up, and the company had doubled the guard at no extra cost.

'Guy out here wants to see you.'

'Sure.' More cops, detectives, Feds; the more the better.

But he wasn't a cop. He looked like an accountant. He opened a briefcase, revealing rows of shiny metal toggle switches, which he jiggled back and forth for an electronic sweep. Satisfied, the guy closed his briefcase and said, 'I represent people who are assuming Cirillo obligations in this area.'

'What are you talking about?'

'I'll be back next week to collect.'

'What are you talking about?'

'God is not coming down to save your ass a second time.'

★   ★   ★

Taggart insisted on meeting the new collector.

'On this, I put my foot down,' Reggie replied.

'I'll wear a mask. I've got to watch my people.'

'But that's what I'm here for.'

Taggart insisted. Reggie told himself that he wanted to retain strict control, but he wondered whether Taggart simply couldn't resist daring the odds. It was one thing to meet face to face, masked, with Mikey Cirillo to consummate the heroin deal, but it was frivolous to tempt fate. Had Reggie the time he might have worried more about Taggart's walk-on-water attitude, but he was too busy. Events were accelerating. No sooner had he displayed the new Rizzolo shylock to a masked Christopher Taggart, than he had a meet, alone, with the outside leader of an upstate prison gang.

'I don't get it,' said the gang leader as he counted the money that consummated their deal. 'South Bronx numbers used to be strictly Cirillo territory.'

'That's right.'

'But now the Confortis and Bonos are stirring the kiddie gangs against them, trying to take over.'

'Correct.'

'So who the hell are you?'

'I'm gentrifying the neighbourhood.'

\* \* \*

Bumpy Fredericks, or 'Bump' to his clients, worried more about robbers than cops as he made his rounds collecting bets and noting the numbers on flimsy cigarette paper. But when a dark van started following him he didn't know what to think. Cirillo numbers-runners all over New York were getting taken off. Up until now, he had liked working for the Cirillos because they kept order. Now he wasn't so sure, because when a Mafia family started fighting its rivals, the neighbourhoods gangs got bold.

The van hung back, stopped when he went into a store, started up when he came out. Being an optimist, Bumpy decided the big boys had sent the van to look out for him as he made his rounds. The drycleaner played his regular 234 and repeated his refrain that it had to come in someday. The liquor store clerks next door slide 285 and 314 through the money slot of their bulletproof glass, the former for his girlfriend's apartment number, the latter for somebody's tag scrawled on an IRT car. The girls on the hotel stoop picked numbers out of the air – 417,630,555,259 – like leaves were falling on them, and pressed the dollars in his hand.

Bumpy rounded a corner and said, 'Oh, shit.'

Three kids from a gang called the Spanish Main were leaning on a storefront. They straightened up when they saw him, as if they'd been waiting. They rarely ventured up to this side of Third Avenue, because it was Devils' territory and the Devils had a protection agreement with the Cirillos. Trouble was, Bumpy thought, the Devils had been getting their asses kicked lately and there wasn't a Devil in sight. Then he realized there were more Spanish Main waiting up the block. He turned back, figuring to head for the more populated Morris Avenue, but two more kids were rounding the corner behind him, at which point he stopped worrying about the money and the slips because his real problem was going to be getting out of this alive. At twenty-eight and nursing a tubercular leg, he was too old to run and too tired to fight. God, send me a cop, he thought. But there were none. He looked for the van which had been following him, but there was suddenly no one on the burned out block but him and them, and they were walking his way.

Bumpy stepped to a parked car, reached carefully into his pockets, and started piling dollar bills on the bonnet. The wind caught them and he lunged, crumping them in his fists. The kids formed a half circle on the sidewalk around the car, watching with dead eyes, and Bumpy felt an anger he seldom indulged begin to well up inside him, a boiling frustration. All he was trying to do was make a small living and these little bastards half his age made him walk in fear. He was not a violent man, though he had seen as much violence as anyone who had grown up in a poor city, but suddenly, if he could, he would shoot them all like Bernie Goetz, the subway vigilante. Not that he could shoot them – he had no gun, just a knife, which he really could not use well enough to defend himself one on one, much less against the six guys now circling him and watching him try to keep his money from blowing away.

'Here. Take it.'

He had made the worst possible mistake, not that he had any choice, by admitting he was defenceless. Their leader, a kid with a three-whisker moustache, said, 'Somebody pop him.'

Two of them pulled guns, huge rusty forty-fives with barrels big as sewer pipes. Forget a flesh wound. They were going to tear holes through his body. He felt like screaming, go away, leave me alone! 'Here's the money,' he repeated softly.

'Pop him.'

Bumpy closed his eyes.

'Whoa! Who be that?'

An engine raced close by and Bumpy opened his eyes. The van was coming. It stopped short beside the car and two black guys in suits and raincoats got out quickly. He thought they were cops, cancelled that, and thought again; maybe, by their business suits and cold faces, they were Black Muslims. But maybe not; maybe something else. They gave the street a quick look and one pulled out a big plastic garbage bag, the other a sawn-off shotgun.

'Pieces in here. You first.'

The thirteen-year-old with the forty-five looked at the sawn double barrels and gingerly dropped his gun into the sack.

'Now you. Don't drop it. Just lay it in gentle.' His partner turned the shotgun on the leader. 'Tell your men to open their colours. The rest of the guns. Then the knives.'

'Hey, man, who the fuck –'

'Who the fuck? What do you *mean*, who the fuck?'

Bumpy saw the dude's polished shoe blur up from the sidewalk high as his shoulder. The steel toe cracked the kid's jawbone and he fell hard and silent to the cement. He wiped the blood off his shoe on the Spanish Main leader's trousers. 'Anybody else say who the fuck?'

He collected the rest of their weapons and told them to pick up their leader. Then he pointed at Bumpy. 'You mark this man? You remember him. If he *ever* has a problem – any kind of problem at all – we'll come back and cut your balls off.' He looked at each kid, straight in the face. 'So that means if you see anybody *else* giving him a problem, you look out for him. Right? He's your friend. Got that? Okay, go on now – Git!'

When they had gone, he turned to Bumpy. 'There's been some changes made.'

'Yes, sir.'

'You'll be delivering your bets to someone else.'

'Yes, *sir.*'

\*   \*   \*

'Mikey, we got trouble.'

Crazy Mikey waited, working his coke spoon with his fingers, repeatedly opening and shutting the miniature breech. Had the bearer of more bad news been anyone but Sally Smart's Ponte, he might have have thrown him down the stairs of the Jackson Heights videogame warehouse he used for meetings. But although troubles were multiplying faster than he could keep up, he still couldn't yell at *Corsigliere* Ponte. As far back as his childhood, the *Consigliere* had been there, his father's closest adviser and his own godfather, a firm, quiet man whose advice always cut to the heart of a problem.

'It sounds like something everyone's afraid to tell me, so they sent you.' Ponte, a darkly handsome lawyer in his fifties, gave him a smile. He wasn't a warm man; were he, Mikey couldn't have trusted him. But he was a man who lent his full attention to whomever he served. 'You're right. They're afraid.' Mikey thought that it was incredible that just when the dope business was going so well, everything else started falling apart. First they had lost Brooklyn books and numbers to the Rizzolos. Now the bastards were moving into the Bronx. But the other families accused the Cirillos of moving in on *them*. Everybody thought he had bombed Joe Reina in retaliation for the Caffé di Catania shooting. Vito Imperiale was barely talking to him, and the Bonos and Confortis had announced that Cirillos were not welcome on their streets – which put all of them one angry Sicilian from open warfare.

'Now what?' he asked Ponte.

'They hit the Chelsea club. Robbed the customers and the take.'

'Who?'

185

'Looks like freelances.'

'Find out who and get them.'

'That's not the problem. After they left and the customers were leaving, some people came up to the high rollers and said they had caught the guys and had their stuff. They brought the high-rollers to another club in the next block and helped them sort out coats and jewellery and even some cash.'

'What other club?'

'A new joint opened during the summer down the street from Limelight. Tommy Lucia's friends had it ready to go. Wheels, booze, broads dealing blackjack – the whole thing. Most of our best customers stayed the rest of the night.'

'In other words, the Rizzolos have moved into Chelsea.' Mikey started playing with the little shotgun model again; Ponte watched anxiously, but Mikey, he was relieved to see, never went near the coke. At last, he said, 'It's time to hit back.'

'I wouldn't rush into anything, Mikey.'

'I ain't rushing. I been thinking about this for weeks.'

'Tommy's just a dumb guinea in the middle.'

Crazy Mikey said, 'Yeah. He's in the middle of Frank and Eddie Rizzolo.'

'We can't afford a war with the Strikeforce on our backs,' *Consigliere* Ponte protested.

'It'll be a short one,' Mikey promised grimly.

'What if it's not the Rizzolos?'

'Then who?'

'I don't know. I think something's going on.'

'What?'

'I don't know.'

'Here's what I know: Memorial Day, somebody turned Vetere in to the Strikeforce and Vetere rattled on Nicky so my father told me to take over. Everybody thought I couldn't handle the family past Fourth of July, but by the end of the summer I got the dope flowing again. But while I'm busy doing that, three guys walked into the Caffe di Catania and blasted our Brooklyn underboss and pretty soon we lost most of his books. By Labor Day they were hitting us in the Bronx. Now, it isn't even Halloween and Tommy Lucia is holding hands in Manhattan with Frank and Eddie Rizzolo. We're going to be dead by Christmas if we don't do something about the Rizzolos.'

\*　　\*　　\*

'Warn Helen and have your people watch her club,' Taggart ordered when Reggie reported what his spies were picking up in the Cirillo camp. 'Follow her when she goes to the restaurants.'

'First of all, they're not likely to attack a woman, especially when they don't know she's the real brains of her family. Secondly, the Rizzolos were defending their enterprises when your father was pushing a wheelbarrow.'

'I'm not taking chances. I don't want her hurt.'

# 14

The Rizzolo's Blue Line bus barn was a steep-gabled nineteenth-century wooden structure built in 1893 to house trolleys. It sheltered an area of Long Island City two blocks long and three wide. Skylights dimpled its vast roofs, like mountain villages of little houses clinging to their slopes. Inside, it resounded from idling engines, shrieking air guns, and low gear whine as drivers jockeyed the buses into the maintenance bays. The air reeked of diesel exhaust.

Helen Rizzolo had always loved the smell. The sharp bite reminded her of rare visits as a little girl to see her father at work in his white shirt-sleeves rolled up his thick forearms, a dark vest, and a loosened tie. Once, to her brothers' dismay, he let her steer a bus while seated on his lap. It was a place that made her happy, and when she came to do the payroll, she always entered through the wooden gingerbread embellishments around the front door. She turned on her headlights and beeped the horn to warn the hustling mechanics, and her Fiat skittered past the bays, dodging the buses like a busy bright-eyed red bug.

The office was a hut in the back, partitioned by thin polywood walls which barely muffled the noise. She could tell by the quiet when the mechanics were on lunch or coffee break. The office had a much lower ceiling than the rest of the barn, windows that looked out on a junk-filled yard, and a back door. Eddie and Frank hung out here since the company was their legitimate employer; Eddie was president, Frank vice-president, and she the finance director.

She kissed them, took her desk, and opened a container of tea she had bought at the deli. Eddie, head in hands, was staring at a sheaf of papers from the city. 'Why the fuck did Pop make us a bus business in Long Island?'

'Now what's wrong?'

'We can't go interstate. The buses in Westchester, they ran the route through two *inches* of Connecticut so they can tell the city to go fuck itself 'cause crossing the state line makes 'em interstate commerce. But we gotta obey every local law the city makes up. Can't use this street, can't use that, no noise, no idling.'

While talking, Eddie was writing a note; they had installed a new telephone line in response to Taggart's warning about the Strikeforce tap, but with the buses coming and going they couldn't count on sweeping every bug. He slipped the note to her: 'Three more Cirillo books came our way last night. We got Brooklyn numbers wrapped up and a lot of the Bronx.'

Helen smiled and Eddie returned a grin which seemed, she thought, almost deferential. Thanks to her deal with Taggart, Eddie and Frank were giving her credit for their prosperity.

'Why don't we go through Jersey?' she asked aloud, writing back, 'Any word on how Mikey's taking it?'

Eddie showed it to Frank, then touched a match to the paper. It burned in his ashtray.

'Well?'

He shrugged. Helen looked at Frank. He shrugged, too, and she realized her brothers were embarrassed to admit that whatever spies they had managed to infiltrate among the Cirillos, didn't know. She reminded herself that her new power was a two-edged sword. She had to be careful not to undercut their pride. They would do something foolish to get it back.

She started in on the computer, but her mind stayed on Christopher Taggart and his scheme. It was almost going *too* well. Between the Strikeforce tearing pieces out of the Cirillos on the legal side and Taggart gnawing away from inside, the huge, powerful family almost seemed paralysed.

The telephone rang. Eddie picked it up, listened a moment, and glanced her way. Helen pretended she didn't notice when he nodded to Frank, and said into the phone, 'I'll be here.'

'Who was that?'

'Nothing.'

'Are you guys dealing again?'

'Shhh! Jesus, Helen. What if —'

''Cause if you are, I want you to stop it. I told you no dope.'

Eddie scrambled about his desk for a piece of paper and wrote, 'Shut up! It's just a little coke deal on the side. Guy's been talking it up for months.'

'I don't *believe* you,' she protested, thinking how could they risk blowing everything for a stupid dope deal. But she blamed herself; she had pushed them too hard. It was like they had to prove something to themselves, like they didn't really need her. Goddamnit, they did. And she needed them.

Eddie wrote, 'We're just going to set up a meeting,' folded his arms and stared obstinately at his desk top. Even Frank wouldn't meet her eye. Seething, as angry at herself as she was at them, Helen pounded the computer keys like an old-fashioned typewriter.

Twenty minutes passed and the phone rang again. Eddie snatched it up. His eyes widened and he motioned to Frank to pick up too. Helen grabbed her extension and covered the mouth piece as the caller repeated, 'I said, "You recognize my voice?"'

It was Crazy Mikey Cirillo.

'Yeah, I know you. What's up?'

'I just want you to know who this is coming from.'

'What's coming?'

'*This.*'

Helen looked at Frank, who sprang to his feet like a panther, reaching into the locker where he kept a brace of legally owned hunting rifles. Then the wall seemed to get suddenly very big as it flew at her. An explosion thundered through the barn.

She found herself on the floor, pinned under the wall, which was propped up by her desk. The computer lay beside her; the winking green cursor blanketed the screen with squiggly shapes she had never seen before. The mechanics were yelling in the barn and something was roaring. A liquid – her own blood, she realized when she touched it – was running down her face.

'Frank! Eddie!'

'Stay there, baby. You okay?'

'Frank!'

'Yeah, I'm fine. Don't move, hon. They might be shooting.'

She heard Eddie crawl past in the dark and yell, 'There's a fire!'

Helen saw the flickering of the flames. The mechanics and drivers were yelling; somewhere a man was screaming. She found the telephone wire on the floor, reeled in the phone, and dialled the lighted dial. When 911 answered she said, 'Fire and explosion. Blue Line bus barn. Ambulance.'

She freed her leg and crawled out of the shelter formed by the wall and her desk. She was surprised to see daylight pouring in the skylights brighter than ever because the glass had been broken. The far end of the barn, the front, was filled with black smoke. The dense, greasy smoke had trapped some forty buses inside. She tried to stand and found she could. Frank grabbed her, his face horrified. 'You're bleeding.'

She wiped at it with her hand. Her head hurt. 'I'm okay.'

Eddie came back with a gun in his hand. 'They're gone.'

Frank yelled, 'I'll drive a bus through the wall there to make a hole for the others.'

'No,' said Helen. 'Help the men out! Leave the buses.'

Frank was wild eyed. 'But I can save 'em!'

'We'll do better on the insurance.'

Her legs started to collapse under her own weight and Frank scooped her into his huge arms. A million sirens seemed to scream at once. Eddie led Frank through the office door. Cradled in his arms, she saw the first plumes of water cascading into the flames. Frank carried her to the paramedics, who swabbed a gash in her scalp. She sat on the back of the ambulance watching the flames disintegrate the gingerbread front of the barn. By then the police were there, plainclothesmen and uniformed cops, and they were questioning Eddie and Frank, who were shrugging a lot.

'Okay, lie down, dear,' a paramedic said. 'We're going to take you to the hospital.'

'No. I'm fine.'

'You might have a concussion.'

She tried to argue, but her hands were shaking and she had the weirdest urge to cry.

She passed out in the ambulance and awakened in bed sometime later to hear Christopher Taggart shouting, 'Get a specialist!'

'You've hired two already.'

'I don't give a fuck. I want the best.'

'I *am* the best, Mr Taggart!'

'Then stick close.'

Some time might have passed before she opened her eyes. The doctor was saying, 'Even a slight concussion is a helluva lot worse than no concussion . . . Hello there! Follow my finger, please.'

He held it a foot from her face, moved it slowly above her forehead and down to her chin. 'Good. Nauseous?'

'No.'

'Good. Now this way, left to right.' She focused and followed his finger to the right, saw it cross his middle-aged face. Behind him was a nurse, a television hanging from the ceiling, an IV rack at the corner of her bed, the bathroom door and wardrobe, a hundred red roses on a table – and Taggart standing in the doorway.

His face was working. He brushed past the doctor, took her hand, and knelt beside the bed so they were face to face, inches apart. He seemed barely able to speak. 'Are you okay?'

'Mr Taggart,' the doctor interrupted. 'If I could finish –'

'Is she okay?' He was holding her hand as gently as a kitten.

'I'm not making any promises. But the CAT scan shows no bleeding.'

Helen tugged him closer and whispered, 'What are you doing here?'

'I was driving around my jobs; heard it on the radio.'

'You're taking chances.'

'Don't worry about it. How do you feel?'

'Okay . . . Where's my brothers?'

'Answering cops' questions.'

'My mother?'

'They didn't want to tell her 'til they knew how you were. Shall I get her?'

She still felt like crying. 'I want to see my mother.'

Taggart signalled someone she couldn't see and turned back to her again and whispered. 'I'm really sorry. I told Reggie to watch out for you.'

'We can take care of ourselves. Isn't that what you're using me for?'

'I figured the fighting would stay at street level.'

'You figured wrong – but we got hurt.'

Her head hurt and it was hard to think while the room made circles, but it seemed important to make him understand what was going on in the rackets. She closed her eyes and pretended to cry. The ruse worked. Taggart leaned closer and the doctor backed away to let him comfort her. 'Why are you surprised?' she whispered. 'Crazy Mikey knows he didn't bomb Joe Reina or shoot Al Conforti, or burn down that fortress Harry Bono had in Westchester. He knows he didn't sell Vito Imperiale's underbosses to the Strikeforce; he knows *he* didn't chase the other families out of Kennedy Airport. And he knows he didn't attack his own enforcers. We've always been enemies and now he sees us getting stronger at his expense. What would you do if you were Mikey?'

Taggart stood up, his face turning cold. 'I'm sorry,' he repeated. 'I'll take care of it. You have nothing else to worry about.'

'Don't fight with Mikey,' she warned him. 'That's our job.'

'I'll be in touch.' His hand tightened on hers and she thought for a second that he would plunge to her mouth. Her body tightened and she started to lift her head from the pillow. But instead of kissing her, he backed away and let go her hand with a little squeeze.

The room started whirling faster. The doctor reappeared and shone a light in her eyes. Helen raised her throbbing head and looked past him at Taggart, who, thinking he was out of sight, had stopped hiding the fury that seared his face.

She saw in that raw expression a side he had hidden last Spring on the Irish cliffs, and again the summer night atop his building. Yet it recalled vividly the night ten years ago at Abatelli's, when he stormed out after Don Richard Cirillo. Christopher Taggart was a man capable of embracing an all-consuming hatred.

It was frightening, and all the more so today because the attack on her had provoked his rage, as if Taggart wanted more than his stated intention that the Rizzolos seize the street. Coming to her club, and now racing to the hospital, he seemed to want to possess her. Helen tried to weigh coolly the additional opportunities that this might present for her family, but deep in her heart she began to fear the price. And she sagged back on the sheets, terrified by her own impulse, when he had taken her hand, to pull him down on top of her.

Outside the hospital, Reggie was waiting in Taggart's car. 'Did the police see you?' he asked.

'Set up a meet with Mikey.'

'But, you're to meet on the boat next week.'

'*Now.*'

'There's only one way he'll agree to meet.'

'I know. Cut him off!'

★ ★ ★

They boarded the boat in Tarrytown at one of the several boathouses Taggart had scattered about New York, and headed down river as night fell. The tide was receding, the Hudson flowed swiftly, and the offshore racer skimmed the water on muted engines. Reggie drove silently until he had concluded the electronic sweeps.

'You surprise me, Mr Taggart.'

'How's that?'

'You certainly didn't expect the Cirillos not to fight back.'

'Right.'

'Is it possible you're over-reacting because the girl happened to be there?'

'Anything's possible,' Taggart replied easily and Reggie felt better until Taggart added, 'He almost killed her.'

'What do you intend?'

'To make sure it doesn't happen again.'

'But you're forgetting –'

'I forget nothing.'

When the boat passed under the George Washington Bridge, Taggart went below and locked himself in the cabin. He wedged his back into the forward V-bunk and waited, while Reggie steered into a private marina at the foot of a New Jersey condo. His anger was rising; he could taste it in his mouth. He listened to two men board and felt the boat turn and gradually pull away. A while later the engines stopped, and he heard the anchor chain rasp out of the winch. Taggart pulled the ski mask over his head just as Reggie unlocked the door.

Their meetings were ritual performances by now. Reggie came first, checked to see that only the red navigation lights were burning, and waited just inside the cabin door. Mikey's bodyguard, a heavy-set Sicilian who had replaced the wounded Buddy, made sure Taggart was alone and ran a quick electronic check, augmenting what he had already done on deck. Then he stood on the other side of the three-step companionway.

Mikey stepped between them and ducked to clear the door. His thin lips formed hard lines in his boney face. He laced Taggart with dark, angry eyes. Taggart stared back.

'Get out!' Mikey told his bodyguard.

Reggie closed the door as he and the Sicilian went on deck.

'Your people are fucking me up.'

'Sit down,' Taggart said.

'Why are they doing this?'

'People I know have a problem.'

'I'll listen. But before I do, you listen to me. Don't jerk me around. You promise to deliver, you better deliver.'

Taggart returned his stare and made no reply. Finally, Mikey asked, 'All right. What's your friends' problem?'

'Somebody threw ten sticks of dynamite at their bus barn.'

'That thing in the papers?'

'The Blue Line in Long Island City.'

'What do you want me to do?'

'Guarantee such a thing never happens again.'

'Guarantee? How can I do that?'

'Put out the word.'

'To who? I don't know those people. I don't know what they're fighting about.'

Taggart felt like he was falling backward, plunging ten years into the past. It was the night on the sidewalk in front of Abatelli's again. Don Richard had denied he had killed Taggart's father and had joked that he hadn't killed anybody in thirty years. He hadn't even known the name, Mike Taglione. As if it were happening now, he saw the skinny old man turn his back, heard the order, 'He's not allowed in,' and felt this same Crazy Mikey pound his face as he joined the Mafia bonebreakers in the fun. Sorrow, rage, and guilt overwhelmed his heart and overcame his mind. He could hardly form the words: 'You hurt a friend of mine. Your people threw the dynamite.'

Mikey didn't deny it. 'That's none of your fucking business. That's got nothing to do with dope.'

'It's got everything to do with dope.'

Mikey looked intrigued. 'How's that? The Rizzolos are gamblers and shylocks. They got freight at Kennedy?'

'If you ever go near them again, I'll cut your heroin supply for good. That's what it has to do with dope.'

'They're none of your business,' Mikey repeated.

'I'm making it my business. Don't ever go near her – ever! Or you're dead.'

'*Her?* Hey, nobody knew the girl was there . . . Is that it?' Mikey sneered. 'You got the hots for their kid sister?'

Taggart bounded off the bunk, flew the length of the cabin, and clawed at Mikey's throat. But Mikey was fast and hit him with a vicious right to the face. Frenzied, Taggart barely felt it as he threw Mikey against the door, which fell off its hinges. Mikey dropped to the companionway, half in the cabin, half in the cockpit. Punching and kicking furiously, Taggart drove him up the companionway, dragged him to his feet, and clubbed him back to the deck in the second it took the Cirillo bodyguard to act.

Reggie and the Sicilian had been standing in the stern, as far from the cabin as possible to allow the bosses to do their business without corroborating witnesses. The tide had turned and the boat was pulling downstream against its anchor, so that the George Washington Bridge lights lit Taggart and Crazy Mikey. The Sicilian drew a weapon in a fluid motion as he moved closer and dropped into a crouch. Reggie chopped his neck. He fell to the deck but slammed Reggie with a scissors kick, which threw the Englishman hard against the gunnel.

Reggie cried out and staggered as he tried to stand. Astonished – in two years Taggart had never seen him hurt, much less stumble – and frightened for him, Taggart turned to help. Mikey used the distraction to kick him in the groin. He collapsed in searing pain, trying to cover up as the mobster hit him with a flurry of kicks and punches. The Sicilian picked up his gun and aimed it with two hands. He shouted for Mikey to move aside, that he had Taggart covered.

Taggart drove the pain from his consciousness, like a debt he would pay later. He seized Mikey with both hands, and held him like a shield. Mikey fought back. The Sicilian looked for an opening. Reggie, hunched over, breathing hard and holding his ribs, moved in sudden swift silence and chopped the Sicilian's neck again. This time the Sicilian collapsed on the deck with a helpless whimper.

★   ★   ★

'He tricked you,' Reggie said bleakly, after they had dropped Cirillo and his bodyguard and the boat was pulling away from the Mill Basin pier on a creamy wake. 'You told him too much.'

'Fuck him.'

'You've gone too far. Until now you had the heroin as a club over him. By showing your concern for Helen Rizzolo, you've given Mikey a club over you.'

Taggart saw he was right, but caught an answer on the wing. 'Maybe so, Reg, but if he thinks I have the hots for her, he won't make the real connection.'

'You're very quick, sir. I only hope he's not. Take the wheel, please.'

Reggie leaned back heavily in the padded seat, holding his ribs, angrily waving Taggart off when he tried to help. Taggart brought the boat back towards the light on Staten Island that he had been steering for. Reggie drew a handkerchief from his pocket.

'How did you leave it with Mikey?'

'He can have dope again, but the price is up to two hundred thousand a kilo – just like we planned.'

'Unfortunately, you've muddied the waters.'

'What's he going to do?'

'He is going to go looking elsewhere for reliable sources.'

'Then we'll take care of elsewhere.'

'Which takes you further away from your goal.'

'Relax, Reg. You're getting way down.'

Reggie put the handkerchief to his mouth, spat, and examined it dispassionately by the red glow of the instrument lights.

'You okay?'

'Maybe I am getting "down", as you put it. The real trouble is, I'm getting old and you're getting out of control.'

# 15

Reggie Rand was right. Just as he predicted, Crazy Mikey asked for a meeting with the narcotics importer Vito Imperiale. He suggested some sort of neutral ground like a Manhattan restaurant, but the word came back: no way was Vito Imperiale coming into the city while a war was on. Instead, Crazy Mikey was invited to Imperiale's house. For Mikey to call on a lesser figure violated protocol, but his father and *Consigliere* Ponte urged him to accept.

'Give a little now, take later,' said Ponte.

Imperiale's driver delivered a garage door opener folded in a map of Alpine, New Jersey.

'What the fuck is this?'

'The garage is attached. You drive inside, nobody sees you.'

Mikey and his bodyguard drove up the Palisades Parkway in a rented Honda. Twenty minutes north of the George Washington Bridge they exited into the bedroom community and found Imperiale's house in a maze of broad and empty suburban streets lined with maple trees that had turned bright yellow. It was a new, three-storey, Tudor-style house with bright white stucco and dark brown beams, set on a fenced four-acre lawn. Across the street a telephone truck was parked beside a stanchion on the grassy shoulder.

The fence reminded Mikey of his father's place on Staten Island, which was bigger and finer-looking, being constructed of brick and marble. Nonetheless, Vito was doing all right. They drove into the driveway, pressed the garage door opener and Imperiale's garage door, which was disguised to look like a stable entrance, opened.

After they had driven in and the door had rumbled shut, Vito stepped into the garage with a friendly smile. He was a fat, pear-shaped man, with a big nose, widely set dark eyes which appeared darker yet because his skin was so white, and shiny black hair. Crazy Mikey left his man in the kitchen with Vito's men and followed his host into the living room. At no point, he noticed, did Imperiale address him by name. He led Mikey through a big living room cluttered with overstuffed beige couches and chairs, and out french doors onto a big stone patio. A high, whitewashed brick wall shielded the patio on three sides. The house blocked the fourth. Overhead was blue sky and the noonday sun, which had warmed the furniture cushions.

'No windows to vibrate when we talk,' Imperiale explained. 'No bugs and taps out here. But shut up if a balloon comes over!' He laughed and poured espresso from a wet bar set in stone.

'What about that telephone truck we passed on the way in?'

'Feds. I leave 'em one phone line to keep 'em busy. Whenever I see the truck, I have a man talk nonsense. Were they out there?'

'Yes.'

'Here, we're safe.'

'You mind if I check?'

'Be my guest.'

Mikey opened his briefcase and checked for transmitters and recorders. When he closed it, Imperiale said, 'So what brings you to the country?' Mikey's father kept telling him to open negotiations slowly, but it was an old-fashioned, stupid thing to do when both of them knew exactly what he had come for. 'I want to buy.'

'I figured that, with Joe Reina gone. How much?'

'Much as you can. Two, three hundred kilos a week.'

'That's a lot of product.'

'It'll save you a lot of trouble if you sell it all to me.'

'What makes you think I got trouble selling it where I do?'

'The FBI, the DEA, and the Strikeforce are doing a number on my middle guys. If my middle guys are getting busted, so are yours. The thing is, I'm bigger and I got more guys, so I can roll with the punch longer than you. And another thing, you're what, fifty-five?'

Vito said, 'Sixty-five,' with a smile, and Mikey felt proud he had scored on that one. 'So what?'

'I'm only thirty. A guy my age is supposed to fight, likes to fight. A guy fifty-five or sixty, maybe he deserves to slow down a little.'

'Maybe,' Vito conceded. 'What makes you think I import so much stuff?' Crazy Mikey smiled. 'My father says you do.'

'You'll need more than me to fill your needs. I don't have that much.'

'My father thinks you might know sources.'

Imperiale covered his annoyance. 'How is Don Richard?'

'Never been better.'

'Forgive me, I say with all respect, that I think your brother getting arrested was good for your father. It makes an old man young to work again.'

Mikey's expression turned complex and Imperiale hastened to sooth him. 'Particularly if he has another son to help him.'

'What do you say?'

198

Imperiale's patio seemed less secure than usual. The world had tracked him down again. The Cirillos must have lost a big supplier. There'd been rumours Mikey had wired into somebody really big. Then suddenly, the street supply had dried up again, as if Mikey had lost that supplier. So now Mikey was leaning on him.

He shrugged. 'I been thinking of easing up a bit. Maybe, if I supply you exclusively, I'd get off the street.'

'It's an easier living,' Mikey replied, amazed by some of the things he heard himself say these days. Six months ago he would have said that if Vito didn't get off the street, he could kiss his street crews goodbye. Today he took his father's advice and spoke softly.

And the amazing thing was that Vito took the hint.

*    *    *

Taggart was in the telephone repair van across the street from Imperiale's house. The white stanchion was the wire closest for the immediate area, which was serviced by underground lines. Reggie focused a laser listening gun on Imperiale's kitchen window. A conversation played through the van's speakers.

'The bodyguards,' said Reggie. 'Mikey and Vito will talk on the patio, where we can't hear.'

'But at least we know they're meeting.'

'Yes, sir.'

'Just don't hurt Mikey.'

'Not to worry, sir. No one shoots his pilot.'

He turned off the laser, which picked up the vibrations of voices rattling the kitchen window, and drove away before the phone company or the Feds came along on their business.

*    *    *

Each new battle of what Vito Imperiale called the Strikeforce War – the Bronx shootout, the Mulberry Street bombing, the Rizzolo bus barn bombing, and the vengeance-fuelled street fights that followed – reminded Vito how glad he was that he had moved his family to the suburbs. They lived like kings in Alpine and didn't have to worry about day-to-day shit. Let his *capos* fight it out in the city. When he was home, he was home free. The house was floodlit and guarded in case some Bronx asshole tried to track him down out here. Even the Feds were co-operating, hanging outside in their phone truck.

Not that it was all a bed of roses. There was always some damned thing going wrong with the house, and out here there was no super to raise hell with or no neighbourhood handy man to set things straight. If a tap leaked you called a plumber and paid thirty bucks just to have him drive in your driveway. No hot water? Up drive the electrician and the plumber, and you kiss goodbye to four or five hundred bucks for a new heater. This morning, he realized, after Mikey had left, the lawn mowers were late. And those who finally did come a little before lunch were new guys who didn't know the property. And as this late autumn mowing would be the last before winter it was doubly important that it be cut right.

They were the blackest blacks Vito Imperiale had ever seen; their skin was so black it was almost grey. He called from the door, 'Where's the regular guys? What's his name, Washington?'

'Washington, his wife be sick.'

Funny accent; maybe from the Caribbean. 'I hope they told you what to do.'

'We know, boss.'

Imperiale closed the door, scratching his head. 'Boss?' Funny accent. He watched suspiciously from the picture window. His wife called him for lunch. 'What's the matter?'

'The landscaper changed the lawn guys. They're going to screw up. They're going to miss the lights.'

They ate lunch in the kitchen with the bodyguards; his wife was always fussing after them, like they were sons or nephews. He was irritable. Mikey was offering a pretty good deal, but he didn't like having to take it. Since the first request for a meeting he had known this was coming and had decided to fight. But with one headache out of the way, he was going to have another, keeping the supply up. Three hundred kilos a week was not smuggled past customs without risk. It took a lot of people and the better they were, the more they tried to lean on him. If he thought about the future, it would get overwhelming, so he shifted his worries to the lawn again. It was flourishing so late in the year, thanks to a wet, warm autumn, and he knew the substitute lawn guys were going to screw up.

Sure enough, after lunch, ragged wisps of grass stood around the high-intensity security lights embedded at strategic points around the lawn. He called again from the door. 'Hey, trim those lights!'

'Yo, boss.'

The one driving the big winged Lock mower swung it around and starting mowing a six-foot swatch towards the nearest light.

'Not with that, for Christ sake! Use the weed eater.' He gestured at their truck where the trimmer was kept. The dumb fuck waved and kept going.

'Oh shit. *No!* You're going to hit –'

The machine ran over the light, mangling the fixture and exploding the bulb with a vaporous *bang*. The Lock mower kept going, yanking the wires right out of the ground. Before it finally stopped, thirty feet of Romex cable was tangled in the blades and Imperiale's lawn was gouged like some monster mole had gone berserk.

'Jesus Fucking Christ!'

Imperiale leaped off the back step and ran across his new-mown lawn. The blacks were walking towards their truck, shaking their heads. The ripped-up earth smelled richer and wetter than the cut grass. New seed would never sprout before winter. It would be mud all winter and frozen ruts.

'You dumb fucks!'

All four turned to face him – crouching, hands extended, cocking the slides on little pistols. They fired in unison.

*    *    *

'I'm told,' Reggie Rand reported with a smile, 'that Mikey beat up the *capo* who brought the news. At any rate, his people are asking to buy from ours again.'

'Not until he agrees to no more attacks against the Rizzolos.'

'He agrees.'

'Good. Raise the price again.'

'I already have. They asked for five hundred kilos. I think they were just a little surprised we had that much.'

'Do we?'

'Barely. We agreed to give it to them at two hundred and fifty thousand a kilo, on consignment. Twenty per cent down and two per cent interest a week, with a month's grace. Next month, Mikey Cirillo will owe you one hundred million dollars plus five hundred thousand dollars interest.'

'Half a million interest a week? That makes me the biggest shylock in the country.'

'Soon you'll have to be the biggest enforcer.'

'Unless he pays me back.'

Reggie smiled again. 'Which isn't likely, sir.'

# 16

Uncle Vinnie's annual contractors' party was going full blast when Christopher Taggart rushed in late. Thirty men in tuxedos were grouped around the spacious Waldorf-Astoria suite, laughing, trading jokes and gossip, drinking at the well-stocked bar, and ignoring the elaborate crabmeat, smoked salmon and caviar hors d'oeuvres. Pier glasses reflected towering arrangements of autumn flowers, chrysanthemums, asters, and purple anemones that stood on consoles at either end of the main room, while the hotel windows offered splendid scenes of night advancing on the city. Bedrooms were available down a long hall – a dozen barelegged girls in T-shirts and high heels circulated – and the party was, traditionally, a mostly Italian and strictly-no-wives affair. When Taggart entered, a group of men near the door pounced on him as if they had stationed themselves there for his arrival.

'Chris! Hey, Chris!'

A cement supplier who had slugged it out with his father pumped his hand; and an electrical contractor who had tried to stiff him in the early days seized his arms, still begging forgiveness for a slight ten years old. Other contractors, suppliers, bankers and fellow developers crowded around, slapping his back, as if by bouncing their hands off his flesh some of the Taggart touch might stick to them.

Uncle Vinnie bounded across the suite, his bulging chest and belly resplendent in a ruffled white shirt and icy black cummerbund. His round face was alight with a proud smile that his star nephew had come. 'Hey!' They embraced.

'Sorry, I got held up – fucking Board of Estimate. I'm going to kill the mayor one of these days.'

'Nice a ya to come. I know you're busy.'

'Would I miss this?'

'Have a drink. Sweetheart, bring my nephew a drink. Watcha gonna have, Chris?'

'Perrier.'

She started towards the bar, but Uncle Vinnie grabbed the hem of her T-shirt, baring her taut behind. 'Bullshit. Bring him a CC on the rocks.' He let her go with a pat. 'That's what your old man drank.'

'My pop drank red wine like any decent guinea.'

'Yeah, but he knew to drink CC in the Waldorf. Wanna meet some of the guys?'

As Uncle Vinnie led him to an expectant group, Chris experienced again the eerie sensation of having men twice his age hang on his every word. Were he to suggest dynamiting the Empire State Building to build a new one with bigger windows, they would nod sagely, and one or two would probably offer their services. 'Hey, what's the matter?' Uncle Vinnie asked, as he herded him towards the next group.

'At these things I think of Pop. He'd still be younger than a lot of these guys.'

'I know. Me, too. I think about him all the time. Ten years? Like yesterday. What are you gonna do?'

Uncle Vinnie beckoned a pretty girl. She hurried over, her nipples pointing through thin cotton. Uncle Vinnie handed her a room key and nodded at a man standing alone. 'Sweetie, there's a fellow there who'd love to talk to you.'

She gave Uncle Vinnie a stoned smile, Chris another, looped the key ring over her little finger, and pranced off. Uncle Vinnie watched until the connection looked secure, then turned back to Chris. 'Funny thing about your Pop. He wouldn't go with the girls. Never when your mother was alive.'

'Really?'

'Only guy I knew never had girl friends. How about you? Want some? There's a blonde with legs right up to her tongue.'

'Naw. I'm fine.' He averted his gaze from a dark girl with a pretty body who looked a little like Helen Rizzolo. Uncle Vinnie noticed and said, 'See how ya feel later. Here's Alphonse.'

Chris shook the ancient Sicilian's hand and bowed his head with respect. 'Hello, Alphonse. We did good with your trucks.'

Alphonse beamed. 'Howsa repairs? Like I promise?'

'My people say, no problem.'

'Listen, Chris.' Alphonse took his elbow and lowered his voice. Uncle Vinnie stepped closer and Chris encircled his shoulder with a conspiratorial grin. A concrete man did not fill a Waldorf suite with half-naked women purely for the pleasure of getting his friends laid. Alphonse had trucks, Vinnie had cement, and the big jobs Taggart Construction did these days often required more cement than Taglione Concrete produced inhouse. 'What is this talk about a stadium in Manhattan?'

'Well, there's still some spaces around.'

'Who owns them?'

Chris shrugged. 'People who control that kind of property tend to keep quiet until they're ready to build.' He winked at Uncle Vinnie because the city was suddenly giving him serious resistance and a little optimistic rumour in the business couldn't hurt.

Alphonse smiled happily, his sleepy old eyes alight. 'I was thinking that if someday, somebody built such a stadium – and it happened to be near some old railroad tracks – we put the concrete trucks on trains.'

'That would certainly eliminate access problems,' Chris agreed, confirming Alphonse's guess, and wondering how in hell he had found out the location. 'As usual, Alphonse, it is profitable to see you. How is your grandson?'

'Aggh. Another goddamned *studente*. Shit on the business.'

'Hey, hey! The food!'

The company mobbed the door as four of Uncle Vinnie's sons bustled in with giant suitcases of food they had smuggled by the Waldorf staff. They spread it out on the conference table; garlic, tomato, onions, pork, veal, and gorganzola filled the air with a pungency no hotel caterer would dare.

Chris sat on a couch surrounded by contractors and devoured a plate of calves brains, sausage, and eggplant. A very pretty redhead kept leaning over the back, refilling their wine glasses and brushing her breasts against his cheek. 'Can I get you anything else? More pasta?'

A cool voice beside her said, 'Pasta's a *New York Times* word. My brother eats macaroni.'

'Jesus Christ,' Uncle Vinnie blurted, sounding equally astonished and embarrassed. 'It's Tony.'

When Chris finally got his head disconnected from the girl's breast, he saw his brother standing there in a dark suit, surveying the party with a fathomless gaze.

'I hope I'm not interrupting, Uncle Vinnie.'

'What do ya mean, interrupting? You're my nephew.' Uncle Vinnie barrelled around the couch, kissed Tony's cheeks and embraced him. 'Hey, everybody. My nephew Tony's here.'

There was a moment's startled silence before the men put their plates aside and stepped over and shook hands, mumbling pleasantries. Tony looked each in the eye and replied with a word for each that implied he remembered not only their names, but their business.

'Hey, it's really great to see you,' Uncle Vinnie repeated when the parade had ended.

Chris pulled Tony down beside him. 'You killed this party faster than herpes.'

'Hungry?' asked Uncle Vinnie. 'Honey. Get him some –'

'I'll get it.' Tony went to the table and filled a plate with small portions from each dish, while the others conversed quietly and pretended not to watch an assistant United States Attorney in their midst. He returned to the couch and picked at the food.

'I was looking for you, Chris. Gotta talk. I didn't realize you were having this kind of party, Uncle Vinnie. I might not have come.'

Uncle Vinnie grinned. 'Hey, can I tell 'em you're off duty?'

Tony looked his uncle in the face. 'No. But I will leave. Chris, when you're ready.'

'Hey, you don't gotta run.'

Tony Taglione said, 'I don't patronize hookers and nobody in this room will talk to me without a lawyer. So I don't see much point in staying.'

'Now wait a minute, these are legit businessmen.'

'So why do they freak when I walk in?'

'You got a rep. But these are straight guys your father worked with.'

'And they'll be the first to remind me. Chris, let's go.'

Chris stood up and embraced his uncle. 'I'm sorry. Tell the blonde with the legs up to her tongue that I feel I know her even though we've never met.'

Uncle Vinnie laughed, smacked them each affectionately on the back of the head and walked them to the front door. Chris waited until they were alone in the elevator.

'Was that fucking necessary?'

'I've saved you a lot of trouble,' Tony replied with a thin smile. 'They'll think twice before they ask for kickbacks and payoffs from Taggart Construction.'

'Was it necessary to fuck up Uncle Vinnie's party?'

'I needed to see you. I called your office and Sylvia said you were here. I didn't realize what was going on till I got inside. Once in, there's no way I'm pretending I don't have eyes.'

'It's just a party, for crissake.'

'Chris, do you think those girls come from the Nightingale-Bamford School?'

'What's the big deal if a girl wants to pick up a couple C-notes blowing businessmen? They're home by ten o'clock.'

'They are supplied by the Mafia. You think Vinnie calls up twelve girls he happens to know?'

'Yeah, or his secretary does. Who knows?'

'The hell he does. He pays a guy with a regular circuit and the guy brings them in from upstate, Atlantic City, New England. The guy is either con-nected or pays connected people for protection. The Mafia gets the money. The girls get drugs and tips.'

'What you want to see me about?'

'Your new girlfriend.'

'What girlfriend?'

'Are you aware you're involved with a Mafia person?'

Taggart laughed. This had to happen sometime, but he had himself to blame for accelerating events by blundering into the hospital. 'A Mafia "person"? Hey listen, man, I don't know what you're talking about.'

'I'm talking about Helen Rizzolo.'

'How'd you hear about that?'

'My agents keep track of criminals.'

'I'll bet they were afraid to tell you they saw me.'

'Chris, are you fucking crazy? You know damn well that Helen Rizzolo's brothers are two of the most vicious bonebreakers in Brooklyn.'

Taggart tried another small joke, while he gauged how much else Tony knew. He would be himself and needle his brother for being so serious, but that resolve lasted for only the briefest exchange.

'Isn't Brooklyn out of your territory?'

'Not anymore. You plan to keep seeing her?'

'Hey, what is this?'

'I'd appreciate it if you didn't.'

'It's partly up to her. I'm not that sure she likes me. As a matter of fact, since the hospital she's been avoiding me.'

'Good. Keep it that way.'

'It's already rolling, man. What happens, happens.'

'What about Pop?'

'Get off my back.'

'Chris, take it to its logical conclusion. You going to bring her home to the family?' Like many trial lawyers, Tony was a great mimic and could paint a scene with his voice. ' "Uncle Vinnie I want you to meet my Mafia girlfriend. You remember the Mafia, they killed my father. And Helen, meet my brother Tony – he sent your father to jail and is hoping to do the same to your scumbag brothers?" '

'Am I supposed to laugh?'

'You're supposed to *think,* you asshole.'

Silent, they walked through the lobby and onto the sidewalk.

'Cab, sir?' asked the doorman, signalling the empty street.

'Two,' Chris snapped, angry that Tony had put him into the false position of pretending he didn't care about his father, when it was his father that lay behind everything he was doing.

It was about eight-thirty and the evening rush for the theatre had ended, but cabs were sparse. They waited in stiff silence. Finally, the doorman got one, but as they argued who would wait for the next, a couple raced out of the hotel, screaming at each other in Texas accents that they were goddamned late.

'Ah told you you should of called the theatre to hold the show.'

Chris stepped back from the cab. 'Be our guest.'

'That's right nice of you boys. You all have a good evening –'

'*Get in*!' his wife yelled, and the cab raced off.

They looked at each other and couldn't help smiling. Chris nodded up Park Avenue where the Taggart Spire sent a lonely line of work lights straight into the sky. 'Want to see the job?'

Tony hesitated. 'Okay.'

Silent still, they walked up Park Avenue and into the site. Chris waved off a superintendent, who was still working with some subs and looked alarmed that the boss had appeared, and made directly for the elevator. Tony stopped him and pointed at a spindly pipeframe outside the building.

'How about the hoist?'

'You got it! Hey,' he called to the watchman, 'send us up.'

They climbed on to the platform. The lift engine roared and the open material hoist climbed up the side of the building, high above the amber lights of Park Avenue.

Chris saw a grin dance on the ridges of Tony's face. 'You miss this, don't you?'

'Don't you? When's the last time you worked the Iron? God, look at it. . .'

'How you been?'

'Working my ass off. Double eights six days a week. You?'

'Same. It gets more every day . . . Hey, Tony?'

'What?' They had climbed to the point where they were looking down on the lower building's roof. The noise from the hoist engine grew soft and a cool breeze sighed in the frame.

'My offers still stand. Offer number one is if you want to be a lawyer, be my general counsel.'

'I told you general counsel's like an employment agent. You end up hiring real lawyers to do your work.'

'Offer number two – and my favourite – is if you prefer to really work hard for a living, be my partner.'

'I already have a job.'

'You're not going to be a prosecutor your whole life.'

'It is my life.'

'Ever peek at your blind trust?'

'You know damned well I don't.'

'You're doing good.'

207

'You push me on that and I'll contribute the whole thing to curing the common cold.'

'Okay, okay. Forget it. But the offers stand, anytime. What was I up to last time? Six-hundred-thousand and hot running secretaries?'

'I got a job. And that's what I want to talk to you about. Very seriously. What is going on?'

'Nothing.'

'You visited her in the hospital. You hired three specialists for a bump on her gorgeous head. Sounds more than nothing to me.'

'What can I say? I flipped, man.'

'But you know who she is.'

'I know about her family. But she's not a hood.'

'But Pop...'

'Whatever her brothers are doesn't make her a criminal.'

Was it a set-up? he wondered. Was Tony onto his shadow Mafia? Or had surveillance just made the connection at the hospital?

The hoist stopped and Tony swung onto the plank floor. Chris watched him wrap an arm around a column and gaze up at Manhattan's pink-black night sky. A forest of columns rose two storeys above the wooden floor, boxed by headers and beams, and dwarfed by three enormous stiff-legged derricks. Their vertical masts and slanting booms, which were jointed at the floor, veered apart as they soared twenty-five storeys above the building to cast V-shaped shadows, as if the Spire herself were flashing jubilant victory signs at the stars.

He wasn't sure he wanted to show Tony the glass apartment. Tony derided anything lavish and sneered at the idea that extravagant design paid back tenfold in free publicity. Taggart thought he had enough condemnation for one night, and it was better to play the Helen thing through to the end. He asked, 'How tough are the brothers?'

'The worst.'

'It's not your problem.'

'You've already made it my problem. How'd you meet her?'

'At a fundraiser for a new parochial school. She was on the building committee.'

'What were you doing there?'

'The Church was hitting me for a low bid. She was hosting the party.' True and verifiable. It was at a jam-packed cocktail party in one of her family's wedding palaces. He had gone for a final look before chosing the Rizzolos for his plan, and had not, of course, actually spoken to her. That came weeks later, after the kidnapping, when he visited her at her club and brought her here to the Spire.

'Didn't you know who she was?'

He made himself sound contrite. 'Yeah, I remembered, you know, from when she was a kid. Remember her that night?'

'I sure do. I also remember her glaring fire at me when I put her father away.'

'Well, I wanted a closer look. I was intrigued. When I got a closer look I liked what I saw. There's a person there who's more than just a Mafia goon's daughter. She's tough, sure. She's strong, she's intensely independent, she's lonely as hell. She loves music and she's beautiful enough to kill for. What else can I say?'

'When was that?'

'I don't know. Around the middle of May.'

'Did you know she was kidnapped about a week later?'

'Kidnapped? What do you mean?'

'Kidnapped. Snatched. She didn't tell you?'

'I told you, we're not that close.'

'Not close? The nurses said you were throwing hundred dollar bills around the emergency room. How'd you hear she was in the hospital?

'Wait a minute. What do you mean, kidnapped? Who kidnapped her?' Tony shrugged. 'It was some kind of family thing.'

'Was she hurt?'

'She was back in a few days and it settled down quickly, so I assume they worked it out among themselves.'

'Does it have anything to do with the bombing?'

Tony shrugged again. Taggart could not guess whether he was denying he knew or was declining to answer.

'How'd you hear she was in the hospital? I'm told you were there twenty minutes after they brought her in.'

'I heard it on the radio. I called the bus bam. The cops told me.' Verifiable again, because it had happened precisely that way. He had heard the news in the car, called, and got to the hospital less than half an hour after she had. Tony said, 'Can I ask you something?'

'Nothing's stopped you so far.'

'Why don't you marry Cheri or Vicky?'

Chris grinned. 'I couldn't marry just one of them; then you'd be back bitching about bigamy.'

'Marry *somebody,* for Christ sake. Settle down a little.'

'Me? What about you?'

'I'm too busy.'

'What if I married Helen Rizzolo?'

'You can go along when she visits her father in jail. Do you know she's the go-between with him and her brothers?'

'I don't know that. And you're probably just guessing.'

'Does she know you helped me send him up?'

'You gonna tell her?'

'I'd love to because it would end it. But I won't.'

'Thanks for the break.'

'It's not a break. You were a confidential source. I promised not to blow your cover.'

'A man of your word.'

'Besides, if I did, her brothers would kill you. And I love you too much for that to happen.'

Tony removed his jacket and necktie, loosened his shirt, and mounted the column, planting his feet against the inside flange and gripping the outside with his hands.

'Where you going?'

Tony climbed straight up to the header, climbed on it, and attacked the next column. Taggart lost him in the dark. He tore off his own bow tie and tuxedo jacket, and started after him. Tony was sitting astride the top header, thirty feet above the plank floor and ninety-six storeys over Manhattan.

'You really believe that about Uncle Vinnie's hookers? That they're just picking up a little spare bread?'

Relieved for any subject change, Taggart leaped into the argument. 'I just can't get on everybody's morality case.'

'Chris, Chris, Chris. You know, sometimes I think you really are what you pretend to be.'

'What's that?'

'Just a clod businessman? A genius at building skyscrapers and otherwise just a dumb, happy-go-lucky idiot. No offence?'

'Sure. No offence.'

They sat, Tony silently gazing at the city, and Chris wondering. Had Tony found himself lonely, as he himself sometimes did, when the action stopped a moment? Was this one of Tony's rare lapses, when he tried to patch things up, feeling a little lonely and seeking the tatters of their family? Did he just want to talk? And took the excuse of Helen Rizzolo?

Tony had no confidants at the US Attorney's office, not with the iceman reputation he cultivated to mask his youth. He worked too hard to have close friends outside of work. Women were drawn to him, as they had been as far back as Taggart could remember; the nymphs were lured by his power, the mothers touched when they convinced themselves they saw something vulnerable at his core. He had almost married in college, the year their father was killed, and again in Washington, when he worked for the Attorney General. Since then, Tony had retreated from involvements, like an old–

fashioned athlete who feared women would suck away his strength. He bounced from woman to woman, dating professionals who were as career-committed as himself, much the way Chris had to admit he would have took, if it weren't for Chryl and Victoria, who in their way stabilized his life. Until now, of course, because connecting with Helen Rizzolo had unhinged everything.

Tony stood up and started across along the header that rimmed the thousand-foot structure.

'Take it easy. It's dark and you've got heels on your shoes.'

Tony walked sure-footedly along the twelve-inch steel girder towards the nearest derrick. Chris followed his brother's dim shadow, feeling a little crazy, a little daring, and more than a little paranoid.

Somehow, tonight Tony did not seem lonely. In fact he was aloof, in charge, and even more pleased with himself than usual. Chris caught up at the derrick which leaned so close he could almost touch it and sat down again, straddling the header. The iron workers had left the boom in a nearly vertical position, so the V between boom and mast was tight, the two arms almost parallel.

Chris reminded himself that devious, convoluted plots were *his* way, not Tony's. Tony constructed his court cases in a straightforward manner, much the same way iron workers erected a steel frame, raising columns, connecting them with headers and beams, laying a floor, hoisting their derricks and raising more columns. If Tony had an inkling of what he was doing, Chris knew he would attack head on.

Without warning, Tony stepped off the header.

'*Wha* —'

'You're playing with fire,' Tony's voice came out of the dark, several feet away on the derrick. He had jumped to the derrick, Taggart heard him ascending. He jumped to the derrick himself and climbed after him, although he couldn't see Tony in the pale light cast up from the city and down from the stars. 'Where the hell are you?'

'Hang on, I got a pen light.'

The little white light blinked to the side. Chris laughed. They had climbed the opposing arms of the derrick. Tony clung to the slightly slanted boom; Chris was on the mast, six or eight feet away.

They held silently to their respective perches as the wind sighed through the steel. Chris remembered something Tony had dodged earlier. 'What did you mean that Brooklyn's not out of your territory?'

'The Attorney General has amalgamated a new *joint* Federal Organized Crime Strikeforce. It now covers the whole city, Long Island, Connecticut, and New Jersey.'

'Who's the new boss?'

'It comes under the Southern District, so Arthur controls it.'

'But who runs it?'

'He offered it to me.'

Taggart stared across the space that separated them. As neither Reggie nor Jack Warner had told him yet, it must just have happened. So that's what Tony was sitting on; no tricks, something unthinkably worse.

'Aren't you awfully young?'

'I'm connected in Washington from when I worked for the AG. They figure I knew enough of the right people to make the agencies co-operate.'

'Jesus, congratulations. That's some honour . . . Have you accepted?'

'We're working out the details. I'm negotiating for as much autonomy as Arthur will give up.'

'Would you please come to work with me?'

'What! Are you nuts? I've fought for this Strikeforce for ten years.'

'Tony, you want to stay in public service and that's good. But you've got to broaden yourself, get more experience, learn business, find what makes things tick.'

'You'd be surprised how much business you learn prosecuting crooked businessmen.'

'But some managerial experience.'

'Chris, I have forty people working directly for me and hundreds of federal agents on tap. With this new thing, I'm running an army.'

'What about politics?'

'What about 'em?'

'A guy like you should go into politics.'

'Maybe someday. But I've got other things first.'

'A stint in business would really set you up with the right people. Hell, the mayor of New York calls me a couple of times a week, I talk to the governor –1 know you do, too, but more as Pop's friend, I'm talking about hondling with them. I can put you in the same room with senators and congressmen, the party leaders. You need them to run for office. I really want you to work with me.'

'But the US Attorney has offered me everything I need to destroy the Mafia.'

'It can't be done that way.'

'You know a better way?'

'Of course not,' Chris said hastily. 'But –'

'So it's the only way.'

Taggart laid his cheek against the cold metal. He looked down and felt a sudden stab of fear. Anyone could fall.

'Is this why you barged in at Uncle Vinnie's?'

'Sure, I had tell somebody.'

The emotion soared between the derrick arms. It felt like Tony had flung him a net. 'Stay there!'

'Wait!'

But Chris had already locked his eyes on the black edge of the boom, gathered his legs, and launched himself into the dark. Something brushed his shoulder and cold steel banged into his bare hands. Then he was clinging to the boom. He set his feet, sucked his palm where he had cut it, and looked around the dark.

'Tony? Where the hell'd you go?'

'Over here.'

His brother's voice came from behind him, on the mast Chris had just left. 'I told you to wait. I jumped, too.'

Chris sagged against the metal, his heart pounding.

'Get rid of that woman,' Tony called.

'What, you got the hots for her too?'

'I'm not joking.'

'Tony, I've got it bad. I'm going to play it out, see what happens. I'm going to do everything I can to turn her on to me.'

'She's trouble.'

'Not for me. Maybe for you, and if that's so, I'm sorry.'

'What if I bust her brothers? Can you imagine what the papers will do when they find out the connection.'

'I suppose it would knock "Nuns Staff Abortion Clinic" off the front page of the *Post*. Are you going to bust her brothers?'

'That's exactly what I'm talking about. It puts a barrier between us.'

'No more Deep Throat?'

'I can't talk to you anymore because I'm an assistant United States Attorney.' 'But I'm your brother.'

'Sharing pillow talk with Don Eddie Rizzolo's daughter.'

'You want to listen in?'

'*Don't fuck with me.* This is serious, Bro. If I could stop it, I would.'

'When we were kids you stopped a lot by dating my girls. Why not Helen?' 'I already have.'

'What?'

'The summer we met her, for crissake, dummy. We went out.'

'Bullshit. You went back to Harvard the next day.'

'I came down from Boston to see her.'

'You prick!'

'Hey, it was ten years ago.'

Taggart was surprised how much it hurt and he felt like a total ass asking, 'Did you hit on her?'

'None of your fucking business.'

'You son of a bitch.'

'What are you mad at me for? She was there too.'

'She has nothing to do with it. I asked *you* not to touch her. You ripped me off, Bro.'

'It was ten years ago,' Tony repeated. 'Forget it.'

'I wish you believed in what was right as much as you believe in the fucking law.'

To his surprise, Tony apologized. 'I'm sorry. That's the last time I did something like that. I told you a few years ago, I don't do that anymore.'

'It must have been weird when you prosecuted her father.'

'Very. I cleared it with Arthur first, of course.'

'Of course.'

'The point I'm trying to make now is, Helen Rizzolo is trouble and until you dump her we can't talk about anything that concerns my office.'

Taggart smiled in the dark. The most important thing was to protect his connection to the Strikeforce, but he couldn't resist making Tony squirm for betraying him. 'We can't talk? What if I told you I heard about a heroin deal going down next week?'

'Call 911.'

'Five hundred kilos.'

'Five *hundred*?'

'That's what I hear.'

'From whom?'

'Not her and that's all I'm going to tell you. Good night, Bro.'

'Wait a minute.'

'I thought we can't talk.'

'*Five hundred kilos*? Where?'

Taggart smiled again. Reggie's people had been pumping the rumour through the law enforcement agencies, and Tony's staff would surely have heard it by now. 'Park Avenue.'

# 17

'I'm so glad you could come, Chris.'

Taggart's host, an elfin man with a gentle handshake and a reputation as the singular music scholar of the last two generations, greeted him warmly in the crowded foyer of the East Side apartment he used for an art gallery and music room. Taggart had read his textbook in college, never imagining that years later he would be one of forty or fifty people invited by him to a musicale. The host introduced him to the composer, who looked equally nervous and happy, and to the soprano in a long green dress who would sing the new work. They raced off and Taggart confessed, 'I've never been asked to something like this before.'

'Dear boy, brace yourself for an avalanche when the word gets out that Taggart Realty is supporting young performers.' He glanced at the foyer where more guests were pouring off the elevator, but inquired, politely, 'Do you know anyone here?'

His guests included young men and women Taggart assumed were musicians, elderly wealthy-looking patrons with dour escorts, and some famous faces – a feminist, an architect, a writer, and a City Hall luminary, the deputy mayor for capital construction who was giving him grief on his stadium project.

'Who is that?'

'Isn't she exotic? I was lecturing at Sarah Lawrence. She came up to me enchanted by a conspiracy theory that a Cremonese scoundrel named Guadignini might have tricked two centuries of violin makers into believing that Stradivari, Amati, and Guarnari used untreated wood.'

'What's her name?'

'Helen Rizzolo. She always comes alone. Shall I introduce you?'

'No, that's okay. You've got more people coming.'

'Well, go into the bedroom and find a drink. They'll bring some munchies and then I'll ask you young men to carry chairs in for the performance.'

Taggart found a white wine and mingled his way back into the living-room. Helen was wearing a black cocktail dress – just a touch hookerish, he thought.

215

Her jet hair was shorter than when he saw her at the hospital and was swept back on the sides in a sleek, stylish manner that Victoria and Chryl would approve. Diamond studs flashed from her ears and when she pivoted towards him, her attention fixed on one of the many paintings, Taggart saw a single, large diamond suspended between her breasts.

Working his way closer, he amended his opinion about the dress. Other women were similarly attired, but she was doing more for hers. A slick-looking European used the painting as an opening, and when she gazed up at him, listening attentively, Taggart felt a powerful jolt of jealousy.

He wandered the room, waiting for the right moment to bump into her to ask if she would sit with him during the performance. The deputy mayor hailed him with a smirk.

'Since when are you a patron of the arts, Chris?'

'I'm getting the inside track on the Carnegie Hall demolition.'

The deputy mayor's wife went rigid until her husband recovered with a belly laugh, at which she drifted determinedly towards the wine room. Her place was taken immediately by Kenny Adler, a PR man who often ran point for the mayor. Taggart had learned to treat Adler as a member of the administration. With one eye on Helen, who hadn't noticed him yet, he asked. 'So what are you guys waiting for on my stadium?'

'Reassessing the risk,' the deputy mayor replied blandly.

'It's not your money. For crissake, can't you get it through his bald head that all I need is the city's enthusiastic permission. I'll raise the money. Just give me a break by making me look good.'

'And if you blow it the mayor looks like a schmuck.'

'Have I ever blown a building?'

'His Honour doesn't want to be in on the first. This is a lot bigger than just a building. And a lot more exposed.'

'You're telling me a Manhattan stadium won't go? Next to the convention centre? Accessed by the Westway and a federally subsidized subway link? What is your problem?'

The deputy mayor glanced around. 'I'm not saying I'm saying this. But there is a feeling that an indoor "Polo Grounds" with million dollar sky boxes is a bread and circus sort of thing.'

'It *is* an election year,' Adler chimed in. 'Again.'

'What does His Honour want from me? A low-income high rise on top?'

'Right next to the convention centre. Perfect.'

Helen was still paying rapt attention to the European who was leading her towards a second painting. Taggart whipped out his wallet, turned to the notepad. 'Mr Deputy, you just gave me a great idea. You want something really hot? Something the mayor can sell? Look.' He drew a round ball with his gold pen. 'This is the stadium, right?'

'The famous white basketball.'

'Now.' He drew a tall, slim triangle on top of the ball.

'What's that?'

'The tallest building in the world.'

The idea had popped full blown into his head. He should have thought of it ages ago – would have if he weren't living half and half. 'A supertall building *atop* the dome. Two hundred floors. Convention centre hotel on the lower levels, condos and executive suites on top. Even some City space in between so the mayor can shack up when the home teams are in town.'

'There's no economies in a supertall,' the deputy mayor protested.

'Don't talk to me about elevators. There are values in a project like this more than the money. Ask Kenny. New York needs the biggest.'

'How much?'

'Think billions instead of millions,' Taggart admitted, 'but it has the pizzaz to draw the money. I'll bet I could pull it off without the Urban Development Corporation. Screw the state. We can do it right here in the City.'

The deputy mayor looked interested because, as Taggart well knew, the mayor hated ceding control to independent agencies like the UDC. Adler asked, 'Does it have a name?'

'It has a name that team franchises will sell their mothers to broadcast from. The Manhattan Super-Spire.'

Adler smiled. 'The mayor would love nothing more than to turn the Jersey Meadowlands Arena back into landfill.'

'Maybe we ought to have lunch, sometime,' said the Deputy.

'I am having *dinner* with the governor next week. Just remember I gave you first shot – catch you later.'

He headed swiftly across the room. The European had been pressed into carrying folding chairs and Helen was inspecting the hors-d'oeuvres. When she reached for a shrimp, Taggart speared it first.

'Excuse me.'

'That is mine,' she said icily. 'And you are a prick for moving in on me like this.'

'I want to see you.'

'I came to hear music. Not for business.'

'Reggie handles that.'

'Leave me alone. My brothers are going nuts waiting for the Cirillos to drive up the street in a tank and you're jerking my strings like a puppet. I really have to get away sometimes.'

'It cost me a hundred-thousand dollars to get invited tonight.'

'What do you mean?'

'You've been dodging me. When I heard you were coming here, I established a lunch hour performance fund for chamber music in my new building. I hired our host to select the performers.'

Helen's lips gathered in a slow smile. 'Just to see me?'

'Worth every penny.'

'And tax deductible.'

'Would you like to have dinner after?'

'No thanks. The guys in my car get nervous if I stay too long.'

\*      \*      \*

Sunlight, stirred by the river, snaked through the tall French ballroom doors of an estate house south of Croton-on-Hudson, rippled on the ornate ceiling, and bounced softly into a humidity-controlled vault where it played on a perfect cone of near-pure heroin. An icy, malevolent mountain, four feet across and a yard high, the heroin looked like enough flour to bake fifty cakes or enough snow to build a fort.

The art dealer from whom Taggart's agents had bought the house had turned the ballroom into a painting gallery and installed the walk-in safe, which Reggie Rand had booby-trapped in case thieves or cops broke in. They had burned the various wrappings which might give clues to the drug's diverse sources – Reggie's Burmese, Chinese and Indian connections – and had blended it all in one anonymous heap. Now they worked with the door open for relief from the fumes and wore surgical masks, rubber gloves, and hospital gowns as they bagged it for Crazy Mikey.

Reggie thrust the nozzle of an Electrolux vacuum-cleaner into the mountain. A deep pucker appeared, as if a mine had caved in inside it, and the slope began to collapse. The grains hissed through the hose. When the filter bag was full the motor shut off automatically. Reggie opened the machine, gently removed the plump sack, which weighed almost exactly a kilogram.

Choosing a bag at random, midway through the job, Taggart slipped an electronic tracker through its slitted rubber diaphram. The tracker was an RF signal-emitting device sold to businessmen worried about kidnapping; it could be secreted in a briefcase, affixed to a car, or, in a miniature nuclear-powered version, implanted surgically under the skin. Reggie's device was modified with a remote-controlled on-off switch; it would enable Taggart to turn on the beeping radio signal from a distance – *after* the Cirillos had finished sweeping the heroin for hidden electronics – and to tell the Strikeforce exactly where Crazy Mikey's dope was headed.

Reggie encased the vacuum-cleaner bag in plastic, using a heat-sealing food wrapper, and laid it beside the others on a dolly. When the dolly was full they

218

wheeled it aboard a silver straight-back truck, which bore the name of a Long Island produce wholesaler.

Taggart knew the risk of dealing personally in heroin, but the risks were even greater with hired hands, because everybody, even professionals, went crazy over the profits. As Reggie liked to remind him, every man carries a number in his head above which he suspends the rules. Thus as a matter of course, Reggie would park the truck at the Hunts Point Market before informing his people where it was and where to deliver it, just in case they were getting ideas; and he would not tell them that tonight they were trafficking in treachery.

★   ★   ★

In the hours before dawn, Taggart and Reggie waited on a narrow sliver of upper Park Avenue that flanked the Metro North-Amtrack rails. The street was crowded with trucks and vans heading uptown to the market. A truck, bristling with radio antennae, pulled into the archway that carried One-hundred-fourth Street under the tracks.

'That's the Cirillo escort,' said Reggie. The men inside it were sweeping the area for police radios and tracking devices. It pulled out and headed uptown, trailed by a battered van. 'Mobile laboratory and the money.'

Next came Ronnie Wald driving the silver truck that Taggart and Reggie had loaded in Croton. It bore the name Sam Gordon Purveyors on the side. A sleek gypsy cab trailed it closely, and the cab in turn was followed by another. Reggie eyed the precautions approvingly. 'I like Wald.'

He eased his own gypsy cab onto Park. Taggart sat in the passenger seat, watching the rear. A truism that ruled the lives of Taggart's enemies now ruled his too: when it came to selling heroin, he worried less about the cops than the criminals. Getting ripped off or killed were the real dangers of the life and far more likely consequences than arrest.

Wald's truck stopped at the One-hundred-twelfth Street market entrance under a brightly painted sign, 'La Marqueta', as the Park Avenue Market, a vast food and clothing emporium housed under the railroad tracks, was known in East Harlem. Wald backed the truck into the building. His men from the gypsy cab followed. The Cirillos, already inside, would analyse the heroin while Wald inspected the down payment, twenty million dollars in cash and bearer bonds.

'Time,' Taggart said, 'to make Jack Warner a hero.'

Reggie drove to a pay phone on Lexington Avenue. Taggart dialled the US Attorney's office and pressed an 'electronic handkerchief' – a portable model of the voice distorter that his secret witnesses used at the President's Commission on Organized Crime – against the mouthpiece.

'Put Jack Warner on the phone. Tell him it's CI-12'

Confidential Informant Twelve was the designation Warner had assigned the scramble-voiced informant who had telephoned a week ago about a supposed Cirillo heroin buy. He had no way of knowing it was Taggart, nor that Taggart and Reggie had carefully spread the rumour by priming numerous agents with a variety of informants. Precise details about the buy, the time and the participants, differed from story to story, but each informant had named Park Avenue as the locale and five hundred kilos as the amount. The hastily formed Strikeforce intercept had been code-named Park Avenue, Reggie had learned, though it was anyone's guess on exactly which of Park Avenue's one-hundred and eighteen blocks the deal was going down.

'It's on the truck,' Taggart said when Warner picked up. His own voice, disguised in the earpiece, sounded as if a third person were on the line. 'I'll call back in ten or fifteen minutes.'

'Any idea where, yet?' came the suspicious reply.

'Not yet. But I know it's going to be five hundred keys.'

Silkily, Warner inquired, 'Want to tell me why you're performing this public service, fella?'

After a long night of sitting around smoking too many cigarettes, Warner and his fellow agents were beginning to suspect they were being jerked around. As he hung up, Taggart gave an answer the bent cop could believe in. 'They ripped me off.'

They drove back to La Marqueta where dozens of trucks were unloading produce. Five minutes later, Ronnie Wald appeared driving the battered van. Wald lowered the window, the signal that it contained the down payment for the heroin, and drove west guarded by his gypsy cabs.

'Are you sure Wald'll deliver the money?'

'No, I'm not,' Reggie replied cheerfully. 'Twenty million dollars is the most tempting amount he's carried yet, though I think I've convinced him that I'm not a man he would want to worry about in the middle of the night. More important than the money is that he simply gets away from here.'

The next moment, the Sam Gordon Purveyors truck full of heroin came out and headed east. Reggie trailed it. But several blocks along, he had to stop for a red light, because a police car was on the comer. The heroin truck kept going, around a corner and out of sight.

'Pray that they've stopped sweeping.' Taggart flipped the tracker switch a and the location device they had buried in the heroin broadcast a loud beep. He unfolded a New York City street map and when the light changed, Reggie steered by the frequency intensity of the sound. They continued east. Taggart compared their route to the street map.

'Phone!'

He dialled Warner again from the corner of First Avenue and One-hundred-twenty-fifth.

'The stuffs heading for the Triborough Bridge.'

Jack Warner was dismayed. 'You said Park Avenue! We're all over Park Avenue.'

'They were on Park. Now they're going for the bridge. It's a silver truck with Sam Gordon Purveyors on the side. If I don't read about this in the papers tomorrow, I'm calling the Strikeforce chief to tell him you screwed up.'

He ran to the car. 'Catch up, in case they blow it.'

They tore across the lightly trafficked approaches to the bridge. The truck was pulling out of the toll booth area. It continued onto the approach, across the span, and turned onto Astoria Boulevard. There was still no sign of the Feds. Taggart reached for the cellular phone.

'Wait.'

A black car shot past, winking a little red FBI light on the roof. The truck sped up and a second car passed Taggart and Reggie. When a NYPD patrol car came screaming out of LaGuardia airport, the truck cut across three lanes of traffic, shot through a police turnaround in the median barrier, and stopped suddenly by the narrow park beside the water. The doors flew open, two men hit the grass running and disappeared in the dark.

Police sirens howled and Reggie pulled onto the shoulder to let them race by. Cruisers ablaze in blue and red light were converging from east and west and pouring from the airport and shortly it seemed as if every third car on the highway had an intent-looking DEA agent holding a red flasher on the roof.

Taggart stabbed a switch, which sent the destruct signal. The beeping turned to a shrill whistle and ceased abruptly as somewhere in the half ton of heroin, the tracker burned. When the Strikeforce examined the dope that they had seized from the Cirillos, the only evidence of treachery would be a knot of charred metal in a glaze of melted heroin.

'I wonder how Mikey's going to pay me back?'

\*　　\*　　\*

The driveway to Don Richard's house had never seemed longer and Crazy Mikey felt like crawling the distance. His father's summons had been curt. A car had glided up to Mikey's Bayside condo and the driver had said, 'Your father wants to see you.'

Mikey, still awake after a long grim night of assessing damage, had shaved and dressed hurriedly and ridden across Queens wishing he had taken the time for a cup of coffee. When he told the driver to stop at a diner, the driver said he wasn't allowed. Mikey snorted a hit off his little shotgun instead.

'If I didn't know better, I'd think you were taking me for a ride,' he joked sourly, to which the tactitum driver had replied, 'Not yet.'

Now the driveway yawned ahead. The car pulled around the circle. The house hulked sombrely in the morning mist. Mikey got out and a servant opened the front door, itself a lousy sign. When things were okay he used the kitchen door. But today, he felt less family than an employee – an employee who had screwed up. His mother didn't even come out of the kitchen to greet him. Instead, a cousin, who worked as his father's secretary, waited in the centre hall.

'Where's my mother?'

'Florida.'

'That bad?'

'Sorry, Mikey.'

He led him to the library, a room with shelves full of knickknacks and photos. His father was sitting in a wing chair, his shrunken profile to the fire, his eyes on the harbour and the city beyond. He faced Mikey with a cool smile and motioned him to a straight back chair.

'I hear you got trouble.'

'What do you got, spies?'

'Spies?' Don Richard asked scornfully. 'I read the newspaper. Biggest heroin bust in history? Who else but you?'

'Us.'

'No. We share the loss – not the blame.'

'Pop.'

'What the fuck did you do?'

Mikey hung his head and worked his big hands. 'I don't know.'

'Did you agree to a vig?'

'Two per cent a week.'

'Half a million dollars a week?'

Mikey looked up. His father had found out the numbers already. There were people still going behind his back. 'A month free.'

'Wonderful. A whole month. Why did you agree to a vig?'

'I needed the stuff. I –.'

'How you going to pay?'

'I don't know.'

'How you going to get more stuff?'

'I got everybody looking. There's stuff around. It's in little pieces. This guy had big pieces. You know?'

Don Richard sighed. 'Tell me about this guy.'

Mikey told his father the little he knew about the guy in the mask, and about the boat, the Brit who fronted for him, the way he shot his bodyguard, and the enormous amounts of heroin he was able to supply. When he was done, his father said, 'That's all?'

'I think so.'

'Has he ever done anything strange?'

'Like what?' asked Mikey. He didn't want to talk about the night he and his best bodyguard got beat up.

'Does he shoot dope?'

'I don't think so.'

'Sniff cocaine?'

Mikey squirmed as his father's gaze burned into his golden spoon. 'No.'

'Nothing?'

'One thing, maybe . . . He's got the hots for Helen Rizzolo.'

'He *knows* her?'

'I think so.'

'I wonder if Helen Rizzolo knows what he does.'

'Pop, this guy is more secret than the Russians. His own mother doesn't know.'

Don Richard touched his fingertips together, sighted the Wall Street skyline over them, let his gaze drift over the harbour, and finally brought his old eyes to bear on Mikey's face. 'But *you* should know when you deal with somebody. You should know who he is.'

'How? I tried, for crissake. Nobody had one bit of postage on him or the Brit. It's like they're from another planet.'

'Maybe you don't concentrate . . . Maybe you sniff too much dope ...'

'I'm not stupid about it.'

'Then maybe you waste your mind on boxing matches ...'

'That was five months ago!' Mikey protested, wondering who in hell had told him. 'Memorial Day weekend. What does that have to do with now? It was just –'

'You put two girls out of work for weeks.'

'Come on, there were guys paying extra to fuck 'em right there in the blood – Pop, we're running a billion-dollar business. Why are we arguing about a couple of whores. Christ, is there anything they don't tell you?'

'That's what I'm trying to teach you. If you don't keep track of details all you got is empty dreams. I want to know everything. Guys know that. They ain't afraid to tell me what they think I should hear. They know Don Richard doesn't shoot the messenger.'

Mikey looked away, out the window, across the water where the city waited to test him again and again. 'I really fucked up, didn't I?' he asked at last.

Don Richard returned a kindly smile; Mikey flinched. It meant his father was resigned to the fact that his kid was not as smart as he had hoped. Don Richard confirmed Mikey's fear with an airy, 'Don't worry about it.'

'What do I do?'

'Order your people to find new suppliers. But you stay clear, because the Strikeforce'll be all over them. Tony Taglione has tasted blood.'

Mikey hung his head. 'You're coming back in, aren't you? You're going to run the business.'

Don Richard shrugged his scrawny shoulders. 'Maybe I retired too soon. Maybe I'm tired of sitting around.'

'What about this guy I owe?'

'I'll get a line on him.'

*   *   *

Don Richard ordered *Consigliere* Salvatore Ponte, 'Sally Smarts', to the Staten Island house. He had recruited the handsome, middle-aged attorney while Ponte was still a college student and had made him his protegé, eventually his counsellor, and finally, when he had retired, mentor to his children. Ponte's fortunes had risen with the family, and being so much younger than the Don, he had stayed on as advisor, first with Nicky and then with Crazy Mikey. If he was disturbed that Don Richard was back, he did not show it, although he took any opportunity he discovered to defend Mikey, for Crazy Mikey was still his best shot at the future. But as the Don put it so well, if they didn't resolve Mikey's screwup there would be no future.

Summonses were issued and a stream of taxis and unremarkable automobiles began decanting visitors who were ushered into the library with the view of the harbour. There Ponte greeted them with the degree of cordiality their station deserved and presented them to the Don, who sat behind a huge desk and peppered them with questions. Strikeforce agents, alert to the traffic, parked outside Don Richard's fence and wondered what was going on. But the visitors kept their counsel, so no one beyond Don Richard's circle knew that the Cirillo family leader was asking precisely the same question: what's going on?

Unlike Crazy Mikey, who had come of age after the Cirillos had seized control of New York narcotics, and knew little beyond the fabulously profitable heroin trade, Don Richard had an overview acquired in fifty years of profiting at a great variety of violent, illegal enterprises. He saw the rackets in the broader sense of a shadow government. He saw the unions as concentrations of money and power, and gambling for the virtual tax it was. He understood loansharking as the foot in the door of legitimate business. He saw where he fit into the society in ways Mikey could not, and saw himself as a wily servant, whereas Mikey, subconsciously at least, was a marauder. Thus Don Richard's visitors hailed from many regions.

His questions, too, were couched in broader terms. To Ponte's surprise, he seemed to ignore the heroin bust. He was much more curious about the Rizzolo rebellion in Brooklyn. Why, he asked a bookmaker, are the Rizzolos daring to take over South Brooklyn numbers? Why, he asked a Bronx loan-shark, have the loans you've written since the summer dropped by half? Why, of a union treasurer, haven't you pressed certain builders to open their payrolls to more Cirillo soldiers? He inquired in detail about the recent killings of Joe Reina, Vito Imperiale and Harry Bono. And he astonished *Consigliere* Ponte with his knowledge of seemingly trivial events – shootouts in the Bronx, street attacks, a firebombing.

Because he confined his questions to loyal associates, the answers were as blunt as they were disturbing. Finally, he confided to Ponte that he was considering demanding a meeting with the Rizzolo brothers, but hated the thought that even the coldest demand would elevate those two *gavonne* to higher planes than they deserved.

'Perhaps,' he mused, 'I could send someone to see Don Eddie in prison?'

*Consigliere* Ponte objected, vehemently. 'Don Eddie's as bad as his sons. Where do you think they learned it?'

'Maybe they're beyond his control. Maybe he doesn't know what they're doing. Maybe it's a simple matter of telling Don Eddie what they're doing. He can stop them with a word.'

'But the Rizzolo brothers aren't smart enough to set this up themselves. Don Eddie's got to be behind it.'

'I'm not sure how smart this all looks,' Cirillo mused. 'All these attacks – while the Strikeforce is hitting too – are kind of stupid, when you think about it. Who wins? Taglione and his Feds. I don't think Don Eddie's stupid. I think these sons of his got a crazy idea while their old man was locked up.'

'Don Eddie betrayed you years ago,' Ponte objected.

Don Richard brushed the air with a bony hand. 'Less betrayal than wanting to be on his own. I can understand that. I can't forgive, but I can understand. . . Look into it.'

*Consigliere* Ponte knew the difference between a discussion and an order. He shut his mouth and assigned people to look into the best way to make contact with the imprisoned Don Eddie Rizzolo. It had to be somebody who could get past the government, get permission to visit the Don, yet of high enough rank so Rizzolo would listen. This was no time for insult, perceived or real; a prisoner's perception would be rutted with suspicion.

The government couldn't deny Don Eddie a visit by a lawyer. Ponte considered going himself, but it seemed foolish to bring such attention to the Cirillos. Besides, Don Eddie knew Ponte hated him for betraying Don Richard and might not see him. That would be a joke, going all the way upstate, nearly

225

to Canada, to be told by smirking guards that Mr Rizzolo wouldn't see him. Then he got an idea and went back to Don Richard to propose it.

'His daughter.'

'Helen?'

'Why not? Invite her here. Treat her respectfully; ask her to carry your message.'

Don Richard thought about it. The last contact he had had with Helen Rizzolo was arranging her marriage to a Las Vegas casino owner's son some ten years ago, when she was only sixteen. It had seemed a good way to stop a war between the Confortis and the Rizzolos. But the marriage hadn't worked. In fact, it had been a disaster, which made him look the fool.

'I doubt she'd come. Besides, even if she would, I doubt her brothers would let her. They probably blame us for the kidnapping.'

'No. They've told people it was something in their own family.'

'I'll think about it.'

When Ponte returned the next day, he was astonished to see a black man in Don Richard's library pacing before the windows and staring at the view like he was on a space station. He was a hard-looking man in his thirties; he wore a suit without a tie, and his hands glittered with heavy rings. Ponte was sure he was the first black man to ever set foot in the house; another reminder that Don Richard was always unpredictable. Don Richard made no introductions, saying merely, 'Tell him what you told me.'

'He's crazy as a bedbug.'

'Who?' asked Ponte.

'Old man Eddie Rizzolo. He's flipped out.'

It hadn't occured to Ponte that Eddie Rizzolo was operating irrationally. Guiding Mikey had given him vast experience in the heartbreaking problems of dealing with a crazy man. On the other hand, they could be controlled by their *consigliere* in ways a brilliant, stable man like Don Richard could not. 'What do you mean? How do you know?'

'Mr Cirillo asked me to see how he's doing in the pen. My people checked him out. He's nuts. Like his brain's gone, like he's senile.'

'Senile?'

The black pointed at a large manila envelope on Don Richard's desk. 'My people stole a copy of Rizzolo's medical report. It's all there.'

Don Richard gave the envelope a grim smile. 'Read it.'

Ponte couldn't believe his eyes. 'Altzheimer's disease!'

'He's gone, man. There's no one home.'

Don Richard ushered the black man out personally, with a gnarled hand on his big arm and a warm nod as they shook hands. Ponte turned away to keep from staring. Seventy-five years old and reluctantly back from retirement,

Don Richard was adapting better than his sons. And he seemed to thrive on it: his appetite was enormous, beaming servants had confided.

The door closed and they were alone again. Don Richard hummed a tune he remembered from the Glen Island Casino. His first job was breaking fingers when musicians welshed on bets and loans; a neighbourhood kid named Oxie held the guy, whose replacement had to cough up initiation fees and dues to the union local. A nice little racket.

'So who's behind it?' Ponte asked.

'The brothers aren't smart enough,' Don Richard answered.

'Then who's running the Rizzolos?'

'I think I'm beginning to understand.'

★   ★   ★

Taggart tracked the Cirillo visits through Reggie's spies in the family, his own friendships with cops and federal agents, and his contacts on the President's Organized Crime Commission. Everyone in law enforcement was intrigued by the meetings. Their subject remained a mystery, however, though a lucky break offered a confusing hint when a retired Brooklyn *capo* limped into the Don's house, leaning on a cane in the silver head of which an enterprising FBI agent had secreted a bug; all they discussed, however, was the Rizzolo takeover of some candystore books on Ocean Parkway.

But Taggart noted that old Don Richard was conducting the meetings himself. While Cirillo soldiers and allies were Staten Island bound on the Varrazona Bridge, Crazy Mikey, the supposed acting boss of the family, was scouring the scummier sections of the Bronx, Brooklyn, and Manhattan for narcotics importers. Taggart concluded that Don Richard was resuming command.

He met Reggie atop the Spire and Reggie agreed, warning, 'He'll attack.'

'No. Crazy Mikey would attack. But the old man will be more careful. He's old and he's tired.'

'But what if he's old and vicious?'

Taggart walked away from Reggie and looked down at the city. It was evening, the night still at bay, and a late autumn haze was drifting into the streets. It carried a cold bite and a memory of football practice after school, pumping up for the Thanksgiving Day game.

'No, Reg. First of all, he doesn't know who to attack. Second, he knows damned well that when Tony and the Strikeforce find out he's back in control, they'll come gunning for him.'

'He may simply attack the nearest irritant,' Reggie countered. 'The Rizzolos. Very well, that's what we recruited them for, after all. As for your brother and the law, don't forget that the Strikeforce is merely *one* of Don Richard's concerns. He's the last of the old Dons and he's regained control of the last of the old Mafia empires. And you've attacked it.'

# 18

Helen couldn't get Taggart out of her thoughts. Tax deductible or not, the man had spent a hundred thousand dollars to sit beside her at the musicale. And he didn't even act resentful when she left early, though a deeply disappointed smile had showed how much he liked her. She liked him too, she had to admit; when she tried to talk about the music, he had listened. And despite his blond looks and Manhattan businessman clothes, he was Italian through and through; how had her Uncle Frank described a guy for an Italian girl? Strong where he should be, but a pussy cat inside? She touched the heart-shaped diamond ring she had put on her finger this morning. Taggart was making her a little crazy.

Suddenly, alerted by a familiar clanging noise in the backyard, she ran to the window. Old Mario, her mother's great-uncle, had come to bury the fig tree. Every November, he arrived in his blue suit and heavy shoes with a shovel, a rope and a big iron stake. He drove the stake into the ground with the shovel. Then he tied the rope as high up the trunk as he could reach, and bent the tree to the ground. It seemed a miracle it didn't snap. Tying it to the stake, he lit a cigarette and started digging earth out of the lawn, which he threw on the tree.

She watched proudly. In a city where poor people slept in the street, her family had room for a simple old man who would never fear or want for anything simply because her parents had reared her and her brothers to take responsibility. When they were children the old man's presence had made them feel secure. Now it was his turn. By the same token, when her lawyers finally convinced the government that her father was truly sick, she would bring him home and they would care for him here, in his own bed, until he died.

The old man worked for an hour – unhurried, heedless of the bodyguards passing between the houses. He worked until the fig tree's branches were buried under a blanket of soil which would protect it through the winter. Come spring he would return, unearth the tree and straighten it up. Every summer it bore fruit.

Taggart riddled her thoughts. Could she have it all with him – a guy and her business? He was no ordinary rackets guy out to rip her off. But what about that other thing she had seen – Taggart's hatred? Combined with his strength it could make him a dangerous opponent.

She gave up working and went to the kitchen. Uncle Mario's muddy shoes were by the back door. Her mother was serving him coffee and cheesecake. Helen greeted him in Sicilian, his only language, and he grunted a reply. Her own Sicilian was good, polished when she had gone to Italy to help with the earthquake relief. Thousands of peasants had died in the wreckage of ancient walls. The disaster had marked her with a powerful fear of chaos, and left her with few illusions about the primitive life; in the morning there a woman milked the cow, cleaned the stable, and cooked breakfast before she woke her husband, which Helen saw as proof that women with no better means to serve their families, served them as slaves.

Her mother poured her coffee. 'That guy Chris called again.'

'What did he say?'

'Same. Wants to talk to you. Who is he?'

'A guy–'

'What's wrong with him?'

Helen shrugged.

'He sounds really nice.'

'You'd love him, Mom. He's a builder.'

'A real builder?' she asked sharply. Helen looked at her. Occasionally, her mother dropped her pretences and admitted that they lived in a world where men who called themselves builders needed a front.

'Yeah. In the city.'

'So what's wrong with him?'

'He's great looking. Real nice manners.'

'So what's wrong?' she repeated.

Helen turned away and engaged Mario in Sicilian. The old man was convinced a cold winter was coming. He wanted to wrap the rhododendron with burlap. She shared a smile with her mother; what Uncle Mario really wanted was to turn the front lawn into a zucchini patch. She half listened, thinking of Taggart, fantasizing that maybe at last she had found a way to have a guy without jeopardizing her empire.

The telephone rang. It was the listed line so her mother answered. She thrust the receiver at Helen.

'It's him again.'

'I'm not here.'

'Yes, you are.' She put the receiver on the table in front of Helen and retreated to the coffee pot.

Helen picked it up with a black look for her mother. 'Hello?'

'It's Chris. The guys get you home okay the other night?'

230

'No problem.'

'Hey listen, you want to go the Governor's Ball?'

'The *what?*

'The Governor's Ball. It's a big fundraiser at the Waldorf. They'll have a good band.'

'That sounds a little heavy-duty. You know?'

'Let me talk you into it at lunch. Are you free tomorrow?'

He's asking me for a date, she thought. Like we're two real people. She held the phone, shaking her head, and wondering what did Taggart want.

'Go on,' whispered her mother. 'What do you got to lose?'

'I'll call you tomorrow,' she said, and hung up.

Her mother looked dismayed. 'I don't understand. What's wrong with him?' 'Bad timing.'

'What, do you think God delivers everything perfect the day you want it?' Helen cupped her mother's soft cheek in her palm, an unusual gesture because the mother and daughter rarely touched. 'Mom. Take my word for it. God didn't make this delivery.'

★　★　★

Tony Taglione's expanded joint Strikeforce hit again, raiding a Kennedy airport hotel room where a big Sicilian smuggler was concluding a sale. They seized forty kilos of heroin and millions in cash, arrested the Sicilian and, remarkably, one of Crazy Mikey's crew leaders. Taggart tracked the US Attorney's press conference on the evening news in his office, which Chryl and Victoria had moved to the third floor of the partially completed Spire. Reggie sat beside him, sipping a neat whisky.

'Mikey is desperate. That man shouldn't have been there.'

Taggart flipped the sound from channel to channel as he hunted for shots of his brother. Tony, as usual, dodged the camera, sitting quietly at the press conference, while Arthur Finch did the talking and introduced the agent supervisors who had led the sweep. When he introduced Tony, Tony's expression said he couldn't wait to get back to his office.

'Come on,' said Taggart. 'Sell yourself a little. Hey, hey, look at Tony!' He turned up the sound. A Channel Four minicam crew had cornered him in an elevator and the reporter was asking with concern, 'As Strikeforce chief, are you aware there is a heroin panic in the streets?'

'I'm aware that Methodone and de-tox programmes are serving double the clientele of a year ago. I am aware that school children don't shoot dope that isn't readily available. I am aware that availability is a major factor in drug abuse.'

'What does it mean in terms of the Mafia?'

'They're losing.'

Taggart clapped his hands. 'Go for it, Tony!'

'He certainly has a way with words,' Reggie observed drily.

'Is it true your office is preparing indictments against the leadership of the Cirillo family?'

Taggart looked at Reggie, whose narrow shoulders lifted in an elegant shrug.

'If it were true,' Tony answered, 'I couldn't comment.'

All three stations went to commercials and Taggart turned them off. 'That's news to me.'

'Ultimately,' Reggie said, 'the Cirillos have to be his target. Who's left?'

'I want the Cirillos myself.' He walked around the room, made a drink and a new one for Reggie, and stared out at Park Avenue. The broad median was ablaze in Christmas trees. Reggie was right; of course, the government was after the Cirillos. But they were his, first.

'I had lunch with Helen today. She says you're bugging her.'

Reggie looked appalled. 'How did she happen to get through to you without me knowing?'

'She didn't. I called her.' He had, in fact, called every day for a week before she agreed to lunch. 'Relax. We met alone at a pizza joint on Ocean Boulevard. Just the two of us. She didn't want her brothers to know.'

'Alone?'

'She slipped her bodyguards.'

'Did you notice anyone following her?'

'I didn't see anybody.'

She had waited in her little red car when he got the slices. While they ate, she revved the engine like Mario Andretti. Taggart had made small talk and had got her to smile by mimicking contractors complaining about his brother's office investigating bid-rigging on a Navy job. Then she had fixed him in her serious gaze and asked, 'Why?'

'Why what?'

'Why did you choose me – forget all that bull you said in Ireland.'

'Why not chose you? I've always worked with women in my business. Why shouldn't I work with one in this business?'

'That's not a reason.'

'Okay, I'm enchanted.'

'That's not a good reason.'

'Oh, it's a good reason,' he replied. 'Maybe not a *smart* reason.' And to his surprise she had smiled again and even touched his arm with her long nails . . .

He could still feel them, electric on his skin. 'It wasn't a major date, Reg. But a beginning.'

'You are foolhardy.'

Taggart grinned. 'I'm indulging a normal human desire to –'

On occasion Reggie had scared Taggart, and this was suddenly one of those occasions when he skewered him with eyes that had seen it all and hated much of it. 'Human? You can't be *human* when you take revenge. You can't risk indulging yourself in a lover or – now that we're on it – your temper, as you did with Mikey, or your arrogance, which you're indulging daily.'

'I remember. Be evil to beat evil?'

'The Devil is organized and disciplined, or he wouldn't have lasted as long as he has . . . Chris, haven't you any concept of the danger?'

'My brother already found out about Helen. What's he gonna do? Indict me for falling for a moll?'

'It's not funny. Being near her doubles your risk. You're forgetting why you recruited the Rizzolos.'

'Reg, you're looking tired. You could do with a rest.'

'I'm quite all right.'

'Take a vacation.'

'Vacations are for amateurs.'

Taggart shrugged and closed the subject. 'I'm taking her to the Governor's Ball. It's a fundraiser. Taggart Construction's buying a table.'

'May I ask why, without being told to go on holiday?'

'Because I want to . . . Hey, it's better being in open contact. Things are breaking faster and faster. Nobody has to know I'm giving her orders while we're dancing.'

Still, he had to consider Tony. If Governor Constanzo did go for the presidency and Arthur Finch managed to beat the mayor out for the governorship, Tony, the leader of the Strikeforce and the man who had the Mafia on the run, had a shot at replacing Arthur as US Attorney. There was no pressure Taggart could exert on Tony's behalf – the office had been fiercely nonpolitical for eighty years – but having a brother publicly dating a Mafioso's daughter wouldn't help. So he telephoned Alphonse and asked the old man, 'Will you lease me a grandson?'

*   *   *

'I've done girls plenty times,' the Vegas hitman assured Sal Ponte at their first meeting. 'But never for you guys.'

Don Richard's handsome *consigliere* was too sharp to go on appearances, but he worried nonetheless that the hitman did not appear formidable. Indeed, nothing about Eddie Berger was threatening, except his reputation. Hand to hand, anyone over five-six and one-hundred-and-forty pounds could have knocked him down easily. And were he knocked down, nothing in his

233

demeanour would reveal that Eddie Berger would be back shortly to kill by whatever means available.

Reggie Rand would have spotted him instantly for that peculiar brand of crazy who had mastered the details of day-to-day life – a lunatic who knew that cops never noticed a little guy pushing a broom – and therefore roamed at will. Abandoned at age three in an Arizona diner, raised as a ward of the state, Eddie Berger had learned early that a child who appeared to obey rules was rewarded. Neatly lettered book reports handed in on time returned praise and affection from teachers, guards and foster-parents; his school mates were less delighted, but unlike the adults, children sensed that Eddie Berger was dangerous.

By nineteen, the ordinary looking little man was an accomplished serial killer, well on his way to his third dozen random murders. Still a rule-follower, neat, clean, well-mannered, he wandered the country, working hard at whatever menial job he drifted into. He had a car, kept up the payments, and neither drank nor smoked. Nothing stood between him and killing people for the rest of a long life. When he learned he could get paid for it, he had turned pro and had, Ponte knew, zapped some very tough people.

'They made me,' he admitted to *Consigliere* Ponte at their second meeting.

'Who made you?'

'Some guy she met by the water. Maybe they heard I'm around, but they don't know why.'

Ponte passed a direct order from Don Richard. 'Do it tomorrow night.'

'Don't take this the wrong way, but I want my fee doubled.'

Ponte's dark face closed up, and his eyes went blank. To those who knew him the look meant danger.

Berger didn't know him and didn't care. 'The reason is,' he explained, 'I'm going to have to drop out after. The word'll get back to her brothers.'

'Don't worry about her brothers.'

'Nobody fools the street. Double or nothing.'

Ponte gave in. It was smarter to pay than to explain that for Helen Rizzolo's brothers to avenge her death they would have to do it from their own graves.

# 19

'Nice table,' said Helen.

'At two grand a plate it ought to be,' Uncle Vinnie said proudly. 'Chris's father was the same way. Nothing was ever too much for Costanzo, even when he was just starting in Congress.'

Taggart's party was sitting at the table next to the dance floor, directly across from Peter Duchin's orchestra. On their right was the mayor's entourage, to the left Governor Costanzo, whose popularity with New York's Italian-Americans had filled the Waldorf's Grand Ballroom to capacity. Television cameras, quiescent while the faithful ate, were stationed against the back wall. Strategically sprinkled among the heavy contributors were former New York mayors and a governor, to whom the passage of time had affixed, like moss, the affection reserved for bold men unlikely to cause any more trouble.

The present mayor was working the room in the hopes Costanzo's presidential ambitions opened up the governor's mansion. He deadpanned that Taggart's Spire was four storeys higher than zoning allowed. And when the governor stepped by for a word about Taggart's stadium proposal, and a look at the women, the mayor bounded back.

'I could build a high school with the taxes he's saving on the Spire.'

Governor Costanzo, who maintained privately that privilege was Manhattan's hottest industry, looked like he wished a *New Yorker* friend wasn't hovering.

'Schools?' Taggart threw his long arms around the politicians. 'I'm already providing jobs, business opportunities, and space for tax-paying tenants. Can't you guys do *anything*!'

He grinned at Helen, who smiled back, and winked at his beaming publicist, who was already rising for a private chat with the lady from the *New Yorker*. He was having a ball. The wine was Italian and Peter Duchin was provoking hundreds to dance between courses. But the best part was Helen Rizzolo, whose solemn eyes had widened appreciably when he had introduced her to the governor and the mayor. She sat at Taggart's left in a red dress, with bare shoulders and diamonds, and had made, even in the incandescent presence of Victoria and Chryl, an impression. Alphonse's accommodating grandson – Taggart's beard – had apparently fallen in love during the limousine trip. Strait-laced Henry Bunker looked so intrigued that his wife started holding his hand.

Uncle Vinnie loved her, but what man wouldn't? Interestingly, so did Aunt Marie, who wasn't fooled by the beard. That Taggart and Tony weren't married was not her fault. For ten years, since Mike Taglione had been killed, she had herded towards them legions of every conceivable variety of Italian girl that Queens and Brooklyn had to offer: old-fashioned family-bred Italian girls; rich Italian girls; 'eighties-slick Italian girls; glossy, college-educated Italian girls with their provocative blend of femininity and iron will. As she had no idea that Helen's family was connected, to her eye Helen was all the wonderful sorts of Italian girls rolled up in one classy little package that might persuade her bachelor nephew to finally make a family.

Chryl and Victoria were rampantly curious; they were thus far behaving themselves, Taggart noted, though repeatedly rapping shoulders and bobbing heads for swift and secret thoughts. Finally, Victoria, who was sitting on his right, beckoned him closer and announced quietly, 'Maybe this isn't one of your bimbos.'

'Do you approve?'

She leaned across her escort – a bearded critic from an architectural magazine who routinely savaged Taggart's buildings and seemed disappointed that the brash builder hadn't broken a champagne bottle over his head – and said to Chryl, 'He's serious.'

Chryl asked him to dance. In his arms she said, 'In our opinion, you have fallen in love, you bastard.'

'You think so?' he asked seriously. If they thought so, it was true. They were in every way his best friends. Only Reggie knew him better. 'She makes me a little crazy.'

'That's a good sign . . . We'll miss you. We'll miss you a lot.'

'I'll be around.'

'Not like that, you won't. A woman like her would cut your heart out for messing around.'

Taggart kissed her. 'Who's telling who to be careful?'

'Not us, kiddo. She 'll know who to blame.' She kissed his cheek, clung to him a moment, and led him off the dance floor. 'Come on, back to your party.'

When Helen excused herself to go to the ladies room, Chryl and Victoria arose smiling to join her and Henry Bunker remarked, 'Nothing they talk about can possibly be to your advantage.'

Taggart excused himself. In the lobby he found a telephone booth, closed the door, and dialled a number Reggie had obtained from a NYREX supervisor. 'Let me speak to Crazy Mikey.'

'Who is this? How the fuck did you get this number?'

'I bought it. A thousand bucks a digit. I already knew your area code. Put Mikey on.'

A hand covered the receiver. Then Mikey came on.

'It's your man from the boat, Mikey.'

There was silence.

'I want to remind you we've got a payment coming due.'

'Hey man, you're pushing the wrong guy. When I got it, you'll get paid.'

'That's not good enough. I'm not selling you another ounce until you pay up.'

'How the fuck am I supposed to earn the money with nothing to sell?'

'That's your problem.'

'Oh yeah. What are you going to do about it?'

'Mikey, you've been a collector. Like the song says, "you can run, but you can't hide". Do I have to send somebody to break your legs?'

'Who the fuck do you think you're talking to?'

Taggart hung up, combed his hair in the men's room, and strolled back to his table. Helen, Victoria and Chryl returned, too. Helen, who had directed most of her attention towards Alphonse's nephew and Aunt Marie, put her hand on his arm, jolting him as she had a week ago in the car, and said with a private smile only he could fully appreciate, 'Your friends made me an offer I couldn't refuse.'

'What's that?'

'They're going to design me a club.'

'You're kidding!'

'You told them I have clubs. They said they've always wanted to do one. We made a deal.'

Victoria, Taggart realized belatedly, had assumed the business look she wore when the design house of Matthews and Chamberlain negotiated a contract.

'Where?' he asked her.

'The lobby of the Taggart Spire.'

'My lobby? But it's an office building lobby.'

'Can you imagine a ten-storey-high dance club? Can you imagine the sound – the *lights* in that incredible space? Ten storeys of music? It's going to be drop-dead fantastic. Hey, Helen, you want to call it that? Drop Dead Fantastic? Maybe just Drop Dead.'

'No.'

'How about Death,' said Victoria. 'That would be nice. Death. I like that.'

Helen said 'No' again, and Victoria said, 'You're right, it's a downer.'

Taggart repeated, 'It's an office building.'

'Not at night. Chryl's got this great idea. Fly the lights and mirrors like stage sets. At night, lower them for the club. In the morning, winch them up out of sight.' Her shapely hand rose airily to the upper tiers.

'Do you know what that will cost, even if you can get it past the city?'

'You can afford it.'

'Me?'

'It's your building.'

'What if I don't want a disco in my lobby?'

Victoria reached over and patted Helen's hand. 'Don't worry, dear. We'll go to Donald Trump.'

'Okay, okay,' Taggart said. 'I'll look into it.'

Victoria showed her teeth. 'Go bounce it off the mayor. Now.'

On his return he saw the party was about to go to hell as the TV crews turned on their lights and eight hundred people who had been having a good time dancing started waving to neighbours stuck home in their rec rooms. Taggart ploughed through the madness, demanded Helen's coat check from Alphonse's vastly disappointed grandson, and grabbed her hand. 'Let's get out of here.'

'What about my date?'

'He's got classes in the morning. Come on, I want to show you something.' Taggart helped her into her black mink, and through the lobby. A nod to one of the many bodyguards Reggie had insisted on secreting about the hotel had produced his white Rolls at the canopy. The clock on the Helmsey Building read one o'clock. Park Avenue was near empty, as were the side streets, but for a sprinkling of taxis and limousines that converged on the Waldorf.

The Spire's Park Avenue and downtown faces were decorated with five-storey trees of hanging work lights, topped by Stars of David to honour Chanukah. 'Next year, when we're occupied, we'll control the lights on a computer to make patterns with the windows – trees at Christmas; hearts on Valentine's Day; rabbits at Easter.'

'What if someone wants to work late in a blacked-out office?'

'He'd better bring a flashlight. It's in his lease.'

The car stopped in front of the construction gate. 'Would you like to see my apartment?'

'The building isn't done.'

Taggart pointed up, out the back window. A solitary gold light shone at the top of the dark tower. 'I finished my place first.'

Helen took his hand in both of hers. He felt her warmth through her kid gloves. 'Could we do something first?'

'Sure. What?'

'Could we look at the Christmas windows?'

'Now? I don't know if they're going; it's after midnight.'

'They are,' she said eagerly. 'My father used to take me late at night; just the two of us. Every Christmas we saw Saks, Lord and Taylor, and Altman's. Sometimes, if it was late enough, we'd be the only people there. Could we?'

'Sure.'

The big car headed west, trailed by an old cab, which Taggart didn't notice. When the Rolls pulled to the kerb in front of Saks, the cab stopped two blocks back. Station wagons were parked in front of the department store; couples were leading small children along the sidewalk. 'Just like we used to,' said Helen.

Saks had done a 'Thirties New York Christmas scene. The first window showed a sleek man and woman going off to a party, bidding goodnight to nanny-tended children in pyjamas; outside the elaborate model house a min-iature Dusenberg waited at the kerb.

'The 'Thirties,' Helen smiled. 'My grandfather was walking the streets. Repeal played hell with the liquor business.'

'Mine was a bricklayer. He got laid off when they finished the Empire State Building.'

She glanced up at him. 'Why do you keep asking me out?'

'Honestly?'

'If you can.'

'I kind of flipped for you.'

'Mr Taggart, I have microphones in my bars to keep my employees from dealing dope. The mikes pick up the customers' conversations, too. I hear that line thirty times a night.'

'It's guys hoping you're listening.'

She laughed, thinking that his compliments always sounded like he meant them. They moved to the next window where the sleek couple was now dancing at the Grand Ball. 'Seriously, why? What's going on with you?'

'Just like I told you.'

'We are in different worlds, man. I met people tonight who if they knew who I was would spit on me.'

'Not in front of me they wouldn't,' Taggart promised in a hard, low voice and Helen saw for a second that capacity for hatred again. It was never far from the surface, yet neither, she had to admit, were his exuberant warmth and the tenderness he radiated towards her. Both made her wary. She doubted he would ever hurt her, but he might someday make her hurt herself.

She said, 'I don't know what's going on. I don't know where you are. And I don't know where you and your scam come together.'

'Do you remember the first time we met?'

239

She glanced around but no one was near. 'Me tied to a chair and you strutting around in a mask?'

'No. In the restaurant.'

'What restaurant?'

'Abatelli's on Woodhaven Boulevard? I saw you on a summer night with your family about ten years ago.'

'My "bethrothal",' she acknowledged with an ironic smile. She hesitated – for she had good reason not to discuss that night further – but by now she cared enough about him to be as straight as possible and wanted to speak the truth in her heart. 'I was wondering when you would mention it.'

'You remember?'

'Of course. You stared at me all night. You gave me a really nice smile. I wondered who you were.'

'You blew me away. I couldn't get you out of my head.'

Helen smiled. Honesty's 'reward' had paid off quickly; Chris's happy expression proved he really meant he liked her, and that he was courting her for more than his scam. She felt like she had for a brief second last spring at Uncle Frank's ball game, wondering if a special door could be opened that she thought forever closed. But the pitcher, whatever his name was, was a guy in that other world, whereas Chris and she had much in common.

'What was going on with you?' she asked. 'What were you doing there?'

'Eating, until I got in an argument with Don Richard Cirillo. Remember?'

'I remember you went out with him. He came back alone.'

Taggart's expression greyed; he looked away a moment, touched the scar on his mouth. Then looked back at her, the grey look erased by one of his easy grins. 'You got stoned in the ladies room.'

Helen smiled. 'No. I got stoned before I came. I got stoned *again* in the bathroom.'

'I guessed they were giving you away.'

'You guessed right.'

'I didn't think that happened anymore.'

'My parents had their reasons.'

'Later, I heard that Cirillo was brokering peace between your family and the Confortis.'

'It was much more complicated than that. My parents would not have "sold" me for peace, I can assure you. They're real Italian-Italian in some ways, but they're not low class.'

'Then why'd they do it?'

Helen shrugged, looked around the sidewalk, stared at a little girl holding her father's hand. 'Marrying me off killed a lot of birds with one stone. I was kind of wild. They knew I'd be nothing but trouble if they kept me home. I was nowhere in school. I was *ready,* you know? Sixteen and everything looked better outside the house.'

'You seemed younger.'

'I was hell on wheels. I had thirty-year-old guys calling me up.' She laughed easily and Taggart decided there was no question he loved her. 'My brothers were spending half their time threatening my boyfriends.'

'What happened?'

'Oh, Christ! What didn't happen? First of all, the whole thing was a Cirillo trick, which I found out later. Second, the poor kid I married was really messed up.'

She moved to the next window and Taggart followed. Here the sleek couple were bidding their host and hostess goodnight, maids were ladling eggnog for the diehards, and outside it was snowing and the Dusenberg had miraculously been transformed into a horsedrawn sleigh.

'My husband was beautiful. A really good person. But he couldn't hack his father, his whole family, all the pressuring. He didn't want the rackets. So he was a doper. Just like with real kids when the parents try to make them be a doctor, so they drop out? I didn't know it at first. I smoked and did a little of this and that, so I didn't think it was any different for him. But it was.' She pushed her hair from her face and shook her head violently. 'The trouble with being married to a druggie is it's so lonely. He was always telling me he loved me, and he did, but three-quarters of the time he was flying.'

'You didn't fly with him?'

'I tried. But I'm not a druggie. I get bored if I get stoned more than a weekend. Two days and I want my head back. So I'd get straight and he was still flying. I was alone 'til I made a friend.'

She moved again and Taggart followed. The sleek couple were tearing across Central Park in the sleigh. Helen looked at Taggart and her eyes glistened. 'You know so much about me? You know who the friend was, don't you?'

Taggart shook his head.

'Come on, you must know.'

'I guess somebody in the casino.'

'Sure. Where else would I meet somebody in Vegas. Guess who?'

'Somebody you fell in love with?'

'Yeah.'

'Then I'll guess his father, the owner.'

'Jackpot. You knew it was my father-in-law -1 wish you wouldn't lie to me. I've been straight, like with nobody I ever talked to. I want you should be straight with me.'

241

'I'm sorry,' he said, and Helen thrilled to his chagrined smile. 'I'm out of practice. We'll work on it.'

'Thanks. That's nice. That's real nice . . . Did you know I got pregnant with him?'

'No.'

She looked up at him sharply, nodded to herself. 'No, no one did. I didn't know what to do. Then I figured, okay, I'll pretend it's my husband's. All I'd have to do was get him off the dope long enough to get it up.'

'Logical,' Taggart replied lightly, finding it hard to handle how harsh she sounded.

'The baby's grandfather would have really been his father. And the baby's father would really have been his brother. Family, right?'

'You make it sound easy.'

'It could have been. Only my father-in-law lover got shot by the god-damned Cirillos.'

She went to the last window, and when a ten-year-old girl looked up at her, she lightly touched her hair. The girl moved on. Taggart joined Helen again. The couple were on their knees on their drawing room carpet, hastily wrapping toys. Champagne was in a bucket and the man was holding the knot while the woman tied the bow. They looked about to kiss.

'So I went home and I told my parents you owe me! You get me an annulment and an abortion. And they did. I don't know what it cost, but they got the marriage annulled. I had my abortion. I made them let me go to college . . . That was funny, Sarah Lawrence College. You should have seen it. This little Italian girl in perfect makeup with hair washed every day, while the real girls are dressing down to look like our kitchen help . . . They taught me about music. They gave me a "don", this woman who played the violin like an angel, and for one whole semester I studied an Italian composer I had never heard of named Corelli. Then your fucking brother sent my father to jail, and I had to come home to help Eddie and Frank run the business ... '

Taggart wished he had not chosen her family to be his instrument of revenge. 'You keep calling other people real. You're real.'

'Not like them. They can make all the mistakes they want. In the rackets, one mistake and you're caught. But who can live a perfect life? . . . Why were you fighting with Don Richard?'

She had caught him off balance. 'I thought he killed my father.'

'Did he?'

Taggart shook his head. 'Somebody got mad and flew off the handle. It took me awhile to see it that way.'

She touched his throat. 'Your pulse is pounding like you're going to explode.'

Taggart escaped the vital lie by kissing her mouth.

She kissed him back, her lips moulding softly to his; he felt her fingers on the back of his head, exploring his hair and drawing him harder against her mouth. Their tongues met, entwining curiously like cats on first acquaintance. She broke away with a satisfied smile.

'Hey. Merry Christmas.'

Taggart felt like he would float across Fifth Avenue if she weren't holding his hand. 'Why don't we go some place and exchange presents or something?'

She was still holding his hand. She probed his face, her violet eyes dark with wonderment. 'I really don't know.'

'Want to see my new apartment?'

She shrugged, as if so sure of herself in most things, Taggart thought, that being unsure about him didn't matter. She almost seemed to revel in the luxury of not deciding. 'Why?' she marvelled, 'Why did I tell you all that?'

'You figured I knew it anyhow.'

She gave him a lopsided smile. 'God, would my mother love you. A nice, rich Italian boy not in the rackets.'

'Half.'

She arose on tiptoes and whispered harshly and bitterly, 'Whose brother put my father in the slammer and who's moving in on the Mafia? Just wonderful!'

'Leave out the last part.'

'Chris, you're crazy.'

'Want to go play?'

'I'll look.'

'Come on.'

She leaned against the door on her side of the car as if debating whether to jump out. Then, to his delight, she moved closer and laid her head on his shoulder. Her hair was shiny and lightly perfumed; when he kissed it it felt like dense folds of silk. Taggart sat back, happy to watch the city slide by the bronzed windows. He hadn't felt like this since – but there was no since. He had never felt like this in his life.

The Rolls drew up to the Spire. A timid-looking little guy in a ragged army jacket was huddled by the construction fence. As Taggart and Helen got out of the car, he started towards them with his hands in his pockets. 'Sir, you got change for coffee, sir?'

The building guard hurried from the gate, saluting. 'Good evening, Mr Taggart.'

'Evening, Johnny. They get my elevator working again?'

'Yes, sir.'

The little guy, backing warily from the guard and Taggart's chauffeur, was

243

shivering, so Taggart slid a pair of C notes out of his money clip. 'Cold,' he said, his father's rough voice echoing in his head. 'Get yourself a coat.'

Helen followed him into the chaos of the lobby. The cement floor and steel supports were lit by bare bulbs; cables and scaffolds cast shadow webs on the poured concrete walls and the lofty ceiling. 'Your club, madame.'

'Can Victoria and Chryl really do it?'

'Given a sufficiently blank cheque, they could arrange tasteful sunsets in the east.'

'Don't worry about the money. You'll make a fortune.'

'Oh yeah?'

'When John Gere's PR man pays a hundred and fifty bucks cash for a bottle in the champagne room, a hundred and twenty of that is cash in your pocket.'

'Right this way, partner.'

She hesitated again. 'You really like them, don't you?'

'We're real friends.'

'More than friends?'

'We've become family. I met them right after my father died. I gave them away at their weddings. When they got tired of the bozos, I provided shark divorce lawyers. Sometimes they're like mothers to me and sometimes I'm like a father to them.'

'They showed me pictures. Victoria's little girl looks a lot like you.'

'That's Annie. Tony says she looks exactly like our mother.'

'Do you –'

'The kids carry the names of rich, old Wasp families. There isn't a door in America that will be closed to them. And until then, they've all got Uncle Chris whenever Mummy needs a man around the house.'

'Do you still get it on with them?'

'Sometimes.'

'Both of them?'

'Chryl and Victoria are a couple. It's both or neither, which was one of the problems in their marriages.'

'It's not something I can get with, but they seem very happy.'

'They're hot in their field, they're getting rich by their own hand, and the jerks they married gave them beautiful children. Damned right they're happy.' 'Will you ever have your own children?'

'Funny you should ask. Shall we go up?'

The elevator shaft was still an open frame, but the car itself was finished in lacquer and chrome. In the comers were crystal flower vases filled with white freesias which perfumed the air, a silver umbrella stand, and a bottle of Moet chilling in a silver bucket.

'Won't they steal this stuff?'

'Private car, straight to the owner's suite. Champagne?' Taggart removed the foil, gripped the cork, twisted the bottle, and filled two tulip glasses. 'Cheers.'

'*Per cent' anni.*'

She smiled at the bubbles boiling from the hollow stem as the elevator started to ascend . . . 'Chris, how rich are you?'

'Never quite as rich as I look, but doing pretty good the last couple of years. And thanks to a maniacally confused city government, I get enough tax credits to keep most of it . . . Swallow if your ears hurt.'

She said in deep seriousness, 'What are you doing it for?'

'What do you do what you do for?'

'I'm protecting my family.'

'Me, too.'

'I find that hard to believe.'

Let this tiger go? Taggart thought. Get out somehow, take Helen and get out. And spend the rest of his life remembering a broken promise? Not while Mike Taglione's killers ruled New York. But afterwards? He shivered, unable to complete the thought, and was saved from further unsettling introspection by the doors opening. He took Helen's hand, which she slipped naturally into his, and led her into the foyer. The doors hissed shut behind them. The air smelled of fresh paint, brand new lacquer, and roses.

'You live well,' she said, and he felt obliged to explain.

'It didn't really cost anything because it's worth a fortune in free advertising. My publicist will get articles about the apartment published in all the magazines. Everybody will hear about the building being the newest and most incredible. That makes it a hot building. Which means I sell an eight-hundred thousand dollar condo for a million-two and promise the owner he'll be able to sell it for a million-five next year because the building has my name on it.'

'I'm in the wrong business.'

'Well, if you ever want to go straight.' He smiled.

'This is yours, not mine.'

She was impressed, he realized, yet not impressed, as if trendy opulence was of the world *stranieri,* too far from her own to have a lure. He showed her the downstairs bedrooms, the kitchen, dining room, and library on the lower levels. On the top floor, down a long hall, appeared a room with glass walls. As they neared it, views of the night leapt from the city.

'Look at the ceiling,' he said, leading her inside.

And for the second time – the first being six months ago when he removed his mask on the Irish cliffs – he astonished her. She looked up; twenty feet overhead the stars shimmered in the glass ceiling. She circled, staring up at them. Her gaze descended through the glass walls and finally to the floor.

She screamed and Taggart caught her in his arm. *'Easy.* I've got you.'

She brought a hand to her chest, gasping, 'Oh, my God!'

They were standing on a glass floor, a thousand feet above Manhattan. The city sprang at them, like a monster rising from the dark with a million gleaming teeth.

'Feel my heart,' she laughed. 'I thought we were falling. Oh, this is fantastic!'

Taggart leaned against a column – the same column from which he had dangled Jack Warner last Spring – and watched Helen prowl the room. It occurred to him that all this stuff was suddenly fun in ways he had never been inclined to notice before. She drifted among the furniture islands, stroking fabrics and polished surfaces, drinking in the views, and looking down repeatedly. At one point she sank into a chair, leaned over the arm, and stared through the floor.

'It still makes me shiver.'

'I know. It took me a week to make my legs behave.'

She prowled again until, near the outer wall, she stopped in a space between two groupings. 'What are these lines?' she asked, pointing at evenly spaced wires in the floor, so thin as to be almost invisible.

Taggart started towards her. 'Touch it.'

She knelt, her gown puddling around her, and felt the glass. 'It's warm.'

'Heaters.'

She stared at the building tops between her spread fingers and suddenly glanced at him with a grin. 'Oh, wow! I just got this incredible idea.'

'I was hoping you would.'

'Have you done it?' she asked.

'Not yet.'

'Truth?'

Taggart sat on the floor beside her. 'Truth. You're my first guest. The place was finished today. Only problem is the floor's hard as a rock. I drove my engineers crazy trying to come up with a soft floor, but everything they tried was cloudy.'

'Will anyone see us?'

'That's up to you.' Taggart handed her a remote control switch. She toyed with the dimmer, smiling, and lowered the lights until the room went black.

'It's like we're floating in the sky,' she breathed.

Above, below, and around them were black night, stars, and lights. Taggart's eyes adjusted and her face took form in the glow from the city. He kissed the soft skin on her shoulder. She moved against him, and he traced the strap of her gown with his lips and tongued her breasts.

'Chris? . . . What do you want of me?'

'How about your body for ten years? Then we'll talk.'

'Don't joke. We're in business.'

Instinctively, though there couldn't possibly be a bug in range, she had whispered the last in his ear. Taggart replied in kind. 'The fact that we're beating the Mafia only makes it better.'

'Beating? You sound like a cop.'

'Making it ours,' he amended, alert to the razors in her voice. *'Look!'* He swept his hand across the floor, as if caressing the lights below. 'We're like barbarians, you and me, galloping our horses over a rise – there's the city, waiting to be taken. It's ours because we want it.'

'You're drunk,' she said unsteadily.

He brought his mouth to hers again, kissed her deeply, and when he stopped they were both shaking. 'Drunks can't kiss. Am I drunk?'

Helen pulled away and sat up. 'You're scaring the hell out of me.'

'You've scared the hell out of me since the day I first saw you.'

'Chris, you can't believe that. It was ten years ago. I was sixteen.'

'I make things real by wanting them.'

'You're crazy.'

'Since my father was killed, I haven't done a thing that people didn't say was crazy. But if I'm crazy, then we're floating here with no floor under us. There's no Taggart Spire, just air over some old wreck of a building I had to knock down to build this one. So if I'm crazy I don't know how we got up here, but we're falling fast.'

She looked at the prize sparkling beneath them. 'Hold me.'

'I can't. We're falling.'

'I have a parachute.' In a swift, graceful motion, she unzipped her gown, slid out of it, and raised it over her head.

Taggart stared. The city glow penetrated the floor and spread soft light on her breasts, which were small, round, and tipped with dusky nipples. Her legs unfolding beside him, were long, slim and shapely. She wore stockings, a garter belt through which her strong thighs flashed like neon, and lace panties taut about her hips. She looked back, a little defiant, a little proud.

'You're not real. We're still falling.'

They came together gently at first, almost tentatively, as Taggart, awkwardly aware of his size, held himself in check because he was afraid to crush her in his excitement. Then dream and reality merged and in the heat of reality, the dream evaporated. She was suddenly and totally three-dimensional, her mouth sure, her breasts soft and warm, her legs strong, engulfing.

\*   \*   \*

Eddie Berger wore black under the army jacket, which he jettisoned in a subcellar – black high-top sneakers, black socks, black sweatsuit, black watch cap, and black makeup base on his face. Nearly invisible in the shadows of the concrete stairs, but for the narrow whites of his slitted eyes, and silent on rubber soles, he climbed ninety-six flights to the top of the Taggart Spire. He had jogged thirty miles a week for jobs like this, and he consequently scaled the last flight breathing lightly.

The top level was a plank floor, apparently destined to become the roof, and there he waited, still as a wall, while his eyes adjusted to the dark. Gradually, he became aware of the construction derricks looming overhead and a glow on the south side of the building. When his eyes could distinguish the girders scattered about, he moved silently among them, heading for the glow. At the edge of the plank floor he found the top of the glass cube jutting from the side of the building, Taggart's cantilevered living room.

It puzzled him at first; he knew they'd come up here, but he hadn't realized that the incomplete building was habitable. Expecting to find Helen Rizzolo holding hands with her playboy boyfriend on the roof, he had discovered instead a luxurious apartment floating in the sky. It took a moment to realize he was looking down at them through a glass roof. Just then the lights dimmed and went out and the glow disappeared. He was left staring at the dark.

Again he waited until his eyes adjusted. Finally, he saw the stars reflected in black glass, like lights on a river. Moving cautiously, careful not to make a sound, he worked his way to the edge of the glass and looked down.

His gut wrenched and he felt his balance going. Beneath the glass, where he least expected it, was the city. He gradually figured out what he was looking at: a cube-shaped room, perhaps thirty feet square, with a glass roof, three glass sides, and a glass floor. He could make out dark clumps of furniture here and there. In the centre was movement. As his eyes grew accustomed to the dark, he saw them in silhouette over the city lights, Helen Rizzolo and the playboy-builder making love on the floor.

Eddie Berger lowered himself to the glass, found it strong, and inched across it. They were little more than outlines in motion, but there was something profoundly erotic about the way they floated in the sky, twenty feet under his perch, as if they and he were the last three people in the world. He watched for a long time, fascinated by the slowness of their movements and the balletic exchanges of position, as if they were indeed floating, adrift in a warm, bouyant liquid. He wished he could hear them, and he was surprised how much he loved them.

Light from Park Avenue below and the heavens above revealed tantalizing glimpses – her thighs flickering as she rolled over, his golden hair, her teeth suddenly agleam in passion, as if a single star were lighting her gasping mouth. Suddenly, they went rigid. He thought they had seen him. A scream pierced the thick glass, another, a long silence, then laughter, and they collapsed, spilling over each other.

He laid his face on the cold glass roof and caught his own breath. But he had watched too long and now discovered to his horror that in his own excitement he had edged out until he was almost on top of them. When they looked up at the stars, as surely they would in such a room, they would see his silhouette, as he had seen theirs.

He froze, afraid to breathe, waiting in terrible anticipation for them to gaze upward and open their eyes. He grew cold. He prayed they'd get up and find a drink or something. But they stayed where they were. They moved closer; slowly they touched and merged, blended, and embraced. Eddie Berger smiled again, his fear evaporating; he wished he could join them. And in a way, he thought, as he slithered off the glass, he would.

He scouted his prospects on the roof. Steel beams were stacked helter-skelter and his mind conjured a vivid image of one of those twenty-foot, multi-ton monsters falling through Taggart's glass roof, through the room, and through the floor – racing their bodies to the street.

The steel-raising derricks projected dark, lopsided V's against the sky. He approached the nearest derrick, which was poised temptingly close to Taggart's apartment. It was close enough to hook around a steel beam, lift the I-beam over the edge, and drop it through Christopher Taggart's glass house. But he had no partner to run the machinery on the ground, for the operating cable that raised and lowered the boom and its hook, stretched the full height of the building and played off a drum at the bottom of the hole. He would have to improvise.

The vast boom was slanting east and Taggart's living room was to the south. A huge iron bullwheel circled the base of the derrick. Eddie Berger gripped the bullwheel, heaved his weight against it, and felt the finely balanced derrick begin to turn. There were rope falls attached to assist turning a heavy load, but the unburdened boom moved easily despite its many tons of weight.

He looked up. The shadowy form of the slanting boom was swinging past the stars. It was much longer than the distance between the foot of the derrick and Taggart's apartment. He kept turning the bullwheel until the boom was leaning over the glass roof.

Then he went to the stairs to search for some sort of cable cutter. Three floors down, he broke into a well-stocked tool shed and found a hacksaw. The blade looked pretty ground up, so he hunted some more until he found a new carbide blade still in its wrapper.

★      ★      ★

249

Somewhere in the silence, Taggart felt a grinding when Eddie Berger turned the bullwheel, less sound than feeling, and he did not consciously connect it with the derrick on the roof. He strained a moment, half-heartedly trying to make sense of it; then Helen touched him and the impression dissolved like perfume on a breeze.

'It's so quiet,' she whispered. 'I can hear our hearts.'

Street noise did not penetrate the thick, air-locked glass. Nor did they hear the ordinarily half-noticed building sounds because the apartment was serviced by temporary mains; the unfinished Spire was deathly still without the normal flow of air, gas, electricity and water circulating through its ducts, lines, pipes and wires.

Memory of the intrusion returned, and with it Taggart's vague feeling of disquiet. They were side by side now, touching fingers, returning slowly from far away. He raised his head and listened hard. But by then Eddie Berger had crept down to the tool shed, and Taggart heard only Helen's laboured breathing. He lay back on the warm floor and lifted her onto him. She whispered, 'Beautiful, beautiful,' and then, with a luxurious smile in her voice, 'Oh, look at us!'

Like magic, the barely perceptible light reflected their bodies in the nearby glass wall. Overhead their images glowed in the ceiling; Helen crouched among the stars. The shadow of a derrick nodded over her like a curious dragon.

*    *    *

The cable which supported the derrick boom was five-eighths braided wire. Shortly after Eddie Berger started sawing, it occured to him he had better stand clear in case the cable end whipped around when it snapped. Since the boom probably weighed five tons, all hell would break loose when he cut the final cable strands and the boom fell into Taggart's apartment. So he stood way back from the shaft through which the cable travelled up the mast and sawed at the end of his reach with short, jerky strokes. He had no real knowledge of the forces involved, but some instinct, keyed perhaps by enormous tension in the cable, made him raise his other hand to protect his face.

It was slow work. He stopped repeatedly to listen in case they heard the noise, but the fresh blade cut smoothly and made a lot less noise than sawing wood. After ten minutes of the difficult, extended strokes, he felt the cut with his fingers and slashed his thumb on the jagged shavings. He cursed and sucked the blood. Despite the cold he was perspiring, and the cut felt as if he hadn't done more than nick the outer strands.

What if the girl had left after all this time? He ran to the edge and looked down on the glass roof. They were still on the floor, still at it, he thought irritably. His thumb hurt and their endless pleasure was making him angry. There was something unfair about them enjoying themselves while he was stuck out in the cold. He hurried back to the cable with new resolve, stepped a little closer, still guarding his face, and sawed with all his might.

Suddenly the tension felt different. He could feel the cable getting ready to part. He sawed harder, watching the top of the boom so he'd know to get out of the way the second it moved.

He heard a rifle-shot bang. The hacksaw blew out of his hand. The strands unfurled faster than the eye. Spinning like a gigantic Cuisinart blade, they lopped off the hand he had raised to protect his face and swiftly ground his head and shoulders into a fine, red mist.

The great boom crashed towards the roof, pivoting from the foot of the mast and gathering speed as it fell.

★　　★　　★

They were sitting face to face, Helen with her knees tucked up to her chin, Taggart holding her within his crossed legs and laughing. 'What are you laughing about?' Helen demanded.

'I'm so damned happy, my bones feel happy.'

'I never knew a guy who laughed.'

'Hey, you know what I'm thinking? You want to sell everything we got, buy a castle in Europe? Make love 'til –'

She touched his mouth and murmured languidly, 'You mean that, don't you? You mean, get out.'

Taggart kissed her fingers. 'Maybe we should talk when this is over.'

'Over?'

'*What's that!*'

The loud bang sounded like a gunshot. Taggart shoved her towards the furniture. She sprawled backwards and screamed. An enormous shadow slashed across the stars and filled the sky. Taggart looked up and knew too late the meaning of the warnings he had ignored – the grinding he had felt and the sight of the derrick leaning where it hadn't been before.

A seventy-foot construction boom was plummeting down on the glass cube. The warnings might have gained him a vital fraction of a second. But his mind screamed empty questions: how had the derrick moved? why was it falling?

He dragged Helen across the cantilevered room, towards the distant shelter of the hallway in the main building. The boom hit the outer wall first, thundering against the steel header. For an instant it was suspended between the Spire's roof and the outer wall of the glass cube. Then, screeching as welds tore and rivets sheered, the boom buckled and collapsed inward, shattering the ceiling.

251

Broken glass rained down around them. The collapsing boom plummeted like a spear and smashed the floor. Chairs, couches, and scattered clothing dropped into the night. Taggart and Helen Rizzolo were scrambling a few feet short of the safety of the entrance hall when the heater wires blew with a white flash. And then, like skaters falling through thin ice, they saw the glass floor disappear beneath their feet.

# 20

Taggart pitched forward, pulling Helen with one hand and reaching towards the lighted hall with the other. She tried to jump, but the floor separated from the side of the building and fell away, growing small and glinting as it tumbled on its thousand-foot journey to the street. The hall appeared to rise as they fell. The cold city roared below.

Lengths of electrical cables, ripped from the falling glass, hung from the subfloor. Taggart clutched one and dangled from it as sections of broken glass hurtled past like guillotines, clanging against the side of the building and drifting into the dark.

They caught the hardwood floor with flailing hands. Taggart got his fingers around the door jamb, rammed his other hand between Helen's legs, and heaved her up onto the floor. He lost his grip and felt himself falling backward, flailing in the dark for the cable. But she was on him in an instant, grabbing his arm with both hands even as his far greater weight started to drag her off.

Kicking the side of the building, he used his other hand to pull himself up to the solid floor beside her. They lay gasping for breath and staring in disbelief at the tangled steel draped over the naked headers of the living room.

'You okay?'

'I don't know.'

'Are you cut?'

'I don't know.'

Taggart felt her body in the near dark. They were naked, their clothes scattered to the wind. She started.

'Hurt?'

'No,' she laughed, half in barely controlled hysterics, half giggling with sheer joy to be alive. 'I don't believe it, but you're turning me on again.'

Looking over the raw edge as Helen reached for him, he felt the same disbelief that he still had eyes to see and hands to feel. The high-pitched sounds of police and fire sirens rose on the wind. They sank to the cold floor.

'If I know Reggie, he's going to be here any minute.'

'Tell him to come back when he finds out who did it.'

* * *

Wrapped naked in her mink, which she had dropped in the foyer along with her heels, Helen waited in the car while Taggart dealt with the police. Reggie had spirited them down a freight elevator, and their story was that no one was in the apartment when the boom fell. Reggie had found a hacksaw beside a mutilated body on the top deck, which confirmed that the boom falling was no accident. By the simple expedient of removing the hacksaw, he had left the police with nothing more than speculation that an unknown person beheaded during the accident might have tampered with the cable that parted.

As soon as the cops confirmed that no one had been killed on the ground, and his own superintendents had reported to take charge of the damage, Taggart asked the senior officer, a one-time protegé of Uncle Eamon, if he minded if he went home. When he didn't, Taggart walked to the Rolls and told his chauffeur to head for Canarsie. Reggie followed in a gypsy cab loaded with selected members of one of his street gangs.

'I'm still shaking,' said Helen.

'Me, too.' Holding her in one arm, he poured a brandy, which they shared. 'Want to hear something weird?' Helen asked.

'What?'

'I had fabulous time tonight. I mean, I haven't been on a date like this ever.' 'Want to go out again?'

'When?'

'Tonight?'

'Jeez, I wish I lived alone. I'd love to take you home and sleep all day with you.'

'How about a hotel?'

'It wouldn't be the same. I'll see you tonight?'

'What would you like to do? Go to a fire? See a plane crash?'

'Boring,' she said with an uncertain smile. 'Maybe we should try something really dangerous ... '

'Like what?' He couldn't read her. Suddenly, she seemed frightened.

'Like talking about that castle.'

Taggart answered very carefully, 'As soon as we finish the Cirillos.'

Helen held his gaze a moment. 'Before you came along, I thought about getting out. I was getting driven out. Now that we're strong it's my choice and it's getting harder. Tonight you're making me really happy.'

'I'm glad.'

'Do you know why?'

'Tell me.'

'You're the first guy I ever went to bed with who didn't act like he was stealing something.'

'Give me a list. I'll make my brother arrest them.'

'They don't stick in my head.'

It was a solid answer and banished his small thoughts of Tony and her together. She seemed poised to say more, and he waited in turmoil, fearing her mood would move her to say, let's get out now. But to his relief – and confused disappointment, for that was what he wanted, but couldn't have – she turned her face instead to the bronzed window. Outside, the city streets were beginning to stir with the earliest joggers, janitors and coffee shop cooks. 'Can they see in?'

'Nope.'

She touched him. 'Do you think you could –'

Taggart reached inside her coat. 'I would love to try . . .'

★    ★    ★

'Cops,' Taggart's driver said in the intercom, as the Rolls turned into Helen's block, and Reggie's car beeped a warning.

Helen pulled away from Taggart, and pressed urgently against the glass. Half a dozen police cars were parked in front of her house, their lights revolving red and yellow reflections upon the two-storey houses, their radios loud in the first silvery light of dawn. Riflemen patrolled the sidewalk. She spotted a couple of federal cars, too, unmarked but for winking red lights suction-cupped to their roofs. Uniformed officers stopped the Rolls Royce and motioned for them to lower the windows, but Helen's attention was riveted to an ambulance, which was pulling out of the driveway, with its lights off, and its siren quiet as death.

She moved out the door before Taggart could stop her, dodged the cops, and raced towards her house. Plainclothes agents grabbed her at her front walk.

'Hold it, Miss.'

'That's my house. Let me go!'

'Who are you?'

'I'm Helen Rizzolo. Let me go! What happened?'

Tony Taglione climbed out of an unmarked car.

'What happened?' she cried. 'Let me go in.'

Taglione put his hand on her shoulder and held her with his dark eyes. 'They've killed your brother Frank.'

She reeled as if he had hit her in the face. 'You're lying,' she screamed.

She knew it couldn't be. It was a mistake – one of the bodyguards instead – and the cops had made a mistake. Then she saw Frank's van in the narrow driveway beside the house. The bulletproof windscreen had been starred in a dozen places by armour-piercing shells, the passenger door was open, and dark blood had pooled beside the tyre.

*I betrayed him*, she thought. *I betrayed my brother.*

'Eddie?' she asked, afraid to hear the answer.

'They shot Eddie, too. He's in surgery.'

'How bad?'

'I don't know. Your aunts are with your mother.'

She turned to the house.

Taglione took her arm. 'Helen. Who did it?'

'What?'

'Who killed your brother?'

She went rigid. 'You bastard.'

'*I* didn't kill him,' Tony shot back. 'People *you* know killed him. *Who?*'

She observed him through a haze of tears. It was her fault. She had manipulated Frank and Eddie to trust her; she had won their confidence; she had convinced them to serve her, so she could serve Christopher Taggart. Frank – her quiet and loyal panther – had been killed while she was at the Waldorf, falling in love with the man who had caused his murder.

'Who, Helen?' Taglione repeated harshly.

She turned her grief and confusion on him. 'You animal! How could you talk to me like that?'

He lashed back savagely: 'Frank's no innocent victim. Neither is Eddie. Neither are you. Your brothers did something to make the killers actually come to your *house*. They could have killed your mother, your relatives. Give me a lead, Helen. What's the war about?'

Taglione's coal-dark eyes mirrored the security lights. It was like looking into the face of a robot. Clearly, Tony Taglione shared his brother's capacity to hate, but not, she realized with aching sadness, Taggart's capacity to love.

She glanced down the street at Taggart, who was standing with the cops. He was straining to come to her. 'I don't know.'

'It's because Eddie and Frank were expanding, isn't it? Because they were taking over Brooklyn? What ever gave them the idea the Cirillos would let them get away with it?'

'Fuck you!'

'Thank you, Helen. Let's talk again – after more people die.'

*Who's left?* she wondered bleakly as the full horror of what she had done slashed through her mind. *I gave them the idea and they trusted me . . .*

Taggart had tried to follow her, not caring who saw him, but the cops blocked the way. 'Wait here, mister. That's a federal prosecutor talking to her.'

'I'm Chris Taggart. He's my brother. I gotta see him.'

One of the cops made the connection. 'Hiya, Chris. Yeah, you probably don't remember me, but we met at a PAL supper. Okay. Let me just go ask.' He approached Tony and Helen and waited close by for an opening. Taggart watched Tony raise a tentative hand to her shoulder, and for a second Helen drifted against him. Then she moved away, her body sagged, and she seemed to disappear within her coat. She suddenly screamed at him, and Tony yelled back. Then they were silent, like two actors caught in the spotlight with no lines to say. The cop caught Tony's attention. Tony glanced towards Taggart and nodded without expression. Taggart ran to her side.

'Helen.'

Her face, trembling and tear-streaked, turned to ice. She turned her back on Taggart and climbed unsteadily up the steps. Her mother opened the door and Helen fell into her arms. Crying, holding each other, the women moved inside. The door thudded shut.

'Wha'd you do to her?'

'I told her some guys killed her brother.'

'*What?*'

'In case you don't remember, Chris, your girlfriend's connected.'

Taggart stared at Helen's house. Every window was lighted, as were the windows in the surrounding houses. Security lamps glared down on the vans parked in the driveway, the backyard garage, and tiny square of front lawn, which had faded to winter straw. The lead van had its windscreen shot out.

'Who did it?'

Tony shrugged. 'They've been fucking with the Cirillo family. The Cirillos joined up with the Confortis and some other scum and hit their books and numbers all over Brooklyn. It was bound to happen.'

Taggart was stunned. The derrick boom had been only part of the attack. The Cirillos had retaliated across the board. Reggie had warned him. He had been too sure of himself. And now Helen blamed him.

'I better go in and help her.' Belatedly, he realized that Tony was as cold and angry as he had ever seen him.

'Chris, what in hell are you doing here?'

'Driving Helen home. She was at my table at the Waldorf.'

'Alphonse's grandson's date?' Tony asked scornfully.

'Why do you got guys following me?'

Tony reached into his car and held the Bulldog edition of the *Daily News* to the streetlight. It was open to a photo on Suzy Knickerbocker's society page that showed Taggart shaking hands with the mayor. To his left were Helen and Alphonse's wide-eyed grandson.

'Her family's in a gang war,' Tony said quietly, almost pleadingly. 'If you don't care about your reputation – or mine – would you please remember that hanging around with her could get you killed?'

Which meant, Taggart realized with relief, the NYPD had not reported the fallen boom to the Strikeforce; the cops had bought the accident story. Now all he had to worry about was Helen. He said, 'I'll take my chances. And the whole point of the beard was to protect your precious rep . . . May I ask what are *you* doing here?'

Tony gave him a look and said only, 'Doing my job.'

'You're not a cop, you're a lawyer.'

'Shut up, Chris. . . Here, get in the car. I'm not having a family fight with you on the street.' They closed the doors and Tony tore into him. 'I can't believe you put that woman at the same table with Uncle Vinnie and Aunt Marie.'

'She's a legitimate businesswoman.'

'And it's just a coincidence that her bus line, wedding palaces, and night clubs are cash businesses which just happen to lend themselves to laundering Mafia money?. . . You're forgetting Pop and everything decent he ever taught you.'

'Oh, now Pop's decent? But not decent enough to work for him, you had to work for the fucking government.'

'Pop *taught* us decent things.'

'He did more than teach.'

'He spoke one thing and did another.'

'What?'

'He rigged bids in the concrete business. And he paid off the Mafia.'

'Shut up!'

'Pop was a crook.'

'*My father was not a crook.*'

'Neither was Nixon.'

Taggart balled his fist. An agent rapped on the window. Tony turned his face, revealing the angry white scar on his cheek. The sight stopped Taggart cold. He sagged against the door. He couldn't do that again, no matter what his brother said. Tony wound down the window, but his gaze burned hotly on Chris's face, daring him to lash out. 'What?'

'Mr Taglione, it just came over the radio. They got old man Rizzolo in jail, too.'

'Christ!' Tony shouted. 'I told them to watch out for him.' He banged the seat with his fist. 'We could have pumped him like an oil well 'cause they killed his son.'

Taggart jumped out of the car.

'Stop him!'

He got as far as Helen's front step. A telephone rang inside just as three marshals tackled him. He fought until Tony caught up. 'Let me go in, Bro. Please. She adored him.'

'Go home, Chris.'

'What are you going to do to her?'

'I'm hoping that maybe, just maybe, with her brother murdered and her father murdered, she'll be willing to talk about who did it. And why.'

'But she doesn't know.'

'Chris, I'm working. Get the fuck out of here.'

Inside the house, women began to keen, an awful, cutting noise. The sound of Helen's rich lovely voice rising to a shrill moan went through Taggart like a lance. He covered his ears; it was his fault. Her voice pursued him. She sounded as if her heart were clamped in cold iron. He couldn't abandon her.

'*Tony,* she needs me.'

'Go home.'

He struggled blindly towards the door. 'I gotta help her.'

'*Get him out of here!*'

The agents dragged Taggart to his limousine and ordered his driver away. As the car turned around, Taggart watched Tony mount the steps and bang hard on the door.

# BOOK III

*Death of a Racketeer*

# 21

'It looks like a giant broad dropped her stocking,' said one of the iron work-ers. Taggart's supers, riggers and engineers eyed the wreckage while chewing Turns. The boom was draped over the outside header. The mid-section sagged into the shattered room; the top dangled over Park Avenue.

Finally Ben, Taggart Construction's senior project manager, voiced the majority opinion. 'Getting it down is easy. Getting it down without drop-ping it, that's the hard part.'

'Get it fucking down,' Taggart ordered savagely. 'Now!'

He had been up most of three nights, running on the ragged edge of sensibility. His face was lined and scruffy, with a yellow stubble. He was wearing jeans and an old Irish sweater, and he reaked of Canadian Club. 'There's a bow in that header.'

'Can you straighten it?'

'I wouldn't in my house.'

'Pull it.'

'Yes, sir.'

Seething, he directed the operations while the riggers and iron workers cut the boom from the mast, repaired the bent bullwheel, and rigged the mast to haul a new boom up from the street. His crews eyed him nervously, thinking it was the damage; but it was actually the wreckage of his plan which fuelled his rage.

Down in the city, Reggie's people were searching for Don Richard to settle the score. For by now it was clear that he had masterminded the joint Cirillo, Conforti, Imperiale fire attack on the Rizzolo clan. So clear, in fact, that Tony Taglione had convinced a grand jury to summon Don Richard to shed light on the affair. But Don Richard had disappeared.

His *consigliere* had been subpeonaed as well. Sal Ponte had turned in his usual skilful portrayal of an aggrieved Italian-American gentleman-lawyer, con-founding the best of Taglione's efforts to paint him as the mobster he was. No, he had not heard from his client for a week. Hardly unusual, he confided to the jury with a folksy smile; the elderly Mr Cirillo was becoming a bit eccentric.

Taggart had found the Cirillos no less elusive. Yesterday, Taggart had blown up at Reggie who reminded him of reality. 'The last time Don Richard dropped out of sight, no one – but no one – saw his face for five years. He ran Brooklyn from 1965 to 1970 like the invisible man.'

'Find him.'

'I'm using every means at our disposal. I've got Sicilians searching Sicily, New Yorkers searching New York, black gangs searching East Harlem where he was born, Ghostshadows tossing Chinatown. Our bookmakers are nosing around Atlantic City, and every retired mobster on my payroll is searching the South. We 're probably closer than the FBI, though not by a lot. There are more of them.'

'What do you mean, the South? Florida?'

'Florida, South Carolina, the Caribbean. He's an old man, they get cold in winter.'

'Ponte.'

'Of course. We're watching Sal Ponte, but it's too obvious.'

Taggart forced a plan out of his anger. 'Contact Ponte. Remind him that Mikey owes us money. Tell him we understand it's a problem, but we want to be paid. Tell him we're willing to discuss a reasonable settlement.'

Reggie sighed. 'You haven't forgotten threatening Crazy Mikey about Helen?'

Finally, early this morning, the third day since the Rizzolo massacre, Reggie's spies had learned that Salvatore Ponte had abruptly cancelled all his meetings. Reggie had thrown a team around his Fifth Avenue office, and Taggart was waiting for the results.

Riley came up and said, 'Those decorating broads are on the horn. I'm supposed to make changes in the lobby? They want enough juice to ran a subway.'

'Cancel it. Tell 'em I'll explain when I get the time.'

Twenty minutes later, Chryl and Victoria appeared on the roof. They surveyed the damage with experienced eyes and joked with the iron workers, comparing it to classic accidents they had all lived through on other jobs. Victoria waved. 'The winner! Even Trump never had one like this, Chris.'

'What do you want?'

'We thought you might be ready for a drink and a nap.'

'I'm fine.'

'Ben says you've been up here three days. Come on, we're taking a break.' She reached under his sweater. 'God, you smell. Make that a *bath,* a drink and a nap.'

'I'm busy.'

'So are we. We want to move on the club. Come on, the jacuzzi still works.'

He turned on them, his mind boiling. *'We're not doing the club.'*

Victoria grinned. 'What, did you have a fight already?'

'Don't you read the fucking newspapers?'

'You know damned well we don't have time for newspapers,' said Chryl. 'When we're old we'll read books about what happened in the papers.'

Victoria reached for him again. 'Listen, fella, you're getting tired. Now come on.'

Taggart whirled on them, the light so violent in his eyes that an iron worker moved to stop him. 'Get off my job! Both of you.'

Victoria backed away, blinking, and fled to the elevator. Chryl stood her ground, white with rage. Taggart said, 'I'm sorry, what did I –'

'Don't you *ever* treat her like that again.'

Chryl raced after her. She held Victoria as the elevator descended, stroked her hair and kissed her tears. 'Hey. He's under a ton of pressure. He didn't mean it.'

'He never talked to us like that.'

'Well. . .' She touched her knuckles gently to Victoria's lips. 'He had to find somebody some day. You knew. I knew.'

'It's not that! It's like he's getting scary.'

*　　*　　*

Reggie returned at nightfall. They retreated from the mechanics who were stringing lights for the second shift and found a windswept perch on the north wall.

'What happened?'

'He got away. He somehow realized our "meter maids" were bogus and lit out the back door.'

'Goddamnit. Who fucked up?'

'Rather than allot blame,' Reggie counselled, 'I would give Don Richard credit.'

'I want him dead. Now.'

'He's gone to ground again, and I'm afraid that is that.'

'How's he going to run things?'

'Don Richard will instruct Ponte. Ponte will pass it on to Mikey. And Mikey will carry through.'

'We made Mikey. The bastard was a lousy bone breaker before we made him the biggest dope distributor in New York.'

'What we did, just for the record, was reactivate Don Richard.'

'I'm going to deactivate him permanently.'

'In terms of your army,' Reggie answered, 'the Rizzolos are effectively destroyed. We haven't the means to attack his whole network.'

'Then attack the top again. Mobilize every foreign group you've got. Fly 'em in on the air ambulances. We'll attack the Staten Island house. Ponte's place in Alpine. Mikey's apartment in Whitestone. Fucking level them. Then–'

'No.'

'What do you mean, no?'

'It's pointless. All the top people have gone to ground. They're not home.'

'I don't care. I'm going to destroy –'

'Kill their wives and children?' Reggie looked at him coolly. 'You don't want that.'

Taggart fell silent. Of course he didn't, he told himself; he was just talking. But he had to do something.

'Get Ponte. Squeeze it out of him.'

'At this moment Salvatore Ponte is better protected than the president of the United States. Besides, the Strikeforce is all over him because they know he'll be the go-between.'

'Fucking wonderful.' He watched the second shift of iron workers trooping off the elevator and mused gloomily, 'How do you suppose Helen would react if I knock off Don Richard?'

'She would sup on his entrails.'

'But would she forgive me?'

'Good evening, sir.'

'What? Where you going?'

Reggie produced an Air France Concorde ticket from his Burberry pocket. 'You suggested recently I take a vacation.'

'Not when I need you.'

'You need a plan, Chris. I can do nothing while you're besotted with that woman. You've lost sight of your revenge. You don't know what you want.'

'I'm not besotted. I just feel I owe her something. Her brother and her father are dead because of me.'

'They were racketeers.'

'Tell her that. She blames me.'

'Nothing happened that you did not initiate.'

'None of this would have happened if they hadn't killed my father.' 'That's more like it.'

'I haven't forgotten.'

Reggie rubbed his moustache and gazed out at the city. The winter sun was setting behind the Statue of Liberty, a red circle in a grey sky. 'Do you recall the night on the boat Crazy Mikey's bodyguard broke my ribs?'

'I recall you pretending he hadn't until you started coughing blood.'

'My first reaction was to hurt him back. But he would have killed me if I had merely caused pain. I had to concentrate fully on the job at hand, which was to immobilize him. Which I did. The same applies to you on a much larger scale. You've simply got to get ahold of yourself, forget revenge for this attack, and stick to your original goal. You don't really care what they did to the Rizzolos. It's your father. Either find a meaningful way to attack the Cirillos, or call the whole thing off.'

'What's your vote?'

Reggie gave him a long look.

'What's your vote? Come on, man, give it to me.'

'Get out while you can. It's only a matter of time until either the Mafia, or the authorities, stumble upon us.'

'The authorities? That sounds like a euphemism for my brother.'

'Your brother is positioned to find out.'

'I won't stop.'

'Then what are you going to do?'

Taggart refused to meet Reggie's cold eye. 'We shylocked Mikey to smoke Don Richard out. I guess I sort of underestimated how the old bastard would react.'

'That's putting it mildly.'

'Why didn't you stop me?'

'Let me remind you of something,' Reggie shot back. 'Their attack on the Rizzolos was originally allowed for in your plan. In fact, it was part of it. You created a shadow Mafia, remember, to attack and absorb attacks. A buffer between you and your chosen enemy. You weren't supposed to fall in love with its boss.'

'Take your vacation,' Taggart answered coldly. 'I'll figure it out.'

*　　*　　*

He had been too successful and the Mafia was the stronger for it. The result of his provoking Don Richard to resume command was that the powerfully led Cirillos were filling the vacuum left by Taggart's devastation of the rival Mafia families.

At the same time, Taggart had made Crazy Mikey more powerful than he would ever have become on his own. For in the course of luring Crazy Mikey into a now uncollectable debt, Taggart had created 'The Man Who Can', as the Black heroin distributors had dubbed the younger Cirillo. Lost shipments notwithstanding, independent smugglers eagerly sought out Mikey's buyers, who now controlled more New York distribution than ever before.

Even worse, Taggart thought, was the long-term stability he had unwittingly helped the Cirillos establish. Having become such a money earner – and having his father's own *consigliere* as his ally – gave Crazy Mikey a power base from which he could seize control of the family the instant that old Don

Richard died. Thus even if Taggart managed to find and kill Don Richard, Mikey's immediate, orderly takeover would actually further strengthen the Cirillos.

Taggart concluded that he had only one hope of wreaking final revenge: destroy all three of the ruling triumverate at once. Destroy Don Richard, Crazy Mikey, and *Consigliere* Ponte in swift and rapid sequence so that their surviving underlings tore themselves apart battling to take control. Tony's Strikeforce would finish the job.

Mikey and Ponte were the more visible targets. While they might be safe from ordinary rivals and law enforcement, Reggie Rand's assassins could eventually gun them down. But attacking Crazy Mikey and *Consigliere* Ponte would still leave Don Richard in firm control of the family. And he might easily live ten more years. It kept coming back to the old man. He had to find Don Richard.

Taggart turned to his law enforcement contacts. He talked to cops, FBI men, DEA agents, a Strikeforce criminal investigator and his friend Barney from the President's Commission. No one had the vaguest idea where Don Richard was hiding; even the rumours were half-hearted. Next he met Jack Warner. 'Forget it, Mr Taggart,' Warner told him, nervously eyeing the city below the Spire. 'The last time he went underground he was gone five years.'

'Everyone keeps telling me that, Jack. I expect more from you.'

'I wish I knew where he was. I could make my career; *and* a fortune from you at the same time.'

'Find out and you can retire.'

'I'm trying, Mr Taggart. But I'll tell you honestly, it ain't gonna happen.'

He tried a different tack. Perhaps Crazy Mike and *Consigliere* Ponte had confided in someone they trusted; or maybe someone in their circle had overheard, or guessed. Taggart was prepared to pay any amount for the information. He tried tapping some of Reggie's spies who had access to Mikey and Ponte; three actually spent considerable time with Mikey – a bodyguard, a friend Mikey often took meals with, and a brothel manager who went whoring with him – but none was privy to Don Richard's location. Reggie had been right; only Crazy Mikey and *Consigliere* Ponte knew where Don Richard was hiding.

How could he penetrate the Cirillos at the very top, something neither Reggie nor the Strikeforce had ever managed to do? He considered the possibility of kidnapping Mikey or Ponte to force him to divulge Don Richard's hiding place. But kidnapping was much more difficult than killing. Both men moved in a war-alert entourage. Ponte seemed the more likely target, yet although he was not a fighter like Mikey, the *Consigliere* was rarely alone. Bodyguards drove him between his Alpine, New Jersey estate and his Fifth

Avenue office. He lunched with associates at Cristos, a short, easily guarded ride to Lexington Avenue. Sundays he drove in convoy to the old neighbourhood in Brooklyn to take his mother to church. The rest of the time he was indoors, his handsome tan apparently maintained under a sunlamp.

Frustrated two Sundays in a row at the church, Taggart drove his rented car aimlessly about Brooklyn until he found himself, as if by accident, in Canarsie. He turned down Helen's street, his pulse pounding.

Her house looked bleak. Dark shades and curtains veiled her windows and black ribbons had been tied to the Christmas wreath on the door. He sensed his car was being watched and when he slowed, men stepped from the neighbouring houses, each with a hand still in the door as if holding a weapon. A van followed him out of the neighbourhood.

He went back an hour later. She was out on the front grass, warming up in a dark jogging suit, surrounded by bodyguards. Several cars were at the kerb, engines running. Taggart kept going, a glimpse of her face seared in his mind. She had looked up when he passed; cold wind had whipped her silky black hair. Her eyes were sunken, her mouth sad and weary. He drove to Canarsie Park, walked to the shore where Reggie had often met Helen. She appeared, running with long, beautiful strides, her breath sharp and white in the cold, her hair glinting in the sun. She was well ahead of her bodyguards and he could easily step into her path and fall in beside her. What could he say? What did he deserve to say? He turned away and hurried to his car.

A third fruitless week passed and suddenly, when he didn't know where to turn, an opportunity to force *Consigkere* Ponte to divulge Don Richard's hiding place came from a totally unexpected source. Uncle Vinnie showed up at the Taggart Spire office carrying a big waxed bakery bag and a thermos. 'Thought I'd come over for coffee.'

'Coffee' meant talk. Taggart was hardly in the mood, but he could never deny his father's favourite. 'Hey, still working,' Vinnie said cheerily, but his big, round face was tight and he kept twisting the bakery bag in his fat hands.

'Only way to get rich. How you doing?' They embraced. Taggart helped him off with his coat.

'Great, great. Really good . . . I brought some stuff from the bakery.'

'What you got there?' Chris cleared his desk top.

Uncle Vinnie laid out Napoleans, cannolis, and a plump Italian cheesecake bursting with coloured citrons. From his thermos he poured pungent espresso into styrofoam cups. 'I thought since your place got messed up you wouldn't have coffee. How's it going?'

'Know anybody who needs an S-boom?'

'What about the guy they found?'

'Half a guy. Nobody knows.'

'I hear sabotage?'

'Was he gnawing the cable with his teeth?'

'Lucky nobody else was hurt.'

'Middle of the night.'

'God's on your shoulder.' Uncle Vinnie popped a cannoli in his mouth and made a face. 'I hate these places that fill 'em ahead of time. The shell's like macaroni.

Taggart bit into one and sipped the espresso. 'So how you doing?'

'Well, I got a problem.'

'Sit down.'

Uncle Vinnie settled, flicked another pastry into his mouth, and studied Taggart's Chinese carpet. 'It's about your brother.'

'Oh, shit. Is he coming down on you?'

'No, no, nothing like that. I ain't done nothing.'

'That's good, because there I can't help.'

'Fix a case with Tony? You'd be in jail ahead a me. No, Tony wants me to set up a sting.'

'What kind of sting?'

'You know, where you set up a phony company to sucker some wiseguy into doing something.'

'Yeah, I know what a sting is. I've helped him with a couple. What's Tony looking for?'

'He was over to supper and he sort of mentioned a sting while Aunt Marie was in the kitchen. Then he looked at me – you know how he looks at you? Like he knows everything bad you ever done and the stuff you're thinking about doing?'

'He looked at me like that when I was born.'

'He expects me to offer to help. Like I'd be a supplier getting hassled by other guys for bidding low. But it means pissing off a lot of people. If it wasn't Tony, I'd say, go fuck yourself. To him I don't know how to say no. Can you talk to him?'

Taggart stared. It was as if God had sent Vinnie, his father's favourite, when he needed help most. For unbeknownst to his uncle, Vinnie had just offered him Sal Ponte on a silver platter.

'Please, can you talk to Tony?'

'I can get him off your back, so he won't ask again,' Taggart answered slowly, his mind racing with thoughts of how best to use this opportunity. If *he* couldn't kidnap Sal Ponte to make him divulge where Don Richard was, why not manoeuvre Tony's Strikeforce into doing it for him?

'Sure, I can get him off your back, but you know as well as me Tony won't excuse you.'

'Shit, I know,' Uncle Vinni said miserably.

'No, the thing is to get out with respect. Right?'

'Right. But how the hell am I going to do that?'

Taggart took the plastic knife the bakery had supplied and cut a wedge of the cheesecake. Go slow, he told himself. Play this carefully. 'Vinnie? You know who Sal Ponte is?'

'The rackets lawyer?'

'Old man Cirillo's *consigliere* is the way I hear it.'

'What about him?'

'You ever hear of him messing around in our business?'

'Sure. You know that.'

Taggart knew, of course, but he asked, 'Doing what?'

Vinnie glanced around Taggart's empty office and lowered his voice. 'You know. They got the Teamsters mobbed up from Jersey to Westchester. They took a big piece of my Newark runway job. So I wouldn't have driver trouble, I had to lease their mixers. Most of it went straight into Ponte's pocket.'

Westchester fell within the Southern District; Tony's territory. Taggart cut another piece of cheesecake, and passed it, balanced on the knife. 'What you got going in Westchester?'

'A store in White Plains; a little office building over in Armonk.' 'Anything bigger?'

'I'm bidding on a new parking garage at the county airport. What's Ponte got to do with Tony?'

'Tony would love to nail his ass to the wall.'

'How's he going to do that?'

'How about extortion? How about bid rigging? How about featherbedding your drivers? How about false billing?'

'Yeah? I don't follow.'

'What if I tell Tony you can't do a sting with him because you're already doing one with me?'

'What do you mean, with you?'

'I told you, I help Tony now and then. Couple of years ago I set the FBI up with a phony electrical contractor to get some wiseguys in Chelsea. We'll tell Tony you didn't want to mention it without clearing it with me first.'

'You think he'd believe you?'

'I'll say I was just getting it started and was going to tell him soon. But first, you and me will bid that airport garage to sucker Ponte into leaning on us. That'll make Tony happy . . . What's wrong?'

'Hey, I don't need trouble with the Cirillos.'

'Don't worry, I'll keep you out of it. Just make sure you bid low enough to get that job.'

'You sure Tony'll go for it?'

Taggart wasn't sure, but Uncle Vinnie could make it sound a lot better than if he alone brought the sting to Tony's office. 'Listen, just between us? Tony and me had it out a few weeks ago. Really bad stuff about Pop, and other stuff I don't even want to talk about it. I've been looking for a way to make it up to him. This is perfect. I'm really grateful you came to me.'

Vinnie still looked dubious. 'So what happens when I get the bid?'

'Then you have lunch with Mr Ponte. To pay respects and talk about making it a smooth job. Tony's agents will wire you and record Ponte demanding payoffs.'

Vinnie got up, pushing the cakes aside. 'No way! You expect me to testify against the *mob*?'

'No, no, not testify. Tony won't go to trial for just extortion against a guy as connected as Ponte. He'll use the evidence to force Ponte to build a bigger case against his bosses. Nobody will even know Ponte's been arrested. The whole idea is the agents arrest him secretly so nobody knows he's turned informant. They do it like a kidnapping.'

'Ponte will know he's been arrested and he'll know why.'

'I guarantee Ponte won't be in a position to do anything about it. Listen, we'll go partners. Who's the general contractor?'

Vinnie named Eastern Casting, a Westchester outfit.

'I'll buy the job.'

'They won't sell the job. They're making out like bandits.'

Taggart laughed. He was Chris Taggart of Taggart Construction, back on track and smokin'. 'If Eastern won't sell the job, I'll buy *them*.'

After Uncle Vinnie left, he wired a Paris hotel that took Reggie Rand's messages: 'Vacation's over.'

# 22

Twelve weeks after Don Richard vanished, Reggie Rand summoned Jack Warner to a Connecticut car pool parking lot, near Interstate 84, which offered a clear view in all directions. The Spring night air was cool. At the edge of the black top was a little marsh, in it peepers were shrilling sharp invitations to mate. The men walked out of the light and patted each other for wires.

It was ten months since the Memorial Day weekend when Taggart had set his revenge in motion by simultaneously tipping the Strikeforce to Nicky Cirillo's crew leader's heroin deal and kidnapping Helen Rizzolo. Reggie imagined that he felt a gathering of forces; one way or another – he worried that he couldn't predict which – Taggart's revenge was about to explode.

'I want to give you something,' he told Warner.

Warner chuckled. 'You want to give *me* something. I'm supposed to give the somethings. You give me the money.'

The burly detective was the first agent to betray the Southern District in over eighty years, an achievement in which Reggie Rand, who admired the elite institution, took pride in engineering. Money was the key to this savvy product of New York's Lower East Side and the elite Stuyvesant High School. Reggie had already deposited 180,000 in his Swiss bank account, but he had calculated Warner's magic number to be a half million, and he intended to keep him from that figure as long as he needed him. Warner was treacherous, but worth the risk. He knew the New York Mafia so intimately that he was regularly invited in on Strikeforce planning operations and had the confidence – to the extent any human being could – of the assistant US Attorney and Strikeforce chief, Tony Taglione.

'So what is it?'

'Salvatore Ponte has a girl friend.'

Warner stopped laughing. 'He does not.'

'He's extremely careful about her. Nobody knows, not even Don Richard.' 'How the hell did you find out?'

'Are you interested?'

'Fucking-A.' This seemingly ordinary piece of information had enormous value because if Ponte sneaked off by himself he could be arrested secretly, without his friends knowing, and persuaded to co-operate. 'What's her name?'

'Ask first why I'm telling you.'

'You got it if you can give it. What do you want?'

'When and if you use this against Ponte, I want the results immediately, within the hour. Do we understand each other?'

'Do I get paid for those results?'

'Of course.'

Warner looked around, scrutinized the highway ramps, the empty shoulders, the few cars still in the lot, each of which he had inspected minutely while waiting for the Brit. A BMW came down the exit ramp and parked beside a Saab. Warner waited until both commuters had left in opposite directions.

'I can see a problem. What if it works? We arrest him secretly when he's shacked up with his girlfriend and we break him down. What if he spills something big? If I tell you and you tell the wrong people, he's going to end up dead. When that happens, Taglione starts screaming, "Who leaked?" '

'He won't be hurt. You have my word.'

'Not good enough. I don't like it.'

'Forgive me,' Reggie said softly,' but I can't take no this time. It must be yes.'

'Sorry, fella.'

'So am I,' Reggie replied, crouching and drawing his gun from his ankle in a single smooth action. He backed up, sheltering the gun against his side, because a New York cop who had survived eighteen years on the street ought reasonably to be considered a dangerous man.

Warner grinned. 'I really don't believe you're going to shoot. I'm not trying to take a gun away from a guy who has no reason to shoot me.'

'Stand still.'

'Sorry.' Warner grinned again, patiently trying to puzzle out where Reggie was heading. Reggie reached into his pocket and tossed him a small metal container. 'Do you recognize that?'

Warner turned it to the parking lot lights. 'Sure. Magazine for your little ankle gun.'

'Have another look.'

Warner tried to remove a slug. 'What is this?'

'Tape recorder.'

Warner felt the blood rush from his head. '*What!*

'I carry it in the gun whenever I'm more interested in recording than shooting, which I have been whenever we've met.'

Warner lunged.

'But not tonight,' Reggie replied, swiftly stepping back and cocking the slide.

'What the fuck are you doing to me?'

'When you report to me what Ponte has told Taglione, I'll pay you three hundred and fifty thousand dollars.'

'Slick, Reggie. Very slick. What are you doing this to me for? I never hurt you.'

'I'm making you rich.'

'There's a big chance I'll get fucked. To get in on the flip, I'm going to have to push to make the arrest.'

'I'll look out for you, Jack. Remember, Mr Taggart still regards you as a most valuable asset.'

Warner ran his hand through his hair and looked at the mud on his hand-made shoes. 'Okay. What's her name?'

'Mrs Hugel. She's married and lives in Great Neck. Ponte seems deeply in love with her.'

'How in hell did you find this?'

Reggie smiled. 'As my friends in the rag trade say, "Does Macy's tell Gimbels?" Now listen. Tell Taglione you can arrest Ponte secretly when they tryst. You might suggest he can use the girlfriend as additional leverage to break him down.'

'I think he'll figure that out himself.'

'Walk to your car. Don't look back.'

Warner started to walk away, but a thought struck him. 'Hey, what makes you think that Taglione has something to arrest Ponte for?'

'I can feel it in my bones.'

On the drive back to the city Warner concluded that the Brit had made a mistake telling him about the tape recorder. The existence of evidence that he had sold information meant that if Taggart were ever caught, Warner had to immediately offer to testify against Taggart in order to plea bargain his way out of going to jail himself. But, he reflected unhappily, he would still be finished on the Force. He comforted himself with the thought that Taggart was too careful to get nailed. And despite the spot Reggie had put him in, Warner found himself wondering how in hell Taggart's scam fitted the weird stuff going down with the mob.

First, Taggart was dating the Rizzolo girl while the Rizzolos were romping over Brooklyn. Then the Cirillos hit the Rizzolos and all of a sudden, Taggart was interested in Sal Ponte – Crazy Mikey and old Don Richard's *consigliere*. Why? Suddenly, he remembered that last year when Taggart had hung him off the building, Taggart had engineered the arrest of Nicky Cirillo. Warner smiled to himself; he was about to spend a long night with his files.

Reggie drove country roads until he was sure that Warner hadn't been followed, then headed down to Auberge Maxime, in North Salem. It was late on a weekday night and the customers were finishing dessert. The exceptions were a company of fat men eating duck at a long table – chefs from the other country inns of Westchester, Putnam and Fairfield counties – and Christopher Taggart, alone in a corner, sipping Bordeaux and reading the menu.

'Wine?'

'Whisky, please.'

A waiter was dispatched.

'How'd you do?'

Reggie covered his face and rubbed his eyes. 'Splendidly, I suppose.'

'What's wrong?'

He shrugged and thought about his answer. 'I hope you know what you're doing. Warner is naturally treacherous. Now we've threatened him, which makes him dangerous.' His scotch arrived. 'Cheers.'

'Cheers. And cheer up. The next thing, Reg, we gotta get Mikey back on the tit.'

'How do you propose to do that?'

'Tell his people we're considering rolling his debt so he can pay it off in new deals.'

'Even if they'll listen, we don't have the heroin.'

'We've got twenty or thirty keys.'

'That's not enough for Mikey.'

'More than enough,' Taggart smiled. 'More than enough. Just get him interested.'

★　　★　　★

'You want to thank me?' Uncle Vinnie asked when Tony Taglione telephoned. 'You have dinner with me and your brother.'

'I'm really tied up.'

'He helped, too. Come on, kid. You owe me. Abatelli's. Ten o'clock. You can work late. You gotta eat anyhow. Then around the corner to sleep.'

Taggart sat across from them, warily. Tony was remote at first – razor slim to Vinnie's beachball round – but his dark eyes warmed with affection as he said, 'Uncle Vinnie, you really started something with Sal Ponte. I can't go into it, but you opened a whole can of worms.'

'Hey, it wasn't just me,' Vinnie protested. 'It was Chris, too.'

'Sure. Both of you. Don't expect to read it in the papers, but you've done a service.'

'Anytime,' said Taggart.

★ ★ ★

Helen Rizzolo was doing warm-up stretches in front of the house. Eddie stood by, instructing her bodyguards. 'If you fuck up, you'll be guarding my uncle in Westport. No bars, no broads, no movies. Just trees.'

'I'd rather do time.'

Eddie forced a laugh as he was forcing bad jokes, working hard to keep up morale, while his soldiers were going nuts waiting for the Cirillos' next surprise. Helen shot him a worried look.

Physically, Eddie still seemed indestructable; the only reminder of three Cirillo bullet holes was a slight limp and an occasional headache. But he seemed lost without Frank, quicker than ever to fly off the handle and, she feared, even more inclined to take wild chances. Frank, in his quiet way, had been a calming influence.

Eddie had taken their father's death hard, too, harder than she would have guessed. Suddenly, in his thirties, he found himself apparent head of the family – which was young for an Italian man with a strong father. He seemed to resent her, as if angry that they had survived while Frank and their father had not. Worse, he seemed determined to prove that he could stand alone. Her mother had suggested that he was afraid of losing her, too, which had the ring of simple truth; but her mother, of course, did not know how dangerous Eddie could be on his own.

Helen motioned him close. 'What are you doing when I'm gone?'

'Digging a hole in the ground.'

'Eddie. No dope deals.'

'Sure.'

'I mean it. I don't want to see any more of these so-called importers coming by the house. All I need is you busted.'

'Don't worry about it.'

'I do worry. You're all I have left.'

She jumped the low hedge and hit the sidewalk running.

Eddie whirled angrily on the bodyguards. 'What are you clowns waiting for? She's halfway down the block.'

Three Rizzolo soldiers bolted after her. Cars followed.

She ran for miles. At last her stomach stopped churning and her exertions dissipated the adrenalin which had seared through her body like fiery knives. She circled Canarsie Park, slowing to study the canvases of the painters who were taking advantage of the day's uncommon warmth to stalk the shore like long-legged water birds. Down the sea wall one painter worked alone. Heart soaring, she walked towards him, tucked her arms under her breasts, and

277

studied his canvas. It was the same gulls over the same barren islands in Jamaica Bay, but this painter had a gift for light, depicting the sun's angle so precisely as to date its swelling rays forever in early Spring.

'You buy this or are you doing it for real?'

Reggie Rand indented a gull with his thumbnail and wiped his thumb on a handkerchief which extended from the sleeve of his neatly ironed smock. They had met this way often up until the Christmas massacre, but this time he was actually painting. 'I took up oils to mend once. Food for the busy soul.'

'Yeah, I know what you mean. I'm learning how to play the violin.'

'Face the water when you speak in case they're using a gun-mike.'

'Yeah, what if they're out there in a submarine? Listen. What's Taggart doing? Does he know what's happening to us?'

'Mr Taggart indicated the risk at the beginning.'

'We're getting killed.'

'Can you hold out a little while longer?'

'How much longer?'

'I can assure you that Mr Taggart has a plan in motion.'

Helen stood silent as long as she could. She hated to ask, but had to. 'Reggie?' He looked at her. 'What is it?' he asked, not unkindly.

'Why won't he talk to me himself?'

Reggie picked up his brush. She wished she hadn't asked. He must think she was a fool.

'Between us?'

'If you say so.'

'He's embarrassed to face you.'

'Embarrassed?'

'He won't until he makes it up. He blames himself. He can't apologize without doing something to set it right.'

'So he sends you.'

'We *are* in business.'

Angry at herself for admitting she cared, embarrassed in front of Reggie, and enraged at Taggart for ducking her, she flared: 'So he puts you in front just like me and you take the heat just like me. While he's clear.'

Reggie twirled the brush in grey paint and worked a moment on the western edge of the island, where the waves had moulded a shallow beach. 'People make a serious error thinking grey is a colour between black and white. Grey is grey, my dear. It doesn't want to be black or white. It *likes* being grey, as I like being Mr Taggart's servant. His youth and exuberance are stimulating. And as I grow older I crave more than the excitement of simply killing for killing's sake.' He showed his even teeth. 'Though I haven't lost the taste. Are we in understanding?'

'Don't threaten me.'

'I'm not. Mr Taggart has "complex" feelings for you. That is all that matters to me. Therefore, you and I are not enemies. And you may take what you dubbed my threat as friendly advice never to try to drive a wedge between Mr Taggart and me.'

Helen looked into the flat pools of the Englishman's eyes and saw herself reflected. 'Do you have any Italian blood?'

Reggie returned a smile as cold and mirthless as hers.

She burst into motion. Her bodyguards streamed after her and when she looked back she saw Reggie dabbing thoughtfully with a long brush. Would the Englishman be as surprised as she how Christopher Taggart filled her thoughts?

Complex feelings? That was putting her own feelings quite mildly. Her father was gone and Frank was gone – reasons enough to hate Taggart. She had tried, but failed miserably, for she could not forget the earlier events of the night her father and Frank were murdered: Chris's pride at the Waldorf ball; the way she had poured her life out to him in front of Saks; making love like molten gold; and his sure, animal reactions when he nearly killed himself saving her on the Spire. Far from hating him, she felt a guilty longing to take him in her arms and curl up in his, share the blame, and start anew.

*   *   *

Jack Warner discovered that Sal Ponte's girlfriend, Mrs Hugel, was a very pretty strawberry blonde of forty-five or so. Her husband owned a Volvo dealership and neither had mob connections. Armed with arrest warrants written by Tony Taglione himself, Warner and a partner followed her for a week. On the eighth day she drove from her Great Neck home to the Box-tree Inn in Purdys, New York, an hour's drive north of the city. She entered the white clapboard inn with a timid flourish and who drove up in a rented Caddy and swaggered in after her, but handsome Sal Ponte?

'Alone,' sang Warner. 'The prick's alone.'

The agents hunkered down to watch from the Metro North train station across the highway. The afternoon darkened and grew cold. They smoked and talked and imagined the couple making love in the empty inn. For Warner she was all the rich women he saw in the department stores, stripped of their fancy clothes and makeup, perspiring freely, gasping their pleasure. His partner's imaginings, relayed in a monotone, were irritating him.

'Think her husband's got something on the side, too?'

'If he does he's an idiot.'

'Think she knows Ponte's a hood?'

'No,' Warner said firmly. He put away thoughts of the woman in bed and reviewed the Taggart situation, which was equally frustrating. It was as if

Taggart had joined the Rizzolo family, but that was impossible; no family took in an outsider at the top level; especially not an old-fashioned clan like the Rizzolos. And why was Taggart on Ponte's case? Could he be looking for old Don Richard?

Warner's partner tried to guess what time she had to be home.

'Six.'

'Her kids are in college.'

'Seven.'

At five, as the northbound traffic thickened, they moved closer, in front of the country grocery. Minutes later, the couple came out and got into their cars, Ponte in the rental, Mrs Hugel in her husband's Volvo. They drove in tandem down Route 684 to the Hutchinson River Parkway, which she took to the Whitestone Bridge and home to Long Island, while Ponte veered onto the Cross County Parkway, tooting his horn and blinking his lights goodbye.

Warner's partner made his move where the Thruway South exit of the Cross County emptied onto a service road in the path of cars attempting to enter the parkway. He tore ahead of Ponte, who had slowed to see if the road were clear, and cut across the Caddy's nose, forcing it into the Howard Johnson's parking lot.

Warner shoved his badge against the windshield.

Ponte took a long moment to hide his relief that they were not hitmen. He pulled a red silk handkerchief from his pocket and dabbed his upper lip.

'Warrant?'

'Four of them. One for your office. One for your house. One for you and one for the car. Open the door.'

Warner handed him the warrants and shoved behind the wheel. 'Move over!'

He handcuffed Ponte's wrist to the frame of the passenger seat, to emphasize he was in deep trouble, and headed for New York, allowing the *consigliere* time to read the charges. He waited until he turned off the FDR Drive into lower Manhattan before he spoke.

'It's RICO, Sal. You're looking at twenty-plus.'

Ponte leaned into the cuff, folded up the warrants and passed them back coolly.

Warner said, 'You want me to call the Strikeforce chief? See if he's willing to talk things over?'

Ponte smiled mirthlessly and shook his head.

'Nobody knows you've been arrested.'

Ponte looked away. Warner hammered at him. 'I can take you straight to prison. Or we can meet the chief. You don't lose anything talking. . . Want me to try?'

'Want you to *try*?' Ponte mimicked. 'Who do you think you're shitting? I know why you picked me up in the middle of nowhere. Tony Taglione wants to deal.'

Jack Warner smiled back. 'Mr Taglione's offering twenty years. You got something worth twenty years?'

Warner parked behind the Metropolitan Correctional Center.

'That's the jail. It's connected to the US Attorney's building there and the Federal Courthouse. And there's a little church.'

'What are you, a tour guide?'

Warner went on casually, 'I like how they're clustered. Always reminds me of a medieval castle. You know? The king's chambers – his court, chapel and dungeon. All of law and civilization right in one spot. Where the king is, so is God, law, and punishment.

'Fuck you.'

'Of course, times change. Goddamned Supreme Court abolished trial by fire. So now the king's only a federal prosecutor. He has to convince a jury to order the judge to chuck you in the dungeon . . . We got you cold, Sal. Why don't you talk to the king?'

Ponte shrugged. 'I'll listen to anybody.'

Warner signalled his partner, who cleared a side entrance. The mobster swaggered across the covered railway into the US Attorney's building, strutted the empty halls, and lounged insolently in the elevator. Upstairs, he cocked an ironic brow at the big STRIKEFORCE sign.

One thing, Warner noticed, gave Ponte pause – a bold colour photograph of a dozen Secret Service agents guarding the President's limousine. It shimmered with a kind of power that Ponte seemed to understand, though he sneered the next moment at the work-beaten furnishings. 'Somebody oughta tell the king he's living like a peasant.'

'Tell him yourself.'

He led Ponte to a cluttered office ablaze in the fiery light of the setting sun. Papers buried the desk, extra chairs, and deep window sills. Filing cabinets lined the walls and were heaped with briefs and transcripts. Evidence boxes overflowed a wire supermarket shopping trolley parked behind the door. Snake nests of cables slithered from a row of battered telephones.

Tony Taglione sat behind his desk in a white shirt and navy tie. His sleeves were rolled up his slim forearms and his tie was loose at the neck. He stared at the mob lawyer like an angry priest, sickened and unforgiving.

'Taps on your secret phone line,' Taglione said, handing Ponte a bound transcript. 'The one in the office down the hall.'

Ponte tried to meet his forbidding gaze, failed, and looked down at the transcript.

'We overheard the number on this bug we installed in Cristo's where you ate steaks with contractors you were ripping off.'

Taglione watched him skim the phone taps. When Ponte turned to the bug transcriptions, he said, 'Your busboy was moonlighting,' and turned on his cassette player, a big silvery ghetto blaster with a sharp treble tone. The mobster's voice filled the room, loud and clear against a background of silver clinking and an ocean-like murmur of conversations at other tables. Ponte stared at the player. Taglione stopped the tape in mid-sentence. 'You were in good voice, Sal. The jury won't even need head sets.'

'That's bullshit. That guy won't testify against me.'

'He doesn't have to. In fact, we're not even going to ask him. But the busboy will.' Taglione allowed himself a chilly smile. 'Profitable investigation, Sal. Extortion led us to narcotics. You did a lot of business at the same table. Richie Cirillo's in the clear, on this one, but *you* are fucked.'

'You can't use this crap in court.'

'Title Three warrants, Sal. Approved in Washington by the Attorney General himself. Scrupulously minimized – when you called your little girl about her sweet sixteen party, the agent turned his tap off. When your godson Mikey Cirillo telephoned about the heroin that gets pushed in the Bed-Study schools, the agent turned it back on. One hundred per cent admissible evidence.'

'My lawyers –'

'RICO, Sal – Racketeer Influenced Corrupt Organizations. It's like your confirmation name.'

'My lawyers –'

'It's a federal crime to organize to commit crime. Every *consigliere* in town knows that's how we got the council. You and little Richie are the last.'

'My lawyers -'

'Your lawyers are going to advise plea-bargaining. I'm advising you to bargain now.'

'You think you can send me to jail?' Ponte blustered. 'Go ahead, send me to jail.'

'That's easy. But I have a better idea. I've persuaded the US Attorney to let me offer immunity –'

'You can shove your Witness Protection Program up your ass.'

'I don't want your testimony.'

'No?' Ponte asked warily, eyes darting towards Warner, who stared back blankly. 'What do you mean you don't want me to testify?'

'I want an informant.'

'Informer? You're nuts. I've been on the other side too long to turn on my people. I'll do the time.'

'Twenty years for the Cirillos? They're not your blood. You're going to tell your wife and children that *twenty* years is okay?'

'I'd rather my kids know I'm a standup guy.'

'Jack, see if Mr Koestler and Ms Gallagher are working late. I want some attorneys to witness our conversation with this gentleman.'

'Here it comes,' said Ponte, when Warner closed the door and they were alone.

'Here what comes?'

'The third choice. If I don't talk, you tell people I talked, anyway. So they kill me.'

'Not in this office.'

'Tell me another.'

'We don't do business that way, Sal. We nail you fair and square in court.' Taglione studied Ponte. He *was* a standup guy. But he was also a fifty-one year old man who had fallen happily and unexpectedly in love, which made the woman the key to flipping him because suddenly he had more to lose than he had ever had in his life. It was a rare lapse by such a criminal, one to be exploited to the hilt. And Ponte knew damned well that Jack Warner hadn't caught him at the Thruway interchange by accident.

'For a man your age, prison is tantamount to life. Even if you gain parole, you'll be in your sixties.'

Ponte pulled a face, but he was suffering. 'What do you do this shit for? You get kicks locking up people you think are crooks?'

Taglione answered civilly to make it easier for Ponte to surrender. 'If you believe in public service, which I do, you naturally believe people have a right to order in their lives. You guys take away that right.'

'Come on. You want criminals, arrest Wall Street.'

Taglione shrugged, though it was getting harder to play the part of an understanding and respectful opponent. 'Democracy's too fragile to survive guys like you.'

'We protect democracy,' Ponte retorted, rising to an avid defence. 'We're like revolutionaries. We protect poor people, protect them from the rich people's rules. You call them crimes, but smuggling's been an American necessity since the Revolution. Jack Kennedy's father was a bootlegger, you know. Union organizing? Where would labour be without our muscle? You got a problem with shylocking? Tell it to the banks who won't talk to the little Guy.'

'*Robin Hood bullshit!* You prey on the weak. You play by your own rules. And then you steal the game. When your victim protests, you murder him.'

'Hey, if we weren't needed, we wouldn't be in business.'

'You're in business, as you put it, by force.'

'We provide services people want.'

Taglione felt his blood rising. 'Stop dicking with me. The mob says: " *We're* here! And *you're* there! *We* take what *we* want." You're the enemy, Sal, a second, brutal society engulfing the first. Maybe I hate you for it, maybe I don't, but I'm sure as hell not going to let you get away with it.'

*'Maybe?'* Ponte sneered. 'Maybe? Everybody knows you hate us, Taglione. The prosecutor's so fucking high–and–mighty 'till it gets personal. Then you want revenge. What could be more Sicilian?'

'If I wanted revenge I'd do what you thought before.' He closed the affidavits in his fist. 'I'd use murder, extortion, dope as my excuse to tell the street you squealed. Let your friends take care of you.'

'So what's stopping you?'

'We're not all greaseball hoods, Sal, no matter what, you've made people think.'

Ponte turned very cold. 'There's an expression I haven't heard in a long time.'

'My Pop used it for wiseguys like you. Behind that fancy so-called law office you're a greaseball hood.'

'Your old man got his ass kicked, so you're going to get back at the whole Mafia?'

Tony Taglione heard the blood start roaring in his head. He pressed his long, tapered fingers to his ears and walked to the window and stared at his reflection. The sun was down, the glass nearly black. Ponte started to get out of the chair. 'Sit down!'

'I don't understand you,' said Ponte. 'Why can't you just accept things like your brother.'

'Careful, Sal.'

'Chris Taggart lets bygones be bygones. He moves ahead. He takes responsibility for his family's business. There's a son your father would have been proud of.'

Taglione jammed his hands in his pockets before Ponte could see them shaking. 'Have you ever seen a man hurt so bad he cried?'

Ponte shrugged. 'I'm a lawyer. I don't know about that shit.'

'There was nothing left of him but the pain to cry. You say you don't know? Let me tell you, Robin Hood, the tears make streaks through the blood, but the sound is worse . . . My Pop finally got the guts to tell some hood to go fuck himself. So some guy like you in your god-damned Fifth Avenue office gave the order and hurt him so bad he died crying.'

'Didn't they make a movie about that?'

'Jack, get in here! Let's get this creep down to arraignment.'

As Warner returned, Tony locked eyes with Ponte, forced him to look at the floor. Then he went back to the window and stared at the blocks of light the cleaning ladies had scattered around the Wall Street towers. He had blown it and lost his famous temper by letting Ponte get to him.

Ponte looked up when the door opened again and a young woman entered. 'Put away your steno pad, sweetheart. I got nothing to say.'

Taglione gave her a stiff nod of gratitude and she lighted like a candle. 'Ms Gallagher's not a stenographer, Sal. She's a prosecutor. In fact, she was on the team that prosecuted Pauly Conforti. Now she's bugging me to let her try *your* case if we can't come to an agreement which meets the approval of the United States Attorney. Ms Gallagher, Salvatore Ponte, or to his intimates, "Sally Smarts".'

Sarah extended her hand, allowed Ponte to run appreciative eyes over her white-blonde hair, and asked, 'What's it going to be, counsellor? Twenty years in prison? Or a little public service, undercover?'

'Pauly's gonna appeal.'

'Not out on bail he isn't,' Sarah smiled. 'And I don't lose appeals.'

Taglione nodded her to the window. Ponte looked a little shaken by the 'Cookie-cutter blitz', the threat that the Southern District could field endless ranks of assistant United States attorneys, élite, mean, and infuriatingly young. Having just made an ass of the Strikeforce chief, he found himself confronted by a twenty-eight year old woman anxious to dedicate long hours to putting him behind bars.

'You're doing all right,' Tony told her. 'Where's Ron?'

'His wife's having a baby?'

'Fuck. I really need him. What are you doing now?'

'I have to write warrants for the FBI bust.'

'They can wait. Come on. Let's hit this turkey again.'

'Do you want me to be nice?'

'Not yet.' He whirled around and levelled the full force of his penetrating gaze at Ponte. 'Who's your girlfriend, Sal?'

Ponte looked alarmed. 'Her husband's a Volvo dealer. Take my word, they're straight.'

'Your word?' Taglione picked up the affidavits. 'Sal, I look at murder, I look at dope, I look at extortion. And I find it very hard to accept your honourable word.'

'I'm telling you the truth. She –'

'You've lied and cheated your whole fucking life, you asshole. You want to finish it in jail or you want things moving almost as good as before we nailed you?'

'What do you mean?'

Taglione drew up a chair and sat down to face him. Perspiration dotted the mobster's tan skin. 'In exchange for immunity from prosecution on these charges – and only these – I want regular reports on Cirillo operations.'

'I can't turn in my friends.'

'You better believe when I find Old Man Richie, he'll turn *you* in.'

'Don Richard has been my friend for –'

'He'd do it to save his kid. . . The line forms outside that door. We're busting left and right. Tonight's your last chance. That's it, Sal. After tonight, you're on your own.'

He nodded to Sarah. She leaned close, striking aside the hair that fell across her cheek, and whispered, as if they three were conspiring which, of course, they were, 'The Cirillos are a big family, Mr Ponte. And they're not all your friends.'

Craft and greed warred with the fear in Ponte's eyes. Suddenly, Taglione gave Ponte what his assistants had dubbed 'the smile'. Wry and fleeting, it hinted that there but for the grace of God I go, that maybe next time the luck of the draw would find the *Consigliere* the prosecutor and Taglione his prisoner. He didn't believe it for a second, but it was very effective with low lifes who liked to think they were really decent fellows underneath it all.

'Sarah's right. You can save your own life.'

Ponte looked from him to Sarah and back. Taglione held his breath. The noises that made silence in an office, the whisper of forced air, the buzz of the florescent lighting, the hum of traffic beyond thick glass, gathered deeply. Taglione listened to his heart, watched the blood pulse through a blue vein in Sarah's temple, watched Ponte's lips grow tighter and tighter. He glanced longingly at the door.

'You're going to get me knocked off.'

'No way. We're going to be very, very careful. You're worth too much alive. Jack will set up a safe house.'

Ponte still hesitated.

Taglione said, 'You just may get out of this mess relatively intact, Sal. You're young enough to retire, start something straight, and maybe make a new life for yourself. We won't stand in your way if you serve us.' He reached into his desk and flashed a shot Jack Warner had pulled down with a tele-photo lens.

'I'll bet *she* thinks you're straight already.'

Ponte nodded.

Taglione handed him the immunity agreement. 'Contingent upon the United States Attorney's approval.'

Ponte gave him a sour smile. 'Pretty sure of yourself. Had it ready to go.'

'Let's just say I was sure you weren't stupid.'

Ponte opened a gold pen and signed. Taglione witnessed his signature, as did Sarah.

Taglione said, 'You have my word. You play fair with me, I'll play fair with you. But if you ever go back on our agreement, you're finished.' He stuck out his hand to seal the bargain.

'Fuck you. I ain't shaking your hand.' He threw his pen at Taglione's brimming waste paper basket. Taglione watched it land on top, nestled on scrap. It looked to be solid gold and surely cost more than any single item in his office.

'You think it's all over when you get us?' Ponte shouted. 'You think you win?'

'We are winning, Sal. We're going to beat you. We're going to break the rackets.'

'You win shit.' Ponte laughed savagely. 'You're digging holes in sand. Guys'll fill our place.'

'Not guys with thirty years experience, *Consigliere* Ponte. Not pros like you.'

'Maybe guys worse.' He lunged blindly towards the door; and Warner followed.

'Sal? Before you go?'

'What now?'

'Where's Don Richard?'

★   ★   ★

Jack Warner made sure Sal Ponte returned his rental car without incident. Then, as they waited for a cab on East Forty-eighth Street, so Ponte could return to his office, his bodyguards and his real life, Warner said, 'Sal, if you ever blow my cover I'll put it on the street about tonight.'

'Fuck you. I made my deal with Taglione. You have to protect me.'

'You made your deal with a lawyer. I'm a cop. You never saw me in your life.' Smiling, he took Ponte's hand – one businessman bidding another goodnight – and ground the *consigliere's* rings until he winced.

A gypsy cab approached. Ponte hailed it, but Warner stopped him and put him in a yellow cab instead. Then he started walking towards Second Avenue. When Ponte's cab had rounded the corner the gypsy caught up and Warner got in.

Reggie Rand was at the wheel, wearing a cap and doper glasses so dark that Warner wondered how he saw in the night. 'What did he say?'

Warner sighed. He hadn't intended to report so soon to Reggie, hoping the FBI would find Don Richard quickly. But when Reggie stopped for a red light, removed his glasses, and turned his empty eyes on him, Warner could not risk lying. 'Little Richie's in Miami.'

'Anything else?'

'Anything else? It's the biggest secret in town.'

Reggie shrugged and returned his attention to the traffic. 'I'm interested in whatever Ponte reports next.'

He was so casual that Warner got alarmed. 'You gonna pay me?'

Reggie glanced in the rearview mirror. 'Of course, Jack. We always pay you. Where can I drop you?'

'Foley Square.'

Reggie let him off a hundred yards from the US Attorney's building and drove blithely into the night. Warner went upstairs, more puzzled than ever about Christopher Taggart's dance with the Mafia. He had been worried they were going to hit Don Richard. Reggie might be jerking him around, but he had seemed genuinely unimpressed by the news of the Cirillo boss's whereabouts. Tony Taglione was still at his desk, though it was nearly nine o'clock.

'Home free?'

'Ponte's fine.'

'Good. Jack, sit down a minute. Stick that on the floor.'

Warner removed the pile of papers and sat down warily. Tony Taglione never asked you to sit down before he got to the point.

'I have a problem. I think you can help.'

Had he screwed up? Had the Brit turned on him? Taglione clasped his hands together and eyed Warner over his fingertips.

'I want to know something.'

'Yeah?'

'Who my brother Chris hangs out with.'

Warner had to stifle a smile of relief. Taglione's *brother* – the freelance racketeer – and he thought the Strikeforce chief was on to him. He said, 'I'm not sure I know what you mean.'

'Just what I said. But I want it done quietly.'

'Any idea what I'm looking for?'

Taglione sighed, clearly upset. 'I don't know. The Rizzolos, maybe. You know about his thing with Eddie the Cop's sister?'

Warner nodded carefully. 'I hear the rumours.'

'Rumours! Try the newspaper.'

'I thought that had cooled down.'

'I'm hoping so, but I want to know about her and whomever else he's involved with.'

Warner hesitated, trying to figure how best to work what could be a very nice opportunity. He said, 'Okay if I talk out of turn?'

'What?'

'Listen, Mr Taglione. It's tough having your brother date a Mafia girl, but when you get down to it, so what? There's no law against fucking a good-looking broad whose brother happens to be a hood.'

Taglione flushed.

'Or are we talking about something more than dating?'

'I don't know. I just don't like what I'm feeling.'

'Can you –'

'No! Just find out who he hangs out with.'

Warner stood up. 'Okay.'

Taglione forced a smile. 'Hey, you did a good job with Ponte. Thanks, Jack.'

'You want I should get down to Miami?'

'No. The FBI's put Don Richard on the ten-most-wanted list. They'll find him. You just check out what I told you.'

Taglione returned to his work, dismissing him. Warner put the papers on the chair and backed out. The funny thing was that he was already checking out Taggart on his own. He walked into Chinatown to a payphone, called Reggie Rand's answering machine, and waited a few minutes for a return call.

'This is worth fifty grand.'

'I'll be the judge of that.'

'The boss asked me for postage on his brother's pals.'

He listened to a short silence. Then Reggie said, 'Your money will be deposited tomorrow.'

'What should I do?'

'Stall him. We need a little more time.'

Reggie hung up and turned to Taggart, who was avidly studying a silenced pistol. 'That was Jack Warner. Your brother is getting curious about your friends.'

'He'll waste six months on Helen. I was right to go public with her.'

Reggie thought that was overly optimistic. 'Perhaps, but –'

Taggart cut him off with a gesture. He was deeply absorbed in the weapon; the silencer screwed on and off the barrel like the finest machine tool, and the bullet-packed magazine was as heavy as a surf casting weight. 'Guaranteed they use this gun, right?'

He extended it to Reggie, who put it in a briefcase where it nested in a green velvet cradle. 'Guaranteed.'

'How do I know for sure?' Taggart demanded.

'Hit men never lie.'

&#42;   &#42;   &#42;

Don Richard Cirillo was sunning in a sand chair on an empty stretch of private beach situated slightly north of Miami. The house behind him was owned by a guy nobody knew. The ocean sparkled in ribbons of pale green and robin's egg blue. Beside him sat Frankie DeLuca. Their acquaintance went back fifty years to Don Richard's apprenticeship breaking welchers' fingers at the Glen Island Casino.

The warm wind drove a brightly coloured beachball towards them. Some distance behind the ball came a girl chasing it. Don Richard saw she was pretty and was wearing a tiny bathing suit. He tried to stop the ball, but it skipped on a footprint in the sand, took flight for a short hop over his sandal and rolled on, blurring red, white and blue like a barber pole. The girl glanced over her shoulder. Way down the beach a child was toddling after her. It was too far away to hear if the child was crying, but Don Richard presumed it was.

'A grand on the ball.'

Frankie DeLuca looked up from the racing form. He rubbed his rheumy eyes, adjusted his sunglasses, and eyed the ball which had rolled well past them. Then he gauged the girl, who broke into a determined run.

'You're covered.'

He had failed to notice the child, as Don Richard had bet he would, because Frankie was closer to the umbrella they'd set up against the wind and it blocked his view; besides, his eyes were going bad.

The girl looked back at the kid and ran even harder, pumping her firm legs in the sand, shaking her breasts. Frankie gestured towards the water, where a catamaran with an orange sail was skimming onto the beach.

'Run on the hard sand! On the hard sand! By the waves! . . . What does she think, she's a mudder?'

She looked over her shoulder again, stopped abruptly, and jogged back to collect her baby. The ball rolled on, a bright dot receding in the distance where a cluster of high-rise condos gleamed like crumpled tinfoil.

Frankie smacked his forehead with his palm and picked up his paper. 'That's why they use jockeys.'

You owe me a grand.'

'Can it wait 'til lunch?'

Don Richard noticed his bodyguards, local boys who were edging nearer as the catamaran skidded onto the beach. The orange sail flapped in the stiff wind, crackling like pistol shots. Four guys jumped off – two rough-looking blacks with twists of dreadknots swinging from their brows, and two whites carrying towels. The blacks were handling the boat. They looked like natives who had sailed straight from Jamaica. They quickly dragged the front of the catamaran around, heaved the twin hulls back into the low surf, and made the sail stop flapping. The whites trotted towards Don Richard, but his bodyguards intercepted them, twenty feet away.

'What's that?' asked Frankie, looking up again at a pair of muffled sounds, like somebody spitting. It was less noise than the sail, but the bodyguards dropped on the sand. The tourists stepped over them and crouched in front of the old men. They had pistols with long, fat silencers under the towels.

'Mr Cirillo?'

Don Richard jerked a thumb at his old friend, Frankie. 'Him.'

# 23

Christopher Taggart stood with his back to the door of a dark LaGuardia Airport hotel room. The wood vibrated against his spine as jets rumbled over. A thin, fuzzy grey line marked where the curtains touched and a red dot glowed on a cigarette the coked-up gunman was smoking. Neither could see the other's face, and for double his usual fee, Don Richard's killer was describing the job. He was a New Zealander who travelled the world as foredeckman on a maxi ocean racing yacht; his accent was mild, as if Reggie's crisp English had been slightly diluted by Ronnie Wald's southern Californian accent. Swiftly, he reported sailing into the beach and shooting the bodyguards.

'Down they go, like stones, and we're over them and up to the old geezers in their chairs. I say "Mr Cirillo?" like I'm paging him for a phone call in the next coconut tree, and do you know what he does? He tells me his friend is him.

'Shit. Two old geezers side by side, no hair, no teeth, chests like spars with ribs, hair in their noses, how the fuck am I to sort them out? Strike me lucky, 'cause when the Pommy gave me the job, he slipped me Cirillo's picture. So I whip out the picture and, sure thing, Cirillo's sending his mate down the river. His mate looks like he's going to cry; really fixed him, doing him in to save his own neck.

'What else do you want to know? Right. I say, "This is for Mike and Helen." Just like the Pommy told me . . . His mate's just sitting there and sort of smiles when it's over, like he won a race by living longer. I look at him and I know for sure that when the cops come, this old geezer will swear he was fast asleep. So I say ta ta and he says ta ta. I give him a little salute and we back down the beach, board the boat, and breeze out.'

'Did he know what you meant?'

'He knew he was going to die.'

'But did he know why?'

'Do you mean, "Say, who are Mike and Helen?" Mate, if he didn't know then, he's got eight billion years in heaven to think it over.'

'Heaven?'

The killer laughed. 'Bastards like him phone ahead. They'll comp him right through the Pearly Gates.'

Taggart walked through a long hall, down the stairs, and into the elevator. The deed was almost done, nearly eleven years since they had killed his father. Sometimes in the night he had wondered whether time would blunt his satisfaction; it had not.

Two uniformed State Troopers intercepted him in the lobby. 'We were about to come looking for you, Mr Taggart. The governor's plane just landed. He wants to ride in your car.'

'We're running late. I'll need an escort.'

'Lights and sirens?' The trooper grinned, knowing what a cop buff Taggart was, and reached to slap him on the back. But Taggart was already striding towards the door, and his cold look told the young trooper that the governor's friend would not welcome being touched today.

They hurried from the hotel across the highway and into a side entrance to the airport. Taggart's driver manoeuvred the Rolls onto the private docking apron as Constanzo's New York State Gulfstream trundled in from the runway. The governor bounded athletically down the ramp and climbed in beside him.

'Welcome home,' Taggart greeted him, waving a split of Moet that he was struggling to open with shaking hands.

'What's the occasion?'

'Pulled off a big one.'

He tore the wire, but he couldn't get his fingers around the cork.

'Let me,' said Costanzo.

Taggart stabbed the partition button and thrust it at the driver. 'Open this. Don't shake it up.'

The driver fumbled.

'Hold the cork and twist the bottle for crissake!'

The cork popped out at last and Taggart snatched the foaming bottle. He filled two glasses, handed one to Costanzo, who was eyeing him curiously.

'Let's drink to my Pop.'

'Anytime.' The governor raised his glass and touched Taggart's. 'Mike Taglione.'

'*Mike Taglione.*'

Taggart drank deep. The car lurched into motion, and they raced out the airport, bracketed by howling state cruisers. The governor settled back. 'Oh, that's delicious. Wha'd you do this time, co-op Gracie Mansion?'

'Don't tempt me. The first sporting event in the Super-Spire Stadium, if I have my way, will be a fund-raiser for Friends of the Zoo – throw that bald son of a bitch to a lion. So how we doing?'

They discussed the stadium project on the way into Manhattan. The governor was returning from Washington, where he'd had some luck with the DOT about the subway spur, but the reality, he reminded Chris, was that the mayor was still lukewarm. When Taggart dropped him at the World Trade Center, Costanzo repeated what he had been saying for sometime. 'You're golden if you get the mayor's support. Without him we're in a nasty fight. I'll back you like I promised, Chris. And I'll lean on the UDC, but you know damned well I don't carry the weight in Manhattan that he does.'

'I'm going to get him, one of these days, for jerking me around.' Constanzo gave him a hard look. 'You seem to be forgetting that politics isn't war, Chris. You don't win by destroying a guy you'll want on your side next time. Ease up . . . Say hello to your brother.'

Taggart ordered his driver to head back to Queens.

At Visions, Helen's club, the bartenders were setting up and vacuum cleaners were whining on the carpets. He pushed through the front door, wrote a note, and told three tough Sicilians guarding the hall to her office to deliver it.

Helen was at her desk, icily beautiful in a white silk blouse and black velvet suit. She seemed older, he thought, tempered, and dark with knowledge. She had changed her red nail polish to lavender, and her lipstick, too, was paler. She was wearing large diamond stud ear-rings. Reggie's people had kept a close eye on her and there was no word she had been going out, but he wondered with a stab of jealousy if the jewels were a gift.

She touched his note with her long fingernails. 'Good news?'

'You know it was Don Richard who attacked your family.'

'I know that,' she said coldly. 'And I know why.'

'He's dead.'

'*When?*'

'Today. In Florida. Shot. The papers will have it soon.'

She studied his triumphant expression before saying, 'My father would have been pleased.'

'How about you?'

'Part of me cheers and says the old men are cancelling each other out. The other part asks what difference any of it makes.'

'I'm bringing the news to the part that cheers.'

'And how do you feel?'

'What do you mean?'

'Didn't you blame him for killing your father, too?'

'I told you I didn't.'

'I never believed that.'

294

Taggart nodded; of course, he hadn't fooled her. 'It's good news for me, too. Very, very good news. A big debt's been paid.'

'And now what?'

'I've paid you a debt, too, Crazy Mikey's next.'

'And then?'

Taggart wanted to say, *We're getting out*, but this was not the moment. There was still Crazy Mikey. He said only, 'We'll talk about castles after Mikey.'

'Castles?' Helen picked up a pencil and drew A's into stars across the top of a letter. 'In the meantime, we've lost territory and momentum. Eddie and I are holding on by our fingernails.'

'I'm aware of that.'

'You are? Has anyone taken your buildings? Has anyone firebombed your plant, your trucks?' She drew the stars harder, gouging lines in the paper. Suddenly she turned the letter toward Taggart. 'See this?'

Taggart's pulse quickened.

The Justice Department seal. And under the text, the razor strokes of his brother's signature. 'It's a "request" to come in for a little talk.'

'He can't make you. Your lawyer can take care of it.'

'I already went.'

'What for?'

'Curiosity. Besides, as my father used to say, "there's answers in questions".'

'What is Tony investigating?'

Helen gave him a strange smile. 'Everything . . . And nothing.'

'What did he ask about?'

'He didn't ask. He told me to keep my "filthy" hands off you.'

'Tony called you into his office just to say that?'

She raised her eyes with a shy smile. 'You know what? I hate to say this. I feel like a fool, but I missed you these three months.'

'Three months, two weeks and one day. I couldn't call until I gave you Don Richard.'

She nodded. 'I think that's one of the things I like about you. . . How are your women?'

'I haven't seen them except for business.'

She stood up, rounded her desk, circled her arms around Taggart's neck and kissed him. 'I'm glad. Thank you for coming back.'

'What did you tell Tony?'

'I told him he was abusing his office. I told him he was taking advantage of his power. I told him I ought to sue the government.'

'You don't know how hard it was for him to do it.'

'I do. He couldn't hide how much he cares for you. For a second I thought, he would kill me right there at his desk.'

'He's only trying to save me from myself.'

'It's way too late.'

She said it with a smile, and kissed his mouth again, and even allowed him to carry her urgently to the couch for a sort of primitive victory feast. But inside she felt chilled by the matter-of-fact way he reported the murder, and frightened by the icy look that turned his blue eyes grey when he promised Mikey was next. The Cirillos were her mortal enemies, yes, deserving to die if anyone did; but Chris seemed unable to see that the time was hurtling near when it would be too late to pretend he was different from them. And too late to pretend that their game of castles was more than a fantasy.

What did she care? she asked herself. And her answer, ironically, was that she had fallen in love – a dangerous state of the heart and mind that revealed beauty in places she had never seen it, and horrors that her father had raised her to ignore.

★    ★    ★

Sal Ponte was driving to meet Mrs Hugel when he heard the news on the radio. He found the Hutchinson Parkway, and headed south over the bridge to Long Island. Crazy Mickey's bodyguards had apartments around his in the town house condo. When Ponte arrived, two of them were watching his front door and three more waited in a car.

Mikey was drinking coffee alone at the kitchen table. It was a modern kitchen with a breakfast nook, all clean and shiny. There was a red-checked oil cloth on the table. The windows overlooked the broad, blue East River and the points spanned by the silvery Whitestone Bridge. Mikey had on a V neck cashmere pullover, his gold chain and spoon, and tight shorts. Ponte smelled perfume, but the girl was gone.

'I got bad news, kid.'

'I just heard. Sit down.'

'Who told you?'

'The fucking radio. Sit down, Sal.'

Ponte sank to the kitchen chair. 'You got any more coffee?'

'*I* knew where he was. And *you* knew where he was. I didn't tell anybody. That leaves you.'

'Wait a minute.'

'Wha'd they give you?'

'Who?'

He saw the coffee mug coming, clenched in Mikey's hand, but couldn't move fast enough. It shattered against his forehead. Hot coffee burned his eyes. The force of it knocked him off the chair and he hit his head against the refrigerator as he went down. Mikey snatched the coffee pot off the stove and held the spout over his face. 'What did the Rizzolos give you to tell 'em where my father was?'

'I didn't tell the Rizzolos!'

He said it with such utter conviction – because, after all, it was the truth – that Mikey hesitated long enough for Ponte to talk. 'I didn't tell the Rizzolos. What the hell would I tell 'em for? You think I'm going leave you and your father for a bunch of South Brooklyn *gavonne*. What am I, crazy?'

Mikey didn't move. 'Somebody told 'em.'

Ponte had prepared an answer in his car. It was thin but he reasoned that if he didn't know that he had betrayed Don Richard to the Strikeforce and that someone on the Strikeforce blew it, he would have made a similar guess. 'Probably somebody spotted him. Lousy luck.'

Mikey shook his head. 'I can't believe that. I can't do business believing in lousy luck. You know what I think? Maybe you didn't tell the Rizzolos.'

'I didn't.'

'So who *did* you tell?'

Ponte died inside. Mikey tipped the coffee pot and half a cup splashed in his face. Ponte yelled and covered his face. His heart started going in his chest like he was going to blow up.

'Sal. I'm not as dumb as you think. Who'd you tell where my father was?' Ponte knew his only chance was to keep clearly stating his case. 'Will you do me one thing for all the years I served your old man?'

'What?'

'Will you listen why?'

It was tantamount to an admission of betrayal and Mikey went rigid.

'*Get up!*'

Mikey wiped the shards of broken mug off the table and found a new one in the cabinet. He filled it for Ponte, and topped up his own cup and put the pot back on the stove. 'Why?'

'For you.'

'For me.' Mikey looked out the window, looked back at Ponte. 'You killed my father for me? I didn't like the bastard, but you know goddamned well I didn't hate him enough to kill him.'

'I also did it for him.'

'Don't jerk me around.'

'I didn't tell the Rizzolos. I told Tony Taglione.'

'Taglione?'

'He had me by the balls. I had to give him something.'

'What do you mean you had to give him something?' Mikey screamed. 'What do you mean "*something*"? Guys take their lumps. Since when is it okay to squeal?'

'I did it for a lot of reasons, not just for myself.'

'You better name a few good ones fast.'

'First of all, to guide you when you take over. I'm no good to you in jail. We've got eight hundred soldiers, Mikey. We'd be in the Fortune Five Hundred if they counted people like us. Half your *capos* think they should have the job. The older guys who've been around, they think you're a kid.'

'I wouldn't have to take over if my father wasn't dead.'

'I didn't mean for him to get killed. I did it to save his life. The Rizzolos would have hit your father sooner or later. How was I to know they had somebody inside the Strikeforce?'

'The Rizzolos couldn't put somebody inside the Strikeforce if he was invisible.'

'Are you saying the Feds shot your father?'

Mikey slammed his fist on the table. 'Don't you understand yet? There's somebody *else* doing this. Somebody *else* inside the Feds. Somebody *else* got my father.'

'Who?'

'How the fuck should I know?' Mikey glared at Ponte and calmly returned to the first subject. 'There's another reason you ratted on my father, you know? With him you were only his adviser. With me, you're older and smarter, and you think you can run me. With my father out of the way, you figure you're almost boss.' He smiled. 'Admit it, Sal, you must have thought that a little.' With nothing to lose, Salvatore Ponte took a chance on honesty. 'A little.' Crazy Mikey looked out the window. His silence stretched to a minute, then two. Ponte watched the second hand creep a third time around the kitchen clock. When he couldn't bear it any longer he asked, 'What are you going to do?'

'Call up Eddie Rizzolo and stop this fucking war.'

'Eddie Rizzolo?'

'Why not? I know he didn't kill my father. He's been trying to get in touch for some time. Wants to do some dope. Why not? We're both young guys. There's plenty in New York for the two of us. And if there is somebody else, we'll get him. What do you think, *Consigliere*? Let's stop the war before the Strikeforce blows us away.'

'Your father thought his sister's running things.'

' *What*? Nobody told me that.'

'That's what he thought.'

'What do you think?'

'Maybe. She has the brains.'

'Fuck Eddie.' Mikey laughed. 'I'd rather do it with her.'

'I don't advise that.'

'I was joking. But why not, *Consigliere*?'

'Your father had me get a guy to take care of her.'

'Jesus Christ. Was that your idea?'

'No.'

'Does Eddie know?'

'The guy missed. I don't know what Eddie knows. I don't know if she told him.'

'She probably didn't. He wouldn't be offering peace.' He laughed softly. 'Guy like Eddie, killing his father and brother is one thing, but if you even *look* like you wanna hit on his sister, he'll challenge you to a fucking duel.'

'So now you know.'

'Thanks for the warning,' Mikey said, and fell silent again.

Ponte inched his eyes to the window, fixed on a sailboat beating across the water. The day looked so beautiful. He hoped –

'You know all the stuff I can do to you, Sal?'

'I know.'

'To your girlfriend.'

'I know,' Ponte said, wondering how Mikey knew about her, but by now he was beyond surprise.

'Even your family, if I have to.'

'My *family*?'

'Sal. You killed my father.'

'I didn't mean to.'

Mikey stood up and stretched, rippling muscle through the arms of his cashmere pullover. Ponte saw him suddenly as the new man events had made him, the warrior prince turned king.

Ponte couldn't stand the silence. Hating the fear in his voice he asked, 'What are you going to do?'

'I'm gonna get in touch with Eddie Rizzolo.'

'What about me?'

Crazy Mikey stepped close to his godfather and Ponte thought he was going to kiss him. Instead, he took his coke spoon, extended it the length of the chain, and gently placed the miniature barrels of the replica sawn-off shotgun between Ponte's lips.

'Add it up, Sal. The best thing for you and me and your wife and your girlfriend is for you to jump in front of a subway.'

*     *     *

Weary, fed up with himself, Jack Warner lay on his bed, staring at the ceiling and waiting for Tony Taglione to figure out who leaked that Don Richard was hiding in Miami. *The New York Post* lay unopened on the rug. The front page had a picture of an E Train for those readers who hadn't seen one, and another of Sal Ponte, described as 'Murdered Mob Kingpin's Adviser, Sally Smarts'.

Once the Strikeforce chief eliminated himself and the new assistant, Sarah Gallagher, and maybe his senior assistant, Ron Koestler – all of which would take about five minutes – he might hit on one of the FBI agents assigned to search for Don Richard. Establishing that an FBI agent hadn't blown it deliberately or just plain screwed up might buy a few days. But in the end, Warner was screwed; or, more accurately, he thought with disgust, he had screwed himself, allowing himself to get suckered by Taggart and Reggie Rand. Of course, they were hunting Don Richard; why else would they have paid him three hundred and fifty thousand bucks? At least, they had paid. He had checked his Swiss account. A lot of good it did him, lying on the bed in the fifth floor studio apartment on East Ninth Street, a block from the tenement where he had grown up. Every time the stairs creaked he looked at the door, expecting his partners to break it down, waving guns and warrants in that order. He had locked his own gun in his gun safe, a two-hundred-pound steel cube under his bed. Goddamned if he was going to kill one of the guys.

When they came he was dozing; it wasn't through the door and it wasn't anyone he knew. A guy swung through the window on a rope, like Tarzan. He was wearing leather, head to toe, which protected him from the broken glass. His eyes gleamed through slits in the mask. He held a gun on Warner, while he unlocked the bars on the fire escape window, opened the sash, and offered a hand to the Englishman. Reggie Rand dropped lithely from the sill and told Tarzan to leave by the door.

'No,' he told Warner, when they were alone. 'I didn't come to kill you.'

'You dropped in to apologize?'

'I gave you my word,' Reggie replied. 'Events moved out of my control. I'll do what I can to make it up.'

'How about a presidential pardon?' Warner hadn't moved an inch, nor did he intend to. He lay there, hands behind his head, wondering why the Brit was going to so much trouble to kill him, when Tarzan could have done it for him.

'Tonight, I'll get you to Europe. You're a fairly wealthy man abroad. You'll want a plastic surgeon. It could be worse.'

'Jail would be worse,' Warner admitted. 'Death would be worse, too.'

'You speak Russian, don't you?'

'*Da*. I picked it up in the neighbourhood.'

'Not to worry,' the Brit said and Warner began to think maybe he was telling the truth. 'If you get bored with your money, there'll be plenty of interesting work.'

'Let me get this straight. You're saving my ass because you broke your word about that prick Ponte getting killed. And I don't have to do anything.'

'One small service.'

Here it came. 'What's that? Hijack the plane?'

'When you land at Orly a lady will point out an American who keeps track of comings and goings for the CIA. You will let him intercept you and, before you vanish, you will volunteer the information that Crazy Mikey Cirillo had a narcotics deal going down on the Hudson River.'

'What does the CIA care?'

'You will make it sound like an apology to your former colleagues.'

'What if this guy doesn't let me vanish?'

'The lady will deal with him.'

Warner swung his feet off the bed and regarded Reggie with interest. Now he knew why Reggie wasn't going to kill him. And at last he had an inkling of what Taggart was up to – though still no clue why – but he had run out of time and was in too much trouble himself to use his theory against Taggart.

'It sounds to me like Taggart's setting up Mikey.'

'Can you think of a more deserving soul?'

★　★　★

Tony Taglione passed a glossy black and white photograph around a gang of agent supervisors who had crowded into his office. Papers had been removed from tables, chairs, and window sills and restacked in the hall. Cigarette smoke loomed in the fluorescent lights. He didn't allow his attorneys to smoke around him, but cops and investigators had different needs.

'What's wrong with this one?' he asked.

Four mobsters were getting out of a limousine. In the background others were standing around the baroque iron gates of a New Jersey cemetery where family and associates had gathered to bury Don Richard.

'Come on, guys. Four hoods getting out of a car.'

'Well, for starters,' a woman answered, 'Eddie "the Cop" Rizzolo and Crazy Mikey are not shooting at each other.'

'Good. What else?' he asked, and the others joined in.

'Eddie's hand is healed.'

'What's left of it.'

'He looks like a punch press operator ordering four beers.'

'Knock it off! Since last summer when the New York families went to war, the body count includes five chiefs dead: Imperiali, Conforti, Bono, Rizzolo and Cirillo. Between us destroying the council and them killing each other, the whole New York mob's been turned inside out.'

'In fact,' a police detective interrupted, 'the guys we indicted turned out to be the lucky ones.'

That got a laugh and a wit from the DEA got another by calling, 'With the possible exception of Eddie Rizzolo, Sr.'

Taglione cut it off savagely. 'None of us can be proud of a jailhouse murder. It reflects as badly on the Strikeforce as goddamned Jack Warner. So let's not pat ourselves on the back.' He iced the room with his piercing eyes. 'But that's water over the dam. The thing is now to capitalize on this bloodletting by continuing to go after the successors while they're still off balance – hopefully before citizens get caught in the cross-fire. But we've got to know who the new leaders will be. Who's taking over?'

'Look at that grin on Eddie's face,' an agent ventured. 'Pretty happy for a guy whose father and brother got killed.'

'The Rizzolos are really throwing their weight around.'

'I hear Eddie's looking for dope again.'

'So do I.'

'Right, right.'

Taglione asked, 'What do you say we shift a ton of people onto Eddie Rizzolo? Let's find out who he's connecting with.'

★     ★     ★

They went out gung ho, but he still worried. When in trouble as he feared he was now, Tony Taglione turned to his boss and mentor, the patrician United States Attorney, Arthur Finch. He left telephone messages. Arthur dropped by the Strikeforce floor, winced as always at the chaos, and asked, 'Time for a drink?'

'No way. Look at these transcripts from taps starting last summer.'

'It's customary in the real world to say, "Not this evening, thank you, Arthur".'

'Look at this.' Taglione shoved him a transcript at random. 'Pay phone outside a Rego Park pizza joint.'

Arthur donned half moon glasses and read in Harvard tones the line highlighted with yellow Magic Marker. '"Pay the fucks what they want. They're connected with the Rizzolos".'

Taglione handed him another. Arthur read, ' "I got some postage on Frankie Rizzolo".' He handed it back. 'I'm always astonished how *lazy* racketeers are. Why won't they simply get in their car and drive half a mile to a safe phone.'

'Arrogance. Here's another.'

' "We're doing good. We got to the Rizzolos".'

'And . . .'

' "You know any Rizzolos? So ask them".'

'Rizzolos, Rizzolos, Rizzolos. Suddenly, in less than a year – while we're chasing Cirillos – Rizzolos are big time, number two in New York.'

Arthur cleared the edge of a chair and sat down. 'Back up. Are you saying the Rizzolos killed Tommy Lucia's boss and Vito Imperiale and Joey Reina and Harry Bono and Al Conforti Richard Cirillo?'

'The Rizzolos benefited.'

'Until Edward Sr. and his son Frank were murdered.'

Taglione held up the cemetery shot. 'But here's Eddie the Cop, big as life at the funeral, as much as saying, let's make peace.'

'Statesman-like.'

'Eddie's a hood. The FBI expected him to be across the street with a rifle.'

'So,' said Arthur, folding his glasses and straightening his lions-rampant necktie, 'we ask, how did a hood get so smart?'

Taglione found another picture. 'His little sister.'

Arthur read Helen Rizzolo's dossier, which covered major events in her life: marriage, annulment, college, visits to her father's prison, and the rumoured kidnapping. Then he looked up with a kind smile. 'I presume you haven't tried this theory on your staff.'

'You heard about Chris?'

'I saw them at the Governor's Ball. Quite the striking couple, his Adonis to her dark Persephone . . . "Woe, Woe to Adonis".'

'What about my theory?'

'I like it. She starts out as her father's messenger. She's intelligent, has some education and a head for business, and she lets her bloodthirsty brothers do the dirty work.'

'Except for one thing. Jack Warner lands at Orly Airport, pulls a James Bond and disappears. Right? By the time Interpol gets on it, some thirty-nine year old burly Irish-American guys who look like New York cops are reported crossing Swiss, Italian, and Spanish borders, shipping out of Channel ports, and cruising the Mediterranean. How the hell did the *Rizzolos* get Jack out of the country?'

'And why did they take the chance?'

'They have their claws into freight forwarding at Kennedy, so maybe they could get him aboard a plane – maybe.'

'But off in Paris? That's what I can't understand. What do they know of the French?'

'And who got Jack papers? The State Department swears there's no way he can flounce around Europe without top-notch forgeries.'

'Actually,' Arthur replied mildly, 'these are questions the Attorney General's been asking me. How, as he put it, did a bunch of Brooklyn "wops" turn into international spymasters? He thinks the Rizzolos have established international contacts.'

'Brilliant. But with whom?'

'Someone she might have met in Europe. Did you know she'd been to Italy for earthquake relief?'

'Years ago.'

'Still, the AG thinks it's worth investigating a Sicilian link.'

'Bullshit. That's the first thing I thought of, but this is much classier.'

Arthur raised an eyebrow.

'Look at the murders,' Taglione retorted. 'Joe Reina killed by a radio-controlled car bomb like in the Middle East. Imperiale shot by Berettas in the Israeli two-shot pattern. The agents told me Imperiale looked like he'd been bitten by a bunch of snakes. Something about how the Israelis teach their killers to shoot.'

'But weren't they black?'

'Then they were trained by Israelis, who're all over Africa. And what happened to Joey Cirillo's goon squad in the Bronx with a rocket launcher? Doesn't this sound way too sophisticated for Brooklyn "wops" or even for Sicilians?'

'Yes.'

'Here's something else the AG doesn't know. A woman I worked with in Washington, who's since moved to the CIA, told me Jack Warner sent a message. Kind of a parting gift – or shot – I'm not sure which.'

'What?'

'Before he disappeared Warner sought out the CIA agent at Orly to tell him he heard that Mikey Cirillo buys most of his heroin right here in New York, from a guy he meets once a week on a boat in the Hudson.'

# 24

Two ocean racers floated side by side in Taggart's Tarrytown boathouse, the stealthy black doper boat Taggart used for his meetings with Crazy Mikey Cirillo, and a bright red luxury model. The newcomer, stolen the night before from the Hawk Racing yard in Mamaroneck, was built on similar lines, though its hull was made of aluminium – which made it a radar beacon.

Reggie had pulled the head off one of the black boat's V-8s, while Taggart was busy stowing kilos of heroin under the floorboards of the red boat. The Englishman was wearing a white shirt and his Drumnadrochit Piping Society tie, and though he was adjusting the valves with socket wrench and calipers, his cuffs were as white as the heroin. 'I'm going to miss you, Reggie,' Chris said.

'Why don't you simply *kill* Mikey?'

'Because someday – probably not when he's arrested, but maybe on the way to court, during the trial, or even on the way to jail – he'll start talking. He knows enough to destroy the whole Cirillo organization and knock some big holes in the Confortis and Imperiales.'

'Why would he talk?'

'Mikey's all that's left of his own blood. His brother's in jail, his father's dead, and Ponte's dead. The rest of the bosses and *capos* are his enemies. And if he doesn't talk, he rots in jail for the rest of his life. So me and my Pop come out even, either way.'

Reggie bolted the head back in place and inspected the wiring to the explosives in the bilge of the black boat. Then he climbed out of the compartment, started the engines and closed the box. Turning to Taggart, he submerged him in the flat pools of his eyes.

'*Then* you will walk away?'

'You asked me that ten years ago.'

'You have a long memory.'

'Always.'

'What about Ms Rizzolo? What if she won't walk away?'

Taggart smiled. 'I'll reform her.'

'And if she resists reformation?'

'I'll kidnap her back to Europe.'

'She can destroy you, you know.'

'She'd destroy herself in the process. But she has no reason. In fact, she might even be in love with me. Want to be my best man?'

'And we'll all live happily ever after.'

'Except for Crazy Mikey.'

'And the redoubtable Eddie Rizzolo?'

'Eddie's another reason to reform Helen. I want Helen clear before the dumb fuck finally gets himself indicted for something.'

'Do it quickly. He's sniffing around for a drug deal.'

Reggie cast off the lines and backed the red boat into the river, which approaching night had turned deep purple.

★    ★    ★

At the hour Taggart watched Reggie disappear down the Hudson, Tony Taglione got a call from the Strikeforce's FBI agent director. An agent planted as an instructor in a Manhattan health club where Crazy Mikey had agreed to meet Eddie Rizzolo had just recorded an incredible tape. Twenty minutes later the agent ran in, flinging open his raincoat. A skin-tight red Spandex T-shirt with East Side Iron Works stretched across his bulging chest drew whistles from the agents and attorneys that Taglione had hurriedly assembled to hear the evidence. Taglione shoved the cassette into his ghetto blaster. It started with a heavy grinding noise, punctuated by sharp hisses.

'Sounds like he's fucking a snake.'

'The heavy sound is the chain pull,' the agent explained. 'The microphone's in the weight machine.'

'What's the hiss?'

'That's the prick breathing. They start talking in a minute. Mikey's on the machine, doing like bench presses. Eddie the Cop comes up and stands over him. All around are their hoods, trying to outpump each other, which is kind of funny 'cause a lot of them are spaghetti bellies. It's a legit club, so regular guys and girls are passing through and using the other machines. You can hear 'em talking in the background. I'm next to Mikey, instructing my partner, Zell, how to exercise her lungs. . . Okay. It starts in a second. Mikey pretends he's surprised to see Eddie, like they haven't set this thing up for a week.'

Cirillo's voice rasped out of the machine. *'What the fuck?'*

The agents laughed. 'Knock it off,' said Taglione.

'Yes, sir. This is Eddie talking now. Mr Subtlety.'

Eddie Rizzolo's voice vibrated with the hearty tones of a radio announcer. *'I hear you owe a guy.'*

*'Where'd you pick that up?'*

306

'The street says, "The Man Who Can" owes a ton.'

'You put out word about a deal.'

' You put out word about peace. Business is the best way to make peace, my father always said. Buyers and sellers don't have to be friends, but they can't be enemies.'

'I don't need your business.'

'The more you sell, the faster you pay off'

'I don't need your business.'

'Brooklyn.'

' What about it?

'If you don't supply me, I'm going to start a heroin detox program in Brooklyn.' 'What?'

'Yeah. It's a new method. Instead of methodone and counselling and all that shit, we set the kiddie gangs on your pushers.'

The weight chain ground. Mikey's breath hissed as he pumped. The agent said, 'Get this. Mikey is really being nice. I mean this is not the Crazy Mikey we know and love. He smiles, like Eddie's joking.'

'How will you know who are mine?'

'Anybody who's not mine. So be my man who can, then we're both happy.'

'Since when do you deal in product?'

'I been waiting for the right supplier. That's you. Hey, listen, I'm offering you the world on a platter. A steady street market from a guy you can trust.'

Another silence was underscored by the sound of the weight machine. Taglione asked, 'There are people around?'

'Yeah, but they're not close. And they're doing their own thing. Besides, what's he said so far?'

'Arrogant bastards.'

' What does your sister say?'

'My sister's got nothing to do with this.'

Taglione stared at the tape machine, aware the others were afraid to look at him.

'Relax. Just asking.'

'Sure you are,' said the agent.

'Shut up!' Taglione leaned over the tape player, but Mikey Cirillo abruptly changed the subject.

'Like I told you. We've fucked each other over. Your father and brother are dead. My brother's in jail. My father's dead. His consigliere – my godfather – killed himself.'

'From grief,' said Sarah Gallagher.

'Who's left? You and me. Hey, like you said, we're two young guys. We're on our own. We can work it out.'

'So when do I meet your man?'

'That's going to be a problem. He said no partners.'

307

'Who is this guy?' asked Taglione. 'Why can't we get a line on this guy?'

'*So we lean on him,*' said Eddie. '*Like I was kidding with you. He can figure out he'll have no customers.*'

'*This guy is independent.*'

'*Come on, he's a businessman. He's not going to fight two families. If he does, we blow him away and then you don't owe nobody anything. So what do you got to lose?*'

'*A goddamned good source, is what I got to lose.*'

'*Sorry, Mikey. If we're going to trust each other, I gotta meet him.*'

The chain ground again.

'Get this,' said the agent. 'Remember, they're standing there in shorts.' '*Eddie? You mind if I pat you for a wire?*'

'So Mikey gets off the bench and pats Eddie for a wire and the whole gym stops. I mean here's these two guys in shorts inspecting each other's asses like—s'

'Where are they meeting this supplier?'

'I don't know, Tony. They went into the sauna. I hung close, but couldn't catch much.'

'Did they say anything about a boat?'

The agent looked surprised. 'You kidding?'

'I'm not kidding. What did they say?'

'Mikey told Eddie, "I hope you don't get seasick".'

Taglione looked around his office. Somebody said, 'It sounds like they're meeting a mothership off-shore.'

'Catch those two together with a load of dope?'

'No way.'

'It can't be. Even Eddie's too smart to get near the stuff.'

'Can you blanket Eddie Rizzolo?' Taglione asked the DEA agent director. 'Take a lot of guys.'

'I don't care if it takes a hundred. I want to know every second where he is. And goddamnit, anybody who gets made might as well join Jack in Europe.'

★   ★   ★

Taggart's plan was simple – strand Mikey on the red boat, in which the heroin was hidden, turn the boat into the Feds, and let the law enforcement agents draw their own conclusions. He left Tarrytown at midnight and steered down river on a cool breeze. At half-speed – an effortless thirty-five miles per hour – the engines were quiet and he could hear the wake falling back on itself in the dark. He passed beneath the Tappen Zee Bridge, spotted the George Washington, and opened the throttles. In half an hour, the George Washington's catenary lights draped the horizon, and on each sweep of the radar screen a massive target blossomed in the lower right quadrant like a huge white flower.

Taggart pulled his ski mask over his face and steered for it. He found Reggie anchored in the red boat, two miles up from the bridge and an eighth of a mile off the Palisades, which loomed darkly on the Jersey shore. Crazy Mikey was lounging in the stern beside a huge man whom Taggart assumed at first was a bodyguard. But as he eased the black boat alongside and Reggie rafted them with a line on their midships cleats, he saw that Reggie had made the same mistake.

Eddie Rizzolo, with arms folded to conceal his missing fingers, was grinning.

'What the hell is he doing here?'

'He was aboard before I realized he wasn't the bodyguard. I decided best to play it through.'

'Did you sweep them?'

'Oh yes. And they swept me. Eddie brought cash.'

'How much time do we have?'

'Time is not our problem. The phone dialler will send the Feds a recorded message with this location when I radio. Rizzolo's the problem. How do we separate him from Mikey?'

Taggart looked out in the dark. The bridge lights would reveal river traffic from the south. But they were sitting ducks from the dark water to the north. 'Get on the radar. I don't like this at all.'

'I don't trust it with the aluminium boat so near,' Reggie warned, swinging aboard the black boat.

Taggart climbed onto the red boat. 'I told you no partners.'

'You want to get paid, you gotta ease up.'

'I don't "gotta" anything. You want to buy from me, you know the rules.'

'All we're doing tonight is talking about changing the rules. No risk to you. I don't want to hear a word about product. Just meet my partner and see if you want to do business with us both.'

'If I'm paying,' Eddie Rizzolo interjected. 'I want to know where my bread is going.'

Taggart had to get Eddie away from the red boat. 'Okay. Mikey, I'm taking Eddie for a ride. You wait here.'

'No way,' Mikey said.

'It's okay with me,' said Eddie. 'I don't mind.'

'I mind,' said Mikey. 'This is my supplier. If you get on that boat with him, you can kiss the street goodbye.'

Eddie grinned, his teeth flashing in the bridge lights. 'Maybe I ought to throw you overboard.' He looked ready to, Taggart thought and he wondered, why not. But Mikey was worth so much more alive than dead.

'Kill each other elsewhere. You coming, Eddie?'

Mikey moved faster, seizing his bug-sweeping briefcase and vaulting over the gunnels into the black boat. 'Okay. Me and the Brit'll take a ride. You two talk.'

Taggart looked at Reggie, who cocked an eye from the radar screen. Did Mikey suspect something or was it animal instinct to retreat from danger? Whichever, Taggart and Eddie were on the wrong boat. Not only was the red boat a radar target, it contained the heroin.

Powerful engines droned on the dark water in the north.

'One of you was followed,' Reggie said calmly as a dozen white dots began to sizzle on his radar screen.

'Cops,' Eddie Rizzolo shouted.

And to the south, a helicopter buzzed under the bridge, flickering yellow and blue in the catenary lights. Taggart saw Mikey shift his attention from the helicopter to the loud drone of the boats, then to the radar screen fairly white with targets, and finally to Reggie at the controls.

'This boat!' Taggart yelled. 'It's faster.'

He cranked the red boat's engines and they started roaring. Reggie scrambled aboard as if his life were in the balance. Mikey seized the wheel of the black boat.

'Jump,' Taggart yelled again. 'This one's faster.'

Mikey hesitated, frantically fingering his shotgun coke spoon.

'Hurry up.'

'Wait for him,' Eddie yelled.

Mikey dropped his coke spoon, snatched up a real sawn-off shotgun he had secreted in his electronics briefcase, jumped into the red boat and levelled the yawning barrels at Taggart and Reggie. 'Get off! Get on the other boat. I'm not getting caught on a conspiracy thing with you guys.'

Taggart and Reggie retreated.

'If you make it we'll talk again. If they catch me and Eddie, we're just a couple a guys going for a ride. Right, Eddie?'

'Right,' said Eddie. Although he looked bewildered, he flung off the rafting line as Taggart and Reggie climbed over the gunnels into the black boat. Taggart had left the engines running and Reggie engaged them.

'I hope he remembers his anchor.'

But they had cut it too close. A searchlight tore the dark like a grasping hand; then another, and a third from the side, a blinding white circle, dead on target. A bullhorn boomed, *Freeze, you fuckers!*

310

# 25

Chase boats loomed out of the dark, a dozen sturdy cutters and sleek new racers, whose decks were lined with rifle- and shotgun-toting agents in flack vests. Bullhorns boomed, warning no one to move. Taggart dived for the locker that held their night goggles as Reggie slammed the black boat's engines to full throttle and put the helm hard over. He saw the red boat pinned in the lights of the raiding fleet, frothing at the stern as propellers fought the drag of the anchor. Crazy Mikey Cirillo and Eddie Rizzolo struggled in the cockpit, fighting for the wheel.

The black boat lifted, stood up on its stern, spun a half circle like a cutting horse. Reggie reversed his helm and drove for dwindling gap in their line. A police boat darted to fill it. But when the fifty-foot black hull slammed down at the space, the little boat fled. The turbochargers cut in with a liquid roar and Reggie ripped through the line, building up speed. Taggart thought they had made it. Then, overhead, a searchlight lunged out of the sky – a helicopter stabbing the dark.

Bullhorns boomed again, their warnings drowned by thundering engines and seconds later by the sharp rapid notes of a machine gun. The air seemed to explode inches overhead. The helicopter's searchlight leaped at them; the spot swept the cockpit and whipped back, but the doper boat's flat, black paint merged with the night, her soft materials and non-reflective surfaces forming a radar sieve. At seventy miles per hour they raced down the river, as the helicopter searched water far behind. Seconds later they were under the George Washington Bridge, and then out of its lights, deep in darkness.

Taggart heard a new sound – a high-pitched drone. 'What the hell is that?' He looked back at the Strikeforce armada circling the red boat in their wake. Reggie pointed at the radar screen where a pair of blips were closing swiftly from the Jersey side. Taggart slipped night goggles over Reggie's head and put his on. Scanning the now bright riverscape, he saw two small pursuit boats trailing enormous wakes like spearheads on creamy white shafts. 'I thought we're not a radar target.'

'We're not,' Reggie yelled back. 'They're using bloody night glasses just like us. And they're going to radio that damned helicopter.'

He steered for the Manhattan side, angling toward the lights of the Seventy-ninth Street boat basin four miles downriver. The black boat poured across two miles in less than two minutes. 'They're gaining,' said Taggart.

Reggie steered within yards of the rocky shoreline, where cars were travelling the West Side Highway. The pursuit boats followed, closing until Taggart could distinguish their crews, one man driving, the other holding a long-barrelled weapon. Reggie glanced back and eased his throttles.

'What are you doing?'

'Look ahead! Find the ice aprons.'

A bullhorn crackled close behind. Taggart searched the water that lay ahead between their boat and the lighted docks. 'There!' Two hundred yards upriver from the ranks of yachts and chunky houseboats was a row of wedge-shaped barriers rising out of the water. Fashioned of bent railroad track to protect the marina from river ice, they emerged at an angle.

Reggie looked back again and when the lead pursuit boat was practically on their stem, pushed his throttles wide open and steered straight at the ice aprons. Taggart gripped the dashboard; the slots between the aprons were narrow and they were approaching at seventy. When they were so close that Taggart could distinguish the individual rails, Reggie flicked his helm to starboard, wove between two aprons, and careened the black boat towards the middle of the river. Taggart, thrown across the cockpit by the force of the turn, looked back. The lead pursuit boat crashed against an ice apron, skidded up the steep incline, crossed a hundred yards of water airborne, and splashed down on its side.

The second boat clipped an apron, rose a few feet on screaming propellers, and landed upright. 'Bloody hell,' said Reggie. 'Are they stopping to help?'

'Yes, he's circling . . . No! There's people on the dock pulling the men out. Here he comes!'

The pursuit boat tore downriver after them, gaining again, though not quite as quickly. The bullhorn boomed, angrily punctuated by a hail of gunfire. 'He's damaged,' Reggie said. A bullet slammed him to the deck.

'Reg!'

Taggart dropped beside him.

'Get the helm!'

'You okay?'

'No. But we're dead if you don't steer! Keep your head down.'

Taggart hunched into the seat and steered, casting anxious glances astern and at Reggie, who was holding his left arm with bloody fingers. 'Head for Twenty-third Street before they get that helicopter. World Yacht Club.'

Two miles. Taggart was competent on the boat, but nowhere near as good as Reggie and he knew he never could have pulled the stunt with the ice apron. They thundered abreast of midtown Manhattan, racing top speed down the centre of the river, the pursuit boat gaining. Taggart saw the golden top of his Spire, riding the rim of the skyline, and wondered if he would ever see it again.

'Are you okay?'

Reggie sat up, his right arm limp at his side. 'Not entirely.' He crawled toward the wet bar on the other side of the cockpit, packed ice against the wound, and hurriedly wrapped it with towels. 'Here comes the helicopter.'

Taggart saw the piers Reggie had indicated coming up fast. He said, 'We can't just get off. We have to send the boat away and blow it up.'

'My thought exactly.' Reggie fumbled a red key from his pocket, inserted it in a panel under the wheel, and moved a series of switches. Each caused a red alarm to blink.

He looked back again. 'We'll round the pier flat out and throttle back. You go over the side. Swim under the pier. We've a motor yacht – *Popeye* – in the yacht basin. Climb aboard on the stern step.'

'What about you?'

'I'll be right behind you, as soon as I set the boat on her way.'

'You've got one arm, Reg. I'll set the boat.'

'Don't argue. I'll steer. Pull the throttles when I tell you.' He took the wheel. The black boat tore past the yacht basin and round the pier that formed its downriver boundary. 'Now!'

The black boat slowed as if they'd hit a wall. Reggie turned the bow back to the river. 'Go! *What are you doing?*'

'Sorry, old chap. I've already lost a father, I'm not going to lose a father figure.' Taggart picked Reggie up, astonished how light he was, and swung him over the gunnel. Reggie fought with his good arm. 'This is what you pay me for.'

'This one's on me.'

He threw Reggie overboard, steered around him, hit the throttles, set the black boat thundering for the river. The pursuit boat rounded the pier and the helicopter flew over it with a spotlight blazing. Taggart rolled off the far gunnel. The black boat ripped past him like a trailer truck. The hull smacked his head and he sank into the bitter cold water half conscious. He heard a roar, saw the dark shape of the pursuit boat coming straight at him and tried to dive. It clipped his back and drove him further under. It sounded like a subway train going overhead. He surfaced, thrashing in the froth of its wake as it tore after the black boat.

The double roaring of the two boats moved swiftly across the river, trailed by the buzzing and thudding of the helicopter. Suddenly, the middle of the

Hudson was lit by a white flash. Flame and thunder split the night. Seconds later, all was silence, but for the frustrated growl of the Strikeforce craft hunting for survivors to arrest.

Taggart swam under the pier and found Reggie clinging to the teak stern step of *Popeye,* an enormous luxury trawler which was moored out of the light. Taggart helped him up. 'Where'd you get this?'

Reggie stood up uncertainly. He had lost his night goggles and Taggart saw him try to smile. 'We never gave second chances, but we always kept a backup. Leave your glasses on; my people shouldn't see your face.'

A tough-looking charter captain greeted them in the salon. Reggie issued swift commands. 'Our doctor, hot baths, dry clothes and a car to the air ambulance.'

An hour later, Taggart rode out of the marina with him. The car stopped at Park and Twenty-third and Reggie extended his hand. He looked grey with pain and fatigue, but his eyes were fathomless flat pools. 'You're done. It's been interesting.'

'Well, let's – if your arm doesn't hurt too much – let's go have dinner or something. Tina's is right around the corner.'

'I really ought to press on. I'll drop you here if you don't mind. I'm just a wee bit knackered.'

Taggart embraced him, suddenly, catching Reggie by surprise. He wanted to say something, but all he got out was, 'Where are you going?'

'Europe.'

'Tonight?'

'Tonight. When your brother and his Strikeforce finish interrogating Crazy Mikey, they'll likely be looking for an Englishman.'

Taggart stood in the street and watched his car drive away. He looked up Park Avenue where the lighted top of his Spire stood like a beacon. Mike Taglione would have loved it, and for a brief second he felt his father's presence, as if Mike's heart were beating in his body. Then he hurried to a pay phone and tried to call Helen to see how he could help with her brother, but all her lines were busy.

*   *   *

Tony Taglione let a United States Marshal drive him home, something he rarely did. Rather than be tempted to abuse the service, he took taxis or drove his own car. But tonight – or rather morning, as a high white disk of sun burned through the fog – he had earned it.

Crazy Mikey Cirillo and Eddie the Cop Rizzolo were caught on a doper boat, thanks to Strikeforce agents sticking to Eddie Rizzolo and bugging the right weight machine. Eddie had thrown a briefcase overboard – somebody should have told him that cash floated. Eight million dollars. And under the boat's floor, were fifty kilos of pure heroin.

Each swore he was framed, which had, Taglione recalled with a weary smile, some of the toughest DEA men in New York in giggles. Now the lawyers' job started. Fifty keys meant no bail. So while some of Taglione's attorneys prepared the drug case, they had time and opportunity to persuade them to flip. Not Eddie, but maybe Crazy Mikey if he were handled properly. It was as good a day as he had had on the Strikeforce.

'Here you go, Mr Taglione, you want I should wait?'

'I'm going to crash for a few hours. Can somebody pick me up at one?'

He staggered up the front walk, picked up two days of newspapers off the porch, and let himself in. Tired as he was, he knew he was miles from sleep. He poured three fingers of CC and sipped it straight. His eye fell on the piano, which he used to play, and on the model of his father's building.

'Hey, Pop. How you doing?'

The little derrick, which Chris had broken the night of Mike's funeral, still lay on its side on the top deck. Taglione swore, as he did each time he noticed it, that he was going to fix the model as soon as he had time. He looked around the room, glad he had stayed in this house. His mother and father were alive here. He had left the living room unchanged. Vicky and Chryl, in one of their attempts to befriend him, had recommended special East Side cleaners and upholsterers who took care of it.

He had to get out of here, someday. It was almost a sin to waste so much space on one person in such a crowded city. But it fitted his needs. Every now and then, when Arthur insisted he submit to an interview, they always asked was he lonely not being married. He had given up on the truth and said his work was everything. It was everything, but here he was connected. The house, and the mark his parents had put on it, and the neighbourhood. Neighbours and aunts kept slipping in the back door to stash casseroles and cheesecakes in the refrigerator. And time went fast. Kids on bicycles grew into earnest teenagers who asked which was the best law school. The paperboy had just graduated from the police academy, and the little girl who weeded his mother's flowers was interning next summer at the office.

He started upstairs, where he had taken over his parents' bedroom. Ii was big and comfortable, had its own bath, and a king-sized bed convenient when he brought a date home. He used his father's desk in one comer and had a comfortable armchair for reading in the other. Heavy curtains blocked the daylight completely.

Either the booze was working or he was blind tired, but he was sitting on the bed, trying to get his shoes off, before he realized he wasn't alone. He smelled perfume and looked up sharply. A lamp flared and there, in his armchair, with her feet tucked under her and her dark eyes luminous, was Helen Rizzolo.

# 26

'Where's your geeps, in the closet?'

He was afraid and that made him angry. Prosecutors had talked about this kind of thing happening. The office employed basic defences – unlisted phone numbers, marshal protection when threatened, even transferring convicts who made threats to harsher prisons to remind them it was not the individual prosecutor, but the government, who meted out justice.

'I came alone,' she said.

'Then leave alone. What the fuck are you doing in my house?'

'My brother was arrested.'

'I know.'

'You charged him with dope.'

'Miss Rizzolo, I want you out of here.'

'He doesn't deal dope.'

'Out!'

'I don't *let* him deal dope.'

'Miss, you are talking to an officer of the court. I have to advise you that anything you say can be used against you. Do you wish to continue informing me about what you allow and don't allow your brother to do?'

'My father is dead. My brother Frank is dead. Eddie is all I have left.'

'I can't help you with that.'

He got off the bed, but a sea of grief and weariness in her eyes made him extend his hand to help her out of the chair. 'You're beat,' he said. 'Go home and sleep. Let your lawyers do their job.'

'My family is dying.'

'What are you saying to me, sweetheart? It's not me. It's them. They hurt people. They take, they subvert. And they got caught. We're going to put them away like the rest of the Cirillos. And like your father.'

She looked up, her eyes liquid, wondering would she be afraid if she had nothing to sell? Would Tony Taglione terrify her if she were defenceless? Would she resign her brother as lost forever? But such questions dodged the issue. She had not entered the prosecutor's house emptyhanded. She had plenty

317

to trade, if she must; more to sell than Taglione could imagine, if she could bear to.

She prayed there was another way. 'My father. . .' She wet her lips with her tongue. 'You never once looked at me during his trial.'

'I was busy. It was the biggest case I ever argued.'

'His lawyers kept saying how good you were.'

'They had to blame somebody.'

'My father didn't blame his lawyers.'

Taglione smiled coldly. 'I forgot. Columbian hoods shoot their lawyers, but Italians hoods understand the power of the court so they shoot witnesses.'

'Why wouldn't you look at me?'

'Getting kicked and bitten by mobster's female relatives is not my idea of courtroom demeanour.'

'You know better than anybody I wouldn't do that.'

Taglione shrugged. He had been unfair. 'Of course, I saw you. You came prim and proper to the courtroom everyday. Little Miss Bus Line Executive in those linen suits and the lavender scarf and the Gucci briefcase. And that gold logging chain around your neck so no one on your side would forget exactly how rich and powerful you really are.'

Helen smiled at him, relieved that somewhere behind his priestly gaze he still had feelings. Taglione felt himself drifting into her eyes . . . floating into the past, ten years back in a shimmering memory, a moment, spontaneous, wonderful and never-ending. . . a crazy moment of his life that started the night Chris got beat up at Abatelli's. It was frightening how she knew what he was thinking.

'Did you ever tell him?' she whispered.

'Tell who what?' he asked, an involuntary smile making a lie of his question. 'Tell your brother how we met in the phone booth?'

'Just last autumn, when you two started hanging out. He was my little brother; he saw you first and flipped. I couldn't do it to him.'

Helen looked away from the bed; Chris had told her the truth. He *had* fallen for her on first sight.

'You never told him before that we went out?'

'. . . I didn't want to. It was mine.'

'Not just yours.'

'But not his. And not my father's. The last crazy thing I did in my life.'

'You opened the phone booth door,' she said. 'And you smiled. You'd already smiled when you went by my table. I thought, "What the hell? They can marry me off, but this is my secret." '

'You came out of the ladies room, stoned to the end of your beautiful hair. God, you were such a beautiful girl.'

'Everytime I see an old Lincoln I think of the front seat of your father's car. . . I never asked you who was on the phone?'

'A criminal investigator with the US Attorney's office. He put me on hold while he checked out your father for me.'

'I always wondered if you were dating me to investigate my family. Am I right?'

'They didn't teach that in law school.'

'How come you stopped calling.'

'Somehow, when I could finally think straight back at Harvard, it didn't seem like a relationship with a future. Besides, you were engaged.'

'I thought it was because I wouldn't go to bed with you.'

Tony smiled. 'To tell the truth, Helen, making out with you in the front seat of my old man's car was better than sleeping with most women.'

'Thanks.'

'Why wouldn't you?'

She laughed. 'You were a turning point in my life, Tony Taglione. It was the first time I was ever smart about a guy. I owe you one. You helped me settle down. I married. And even though that didn't work out, I became a real woman, so I was ready when my family needed me. Maybe my whole family owes you.'

Tony stiffened and the humour went out of his eyes.

'Did you think of me when you persecuted my father?'

'The word is *prosecute.*'

'Sorry.'

'Of course, I did. I think of it often. I'm in your debt for a memory that pops into my head at the oddest times. It's a moment I still cherish . . . You are an achingly beautiful woman.'

'You never mentioned it when you warned me off your brother.'

'It happened years ago. It's not my life anymore. Nor yours.'

He met her eyes and they stared at each other for a long time, in silence. 'I'm in love with him,' she said. 'It's for real, with both of us.'

'That's what you came here to tell me?'

'I didn't ask for it.'

'I'll tell you right now I can't come to the wedding.'

'We're not quite there, yet.'

'I'm told you haven't seen him since your father was killed.'

Helen nodded, although he could be lying; agents could have seen Chris come to her club after he had killed Don Richard. She said, 'It's been a terrible time.'

'Yeah.'

'So where are we?' she asked.

'Where we've always been. Across the street from each other.'

'Tony, can't we work something out?'

'Because we were going out ten years ago?'

'It makes it easier to talk. I didn't bring a lawyer.'

'Even your lawyers wouldn't break into my house.'

'The back door was open.'

'What did you have in mind?'

'My brother.'

'What are you offering? Testimony?'

'I'll testify against Mikey Cirillo.'

'Pertaining to what?'

'Whatever you need.'

'You mean you'll lie on the stand?'

'What do you want?'

'You'll make something up?'

'Tell me what you want.'

'I already have what I want – both those sons of bitches in jail.'

'You still have to convict Mikey. He's the biggest boss in New York. My brother's just a dumb guy.'

'Do you really believe I would let you lie on the stand to make a case? Helen, you are further away than I thought.'

She faltered, realizing she had mishandled him badly. 'Give Eddie back to me. Please.'

'Have you talked to your lawyers? Have you seen the charges?'

'He got suckered, Tony. Crazy Mikey set him up.'

'How do you explain that Mikey's in the next cell?'

'One of Mikey's enemies double-crossed him.'

'Your brother was arrested on a boat in the middle of the river with fifty kilos of pure heroin.'

'He was tricked.'

'I've been speculating about your brother's enterprises for a long time. Mikey's, too. But I'm done speculating. I've got them both. At least six investigators will swear they saw him heave a briefcase full of money into the water.'

'They're lying.'

'Here, you want to see?' Tony reached down for the briefcase he had dropped beside the bed. He pulled out a glossy black and white photograph and thrust it at Helen. The paper was still soft from the chemicals.

She screwed her eyes shut, but not before the image seared itself in her mind; Eddie swinging a briefcase over the side of a boat, his face frantic in the glare of searchlights, like a frightened little boy caught with a girlie magazine by the priest.

'Forget it, Helen. He made a dumb mistake and he got caught. Even your five-hundred dollar an hour junk lawyers had nothing to say when they saw this.'

She opened her eyes. 'What can I do?'

'You want my advice?'

'I'll do anything.'

'If you're in, get out. We're rolling up the Mafia. We got the old ones and we'll get the new ones.'

'I'm not in,' she retorted automatically.

Taglione took back the picture and closed his briefcase. 'I'll give you one thing, Helen. Not for old times, but for my brother. Fair warning. You see, I think you're Eddie's *consigliere*. Maybe even more since your father died. Get out of it! Because when I find the evidence that you're running the Rizzolos, you're next. I'll get you like I got the Cirillos, and the Bonos, and the Confortis – and your father. When I can prove it, you're going to jail, too.'

She wondered if Taglione would accept her, right now, in trade for Eddie? The question was on her lips, but reality stifled it. Who would protect the family? She couldn't trust Eddie alone. Without her to watch over him, he would get caught again, and her mother, the old people, the businesses would all be cast into the world.

'Get out,' said Taglione. 'Get straight. And go away.'

'Where?' she asked bleakly.

'You could try your uncle in Westport. He's a decent guy.'

'It's kind of nice how you keep track of me.'

'I keep track of every hood in this town.'

'You missed one.'

'What is that supposed to mean?'

Helen Rizzolo returned a cold smile, but she felt her mouth begin to tremble, as if her body knew before her mind that there was no way out, no other way to save her family. 'I came here for my brother. I want Eddie home.'

'You can't have Eddie home.'

'I want him free, the charges dropped. I'm willing to pay.'

'Hold it!'

'I'm willing to pay.'

'Pay? You're going to pay *me*. That's a bribe. Helen, surely you don't mean–' Her eyes filled with tears. '*I'll pay.*'

'There's nothing for sale in this house.'

'Yes, there is.'

'Nothing.'

'There is always something. Even when a guy thinks he's God.'

'You are warned. I'll charge you with attempted bribery if you say another word.' He stood up and took her roughly by the arm. 'Get out of my house.' Helen tore away. 'I'm here to bargain, you bastard! I've got something to bargain with.'

'What?' he asked scornfully.

'Chris.'

Taglione felt the blood rush from his face, leaving his cheeks prickling with cold and his heart afire. Of the thoughts racing through his head, he blurted the first he could accept:

'You're lying!'

'About what?' she asked. 'I haven't told you yet.'

'You're *lying*!'

'*Your brother for my brother.*'

'My brother isn't a criminal.'

She saw by Taglione's agonized expression that she had won. Her heart withered, but it was the only way. 'Shall I start with the day his people kidnapped me? Or the day your father was killed?'

# 27

'Chris? It's Helen.'

Sylvia had reached for his private line. Taggart beat her to it and when he heard Helen's voice, he shooed her out of his office.

Sylvia mouthed, 'What about the mayor saying no?'

'Excuse me.' He covered the phone. 'Fuck him,' he said savagely. 'Fuck his whole City Council. I've had it. Let him build his own stadium.'

'Chris, listen a second. Henry Bunker's on the other line. Kenny Adler called him to smooth things over.'

'I don't need his garbage.'

'It's *Henry*. Talk to him, please.'

'Goddamnit. Okay, I'll talk to him – Helen, hold another second –' He stabbed the button. 'Henry?'

'Chris. Look, I'm as angry as you are. But Kenny called. His Honour thinks maybe things got out of hand between you.'

'We agree at last.'

'That's a big concession for him; don't forget he's a hot-tempered guy who happens to own a twenty per cent plurality in this town. He'd like you to know he's sorry. Maybe we can get the project going next year.'

'I got to wait a year?'

'Years go fast.'

'Would you give him a message, Henry?'

'Sure.'

'The message is: "Fuck you, Your Honour".'

'Chris, let's not be crazy.'

'I'll have Sylvia send a confirming letter.' He banged down the phone. 'No more calls.' Sylvia backed out, dismayed. Taggart composed himself and returned to the phone.

'Hi. I miss you a lot.'

'Yeah, well, I've been hassled.'

'How's your brother doing?'

'Not great. He's getting into fights with the guards. How's yours?'

'The darling of the New York *Post* – "Battlin' Tony." Too bad he hates publicity.'

'I want to see you.'

'Is half an hour too soon?'

'Could we go away for the weekend?'

'That's like the original Helen asking a Greek shipbuilder if he's got anything that floats. Let's go up to the country. Cold as hell still, but we'll build a fire and –'

'Take me to Atlantic City. I want to go to a casino.'

'Casino? I'll take you to Monte Carlo.'

'No. AC's fine.'

'Hey, I'll charter a Concorde. Hit Monte Carlo, Macao, and AC on the way back.'

She laughed. 'The only travelling I want to do is between bed and the blackjack table. I want to beat the house and blow it all on dinner and presents.' 'Okay. I'll call Trump and get his top floor.'

'One big bed in a private suite will be perfect. I'll drive.'

'No way I'm getting my hand caught in your gearshift. I'll pick you up with the Rolls. And wear something loose. It's a nice long ride.'

\*　　\*　　\*

Helen cradled the phone, her head resounding with the trust in his voice. 'You heard.'

Tony Taglione, Marty, the broad-chested agent of the East Side Iron Works FBI bug, and Zell, his platinum blonde partner, removed their headsets.

'That means we have to wire her,' said Marty. 'I was hoping we could do the car.'

'Wire me? Didn't you hear his voice? The guy loves me. Am I supposed to slap his hand?'

Tony Taglione had refused to believe her. He demanded proof she hadn't concocted a story about Taggart's scam to get her brother's charges reduced. He wanted his brother's guilt in his own words. So the price to free Eddie Rizzolo had gone up; Helen had to trick Taggart into admitting – on tape – how he had seized control of the New York Mafia.

'Zell?'

'Yeah, we have something new she can wear. It's soft and it's kind of pretty. Goes with your colouring . . . You *are* a natural brunette?'

Taglione said, 'They're intimate. A wire's too dangerous. What if he finds it?'

'He won't hurt me.'

'I wouldn't bank on that,' said Marty, and Zell nodded firm agreement.

Helen turned on Tony. 'Let's get something straight. You know damned well he wouldn't hurt me.'

★   ★   ★

The act was easy. She had to pretend she wanted to be with him, which she did, and pretend she wanted to sleep with him, which she did, and behave as if she adored him as he adored her. The hard part was concealing the secret knowledge of how it would end. Harder still was hiding the sorrow.

They made out like kids in the back seat of the Rolls on the drive down. Their suite had a pool table, on which she beat him twice, a hot tub they abandoned for the cool sheets on the mirrored bed, and a white piano that Chris said he wished he knew how to play. He took her out to dinner, but still, Friday night turned to disaster; she spent it crying in his arms. He comforted her, thinking she was crying only for Eddie.

Saturday morning they made up for it, in bed till lunch, then back for more. By Saturday evening, Taggart was sprawled happily on the sheets enjoying the sight of her chosing a dress for dinner. 'I never knew a girl who wore a garter belt.'

'Just on special dates.'

'Need help?'

'You stay there.'

'Aren't you cold?'

'Back. Back.'

'Exhibitionist.'

She glanced over her shoulder, 'That's a fancy word for tease.'

'I told Reggie I want to marry you.'

His words went through her like ice. She teased him, to hide her agony. 'What is it with Italian boys? As soon as they pass thirty they have to get married?'

'I would have asked you when I was ten.'

'What did Reggie say?'

'He agreed to be best man.'

'First, we'd have to find him. Where is he?' Tony Taglione and his eager assistants had agreed that the existence of Reggie Rand would do a lot for her story. But Taggart, she knew, would never knowingly betray the Englishman.

'Will you?'

'Will I what?'

'Marry me.'

'No.'

'Why not?'

325

It killed her that he was making it easy, setting himself up in his inno-
cence. She forced her mind to an image of Eddie bloodied on a concrete
floor in a battle with the guards. It gave her the strength to seize the opening.
'Because there's stuff going down you don't know about.'

'Like what?'

'Like I have to see people.'

'Who?'

'Philadelphia people.'

'Hang on a minute.' Taggart got off the rumpled bed and pulled a briefcase
out of his two-suiter. 'Certain habits don't go away.'

'What are you doing?'

'Sweeping this room.'

'We took it at the last minute with phony names. Who's going to bug us?'
'I didn't know we were doing business,' Taggart replied, unlocking the case.
'We're not.' Helen picked up her dress, sauntered around the bed and wrapped
his naked body with hers. 'We came to play. I'm just going to check them
out. Can you fix this damned zipper?'

'If I can do it without letting go. When did you connect with Philadelphia
people?'

'Are you kidding? They connected with me. They came right up to me
at the blackjack table the second you went for a walk.'

'What if they're cops?'

'Oh, no. I recognized them. I'd seen them in Vegas and once in New
York.' 'Wha'd they say?'

'You should hear them. They're like from another country. They talk out
of the side of their mouth.' She mimicked, ' "We hear you're doing real good
in New York. Maybe you want to come in with us down here." '

'How do they know about you?'

'You can't fool the street, Chris. Everybody knows the Rizzolos are tops.
Philly and New England have to connect in New York. Inviting me to take
a shot at AC is like a peace offering. Of course, I'd have to fight to keep it,
but we're talking gold, man. This place is making Vegas a ghost town. The
only problem is the connected people can't get their act together. The Philly
*gavornne* are killing each other off, messing up the image and wasting a great
shot. Anyhow, that's why I'm getting dressed. I'm meeting a guy for dinner.'

'What guy?'

'One of these guys.'

'Mind if I come?'

'Relax, he's with his girl.'

'I'll come along, anyhow. Sounds interesting.'

Their hosts were waiting in an Italian restaurant a block from the Boardwalk. Marty had a broad chest and a hearty conspiratorial laugh. He reminded Taggart of a young version of his Uncle Vinnie the way he said, 'It don't look like much, but it's nice and private and the food's good.'

Marty's girlfriend, Zell, looked loud, but said little. She got flustered when Taggart grinned at her for staring at the love bites Helen had left on his neck. 'I know you,' said Marty. 'You're the builder.'

'What do you do?' Taggart asked.

'I'm a builder, too. You wouldn't a heard a me, yet. I'm not as big.' 'Around here?'

'Pennsylvania. This is just fun down here, but I was talking with Helen earlier about what a future this place has.'

'I'm a builder, too,' said Zell.

'What?'

'Honey . . . She's got a plumbing outfit. You know, affirmative action.' 'But I really run it,' said Zell.

'Honey, pipe down. Do you do that up in New York, Chris? Front companies for the civil rights quotas?'

'I don't.' Taggart looked at Helen, who hadn't said a word since they sat down. She lifted her shoulder in a minute shrug.

★　　★　　★

'They kept trying to steer the conversation,' Taggart said on the ride back to their hotel. 'Like they were looking for quotes.'

'I didn't like them, either.'

'Too busy establishing credentials,' he said in the room. 'I think they're phonies.'

'What do you mean?'

'Smalltime hoods trying to get a free ride off you.'

He went out on the terrace and stared at the dark ocean awhile.

She came out and stood with him, shivering until he wrapped his arms around her. 'You're not really interested in Atlantic City, are you? We could go to Europe and –'

She turned her face. She wanted to scream, yes. Let's go. Now! Run!

'It's a gold mine, Chris.'

'But –'

'I could set up here and get the hell out of New York. Less heat.'

'You really think so?'

'I could really take control. End the fighting here. And no one would ever try to take it away. It's like a gift for the right family.'

They went in and had a drink. Taggart was quiet. He went to look at the ocean again. She watched him, her heart pounding. He leaned over the terrace railing so he could see the bright lights marching along the beach. He looked at New York that way, she knew, hunting dark spots to fill with new buildings.

She had done it. She had wedged the idea into his head that the prize was worth taking. And, best of all, she thought bitterly, she supposedly came with it. A poisonous pot-sweetener. She thought of her brother and her family. Had she not, she would have walked out on the terrace and thrown herself into the night.

Taggart stayed outside a long while, thinking. When he came back, she was hanging up her dress. He came up behind her, cupped her breast and her belly, and touched his lips to her ear.

'I'm going to make you an offer.'

She turned swiftly in his hands and covered his mouth. 'We'll sleep on it.'

'It's wild. You'll love it.'

She drew him to the bed. 'Not another word 'til morning.'

'I'm serious.'

'Shut up. Everytime you open your mouth, I'm going to put part of me into it. Shhh.'

'Listen —'

'I warned you . . .'

$$\star \quad \star \quad \star$$

In the morning, she awakened early and phoned quietly for coffee. Chris stirred sleepily when the waiter arrived. She pillowed his head on her thighs and sipped the coffee and stroked his hair, wishing they could sleep forever.

'Can I talk yet?'

'Tell me at breakfast.'

'It'll be brunch by then.'

Finally, at brunch in a hotel dining room with a gold vaulted ceiling, huge chandeliers, and the flashing casino lights visible through many doors, Helen Rizzolo spread a pink linen napkin on her lap, clinked her mimosa glass against his, and listened to Taggart with sombre eyes.

'If you want Atlantic City —'

'I don't know,' she whispered. 'Maybe you should —'.

'You got me thinking. I've been thinking about how Las Vegas was years ago. With your support, I could be like the Howard Hughes of Atlantic City. We could own this town. It's a great place to build hotels, especially when the woman I love is in a position to help me with zoning. The town's got more class already than Vegas ever did, and it's near our stuff in New York. We'll run this place exactly the way we want it. We'll own it. No government bullshit.'

328

'Chris, are you sure?'

'Consider it a wedding gift. If you want to take over Atlantic City, you've got Atlantic City.'

She looked away, because if she looked in his eyes she would cry. But so far, nothing she had coaxed him to say would make a case for Tony Taglione. It was now or never.

'What do you say?' he prompted.

'How would we do it?'

'Exactly like New York. The hell with those clowns last night. We don't need them. We'll do it our way. Find a nice, tight family like yours to front the street for us. If we can't find one, organize one or bring in our own people. Then I'll talk Reggie into supplying the dope and the muscle to bust them up on top. We'll take this town in a month . . . If you're sure you want to do this again?'

'I don't know,' she whispered. She took his hand and pressed it between her thighs, covering the bug, but it was too late. She saw them coming from the doors.

'I'm sure,' said Taggart. 'I could build for ten years here if we controlled the government. It's a dynamite opportunity. And the best part is we'll do it together.'

Helen leaned across the table and took the back of his head in both hands. She stared into his eyes. Taggart was astonished to see tears fill hers.

'What?' he asked. 'What's wrong?'

She crushed his mouth with hers. When he opened his lips she pulled him harder. Her body shook with the strain. He felt her teeth and tasted blood. With a convulsive shudder she let him go. When they parted he thought he would die.

'*Jesus*. Come upstairs.'

'I'm sorry,' she said. There was blood on her lip, bright red, his or hers he would never know. 'I wish it never happened.'

'Why?'

She turned her face. He looked up, his heart still pounding, and broke into a startled smile. 'Tony! There's Tony! Hey, Tony! What are you, on a junket? Sit down, man. Grab a chair. Waiter!'

The waiters had retreated to the wall. They were watching for something to happen. Taggart looked at Helen. Her face was white, her mouth a rough line crumbling at the edges. He turned back to his brother, saw the agents spreading out behind him, and thought, they got to Jack Warner. There were four big guys with Tony and agents at every door.

'What's going on, Tony? Who's the heavies?'

'They're going to arrest you, Chris.'

'What?'

'I came to read you your rights. You have the right to remain silent. You have the right to legal counsel. You have the right –

'What the hell for?'

'Heroin trafficking.'

'Hey, I'm just a businessman,' Taggart laughed. No way they could ever prove that.

'Racketeering.'

'Forget it.'

'And murder,' Tony finished coldly. 'I didn't believe her . . . I didn't *want* to believe her. So I needed this to start a case.' He pulled a Sony out of his pocket and turned it on.

'*Exactly like New York. The hell with those clowns last night. We don't need them. We'll do it our way. Find a nice, tight family like yours to front the street for us. If we can't find one, organize one or bring in our own people. Then I'll talk Reggie into supplying the dope and the muscle to bust them up on top.*'

Tony turned it off. 'Who's Reggie?'

Taggart felt a sickening sensation that the casino lights were whirling around him. He looked at Helen. A tear skated down her cheek. She pulled back when he reached for her hand.

'Where'd you hide the wire?'

'Garter belt.'

'I'd like to hear the rest of the tape, if we didn't melt it. Want to tell me why?'

'Don't say anything. They'll use it against you.'

'I want to know why.'

'Eddie. It's a trade.'

'But we –'

'We are *stranieri*,' she whispered. 'A wife is one thing, a sister something more.'

330

# 28

A pair of agents stepped towards the table. 'Stand up, please.'

Taggart pointed a big, blunt manicured finger at his brother. '*You* know and *I* know, they owed us.'

'They owed the law. And so do you. Make it easy for me and I'll do what I can to make it easy for you – Who's Reggie?'

'Reggie?' The whole room was spinning. Helen in the centre, tears splashing the hands she held to her lips. He wanted to make her smile. 'Reggie? Isn't he the rich kid in the Archie comics?'

Helen felt as if an earthquake had cleaved the gaudy room. With that joke he had forgiven her betrayal and the betrayals to come at his trial. It made it even more terrible that she could never see him again.

Except, like her father, behind faraway prison walls.

\*     \*     \*

They locked his handcuffs to a chain around his waist when they boarded the chartered plane. The NYPD escorted them with lights and sirens from LaGuardia Airport to Foley Square. Cops with shotguns lined the steps of the Federal Court House shouting, *'Get back! Back!'*

Barred, ethically, from participating in his brother's case, Tony Taglione observed Taggart's arraignment from the public area of the magistrate's courtroom. He maintained a scrupulous silence as the Strikeforce agents swore their complaints but his gaze, alternately angry and stricken, flashed like high beams on ice.

Taggart pleaded not guilty. He was still deeply shaken by the arrest, and awed by the finality of the handcuffs; every few minutes he had to struggle with himself not to tear at the metal.

Taggart's lawyers – 'graduates', themselves, of the US Attorney's Office, Criminal Division – moved to seek bail.

Tony's assistants acted swiftly to dominate the bail hearing. They characterized Taggart as an international criminal with means to escape the court's jurisdiction before the government could finish investigating the scope of Taggart's conspiracy.

The head of Taggart's defence team rebutted: 'To characterize the government's case as thinner than the thinnest ceramic wafer on the smallest chip in the tiniest component of a microscopic electronic element would be to overstate its validity many-fold. We will not dignify this entrapment by a woman scorned – a woman whose racketeering brother is in the slammer, a woman herself on the brink – by ever mentioning it again. Your Honour, Mr Taggart seeks bail solely on the grounds that his roots are deep in the community.'

He sat down whispering, 'If this ever goes to trial, we will eat their "accomplice witness" for breakfast.'

'Just keep me out of jail.'

Tony's assistants offered their second argument. The accused was a danger to the community.

Taggart's lawyer rose again chuckling. 'A *danger* to the community? Perhaps the prosecutor has confused the breastbeating of a disappointed Landmarks Commission with reality, but I really can't accept that Mr Christopher Taggart, developer of some four Manhattan skyscrapers this year alone, a Queens high school, and several thousand units of Bronx low-income housing is a danger to the community. Good lord, Your Honour, Mr Taggart *is* the community.'

The magistrate, an ordinary-looking, round-faced woman in middle age, replied: 'Obviously, the charges are extremely serious. And just as obviously, what the accused characterizes as roots in the community could also be construed as the wealth and power to escape the juridiction. Therefore, the accused will surrender his passport to the US Attorney. And bail is set at eight hundred thousand dollars.'

Taggart held up his hands. 'Could Your Honour have these removed so I could write a cheque?'

# 29

'And of course,' said the bar fly, 'you've heard of the Eton boy who ran away from school? Disguised himself by closing the bottom button on his waistcoat.'

Jack Warner felt his waistcoat – the goddamned thing was buttoned – finished his flat beer in the dreary pub near Charing Cross station, and wandered unhappily into the cold damp streets of London. He hated not knowing the rules. And he didn't really want to learn new ones. Loathing his weeks in Europe, he had retreated to England, and liked it even less. It was all, in a word, bush. Or, in three words, not New York. He missed Puerto Ricans, Blacks and Chinese. He missed fast, dirty streets and Italian guys on the make. He missed knowing who was good and who was bad. But most of all, he missed being a cop.

Heading for a newsstand to buy a map of Ireland, he was amazed to find Christopher Taggart's picture plastered on the front pages. How in hell had they nailed the slick bastard? Warner started to read the story in the *International Herald Tribune*, but halfway down the first column, he bolted into the street, hailing a cab with the paper.

'Heathrow Airport!'

'What's in the news, Guv?'

'My ticket home.'

US Customs didn't even blink at the forged passport Reggie Rand had supplied him when he had fled New York. Warner ducked the Immigration guys working Kennedy and caught a cab to his lower East Side apartment. Slipping in unnoticed, he wedged himself into his kitchen closet and opened a tiny wooden door in the back, behind which sat the ancient fuse box. Helen Rizzolo might have told Tony Taglione *what* his brother had done, but knowing and *proving* were different matters, as any cop could tell you.

Five malevolent-looking glass fuses studded a metal frame. He disengaged the main switch; the lights went out and the refrigerator stopped with a shudder that shook the floor. Working by flashlight, he unscrewed the face of the fuse box, reached into the hole and removed a long mailing tube. Then he

333

stuffed the cardboard tube in the inside pocket of his raincoat, and headed for St Andrew's Square.

The Strikeforce receptionist regarded him uncertainly.

'Tell Taglione it's Detective Jack Warner, NYPD, and I guarantee he'll drop everything.'

As a cop, he had broken many a prisoner down; the coin of the realm was, *I will send you to jail*, and there was only one winner in the race to cooperate. An FBI agent he knew came out and frisked him warily. He even peered inside the mailing tube.

'I'm not here to shoot him, asshole.'

'I wish you were so I'd have an excuse to shoot you. Here's a warrant for you.'

'Save us both some trouble and wait 'til I've seen the boss.'

Taglione was on the phone. Some exhausted-looking assistants were waiting with papers. Agents were pacing the halls, smoking too much. Warner smiled. Just as he had suspected when he had read the first news story – all the trappings of a big case turned sour.

Taglione covered the mouthpiece and drilled him with his piercing eyes. 'Are you turning yourself in?'

'Alone.'

Taglione studied him with dark contempt, muttered something in the phone, hung up and asked his assistant attorneys to come back in five minutes.

Warner closed the door and leaned against it. 'All I want is my badge.'

'Your *badge*? You'll be lucky to pull ten years. Why should I give you your badge?'

'Because without me, you got shit on Taggart.'

'We have an accomplice witness. I don't call that a weak case.'

'You have no corroboration.'

Taglione stared.

'Hey, I worked for your brother. I know how careful he was. He didn't give the broad anything she could use on him. All she's got is a story. No proof.'

'Jack, you betrayed the most prestigious office in America. You sold out and you ran for it. I can't give you your badge.'

Warner shrugged. 'So your brother walks.'

'And you go to prison.'

'Great. The big guy gets away and the little guy gets the slammer. Maybe the US Attorney for Kansas plays that way. But the Southern District of New York..?'

Taglione reddened and Warner knew he had him. Taglione said, 'Even if Arthur Finch goes along, the cops won't. Everybody knows you ran.'

'I didn't run,' Warner smirked. 'Where'd you get that idea? It was a setup. I was working a deep cover sting for you.'

'*You were not.*'

'But if you and Finch tell 'em we had to make it look like I ran, then I'm home free and you make your case.'

Taglione glared, ready to kill, but he was stuck and he knew it. 'You'd have to do a hell of a lot to get us to go along with that.'

Warner laughed. 'Hey, nobody knows more about the Maf than Jack Warner.'

He pulled the mailer from his new trenchcoat, pried off the cap, and spilled the contents across Taglione's desk – notes, xeroxes, recording transcripts, phone records, names and dates.

Taglione shifted through them with both hands. 'What does this mean?'

'It means if I keep my badge, I can use my files to steer your investigation in seventeen directions your brother went. Helen Rizzolo don't know the half of it.'

★   ★   ★

US Attorney Arthur Finch invited Taggart and his lawyer to meet in his office. Tony Taglione was there when they arrived, sitting on a couch, his dark eyes burning. Taggart's lawyer walked around, sniffing the wind while he rolled a cigar pugnaciously between his fingers. Taggart stood quietly by the window gazing upon the Brooklyn Bridge, waiting to hear what had gone badly wrong. Arthur took the seat behind his desk.

'I'm going to let your client cop a plea.'

'We're not copping any plea.'

'You'll be begging to when you hear what we've got.'

'You've got shit, Arthur. This is a charade to scare my client. You've got an asshole case and you're going to look like assholes in front of the grand jury. I'm moving to get this whole trumped-up mess dropped tomorrow morning.'

Finch's eyes turned steely grey, and for the first time in the years he had known him, Taggart understood how earlier Finch generations had acquired railroads. 'Are you quite through, Counsellor?'

He held Taggart's lawyer's eye until the man looked away.

'Up until now, we knew your client did it. Now, we can prove how.'

'If you're that sure, Arthur, how come you're talking plea?'

'Because I would much prefer a full list of all the government people your client corrupted and the Mafiosa he elevated and the dope networks he spawned, as well as your client himself under immediate lock and key.'

'Should we throw in a cure for cancer?'

'We've cut a cooperation agreement with one of your client's helpers. He's steering us in every direction we need. The conspiracy is much bigger than we thought.'

'Come off it. What "helper"?' He glanced at Taggart, who shrugged and thought, *Jack Warner*.

'I'm willing to consolidate all the charges – those made and those to be made – into two RICOs on heroin trafficking, twenty years apiece, to be served concurrently. The *full* twenty. I don't want to see your man on the street before he's fifty years old.'

'I don't believe you guys. What "helper"? Who is this "helper"?'

The room was stuffy. Taggart unlatched the window and swung it open a crack. He held his face to the cool breeze, then turned to study the men debating his fate. Arthur glared back and Taggart realized that even as he tried to put him in jail, the US Attorney was hoping to save Tony's career. His own lawyer's mouth was a tight, worried line. And Tony's mask was slipping; a tic that Chris remembered from childhood was tugging at his brother's cheek. 'Sid, would you please leave the room?'

'Mr Taggart –'

'Out! Please.'

'I really strongly advise –'

Taggart glanced at Tony and Tony stood up. 'Arthur? Why don't Chris and I take a walk?'

'Fine with me. Counsel and I can pass the time recalling the good old days before he left public service to get rich.'

'Some of us weren't born with a silver suppository up our ass,' Sid shot back. 'Mr Taggart, what you're doing is dangerous. I strongly advise–'

'I'm just going for a walk with my brother.'

While riding the elevator and walking through the lobby and on to the paved plaza, Taggart could feel Tony assessing him, as if he was hunting the best approach to get him to open up. 'No escort?' he asked.

'You're still out on bail, for the moment, Mr Community. What do you want? Walk? Drink?' He nodded towards Police Headquarters, behind which nestled a cop bar. 'Hamburger at the Mick's?'

Taggart raised his eyes to the building tops. 'Let's go to the Spire.'

'You gonna talk to me?'

'Yeah. We'll work something out. I want to see the job.'

They hurried to Center Street and got into a cab. 'Okay,' Tony said, shutting the driver's shield. 'Just us. It's all true, isn't it?'

'What do you think?'

'But *why*? Why'd you do it?'

'For Pop.'

Tony stared. 'Revenge?'

'I told you ten years ago. They owed us.'

'All for Pop?'

'All.'

'What about the money?'

'What money? I spent more than I ever made.'

They sat silently until the cab reached Union Square. Tony said, 'You don't understand what you've done wrong, do you? You still don't understand the crimes. You sold dope.'

'Bait.'

'You killed people.'

'Greaseball hoods.'

'You corrupted –'

'I got caught.'

'But don't you understand what you've done?'

'Yes. I destroyed the biggest Mafia family in New York.'

'You can't do that!'

'I did it. The Cirillos are broken, man. Pick up the pieces.'

'It's wrong that way.'

'It *worked*.'

'You undermine everything. Why have a government if you can just run out and blow people away to satisfy your revenge? Why 'You tell me.'

'Because a guy can always be wrong. And the rest of us have to be protected from a guy who can be wrong.'

'But I was right. And you know it. We fought on this from the beginning. You're still trying to force theories on truth. But you know I was right.'

'Not quite. You're going to jail.'

'We'll see.'

'Oh, you're going all right. You belong to the law now.'

'The same law that did nothing when they killed Pop.'

'Pop!' Tony yelled. 'Blame it on Pop!'

'They killed Pop!'

'Pop! What about *me*.'

'What?'

'You used me. You used my office. You ripped me off, Chris. You tricked me into doing your dirty work.'

'I gave you real leads.'

'Thanks a lot. You two. You and Pop. Remember joking about me? Big joke. Tony's honest? Tony's straight? He's like a priest? Got it from Mom? And then in the next breath, Pop going, "Tony's gonna be my lawyer".'

'What's wrong with that? He loved you. You were his first-born son.'

337

'Pop knew I couldn't have been his lawyer in a million years. Didn't you ever wonder? Who did he appoint executor of his will? You. I was studying law and he put you in charge of the money.'

'I was in the business,' Taggart protested, but he too had wondered at the time, and despite the pride of being chosen, he had felt for Tony. Now he wished he had said something then, when it had mattered.

'And straight Tony was too honest,' Tony said bitterly.

'*I* wanted you to be my lawyer. I asked you fourteen times.'

'You didn't want a lawyer, you wanted a manipulator. You wanted to find the ways around the law like it's a game, and if you're smart you win. Well, that's bullshit. The law is supposed to protect helpless people from people who are so strong they think they can do what they please . . . People like you, Bro. Scary people. . . Admit it, man. You wanted me off the Strikeforce because you knew I'd nail your ass in the end.'

'All Pop or I ever wanted was you to be part of the family.'

'You used me. You lied. You talk about family, but you treated me like I was one of your fucking women.'

'Hey. Don't talk to me about women. You don't know them.'

'You *do*?' Tony exploded. 'You arrogant bastard! Do whatever you feel, whenever you feel. That's how you see life. If you get mad, kill somebody – right, Bro? It's obvious you killed Rendini, or had him killed. You meet a Mafia girl, bingo, fall in love. Your brother, who you say you love, gets established in something he loves, so you use the dummy. You have no standards. You have no restraint. No *character*. Look what you've done. You've blown it all. The company. Us. Even Pop. I loved him too, you know. I didn't have to agree with him to love him. Do you think Pop would back you on this shit? Don't you see how far wrong you've gone? Do you think Pop would *approve*?'

'The only thing I regret is making you trouble,' Taggart retorted angrily. 'I am really sorry. You wouldn't have been hurt if I didn't get caught, and believe me, Tony, I did not intend to get caught.'

'What are you, God? Of course, you got caught.'

Taggart flushed darkly. 'Only because Eddie Rizzolo homed in on that phony dope deal. When you investigate you'll see I had Crazy Mikey set up. He was the last. I got Don Richard. I got Sal Ponte. I blew that whole stinking family apart. Then I was home free. Out and done. With my father's murder avenged . . . Our father. *I don't apologize for avenging Pop.*'

'But you couldn't let it go,' Tony shouted. 'You love the power it took to beat them. *The Howard Hughes of Atlantic City!* '

'I –'

'How 'bout the Al Capone of Chicago? Why not the Mussolini of Italy?'

Taggart stared back as long as he could. What could he say? For Helen? Partly. But as much for himself, he had to admit. A castle in Europe was a fantasy. He had to work. He had to build buildings. And what a temptation to build them without restraint.

'Do you deny it?'

'You've got it on tape,' he admitted. For a long moment the only sounds he heard were the taxi's tyres pounding asphalt and a bubbling murmur from its rusty muffler.

'Maybe that's the crime of revenge,' Tony said softly. 'It feels too good to stop.'

Turning away, Taggart suddenly thought he saw his father standing at the bars of a prison cell. The image was so real. Mike Taglione had his coat over his arm and his eyes were dismayed, even as he tried to offer an encouraging smile.

'Chris? . . . Chris!'

The hallucination dispersed, and Tony was there again, beside him in the cab. Taggart's hands began to shake with a violence that frightened him. He looked at the plastic shield and the windscreen beyond. His Spire was growing tall in the distance.

'What is it?' he asked dully.

'We've got you cold,' Tony whispered. 'It's just a matter of time. If you don't co-operate, Arthur will put you away a lot more than twenty years. He'll put you inside forever. And my outfit will have to help him.'

Tony's whisper faded, like the voice of a child on the verge of tears. Taggart abruptly realized he would never get out of this. Fight as he would, the Strikeforce would put him in prison. There was no way to win. His hands were still shaking.

Tony noticed. 'We gotta talk,' he said. 'Make the best deal for you. Chris, it's all I can do.'

Quickly, as the cab snaked through the Helmsley Building and up Park Avenue, Tony described in detail the range of informtion that Arthur Finch would require to cut a cooperation agreement.

'There's a lot of stuff I don't know. I didn't walk around with a gun in my hand.'

'Okay, who does know?'

Taggart shrugged. 'Talk to Jack Warner.'

'We already have. Who's Reggie Rand?'

'Forget it.'

'Chris, this is your life.'

'Sorry. I don't turn on my friends.'

'Do Cheri and Vicky have anything to do with it?'

'Christ, no.'

'Sylvia? Your supers?'

'No. The business is legit.'

'It turns on Rand, doesn't it?'

'Forget it.'

'You have to make a deal. You'll go away for ever if Arthur takes you to trial.'

The cab slowed in heavy traffic and Taggart sank into a deep silence that lasted, despite Tony's exhortations, until they finally arrived at the construction gate. There he surprised Tony, exploding back to life, tossing money at the cab driver, springing onto the sidewalk with all eyes for the job. Like their father, Tony thought; the boss – just like Mike Taglione.

Already Chris was charging through the gate. Tony scrambled after him, as he used to try to keep pace with the two of them. He caught up when Chris beckoned a foreman. 'Charley, it's your ass if that dumpster catches fire. Get it out of here!'

'Sorry, Chris, the truck's on its way.'

'Fuckin' better be. How's the kids?'

'*They're trying out for Little* League.'

'Talk to Sylvia about uniforms. Hey, this is my brother, Tony. Maybe you can get the US Attorney to sponsor a team, too.'

The foreman, who read the newspapers, stared. Tony grabbed two hard-hats and followed Chris into the site and aboard an outside hoist which had already started rising. As it clanked up the nearly completed building – ten, twenty, forty, eighty floors – Taggart grew pensive again as the city thrust crisp edges into the deepening afternoon light.

'I'll miss this,' he said softly. 'This time of day the sunlight makes the buildings better than the guy who built them. For a second each stands alone.' He smiled at Tony as the elevator stopped. 'And that's when the whole story looks best.'

The roof was deep in fresh, white pea gravel. They crossed to the edge and climbed onto the only bare steel remaining, the new beams replacing those damaged in the attack on Taggart's cantilevered penthouse. He walked a narrow header to the far edge and rested against a column that stood alone. Tony caught up, swung gracefully around him and leaned on the other side. The wind plucked at their jackets, tugged their hair. Tony slapped the steel. 'What's this?'

'I had to pull a header that got creamed in the accident – which it wasn't, by the way; Don Richard sent a guy to kill Helen – so I figured what the hell, while I'm making the repairs I'll add a room.' He started to make a joke about slipping an unauthorized floor past the mayor, but suddenly the grief he had felt since

Atlantic City swelled and rolled over him like a wave. He could only manage to say, 'It was supposed to be a surprise – a little music room in the clouds.'

Tony gathered his resolve and forced himself to look at Chris's face. He leaned around the column and saw what he had feared for days. There were guys who made it through prison and guys who couldn't. His brother would waste away like a tethered falcon.

'*How could you be so stupid as to trust Helen Rizzolo?*'

Taggart looked at him, puzzled, as the words sank in. 'You're not talking about right and wrong, now. You're talking about getting caught.'

'You heard me.' Tony was trembling. 'How could you be so stupid? She handed me your ass on a silver platter.'

'I'm not sorry I fell in love.'

Sweat glazed Tony's palms. They were suddenly so wet that his grip began to slide on the steel. He dried them on his trousers and grabbed hold again. He was the only force on earth that could save Chris, but the price was all he believed. He tried again to make something work.

'Listen. If I could maybe persuade Arthur to come down a few years, would you give him what he needs? You know, maybe you'll get out on parole in a few years.'

'I can't give him Reggie Rand.'

Tony wiped his palms again. 'I didn't think so,' he whispered.

Chris felt his brother's hand, and looked down as Tony pressed a slim blue booklet in his palm.

'What?'

'Take it!'

Taggart stared, utterly astonished. It was his passport.

'I'll give you three hours.' Tony's lean face was working, his dark gaze opaque. 'Three hours. Get on a plane. Go away. *Don't ever come back.*'

'What happens to you?'

'It's a little late to start worrying about that. Go! From what I know already, you can disappear in style.'

Taggart thumbed the stiff pages. The wind seized them, flipping them like a slick-fingered dealer; the entry stamps of two dozen nations were a blueprint of all he had done to avenge his father. Now it was he who leaned around the column to see his brother's face. The tic was leaping in Tony's cheek, and the fire in his eyes was going out.

'What about the Law?'

'I can't make it fit you.'

'What about your office? What about the Strikeforce?'

'I can handle it.'

'No, you can't. The Law is your family, like Pop was my family. You can't betray it.'

'Only for you.'

Tony's need to sacrifice hit Taggart like a sledgehammer. 'That's how I felt about Pop! *That's why I did it.*'

'Go!'

'No. I can't let you pay my dues.' He tried to wedge the passport between the steel and Tony's fingers. Tony jerked his hand away.

'Don't be crazy, Bro. You'll spend the best part of your life in jail.'

Taggart shuddered. Helen would make a loyal visit, once a week, forever. For in a terrible, relentless way he would become part of her family and she would serve him. But he could no sooner ask that of her than let Tony betray himself.

'If I run, you'll be finished with the Law. And dead in your heart.'

Taggart retreated to his side of the pillar and gazed at the city. His eye fell on beauty wherever it roved – the evening skyline, the sunlit forms, their shiny coloured glass skins, new concrete racing upward. He leaned out to see the ground. A quarter of a mile down, Park Avenue was a broad river between shores of glass. Long beds of daffodils drifted down the middle of the avenue like a string of yellow barges. There was so much to remember.

'But you'll die in prison,' Tony pleaded. 'Let me do this for you.'

Taggart knelt on the header and tucked the passport within the flange of the pillar where it was safe from the wind. He arose lightly, cupped his brother's face in his big hand. 'I think it's more than I deserve.'

'*Chris!*'

Tony reached for him, but it was too late.

'I love you,' Taggart said, stepping into the sky.

# EPILOGUE

*Saints avenged,
angels seduced*

A white Rolls-Royce drifted slowly down Mott Street.

Jack Warner was out of breath, having toiled up the Mosco Street hill on his regular route from Police Plaza to Hunam House. His mind was on a stiff drink and a cold Chinese beer, so he didn't notice the limousine until they met in front of the restaurant.

'Jack!'

Warner flinched. Reggie Rand was sitting in the limousine.

Caught flat-footed, Warner knew he couldn't run, so he did the only thing possible. He charged, hurled himself into the passenger compartment, and rammed his gun into Reggie's belly.

'*Jack*! Easy.'

Instead of a pistol, Reggie was holding an old-fashioned glass, and he looked and smelled like he had had a few. Warner frisked him thoroughly, nonetheless, but his ankle gun was gone, as were the holster and a throwing knife he sometimes carried in the back of his belt.

'Would you like a drink?'

Warner closed the door and holstered his weapon. The partition was up, the driver invisible, and the air conditioning was comfortably cool. 'What are you doing in New York? Half the federal agents in America are looking for you.'

'Leaving shortly. Tying up some loose ends. I saw you on the street and thought –'

'Where'd you get the car? I thought the Feds confiscated it.'

'We maintained several in the event we were followed. In fact,' Reggie added drily, 'I recall we lost *you* a couple of times that way. Whisky?'

Warner nodded, debating whether to arrest the Brit himself. Tough decision. He was valuable either way. Unless he was over the hill, in which case he was worth more in jail. He studied him as Reggie opened the bar, refilled his own glass first with a shaky hand, and poured another for him, neat.

'What shall we drink to?' Reggie asked with an ironic glance, tossing his whisky back. 'Survivors?'

'Okay. Survivors.'

'Have the other half,' Reggie said, pouring again. 'Ice this time?'

'Yeah.'

'Pardon my fingers. Someone pinched the bloody tongs.'

Warner took a long sip and sat back to let the stuff do its work. Better . . . much better. No denying Reggie had scared the hell out of him – nice reflexes, though. Even if it had been a rubout, he might have saved himself by his quick action.

'What are you going to do?' he asked. 'Got anything lined up?'

'I'm not really sure,' Reggie replied. 'This has all been rather a sudden shock.'

'Well, if you get something, stay in touch. You know?'

Reggie swirled his glass and stared owlishly into the liquor. He drank some more, refilled, and added a splash to Warner's.

'Funny thing,' Warner said, breaking the silence.

'Funny?'

'The wiseguys always say, "Never trust a woman".'

'Helen? Oh, I don't know about that. Her family came first. That was her code and one has to respect that she adhered to it.'

'Italian women never forget. Screw them once and they make you pay. He musta done something to her.'

Reggie put down his glass. 'Whatever there was between Helen Rizzolo and Mr Taggart, Helen *sacrificed* to save her brother. One must respect her strength as well as her . . . honesty?'

'She turned the guy in.'

'She honoured the greater whole. That is far different than treachery for one's own sake. Different than squealing on Mr Taggart purely for your own advantage.'

'What?'

'Jack, Mr Taggart would have beaten the charge if his brother had not received additional evidence. Evidence which only you or I could have supplied . . . I didn't.'

The car started moving.

Warner reached in his jacket and touched his gun. 'You got some crazy idea of doing something about it? Hey, fellow, you're talking to a cop. I'll blow your head off and deliver the carcass to the nearest station house.'

'You betrayed your badge. You betrayed your fellow officers. And you betrayed Mr Taggart. All for Jack and only for Jack. You serve no one . . . I might feel sorry for you, if your selfish treachery hadn't destroyed my friend.'

'What are you going to do about it?'

Reggie raised his arm, wincing as if it had been hurt recently, and slid the

French cuff off his wrist watch. A sweep timing hand was whirling around the face. He pressed a stud and the hand stopped, quivering. 'It's already done.'

Warner blinked. Reggie seemed suddenly very sober. The car slowed for a red light. Chinese people and tourists wandered by, gazing blankly at the mirrored windows.

Warner's throat felt tight. He looked at the drink. 'Tastes funny.'

'It's the poison,' Reggie said gravely.

Warner reached for the door. It was four or five miles away. Reggie appeared to be falling down a deep hole, getting smaller and smaller. When Warner tried to speak, his voice was a whisper, and it hurt terribly. He pried a question like claws from his throat. 'How come you didn't just shoot me?'

In answer, Reggie lowered the chauffeur's partition, and Warner saw to his astonishment that the Englishman had a new boss. Helen Rizzolo turned from the wheel, her silky black hair cascading from a chauffeur's cap.

'That wasn't a choice I could live with, Jack. Mr Taggart would have wanted you to know that he had been avenged.'

'She won it all,' were Warner's dying words.

And perhaps, thought Reggie, she had – what little Taggart had left of it – but her sombre eyes were dark with a thousand years of sorrow, her voice as lonely as the stars.

Printed by RR Donnelley at Glasgow, UK